NOT A
CREATURE
WAS STIRRING

Baptim 96
Deadly Beloved 97

NOT A CREATURE WAS STIRRING

A Gregor Demarkian Holiday Mystery

Jane Haddam

A Perfect Crime Book

DOUBLEDAY

New York   London   Toronto   Sydney   Auckland

A PERFECT CRIME BOOK
PUBLISHED BY DOUBLEDAY
a division of Bantam Doubleday Dell Publishing Group, Inc.
1540 Broadway, New York, New York 10036

DOUBLEDAY is a trademark of Doubleday,
a division of Bantam Doubleday Dell
Publishing Group, Inc.

All of the characters in this book are fictitious,
and any resemblance to actual persons, living or dead,
is purely coincidental.

Designed by Joseph Rutt

Library of Congress Cataloging-in-Publication Data

Haddam, Jane, 1951–
    Not a creature was stirring : a Gregor Demarkian holiday mystery /
    Jane Haddam.
        p.   cm.
    "A Perfect crime book."
    1. Demarkian, Gregor (Fictitious character)—Fiction.   I. Title.
PS3566.A613N6   1993   93-19244   CIP
813'.54—dc20

ISBN 0-385-47036-3

December 1993

2   4   6   8   10   9   7   5   3   1

First Edition

NOT A
CREATURE
WAS STIRRING

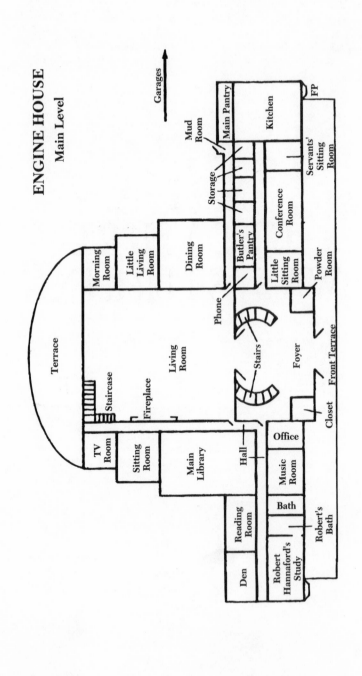

ENGINE HOUSE
Main Level

Garages

Terrace

TV Room

Sitting Room

Staircase

Fireplace

Main Library

Hall

Living Room

Stairs

Foyer

Reading Room

Den

Robert Hannaford's Study

Bath

Music Room

Office

Closet

Robert's Bath

Front Terrace

Powder Room

Little Sitting Room

Conference Room

Servants' Sitting Room

FP

Kitchen

Main Pantry

Mud Room

Storage

Butler's Pantry

Phone

Morning Room

Little Living Room

Dining Room

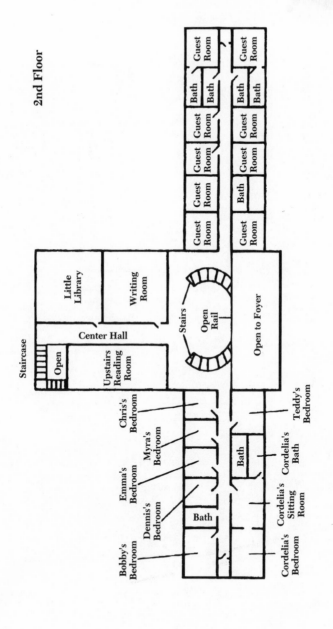

2nd Floor

PROLOGUE

THURSDAY, DECEMBER 1

THE TELEPHONE CALLS

ONE

1 "Listen," Myra said, as soon as the phone was picked up, without waiting to find out who had answered it. "I've had a phone call from Bobby. Something's screwy up at the House."

There was a tiered set of wire baskets hanging from a hook in the kitchen ceiling, filled with boxes of Celestial Seasonings teas. Emma Hannaford took out the Morning Thunder and put it on the counter. Myra, for God's sake. Emma kept in touch with only one of her sisters, and only because she and Bennis had always been close. She didn't hear from the rest of the brood from one year to the next, and she thought that was just fine. Still, when she did hear from them, the one who called was always Myra. Myra was a combination gossip service and witch. She knew things about people they didn't know themselves (usually because they weren't true). She also knew things about people they'd never told anyone, which was—well, weird. Emma dumped a tea bag into the bottom of her best oversize ceramic mug, the one with I CAN BEAT THE WORLD in big red letters on both sides of it, and took the kettle off the stove. If she'd been asked to name the one thing she was least able to deal with after a day like today, she would have had to say Myra. If she'd been asked to name the second thing, she would have had to say a double dose of Morning Thunder (caffeine overload guaranteed) at eight o'clock in the evening.

"Emma?" Myra said. "Emma, are you there?"

"Yes, Myra. I'm here."

"Well, good. For a minute there, I thought you were being raped or robbed or something and I had the mugger."

Emma let that one pass. One of Myra's major monologues, ever since Emma had graduated from Bennington and moved to New York, had to do with how long it would take before Emma got herself killed. Useless to explain to Myra that the Upper West Side, especially this part of it, was probably safer than Vermont had ever been. Useless to explain anything to Myra, really, because Myra only listened when she thought she was getting "important" information. The fact that her youngest sister was living in one of the fanciest neighborhoods in Manhattan was not "important" information.

Emma picked up her tea and the phone and went into the main part of the apartment. It was a room approximately ten by ten feet and, aside from the kitchen (which was an alcove) and the bathroom, it was the only room in the place. At $900 a month, in this neighborhood, it was even a bargain. One of the things Emma had decided when she moved to the city five years ago was that she was going to get along on her own money. Bennis was making a mint and Myra had married a rich husband and the boys had those trust funds, but she was going to have to make her own way eventually. Now she was settled and (she thought) comfortable. She never gave a thought to the fact that she'd grown up in a forty-room house. Or that her bedroom at home was three times the size of this apartment.

She sat down on the couch and stretched her legs, good dancer's legs that wouldn't be so good if she kept cutting class the way she had tonight. Emma Hannaford had good dancer's legs and a good dancer's body, even though she wasn't a dancer, and wild black hair that was a throwback to the first Robert Hannaford, the one whose portrait was on the wall above the mantel in the main library back at Engine House. Engine House was what Robert Hannaford had called the place he'd built in Bryn Mawr, Pennsylvania, after the railroads had made him rich. The first Robert Hannaford had been like that.

The fifth Robert Hannaford, otherwise known as Daddy, wasn't like that at all.

"Emma?"

"I'm still here, Myra."

"I saw that commercial of yours. The one where you get the cereal all over your hair? I thought it was silly."

"It paid a lot of money. And it pays residuals."

"Well, I suppose you need money. I just don't understand why you don't marry it, like everybody else."

Emma let that one pass, too. Myra had married money, but Bennis had made hers, and the boys had been handed theirs courtesy of Daddy. Anne Marie had simply sidestepped the whole question. Anne Marie still lived at Engine House, like some kind of post-debutante twit.

Also, Emma had a fair idea how Myra felt, under all the verbiage and sisterly concern, about being married to Dickie Van Damm.

Emma took a sip of tea and tucked her legs under her. "Is this about something in particular, or did you just call?"

"Of course I didn't just call," Myra said. "There is something screwy up at the House."

"Myra, there's always something screwy up at the House. Our father is a fruitcake. He gets to be more of a fruitcake every year. What else is new?"

"Emma, listen. Bobby called me. Mother was in the hospital—

now, don't jump to conclusions. She's out again now. But from what Bobby's been telling me, things are very strange. She stays in her room all the time and Anne Marie won't let anyone see her and Daddy's going crazy. He's doing things. *Financially."*

Emma stared into her tea. Mother sick. Mother in the hospital. It was like seeing those pictures of baby seals dead on the ice. It made Emma feel sick and numb and very, very frightened.

"Myra?" she said. "What was Mother in the hospital with?"

"I'm not sure."

"Don't you think you ought to find out? That's the important thing. Daddy can't really do anything, financially or otherwise. He's in that wheelchair. And he took care of the money years ago."

"Bobby's worried," Myra said stubbornly.

"Bobby's always worried," Emma said. "That's what he does with his life. What does Anne Marie say?"

Myra paused so long, Emma thought she'd hung up. When her voice came back, it sounded strangled.

"Anne Marie," she said, "is hysterical. You know Anne Marie."

Actually, Emma didn't know Anne Marie. There was fifteen years' difference between them and an even wider gulf in personality. Emma did whatever came into her head. Anne Marie thought things through and found some reason not to do them.

"Emma," Myra said. "You know Bobby. He's not an alarmist. If he says something's wrong, something's wrong."

"Maybe," Emma said, "but he's an old lady about money. And there's nothing to worry about. The money's all locked up. Daddy did it himself."

Emma waited for Myra to say it was all her, Emma's, fault.

Instead, Myra said, "Emma, I really think we all ought to go out there."

Emma paused with her mug of tea halfway to her lips. She had heard that tone in Myra's voice only once or twice before. Mostly, Myra was harmless, but there were times. . . . Emma put her mug back on the floor, feeling distinctly uneasy. She thought of her family as a collection of benign kooks. Too much money over too many generations had left them a little addled, but in pleasant, amusing ways. Of course, there was nothing pleasant about Daddy. He was a nasty, vindictive old man. But—

But. When Myra got started—and praise God in Heaven it didn't happen often—things could get damn near lethal.

"Myra," Emma said carefully, "I don't think—"

"Oh," Myra said, "you never do. But I do. And I think we ought to go up there. For Christmas."

"Daddy will throw us out," Emma said.

"No, he won't. You know how Mother is about Christmas. We could go up Christmas Eve and stay till New Year's. By then we'd have everything straightened out."

"Maybe Daddy doesn't want everything straightened out."

"Daddy doesn't know what he wants. If he did, he wouldn't have done all that about the money. Now, Emma, I don't want any arguments. Just be on the five-seventeen when it gets to Bryn Mawr December twenty-third. I'll pick you up at the station."

"Myra—"

"Bring woolies. It gets cold up there this time of year."

Emma stared into the phone and sighed. It was infuriating. No matter what she did, they always got to her. Family, home, position, security, money—she hated to admit it, but the thought of going home for Christmas had improved her mood enormously. Even after all that terrible stuff about Mother.

Even after Myra had made her think about the money.

Emma stretched out on the couch and stared at the ceiling. Large rooms. Fireplaces. Mattresses and box springs. Four-hundred-dollar down comforters. Oh, Lord.

She felt about as independent as a baby kangaroo.

2

When Bennis Hannaford hung up on her sister Myra, she was thinking not about what Myra had said (Myra never made any sense), but about the phone call she'd had only half an hour earlier, the one from the nut. She put her hand to the back of her head and released her black wiry hair from its barrette. Through an accident of genetics, she had all the really good Hannaford features and none of the bad ones. Her bones were fine and fragile. Her eyes were large and widely spaced and almost a deep purple. Her cheekbones were high and her cheeks just a little hollow. She was a beautiful woman, and she knew it.

The nut on the phone had given her a flawless description of her living room as it had existed six months ago, which meant he was one of the people who had attended the fantasy fan convention in Chicago last June. That meant he could be either harmless or not, depending. Depending on where he was. Depending on his psychiatric history. Depending . . .

Bennis brushed it off, irritated. The way she reacted to these calls always made her feel like a hypochondriacal old maid. And it was so asinine. This idiot hadn't been in her apartment. If he had, he'd know it had been redecorated. Still . . .

She headed for the living room, down the long hall bracketed by built-in bookshelves holding only the books she had written. One shelf was given over to copies of *Chronicles of Zed and Zedalia,* her second novel and the first fantasy ever to make *The New York Times* hardcover fiction best-seller list. She prodded Michael Peteris with her toe as she passed his place on her Persian rug and dropped down on a green plush Louis XVI chair she'd bought because it "went with the room." That was before she realized nothing would ever go with this room, because it had been built at a time when people who knew nothing about history were trying to invent it.

"Michael," she said, "tell me what to do about the nut."

Michael turned over and put his hands behind his head. If he hadn't been as tall and broad as he was, he would have been ugly. He looked, as Bennis explained to Emma when Emma asked, "very Greek."

"What you're going to do about the nut," he said calmly, "is what you always do about the nuts. Call Jack Donovan down at the station. Get a tap put on your phone. Then—"

"I'm tired of this, Michael. I really am. I want to be Stephen King and not have to go to conventions. I want—"

"From what you tell me, Stephen King does go to conventions. And if you're tired of this, move."

"Oh, hush," Bennis said.

Michael shrugged and turned away. This was an argument he had no interest in repeating. Of course she should move. She'd known that the first time a nut called—the one who said he'd put a rogue troll in her underwear drawer—even before she'd asked him and he'd told her.

"Who else was on the phone?" Michael said. "I heard it ring twice."

"What?" Bennis said. "Oh. That was my sister."

"Emma, Myra, or Anne Marie?"

"Myra."

"You are going to be in a bad mood tonight. Oh, well. What did she want?"

"What?" Bennis said again. "I'm sorry. My mind's wandering." It was, too. She was thinking about Daddy. She shook it out of her head and said, "Myra. Well, she wanted me to come home for Christmas. For the whole week between Christmas and New Year's."

"But that's wonderful," Michael said. "You call Jack. You get the tap put on the phone. Then you pack up and go to Sewickley, or wherever."

"Wayne. That's not what she wants me to do. She wants me to go out to Engine House. My mother just got out of the hospital."

Michael sat up. "Do you realize what you just did? You told me about the nut first."

"And that shocks you," Bennis said.

"It would shock anybody."

"Not if they grew up at Engine House." Bennis stood, went to the drinks cabinet, and fished her cigarettes out from behind the gin. So much for cutting down on smoking by keeping your cigarettes in an inconvenient place. When she got a real nicotine fit, there was no such thing as an inconvenient place.

She went back to the chair, lit up, and said, "Besides, this isn't exactly news. I've been living with this thing of Mother's for a long time."

"How long?"

"Fifteen years."

"What's she got?"

"Some kind of multiple sclerosis. I don't understand it exactly. She's been in and out of hospitals for years."

Michael blew a stream of air into the room, like a pregnant woman hyperventilating to take her mind off labor. "Jesus God," he said. "And half of you live out of town. What are you people, anyway?"

"Down dirty furious at my father, for one thing," Bennis said. "Besides, I don't think the rest of them know. I mean, Anne Marie knows. That's why she's never left home. Daddy knows, because he'd have to. I know because I was home once when she had one of those attacks." She considered it. "Bobby might know. I'm not sure."

"You mean your mother hasn't told anybody?"

"Of course not. She wouldn't want to be an object of pity."

Michael shot her a look that said this attitude made no sense to him at all, and Bennis shrugged. Of course it didn't. He came from an absurdly extended family, full of immigrant great-aunts and just-off-the-boat quasi uncles, people who stuck together because they were trying to get someplace. He would never understand how the Main Line worked.

Bennis stretched her legs, crossed her feet at the ankles, and said, "The thing is, no matter how much I love my mother, a week at home with Daddy would just about kill me. That old son of a—never mind. If you could come with me—"

"I can't. I've got the Andrekowicz thing."

Bennis made a face. She didn't want to hear about the Andrekowicz thing. Bodies in pieces all over the South Side. "Well, there you are. I don't want to see my father, and no matter what Myra says, he doesn't want to see me. He only talks to Bobby and Anne Marie because he has to. He wrote the rest of us off years ago."

"That's a hell of a thing to say about an old man in a wheelchair."

"The old man in the wheelchair is going to last another twenty years," Bennis said. "A lot longer than Mother. And he deserves it less."

"Which is supposed to mean what?"

"Which is supposed to mean I think I'll go call my brother Chris. Myra must have called him. Maybe he got more out of her than I did."

"I like your brother Chris," Michael said. "Only don't tell him I always think his poems are jokes. He gets weird about it."

Bennis hauled herself out of her chair and headed back toward the bedroom and the phone.

When the light went off on his console for the third time in fifteen minutes, Chris Hannaford told his listeners (all 226 of them) not to forget to boycott grapes, started a Grateful Dead record, took off his sweatband, and dropped the sweatband over his light. A little later, he would read some of his poetry, and that would be nice, but what he wasn't going to do any more was answer the phone. Oh, no. First he'd been stuck with his sister Myra, which was a little like accidentally ingesting a triple dose of Benzedrine. Then—

He felt his stomach start to cramp and leaned over, counting until it went away. He was losing his nerve. He was coming apart. And that second phone call hadn't helped.

They were going to kill him.

The Dead record was winding to an end. He got another from the stack and flipped it on without introduction. The masses never minded getting their music straight. Mostly he wouldn't oblige them, of course. Just because the idiots wanted to pretend that literature began with Paul McCartney and ended with Bruce Springsteen didn't mean he had to agree with them. He'd won four dozen awards for his poetry, been published in everything from *The Atlantic* to *The New Kionossa Review,* and was (if he had to say it himself) the driving force in the survival of poetry in post-Reagan America. Actually, someone else had said it for him, in *The Yale Review.* A friend who still lived in New Haven had sent him the article. He'd been embarrassed as hell at first, but after he'd thought about it he'd realized it was nothing but the truth. Who else was there?

His stomach cramped up again, and he forgot all about it.

They were going to kill him. They had practically said so when they called. How in the name of God had he got himself involved with these people? What was he—aside from the driving force, etc.—but an ex-preppie Yale boy with a little family money and even fewer brains? He must have been tripping.

Except that he didn't trip. He didn't do much of anything but smoke marijuana, write poetry, show up for work—and gamble. When he put it like that, it made him want to laugh. Gambling was what got people in trouble in thirties detective novels. Getting in hock to mob-connected bookies was a hard-boiled private-eye cliché. That kind of thing didn't happen to people in real life. It didn't exist in real life.

(We don't hear from you in four days, we're gonna take your thumb.)

He flipped the second record for a third, still not able to talk. The spasms were so bad, he had to put his head between his knees to keep from vomiting. That comic-opera voice on the phone, for God's sake. The thought of his thumb (right or left?) lying on the pavement in Santa Clara in a mess of blood and pulp. Four days.

He felt the sweat break out on his forehead and knew he was going to be better. The sweat always hit him just before and after these attacks. He sat up, waited for the record to finish, and said,

"That was the Dead times three, ladies and gentlemen. 'Truckin,' 'Sugar Magnolia,' and 'Uncle John's Band.' Give me a minute here, we're going to have a Chris Hannaford special. An uninterrupted album. *Sgt. Pepper's Lonely Hearts Club Band.*"

He chose it because it was sitting right there on top of his stack. He spun it onto the turntable, flipped off his mike, and sat back, a tall, cadaverous, long-limbed man with the trademark Hannaford hair and a face that had seen too many bars, too many late nights and too much trouble. Now that the attack was over, he could think.

Myra was out there somewhere, getting a bug in her ass about dear old Daddy. Myra always had a bug in her ass about something. That was her thing. Just like being a first-class son-of-a-whore was Daddy's thing.

Just like gambling was his thing.

He thought about calling Bennis and decided against it. She'd got him out of the hole that first time without asking questions. She'd get him out of this one the same way. He wasn't going to ask her. In direct contradiction to the way he lived and the things he said when he had anyone but Bennis for an audience, Chris had a streak of moralism in him. Bennis would let him bleed her forever. For precisely that reason, he couldn't go to her. After all, he was the one with the nice little chunk of family money. Bennis had what she made and nothing more.

(We're gonna take your thumb.)

They were going to take his thumb. Yes, they were. And after they took his thumb they were going to take the rest of him, piece by piece, because this time he was in for $75,000 and there was no way he could pay it. Not now, not tomorrow, not two days from tomorrow. What the hell had he bet in on, anyway?

Did they know about Engine House? Probably. But he knew his father. Engine House was a fortress. Daddy was the ultimate paranoid.

He rubbed his hands against his face and went back to trying to think.

4 "You must understand," the chairman of the English department was saying, "no matter how liberal the times have become, we cannot, in cases like this, ignore the traditional consequences."

The chairman of the English department looked like a fish wearing a toupee. At least, he looked that way to Teddy Hannaford, and Teddy had always prided himself on his powers of observation and his ear for a good metaphor. Simile. Whatever. The chairman of the English department was a turd, and all Teddy wanted on earth was not to have to listen to him.

Unfortunately, at the moment he had no choice. He sat awkwardly in the chairman's visitor's chair, his right leg in its brace as stiff as a length of hardwood, thinking they could have saved half an hour if the chairman had just fired him outright. Instead, the fish was making a speech. And a banal one at that.

Teddy started to put a hand to his head and stopped himself. Unlike everybody else in the family, he had not been born with hair that flourished under any and all conditions. He was going bald at the top and thinning in every other place. It was not something he could think about with charity. They, after all, were just fine—Bennis and Emma and Bobby and Chris and even Anne Marie. He never counted Myra, because Myra was a housewife. Nobody took housewives seriously. But the rest of them—. Emma was young and pretty. Chris was screwing every blonde in Southern California. Anne Marie was always in the society magazines. Bobby had been given the biggest chunk of money. And then there was Bennis.

Sometimes, when he went into the Waldenbooks in Kennebunk and saw all those ridiculous books taking up more shelf space than Dreiser, he wanted to scream. Bennis had been the pain of his life for as long as he could remember. Here she was again, making idiots of them all with stories about unicorns and knights in shining armor. They even carried her trash in the college bookstore. And *The New York Times Magazine* had done a silly article called "The New Face of Fantasy Fiction" and put Bennis right on the cover.

No matter what the chairman of the English department said this interview was about, it was really about Bennis. Teddy knew.

He also knew it was Bennis's fault his leg was in a brace and his knee wouldn't bend. He hadn't figured out how that worked—Bennis had been in Paris the day Daddy had taken him for a ride and tried to kill him—but he was sure he would be able to unravel it if he put his mind to it.

The fish squirmed in his chair, cleared his throat, and tried a smile. "There is also," he said, "the question of your alleged motive in this, uh, action."

"Motive?" Teddy could practically feel the antennae rise up out of his head, like the retractable ears on a Martian in a fifties alien invasion movie.

"Miss Carpenter," the chairman said, "claims you made this suggestion to her as the means by which she could receive credit on a paper you were writing for *NEJLA* with research you had used from her final project in Victorian Authors."

NEJLA was the *New England Journal of Literary Arts*. What the fool was trying to say was that Susan Carpenter claimed Teddy had told her she'd have to sleep with him if she wanted her name on the article he was submitting to *NEJLA* on women in the Victorian novel. Where the fish had it wrong was in that bit about "using some of Miss Carpenter's research." He had not used some of Miss Carpenter's research. He had stolen her paper outright.

He hadn't told Susan she'd have to sleep with him if she wanted her credit, either. He might have implied it, but he hadn't said it. He never made promises he had no intention of keeping.

"Miss Carpenter," the fish was saying, "has submitted to us a photocopy of this—"

Teddy closed his eyes. A photocopy. Yes, he'd been waiting for a photocopy. After all, Susan Carpenter wasn't the first. She wasn't even the twentieth.

"Professor Hannaford," the chairman said solemnly.

Teddy looked up quickly. He had broken out in a cold sweat.

"You understand," he said, "that every professor has this problem from time to time with students, especially female students, who think they haven't received the grade they, uh, deserved."

"It comes up," the chairman agreed, and then spoiled it by saying, "rarely."

"Yes," Teddy said. "Well. Rarely or not, it comes up. If you've read Miss Carpenter's paper—"

"I have not."

"Well, read it. You'll see it's nothing *NEJLA* would be interested in. Miss Carpenter's, ah, communications skills are not of the highest. As for research—"

"Yes?"

"There isn't any," Teddy said. "It was an exposition. Textual analysis."

"And Miss Carpenter's analytical skills are not of the highest?"

"They're nonexistent."

"Ah." The chairman sat back and folded his hands over his stomach. He no longer looked like a fish. He looked like a pregnant frog.

"I see," he was saying. "This should be relatively easy to clear up. We have Miss Carpenter's paper. We have your article—has it been published yet?"

"No," Teddy said, knowing this was the worst luck of all. "It's due in their spring issue."

"I see. Do you have a copy?"

"Of course."

"Fine, then. We'll have both the paper and the article. We'll have copies made before the hearing. Then, at the hearing—"

"What hearing?"

"The departmental hearing," the chairman said. "There'll have to be one. If the charges had any merit, there'd have to be a hearing in the Faculty Senate as well, but as you've assured me—" The chairman didn't look assured. He looked, in fact, rather smug. Teddy was suddenly sure the chairman had known about his papers for years.

Just then, the buzzer went off on the chairman's phone. The chairman picked up, grunted a few times, and then hung up again.

"That was Miss Holcomb in the office," he said. "It's a Mrs. Richard Van Damm. She says she's your sister. She says it's urgent."

The chairman looked as if he thought Teddy had fixed this up just to escape from the interview, but Teddy didn't care. Myra, of all people. Bless her malicious little heart. Myra could make an emergency out of a lost earring, but Teddy wasn't going to tell the chairman that.

After all, for the moment, she was his salvation.

5 When the phone rang, Bobby Hannaford was sitting on the king-size bed in the second-floor master suite of his $1.5-million house in Chestnut Hill, trying to extract forty-two $100 bills from the waistband of his boxer shorts. It would have been easier if he hadn't been so edgy, but he was always edgy on the days he saw McAdam. When the bell

went off, he jumped half a foot in the air, scattering bills everywhere. He had to get down on his hands and knees to rescue the
two that blew under the night table. When he got up, he was
breathing heavily, and he still had money in his underwear. He
snatched at the receiver with all the good humor he could mus-
ter, which was none at all.

"Bobby? Bobby, I know it's probably a bad time, but I've got
to talk to you."

Bobby paused in his struggles with elasticized 100 percent cotton. He'd know that voice anywhere. When he died and went to
Hell, it would be waiting for him in the fiery pit, right along
with Donald McAdam.

"Shit," he said, extracting another $600 from his shorts. He
didn't need Myra. He needed to think about McAdam. McAdam
was getting crazy. If he got crazy enough, they were both going
to get caught.

Bobby knew exactly what getting caught would mean. He'd
gone about white-collar crime the way he went about everything
else. He'd done a cost-benefit analysis. The benefit: three-quar-
ters of a million dollars so far, in cash, most of it still in the
tempered steel wall safe in his room at Engine House. The cost:
either nothing, or public exposure, an IRS judgment, a criminal
trial, and Leavenworth.

Leavenworth, in the name of Christ Jesus.

"Bobby," Myra said.

"I'm here," Bobby said. "Just a minute. I was changing when
you called."

"Stop changing for a minute. This is serious."

"Myra, with you everything is serious."

Myra snorted. "Stop acting like my algebra teacher. You're as worried about this as I am. And you know it's important. You said yourself—"

"I remember what I said, Myra."

"When you want to," Myra said. "I've called them. They're coming. Whether that's going to do the trick, I don't know."

"It can't hurt. At least it will take his mind off us. If he runs that audit—"

"I don't know," Myra said. "The company has to be audited sometime."

"This would be a directors' audit," Bobby said, "not the usual annual pain in the ass. You know he just wants to cause trouble—"

"Maybe he does," Myra said, "but—"

"And don't forget. You're the one on the books with thirty thousand nobody knows where it came from. Except you, of course."

There was a pause on the line. "That was low, Bobby. That was very low."

"I'm not your husband," Bobby said. "You can't fool me. If you hadn't had a stake in this yourself, you'd have left me to paddle my own canoe."

"Maybe I should have."

"I could answer that, Myra, but I don't want to be indiscreet over the phone."

There was another pause, a longer one this time. Bobby felt a little spurt of fear climb up his spine. Myra was a smart woman, and a vindictive one. And right at this moment, he needed her. He needed her more than she could know.

"Listen," he said. "I'm sorry. It's been a long day. And we don't have anything to worry about now. They're coming. It'll take care of everything."

"I hope so, Bobby."

"I know so. He'll be so worked up over Bennis, he won't have time for us."

"Are you sure there isn't something you're not telling me?" Myra said. "You haven't, oh, fiddled with the books or anything? Because if you have—"

"What would I have to fiddle with the books for, Myra? Remember me? I'm the one who got the most money."

"I remember. You'd think the old goat could just have made a will like everybody else. I wish he had. Maybe somebody would have killed him for it."

"That's a very indiscreet thing to say over the phone."

"Only if he shows up murdered," Myra said. "All right, Bobby. It's all set up. Anne Marie's expecting you on the twenty-third. Try to make it for dinner. There's a guest."

"With Mother this ill?"

"You know Daddy."

The phone went to dial tone.

Bobby replaced the receiver. His mouth felt dry. His chest felt heavy. It hit him suddenly that he was forty-four years old, no longer too young for a heart attack.

6

In the telephone stall off the first floor sitting room at Engine House, Myra stared at the old-fashioned metal phone and wondered if she'd done the right thing. Get them here, Bobby had said. She had certainly done that. Or would have, when they arrived. Which every last one of them would.

Still, it might have been better if she'd told them the truth. The whole truth. Like the fact that Mother wasn't securely home from the hospital and doing just fine, but dying. Like the fact that Anne Marie was having some kind of nervous breakdown. Like the fact that Daddy was on the warpath for real this time.

Of course, with that kind of information, some of them might not have come.

She tapped the phone table restlessly, then reached up to stroke the brooch she was wearing, a shiny tin Christmas ball Mother had made as a child. On the table's polished obsidian surface lay an oversize white visiting card, scribbled over and splotched with fountain pen ink. *"Gregor Demarkian,"* it said. *"Head, Department of Behavioral Sciences, Federal Bureau of Investigation. Retired."*

Here was something she hadn't told anyone about—Daddy's dinner guest. Two hours ago, she'd never heard of him. Now she just wished she hadn't. There he was: a man with a funny name who had held the second-most-important position in the most Irish Catholic organization in the U.S. government, a man with a reputation for being both obsessive and fanatical about his work, a man with an even bigger reputation for being right. Myra wondered what he looked like. Myra wondered what Daddy wanted from him.

She tucked the card into her shirt pocket and got up. Anne Marie had taken to listening in on phone conversations, and Myra had no way of knowing if she'd listened in on that last one. She hoped she hadn't. Things were in enough of a mess already.

It was going to be a hell of a Christmas.

PART ONE

SUNDAY, DECEMBER 18–SATURDAY, DECEMBER 24

THE FIRST MURDER

ONE

1 When Gregor Demarkian was very young, his mother
told him stories about Armenia. Her Armenia wasn't the
historical Armenia, because she'd never seen that. She
had been born in Alexandria and come to the United
States before she was twelve. It was Gregor's grandmother who
had been in Yerevan that November of 1915 when the Turks had
come. Blood everywhere, horses everywhere, a million and a half
dead in less than a year: the stories had come pouring out into
the dark of Gregor's room every night when his mother came to
put him to bed. Even now, after more than forty years, he could
smell the stink of dying. He thought his grandmother must have
been a truly great storyteller. Either that, or his mother had had a
genius for imagination. Whichever it was, he found himself—at
the age of fifty-five, after a bachelor's degree at Penn and a master's at Harvard and a twenty-year stint in the FBI—firmly anchored in the agony of a country he had never seen.

Gregor had been four years old the first time he had heard
about the New Armenia—four years old and sitting in this very
church, in the second pew from the front on the right—and he
remembered that even then he'd thought the idea made no sense.
They wouldn't march back to Asia Minor. They wouldn't re-
claim their land from whoever had it now. They would simply
stay in America and build a Real Armenian Culture, distinct but
not separate from the Armenian culture around them. How they
were supposed to do this, no one knew—especially because the
children were having none of it. Still, it inspired them. There
would be a Great Cause and a Great Effort, complete with Virtu-

ous Sacrifices. Whatever else was going to happen to them, they weren't going to get rich.

And now, of course, they had.

Gregor put his hands up to his eyes and rubbed. The liturgy was nearly over, and the church was full of incense. As far as Gregor knew, the peculiar scent of that incense was used only in Armenian Christian churches. He had never encountered it anywhere else. Now he wondered if it was contributing to his feeling of incipient schizophrenia. The smell was right. The words of the service were just what they had been for more than 1,200 years. Even the little priest was right, standing in the center door of the iconostasis, dressed in blue and gold and carrying a great golden cross on a long shaft. It was everything else that was wrong.

He didn't know what he'd expected. He'd left this small ethnic neighborhood in Philadelphia just after he graduated from Penn. In the thirty-four years since, he had been back exactly twice— once for his wedding, right after his two-year hitch in the army; once about five years after that, in 1962, to see his mother buried from Holy Trinity Church. The years between had been full of changes, for himself and everyone else. He had no right to be disoriented by a Holy Trinity that was not just what it had been when he left.

On the other hand, it was entirely possible that it wasn't the fact that things had changed that was bothering him, but the way they had changed. When he had first decided to come back to this neighborhood—to come home—he'd half-expected to find nothing to come back to. He'd pressed on simply because he'd had nothing else to do. Elizabeth was dead, fading away finally after years of terror and futility, anger and pain. His job was gone. He'd taken a leave for the last year of Elizabeth's illness, and when she'd died he'd had neither the energy nor the inclination to go back to work. Then he'd woken up one morning to find himself in a nearly empty apartment in a high-rise off the Beltway, with no idea what day it was or what he was going to do with the day now that he had it, and it began to occur to him that he had to get going again.

He'd been ready to find Cavanaugh Street changed into an Hispanic neighborhood. He'd been prepared to accept it as a battleground for teenage gangs, a strip for prostitutes, a drug bazaar, a burned-out hulk. He'd steeled himself against just about anything, except the sight of Lida Kazanjian Arkmanian in a three-quarter-length chinchilla coat.

The congregation had begun to go up to Communion, making two lines in the outside aisles. The little priest—that would be Father Tibor, the one who had called him—was standing in front of the iconostasis again, holding a large gold cup and a small gold spoon with a handle like an elongated letter opener. As Gregor watched, a boy of no more than three stepped up, closed his eyes, and opened his mouth.

The line reached his pew. If he was going to receive, he would have to go now. Lida slipped out of the pew in front of him and turned, nodding her head vigorously. Gregor hesitated and then shook a negative.

The last Armenian liturgy he had attended had been Elizabeth's funeral. It had been the last he'd intended to attend. He'd only come here today out of some kind of whim, the way he'd come back to Cavanaugh Street.

The people who had received Communion were leaving by the center aisle. They were moving quickly, in a hurry to get to the church steps and the permissible zone of conversation. One or two of them looked him over as they passed. Many more looked back at him when they thought they were safely beyond his field of vision. His scalp was beginning to tingle. God only knew what kind of stories had been floating around this neighborhood since he'd come back.

He spied a gap in the stream of people and felt a little better. At least he was going to be able to get out. He wedged himself between a tiny grandmother in archaic black and a boy in Ralph Lauren Polo and headed for the vestibule.

Going toward the door, he began to wonder what would happen if he did something "really radical," as his favorite niece would say—if he started singing Bob Dylan songs in his deep baritone voice, or talking in Armenian.

Madness.

2

Actually, Gregor thought a little later, climbing the stairs to the second floor and Father Tibor's office, what was really madness was his state of mind. For the two years of Elizabeth's last crisis and the two more that followed her death, he had had absolutely no interest in the work that had taken up most of his life. That had begun to change. Maybe it was because he was settled, with a real apartment and a real address. Maybe it was just a matter of time, and he was getting bored. Whatever the reason, he was feeling distinctly itchy—and in his itchiness, he was beginning to do some very strange things.

Now he did something that wasn't strange at all. He poked his head through the door of the big room where he had once attended Sunday school. It had been divided up by slick new baseboard partitions, each hung with a green chalkboard and decorated with construction paper cutouts of the dove of peace. Gregor backed into the hall again. The older he got, the more depressed the world made him. The big things didn't bother him so much. Crime and drugs, war and brutality—he'd read enough history to know all that had happened before and would probably happen again to whatever civilization replaced this one. It was the little things that made him crazy. When he'd been at Sunday school here, the room had been decorated with icons and the words on the blackboard had been in Armenian. What was in there now could just as easily have been part of a Methodist Church in Pederucah, Tennessee.

Gregor heard a sound on the stairs and looked into the well. The little priest was there, hurrying, the tattered hem of his day robe catching on the stair runner every few feet. Gregor made a mental note. He'd known from the sound of the voice on the phone that Father Tibor was an immigrant. The day robes told him Father Tibor was an immigrant from a Communist country. It was only in places where the Church was suppressed that the clergy still felt the need for religious dress.

Gregor leaned over the railing. "Father Tibor?" he called down.

"Yes, yes," Father Tibor said, still hurrying. "Mr. Demarkian. I'm very sorry. I was coming right up, but Mrs. Krekorian was there at the bottom of the stairs—"

"I know Hannah Krekorian," Gregor said.

Father Tibor looked up quickly and smiled. "Everybody knows Mrs. Krekorian," he said. Then he raced the rest of the way up and emerged, puffing and red faced, on the landing. "There. I should have told you to go into the office and sit down. The door is open. It sticks a little."

"That's all right," Gregor said. It was, too. He was beginning to feel as if he spent his entire life sitting down. "I was looking at all the renovations. You've done a lot of work around here."

"Work," Father Tibor said, as if there was something particularly nasty about that word. He brushed past Gregor and walked to the far end of the hall, to an old-fashioned door that had been newly painted black. Then he twisted the knob and pushed, hard.

"Mr. Kashinian had the office remodeled," he said. "It was a very fine remodeling. It's my own fault I can never get this door open."

"Howard Kashinian?" Gregor said.

"That's right." Father Tibor nodded. The nod was vigorous, almost frantic—but everything Father Tibor did was almost frantic. "I keep forgetting. You grew up here. You would know these people."

"What I know about Howard Kashinian is that he used to be the biggest juvenile delinquent on Cavanaugh Street. He got sent to the reformatory when he was twelve and his mother wore black for a year."

Father Tibor's face became a mask of infinite innocence. "There was a little contretemps with the Securities and Exchange Commission," he said blandly, "but that was nearly two years ago, and the charges were dropped. Please come in."

Father Tibor smiled. It was a smile with intelligence in it, and humor, and the acid of a tempered cynicism.

Well, Gregor thought, at least this is going to be interesting. And then, because he had been brought up to it and it's never easy to get rid of what you have been taught in childhood, Gregor grabbed the handle of the door and motioned the priest to go in before him.

3 Father Tibor's office was full of books—great floor-to-ceiling cases crammed until the wood cracked, great stacks scattered across the floor, small piles on chairs and tables and even an umbrella stand. Tibor had to clear a place for Gregor to sit. When he did, Gregor saw the books were in at least five languages, or maybe six. There were two books in Greek, but Gregor had the impression they weren't in the same Greek. Was it really possible that this man read both ancient and modern Greek? It was an eerie thing, like being presented with the ghost of one of the desert Fathers.

Father Tibor sat behind his desk—he had to take a few books off that chair, too—and folded his hands. It was a classic priest's pose, but Tibor couldn't really look priestly. At his best, he looked like a scholar. At his worst, he reminded Gregor of the old men who had lined the halls outside the Immigration and Naturalization Service in the hottest days of the cold war.

"Well," he said. He looked at the ceiling, and the floor, and his hands. "Well," he said again.

"You wanted to ask me a favor," Gregor prompted him.

Tibor cleared his throat. "Well," he said for the third time. "This is very hard for me to say. I told you this had nothing directly to do with the Church?"

"Yes, you did," Gregor said. He didn't say he didn't believe it. In his experience, Armenian priests professed to believe that ev-

erything, even the shifting rules of sandlot baseball, had something to do with the Church.

"Well," Tibor said yet again. "I don't know if I should have
put it that way. My English is still—I read well enough, but I
don't speak . . . precisely . . . all the time. I get . . . in my
life, I've had to live in Russian and French and Hebrew and
English and sometimes even Armenian. I get . . . confused."

"I shouldn't wonder."

"I don't wonder. I just lose my patience. Yes. Well. Maybe it
would be easiest this way. Do you know a man named Robert
Hannaford?"

Gregor hesitated. Hannaford. The name was familiar, but he
couldn't figure out why. He slid, automatically, into what he had
been trained to do. Known criminals, suspected criminals, candi-
dates for investigation: the list was appallingly long, but the name
Hannaford was not on it. Hannaford wasn't the name of anyone
he'd known at the Bureau, either, or any of the victims of crimes
still unsolved when he'd taken early retirement. God only knew,
there was nobody named Hannaford connected to that last mess
of a job he'd left unfinished to sit at Elizabeth's deathbed.

Tibor swiveled in his chair, nearly fell out of it, and finally
managed to retrieve two paperback books from the case behind
his desk. He pushed them across the clutter to Gregor. This time,
Gregor was really surprised. These weren't theology, or history,
or even literature with a capital L. They were sword and sorcery
popular novels, complete with gold foil lettering and embossed
unicorns. *Chronicles of Zed and Zedalia,* the closer one said. The
other was called *Zedalia in Winter.* On that one, the author's
name was above the title, writ large: Bennis Hannaford.

"Bennis Hannaford," Gregor said.

Tibor was bouncing up and down in his chair, making Gregor feel a little dizzy. "She's one of the daughters," he said. "The middle child, I think. Mr. Hannaford has seven children. This one is very successful, a best-seller all the time—"

"I've seen her books. They're all over the newsstands."

"They're all over everywhere. And she has a brother, an older brother, and he runs the family business—"

"I remember," Gregor said, jolting up a little in his chair. That was why he recognized the name—not from the Bureau, but from his life before the Bureau. "Hannaford of Engine House. They made their money in railroads. Rich people out on the Main Line."

"Very rich people," Tibor said, and then, "Protestant, of course."

Gregor bit back a smile. If he knew anything about rich people —and he did; that was one thing a twenty-year stint in the FBI had done for him—the Hannafords were Protestant the way he was Armenian. It was part of the definition.

"Of course," he said.

Father Tibor sighed. "I don't suppose it matters in America. Religious pluralism, they call it. I'm having a hard time getting used to it."

Gregor studied the old man, curious. "Is that what all this is about? Robert Hannaford being Protestant? Your note said—"

"Wait," Tibor said.

"I'm sorry." Gregor settled into his chair, as well as he could. He was so big, and the chair was so small, he felt a little like a beach ball trapped in a paper clip.

Across from him, Tibor took in an immense breath, let it out again, seemed to count to ten in his head, and stood up. "I have talked to Lida Arkmanian," he said. "She says you are a very famous detective."

"Famous?"

"That you once had your picture on the cover of *Time* magazine."

"Yes, Father, I did, but that was—"

"She said you were very intelligent. I think in this matter you are going to have to be very intelligent."

"Why? What matter? Father—"

Tibor sat down again. "I have had a communication from this man Robert Hannaford. He came here to this office one day last week. He was in a wheelchair. He had a driver with him and he had to be carried up the stairs. But that was just because of his legs. He was not a weak man. Even at his age, over seventy, he is not a weak man. He's not going to die tomorrow. Or next week. He must work himself very hard. The upper half of his body is—" Tibor made a wide motion with his hands and arms. "You see?"

Gregor didn't see anything. Talking with Father Tibor Kasparian was like swimming in ink. It didn't make any sense, and the world was dark. But this was a direct question, and one he could answer, so he did.

"That's not so strange in America," he said. "Disabled people here seem to go one way or the other. Either they give up entirely, or they become obsessive about building up what body they have—"

Tibor brightened. "As a method of control? Yes, that's what I thought it was. All through our talk, I got the impression Mr. Hannaford was a man who loved to be in control—of himself, of me, of everything. It was not pleasant."

"No," Gregor said. "It wouldn't be."

Tibor drummed impatiently against the desk. "I don't think this is a good man," he said. "I'm not saying that just because he reminded me—reminded me of other things. I've had a very long life, Mr. Demarkian. It was a bad life, but I think this man was worse. He—I don't know how to say it—it was as if everything he did was a lie. Even the expression on his face, that was a lie. And yet, you know, I think he was telling me the truth, when he talked. The exact truth as he knew it. I don't think he said anything false."

"Yes," Gregor said. This was something he understood. He'd met a number of people who fit this description when he'd been at the Bureau, and most of them hadn't been on the criminal lists. Politicians were the worst, but they weren't the only ones. Lobbyists, businessmen, the head of a large consumer-advocate group: acculturated psychopaths. No intelligent psychopath had to murder a dozen little old ladies to get his kicks. He could wreak far more havoc by going into government work.

Gregor didn't think Tibor needed any of this explained to him. If he hadn't already figured it out, it had to be because he didn't want to. Besides, there were more immediately interesting things going on here.

"What did Robert Hannaford want with an Armenian priest?" he asked.

Tibor flushed, bright red. Gregor felt the ink seeping back into his life.

"Father," he started, cautious.

Tibor waved him to silence. "No, no. You must understand. You are famous—"

"I am not—"

"Yes, you are. I've read the articles. Mrs. Arkmanian kept every one. I realize you are very modest—"

"Father, I am not modest. I've never failed to take credit for something I've done right in my life. And that *Time* magazine article—"

"Yes?"

Gregor felt himself hunching up. He'd always been uncomfortable about that damn *Time* cover. No, worse than uncomfortable. He was not a natural extrovert. Left to himself, he even tended to be something of a recluse. The first time he'd seen that magazine on a newsstand, he'd wanted to go home and hide in a closet. Permanently.

"It was when we were setting up the Behavioral Sciences Department," he told Tibor. "That's what I did most of my last eight years at the Bureau. I helped to coordinate investigations of serial killers. It was the serial killers *Time* was interested in, not me."

"I read the article," Tibor repeated, chiding.

"You should have read the one two years ago. That time, they called me an irresponsible son-of-a-bitch for walking out in the middle of a case just because my wife was dying."

"That case never got solved. Maybe that's what they were worried about."

"I'm sure it was. And child murders are a particularly nasty kind of case not to get solved. But—"

"Stop," Tibor said. He got up and walked to the window, a narrow bar of glass that looked out on an air shaft.

"I have read this Bennis Hannaford's books," he said after a while. "I like them very much. Whatever her father is, she is not the same. Do you see?"

"No."

"He came here, and he sat in his wheelchair, and all the time I am thinking he has seven children, and maybe none of them are what he is. And he has a wife, who is very sick, and she spends her life doing good works. This I see in the paper all the time, too. He is—intent about his wife. And he comes here and talks to me, and he makes me an offer. A very strange offer. He takes out his briefcase and he opens it up, and inside he has money. One hundred thousand dollars in money. He counts it out for me, and then he asks me a favor, and he says if I do this favor the church can have this money."

"A hundred thousand dollars in cash?" This wasn't ink. It was Krazy Glue.

But Tibor was nodding. "Yes, Gregor. A hundred thousand dollars in cash. With money like this—there is a lot going on in Armenia now. The Turks. The Soviets, who are worse than the Turks. The problems caused by the earthquake. The people—"

"Father," Gregor said, "what did Robert Hannaford want you to do for that money?"

Tibor smiled. "You're thinking he wanted me to commit a murder?"

"Or something worse."

Tibor's smile got broader. It made Gregor realize he'd lost a lot of teeth.

"Well, Gregor," he said, "I will tell you. He didn't want anything from me. He wanted something from you."

TWO

1 On the corner where the Halakmanian grocery used to be, there was now a gift shop—a great big plate-glass–windowed, tinsel-trimmed shop full of colored glass Christmas ornaments and flower vases made of seashells. Gregor didn't know if he liked it or not. If he'd still been living in Washington, the question wouldn't have been worth asking. In a sophisticated city among sophisticated people, it was obligatory to deplore the "commerciality" of Christmas. Sweet little girl angels with feathery wings, bright tinfoil stars, tree lights that winked and blinked like the neon signs of roadside motels: Gregor could hear Mrs. Senator Thomaston now, going on and on about it in her hoarse society caw, as if putting blinking lights on Christmas trees was tantamount to letting a four year old attack the Sistine ceiling with bubble gum. Mrs. Senator Thomaston had been Marianna Winford before she married, and what she liked in Christmas ornaments were little mud-colored figurines made by peasant women in Honduras.

What the children liked was flash and dazzle, the flash and dazzle of blinking lights especially. There was a crowd of them watching from the sidewalk, pressing their faces to the glass like street urchins in a Dickens novel. Even the ones in Ralph Lauren Polo had lost their studied jadedness. In fact, all of Cavanaugh Street had lost its studied jadedness. Back in May, when Gregor first moved into his apartment, the neighborhood had seemed not only newly rich but newly nervous. The triple deckers had been turned into private houses or renovated beyond recognition

into what their new owners insisted on calling "flats." The cars
in the cramped garages were made in Germany and various
shades of maroon and grey. The women had switched their alle-
giances from Sears to Saks. Cavanaugh Street had been a theater
of grinding poverty in the thirties, a prison of lower-middle-class
anxiety in the fifties. This latest change should have been a happy
one. Instead, the people Gregor met, even the ones he had
known for years, lived behind defensiveness and cynicism, as
jumpy and frightened as guests at a Washington cocktail party.

Maybe that was why he had made no effort to develop a social
life. Maybe he had found no one here he wanted to socialize
with. On the other hand, "socializing" had never been one of his
strong suits. While he'd had Elizabeth, she'd been enough. Once
she was gone, he'd found it hard to connect with other people.

He climbed the five stone steps to the door of the small house
where he had his apartment and searched through his pockets for
his key. It was after five and getting dark. He could feel a wet
sting against his hands that was the first of this winter's snow. He
was beginning to regret his months of coldness. With the coming
of the season, Cavanaugh Street had been transformed. He'd
missed Christmas, he realized—not Christmas as it was celebrated
in Washington and New York, but real Christmas with children
and grandmothers and too much food, with colored lights strung
in windows and ribboned wreaths hanging on doors. That, Cavanaugh Street had not lost.

He got the door open—he'd had so much trouble with it because it hadn't been locked in the first place—and as he swung
into the vestibule he heard George Tekamanian fumbling at the
first-floor apartment door. Gregor shut the outer door against the

wind and waited. George was quick for eighty-six, but he was still eighty-six. And just now, Gregor wanted to talk to someone. Badly.

The door scraped, screeched, popped. George stuck his tiny grey head into the vestibule, looking for all the world like a geriatric punk.

"Krekor," he said, using the Armenian pronunciation, the way all the old people did. "I thought it was you. Come in, come in. I have the rum punch, yes?"

"Does your doctor let you drink rum punch?"

"If it was up to my doctor, I'd live on grass." George swung the door wide and grinned. "Hot rum punch," he promised. "Real butter. Cholesterol city."

Gregor shook his shoes off on the vestibule carpet and followed George into the apartment—the Impossible Apartment, he thought of it, because the first time he'd seen it he'd thought he was hallucinating. George's grandson Martin had made a killing in the stock market—six or seven killings, from the look of it—and since George had adamantly refused to leave Cavanaugh Street for the Main Line, Martin had decided to bring the Main Line to George. George's apartment had been gutted and remodeled, its rooms made larger and airier, its soft plywood floors replaced with polished oak, its plain walls adorned with plaster moldings. In its present incarnation, it could have been a cover for *Metropolitan Home,* or a page from one of those catalogs for Yuppies Who Have Everything. Martin had bought George a "total entertainment center" in a walnut cabinet, complete with forty-inch TV and compact disc player. There was also an electric pencil sharpener, an electric waffle maker, an electric yogurt maker, a food processor that did nothing but roll meatballs and a set of sterling silver swizzle sticks in the shape of miniature golf clubs. There were also paintings, but both Gregor and George tried to ignore those. Martin had an unfortunate passion for postmodern art.

The rum punch was in a Baccarat crystal bowl surrounded by half a dozen matching cups—$8,000 worth of glass. The bowl and cups were sitting on a sterling silver serving tray—another $2,000. The tray rested on a butler's table that looked like a museum quality-antique—with a price tag Gregor couldn't begin to guess at.

He dropped into a needlepoint-embroidered wing chair. The fire was going, meaning Martin and his wife had been here not long before. The five-pound bag of sugar and the Hostess Twinkies were out, meaning they had been gone long enough for George to get comfortable. Sometimes Gregor wondered why he spent so much time in George's apartment. It might be the pleasure of George's company—which was considerable. It might also be envy.

George poured a cup of punch, dropped an immense dab of butter into it, and passed it over to Gregor.

"So," he said, "you went over to see Father Tibor. How was he?"

Gregor knew better than to think George wanted a report on Tibor's health. "He wasn't what I expected," he said. "I thought—"

"You'd find old Karpakian?"

Gregor smiled. Old Karpakian had been the priest at Holy Trinity while he was growing up—and the smelliest, most malicious old man Gregor had ever known. Armenians are respectful of their priests. Armenia was, after all, the first country to adopt

Christianity as a state religion. Karpakian had been that anomaly of anomalies, a priest who was genuinely and universally hated.

Suddenly, Gregor had a flash, a memory that hadn't surfaced in God only knew how many years. And it was just as funny now as its reality had been on V-E Day.

"Oh, God," he said, starting to laugh. "George. Do you remember the donkey?"

"Of course I remember the donkey," George said. "I—" He sat forward in his seat and tried to frown. "Krekor. The donkey. Was that you?"

"Me and Lida and Howard Kashinian," Gregor said. He was laughing so hard he was choking. "Lida and I weren't supposed to play with Howard Kashinian, but we needed him. He knew where to find the donkey. And he was the one with the criminal mind."

"But Krekor—"

"Well, old Karpakian deserved it," Gregor said. "The day before we'd had this church school class, preparation for something, I don't remember what. And Lida's sister Mary had a cold. She was sick as a dog and her mother had given her something for it that kept putting her to sleep. So she fell asleep at her desk and Karpakian came thundering down on her with a ruler and practically broke her fingers. And Lida said—"

"Krekor, old Karpakian may have deserved it, but I didn't deserve to spend my Sunday afternoon getting a donkey off the second floor of a church. Never mind out of that little room."

"He certainly knew what the little room was for," Gregor said. "That's the first thing he did when we got him in there."

George sighed. "Drink your drink, Krekor. And try to remember I'm an old man. I don't want to die without knowing how it was done."

Gregor took a long pull on his rum punch. "Oh, well," he said. "Tibor. I suppose I expected an illiterate peasant. I got a scholar. It's unusual."

George hesitated, as if he wanted to take up the matter of the donkey again. Then he said, "Tibor is unusual. When they sent him we got a report from the bishops. You know how that is?"

"I didn't know they let old wrecks like you on the parish council," Gregor said.

"The parish council is all old wrecks like me," George said. "The young men want to give the church gold-plated icon stands. There was a wife, you know."

"I wondered about that. I thought we liked them married."

"We do. Tibor's wife was just as crazy as he is, from what we hear. Crazy in a good way. She died in prison in the Soviet Union."

"That's interesting. What was she in prison for?"

"We don't know. I think this man may be a saint, Krekor. A real one, not the plasterboard kind they like to tell us about in church."

"I find it hard to believe you don't know all about him," Gregor said. "Everybody always knows everything about everybody around here. They used to say Lida's mother knew who was going to have a baby before they even conceived."

"Father Tibor," George said, "talks a lot. But not about himself."

"What does he talk about?"

"Many things. What did he talk about with you?"

Gregor shot the old man the look he used to give subordinates who'd asked questions they'd no right to the answers to—and then stopped himself. Under the circumstances, that was a particularly stupid reflex. He wanted to talk to George, and not only because he was lonely—although he'd come down to this apartment for that reason alone often enough. George was old and basically uneducated, but he would have made a better agent than most of the men Gregor had trained. Come to think of it, Father Tibor would have, too. They were both perfect straight men, the kind who knew when and how to get creative.

Gregor held his now-empty cup in the air, got an affirmative nod from George, and passed it over. He hated to admit it, but since he'd started thinking about Robert Hannaford, he'd been feeling better. It was like eating a really big dinner after being on a diet for months. He felt alert, awake, energized. He felt—

George handed him a cup full of rum punch. "So," he said, "are you going to tell me or aren't you going to tell me?"

"Oh, I'll tell you," Gregor said. "I just don't know if it will mean much."

"It wasn't just a lecture on how you should go out and do more?"

"No." Gregor cast around for a way to get into it, and came up with the same one Tibor had. Of course. "Do you know a man named Robert Hannaford?" he asked.

"The robber baron?" George brightened.

"The great-grandson of the robber baron," Gregor said. "The one who's alive now."

George frowned. "Robert Hannaford can't have a great-grandson," he said. "He's only—forty something. I read it in the paper."

"Forty something?"

"In *The Inquirer*," George said.

"This Robert Hannaford who was in *The Inquirer*," Gregor said, "was he in a wheelchair?"

"Oh, no. He'd just won—a tennis championship, I think. It was in the paper, Krekor. I read it."

Gregor thought it over. "That's probably the son," he said finally. "The son of the Robert Hannaford who came to see Father Tibor. Tibor said he, this Robert Hannaford, had seven children—"

"Then he's not my Robert Hannaford," George said. "They called this one an eligible bachelor. You know what that means. Not married and making whoopie with every girl he meets."

"Yes," Gregor said. "But a robber baron?"

"A corporate raider," George said helpfully.

"Ah," Gregor said. "This is getting interesting. Seven children, one of them a—robber baron. One of them a famous novelist—"

"Bennis Hannaford," George said, excited. "Father Tibor gave me her books. She's very good, Krekor. Very exciting."

"Does everybody around here read those things?" Gregor asked. It was remarkable what cultural climate could do. He had no interest whatsoever in fantasy fiction, or in fiction of any kind, but he was getting the urge to read Bennis Hannaford's books. He took another sip from his cup. "Mr. Hannaford asked Father Tibor to get in touch with me. He wants me to go out to his house and have dinner there on Christmas Eve."

"That was it? Just that you should have dinner there?"

"That was it for the request. He gave Father Tibor his card, and Father Tibor gave the card to me. I'm supposed to make a phone call. But Tibor said Hannaford insisted, and he stressed the 'insisted,' that there was nothing more to it but one dinner on the Main Line."

"Maybe it's because you're famous," George said, repeating the inaccuracy that was apparently believed by every resident of Cavanaugh Street. "Maybe he wants to impress his friends by bringing you out to dinner."

"Maybe."

George threw up his hands. "So what is it? It has to be something. What did he do, threaten Tibor with a gun?"

Gregor sat back, stretched out his legs, and told George all about the briefcase, the money, and the deal. His powers of narration seemed to have increased since he left the FBI. He'd never claimed quite that degree of attention from his listeners before.

By the time Gregor was finished, George was up on his feet and pacing—something, given arthritis and the general creakiness of old age, he never did. "But Gregor," he said. "That's crazy. That's the craziest thing I've ever heard."

"It's even crazier than you think it is," Gregor said.

"I don't see how it could be. It's crazy enough to start."

Gregor held up his glass and let George take it from him. He wasn't in need of another drink, but watching George pace that way, in such obvious pain, made him feel terrible.

"Listen," he said. "If Robert Hannaford had been a self-made man, I might have looked at this thing and decided it was crazy but not impossible. But Robert Hannaford is not a self-made man. Do you see what I mean?"

"No," George said.

"Self-made men sometimes think anything can be solved by money. Their whole lives have been motivated by money. A man

I knew, a congressman, told me once it was true that anyone can get rich in America—as long as that was all he wanted to do. That's the kind of commitment it takes, to be Carl Icahn, say. But the hereditary rich are different. They have money."

"So?"

"So they learn early that there are a hundred better ways of getting what they want than shelling out cash. They have family connections—in Washington, in New York, in government and industry and the security services. If Hannaford wants me out at Engine House for Christmas Eve dinner, why not just call somebody who knows somebody at the Bureau? The Bureau knows where to find me. What's more, anybody with any sense has to realize I owe those people."

George nodded. "All right. So why?"

"My considered judgment?"

"Yes, of course."

"Gossip," Gregor said definitely. "Whatever's going on with Robert Hannaford has to be sensitive enough so that he doesn't want any gossip. Which means it's probably actionable. You know what I'd do, if this had happened when I was still working?"

"Send Mr. J. Edgar Hoover after them?"

"J. Edgar," Gregor said, "is blessedly dead. Blessedly for the rest of us, I mean. No, what I'd have done is go straight to the senator I thought I could trust most. And I do mean straight."

George had settled himself in his chair again. The part of him moving now was his head. It was going back and forth like a door swinging on its hinge in a stiff wind. "Krekor, you're talking as if this is about spies."

"Spies is one of the things that might explain it. I can think of two others."

"What?"

"That one of his children is involved in a plot to kill the president. Or that one of his children is involved in major fraud."

This time it was George who took a long pull on his drink. He looked like he thought he needed it. "Krekor, in your voice I can hear it. You don't believe any of those things. I don't believe any of those things, either. They sound like science fiction. Miss Hannaford's unicorns are for me more real."

"Well," Gregor said, "that sort of thing is real enough for me. I've spent most of my life living with it in one way or another. What bothers me is that I don't think any of it is real in this case."

"Why not?"

Gregor waved a hand in the air. "For serious espionage, you need access. From what I've been able to figure out so far, neither Hannaford himself nor any of his children have it. As for the other things—Tibor thinks this man is, I wouldn't say an agent of the devil, but close. He didn't like Hannaford at all."

"Then there's probably nothing to like," George said. "Tibor isn't a practical man, but I would listen to him about people."

"So would I," Gregor said. "Tibor thinks Hannaford hates his children. Hates them unreservedly."

"And?"

"And a man who hates his children doesn't throw a hundred thousand dollars in cash around to get them out of trouble."

"Ah," George said.

"Exactly," Gregor said. "I thought about the wife, but Tibor says she's some kind of invalid. Very social and very involved in

good works, but basically domestic and too ill to get around and
do things. I think she gets written up on the society pages a lot."

George sighed. "So," he said. "Here we are. Maybe the man is
just crazy in the real way. Maybe he belongs in an institution."

"I don't know, George. I just know I don't like this thing. I
don't like him involving Tibor, and I don't like—well, what it
feels like."

"Do you know what you're going to do about it?"

"No."

"I don't know what you're going to do about it, either. Have a
little more rum, Krekor. It's good for the brain."

Gregor doubted it, but he knew it was good for the nerves. He
needed something for those.

2 Half an hour later, Gregor climbed the stairs to the
third floor, unlocked the door to his apartment, turned
on his foyer light, and found himself staring at Robert
Hannaford's card. The damn thing seemed to have appeared in his hand of its own volition.

He shut the door behind him, threw his coat on the rack, and
walked down the narrow hall to his living room. It looked white
and dead, but through its windows he could see the decorations
on Lida Arkmanian's town house. Lida had outdone herself—she
had a plastic Santa with eight reindeer and Rudolph on the roof;
a curtain of red and silver tinsel hanging from the fourth-floor
balcony; string after string of colored lights—and it was a good
thing. The reflected glory of her facade was all that made
Gregor's bare space look habitable.

Bare walls, bare floor, one couch, two chairs, and a coffee table in a thirty-by-twenty-seven-foot room. It reminded him of the way dance studios looked between classes.

He dropped into a chair, stretched his legs, and turned his body slightly so he could go on looking out the window. They had warned him he would lose the details of her—the way she looked, the way she talked, the way she moved—but it hadn't happened. In the dark, he could always hear her voice.

In this dark, he could hear her half-singing, half-humming under her breath, the way she had every night while washing dishes. She was in the kitchen, stacking plates away in tall oak cabinets. If he didn't try to follow her, she would stay.

Gregor closed his eyes. He had started out afraid of this. He had put her pictures in a drawer, put the sweaters she'd made him into storage with their furniture, taped her books into packing boxes. He'd thought he was losing his mind, and every time he'd felt her with him he'd wanted to drink.

Now he hoped only that she'd never leave him. He needed her as much as he ever had, beyond all considerations of pain and comfort. Better to ache for her than to feel nothing at all.

Elizabeth. Elizabeth. Elizabeth.

He opened his eyes again. The apartment was full of her, but for some reason that no longer relaxed him. He was restless and dissatisfied, distracted and tense. *Listen,* she'd told him once. *You need to do what you do. You need it more than you need me.* That wasn't true, of course. Before she died, he hadn't believed there was pain like that in the universe. But—

But.

He got out of the chair and headed down the back hall to his bedroom. The bed in there was unmade, something Elizabeth would have hated, but for once he didn't let himself feel guilty about it. He went to the dresser and took her pictures out from under the laundry-folded piles of shirts.

Elizabeth in her wedding dress, covered with satin and petit-point lace. Elizabeth on the boat they'd rented that summer on Martha's Vineyard, her fine grey hair blown into a cloud around her face. Elizabeth with her niece's tiny daughters, painted white and orange to look like a clown. Elizabeth. Elizabeth. Elizabeth.

He would have to get the sweaters out of storage, and the furniture, too. He would have to get new frames for the pictures. He would have to do a lot of things. At the moment, he only had to remember how much she had liked hearing about his work. It had been over two years, and it was time.

He'd dropped Robert Hannaford's card when he came into the bedroom. He bent over and picked it up off the floor. It was silly. It wouldn't lead to anything serious. It wouldn't provide him with something to do with his life. On the other hand—

On the other hand, at the moment, it was the only option he had.

There was a small black phone on the night table next to his bed. Gregor put Elizabeth's pictures where he could see them, picked up the handset, and started dialing.

THREE

1 "Listen," Myra said, throwing overpacked pieces of Gucci luggage into the foyer with one hand and holding her sable jacket closed with the other, "I know what time it is. Of course I know what time it is. I just don't *care* what time it is."

Anne Marie Hannaford backed up until she was standing against the wall. It was six o'clock in the morning, a good half hour before any of the staff was due to be on call, a good two hours before the kind of staff Myra needed would be around to help her. Like all large and formal houses—and this was that: forty family rooms, 26,000 square feet in the main wings, six double garages, a servants' wing the size of a small apartment building—Engine House was run on a rigid schedule. Anne Marie had been administrating that schedule for almost twenty years. She knew Mrs. Washington would "open" the kitchen at six-thirty and lay out breakfast on the sideboard in the dining room at seven. She knew Morgan, the driver, and Marshall, the butler, would both appear out of nowhere at exactly eight o'clock. She even knew which of the fourteen bedrooms each of the five upstairs maids would be cleaning at any given moment of the morning. What she didn't know, and couldn't figure out, was why *Myra* didn't know.

Of course, Myra never seemed to know anything. That was one of the things Anne Marie thought of as "seminal" to Myra's personality. There was a dress code on the Main Line, unofficial but tacitly enforced, and Myra always broke it. Instead of good tweeds and low shoes and a plain cashmere sweater, Myra had spikes and sable and large diamond earrings before dawn. Instead of a neat, little, hard-edged shoulder bag, she had a mammoth tote that could have been used to move furniture. Instead of a chignon, she had something that looked like a mushroom cloud in an advanced state of disintegration.

Anne Marie folded her arms over her chest, stroked the antique tin angel brooch on her collar, and waited. With Myra, waiting was always enough. The woman quite literally couldn't keep her mouth shut. And *that* broke the code of the Main Line, too. For Myra, there was no line of demarcation between the public and the personal.

Myra had finally managed to get all her suitcases into the house. Now she turned around, grabbed the foyer door, and slammed it shut.

"There," she said. "Now we can get down to serious business. *Is* there any coffee in this house?"

"Mrs. Washington's coffee will be out in an hour," Anne Marie said. "If you want something immediately, you'll have to go to the kitchen and see if Bobby's figured out how to use the Dripmaster yet."

"Bobby's here?"

"Everybody's here, Myra. And none of them were due until this afternoon."

"I wouldn't complain about good luck if I were you, Anne Marie. You don't have much of it."

If Anne Marie could have backed up any farther, she would have. Things being what they were, she had to stay where she was. She felt the throb in her head and rubbed the heel of her hand against her temple. Myra always gave her a headache, and the headache was always impervious to aspirin. Or Tylenol. Or any of that stuff. Anne Marie thought of it as a physical manifestation of a moral complaint. In all justice, it was Anne Marie who should have been married to a rich husband and living in Wayne.

Through the long, narrow windows on either side of the front doors, Anne Marie could see snow, the thick kind that fell for hours and stuck for weeks. She patted stray hair back into her chignon and tried not to think of all the other things that gave her headaches. Mother, upstairs in her private suite, barely able to get herself out of bed in the morning. Daddy, fallen asleep in his wheelchair in his study for the third time this week, likely to awake at any moment in a perfectly foul mood. Even the sight of Engine House decked out for Christmas—the wreath on the outside panel of the door Myra had just slammed; the bowls of holly on the foyer tables; the delicate crystal angels hanging from invisible threads from all the common room ceilings—gave her no joy.

In the early days, when Mother was periodically ill instead of periodically critical, Anne Marie had almost always enjoyed her life. Where Mother went, Anne Marie went—visiting and charities, parties and volunteer work, all within the carefully proscribed circle of Main Line women of good family. Anne Marie had found that period far more satisfactory than her two aborted years at Wellesley College. At college, her roommate had been a scholarship student from Detroit with pronounced ideas on politics and personal hygiene, and all her professors had seemed to lean determinedly leftward.

Unfortunately, as Mother's illness had worsened, her taste in charities had undergone a radical change. Benefit balls for the American Cancer Society and the Philadelphia Art League had been replaced by forays into the inner city—to free clinics, half-way houses, counseling centers, women's shelters. Organizational luncheons had disappeared from Anne Marie's schedule, supplanted by back-room meetings with middle-aged harridans who never wore makeup and smoked while they ate. Even the things she had enjoyed most, like her long conversations with the girls she'd once gone to school with at Agnes Irwin, had been crowded out of her life. These days, if she had a chance to have a long conversation with anybody, it would most likely be with a bag lady. Bag ladies littered the halls of all the "people's projects" her mother now visited.

Bag ladies. Anne Marie shook her head. The last thing she wanted to do was get herself started on the bag ladies. Thinking about them always made her wonder if she was losing her mind.

She looked up, expecting to find herself alone—surely Myra had wandered off to rant and rave at Bobby by this time—and found instead that her sister was still with her, standing in the middle of the foyer's checkerboard marble floor and looking her over like the head nurse at a diet center, eyes riveted on that damn tin angel. It made Anne Marie feel clammy and even fatter than she was.

"For God's sake," Anne Marie said. "What are you staring at?"

"You're the one who was a million miles away." Myra sounded uncharacteristically reasonable. "I've just been trying to get you to tell me what you meant by saying everybody was here."

Anne Marie sighed. "Everybody's here. Bennis and Emma came in right after dinner yesterday. Teddy wandered through at about midnight. Chris called up from Newark at two o'clock in the morning because his car broke down and I had to wake Morgan to go get him. Everybody's here, Myra."

"Are they up yet?"

"Of course they're not up yet. I wouldn't be up myself if Bobby hadn't come banging on the door at quarter to six."

"Have you talked to any of them?"

"If you mean did I sit them down and grill them about their lives, Myra, the answer is no. I never did much go in for gestapo tactics."

"You never did much go in for self-denial, either," Myra said. "You'd better put away the chocolates for a while, sweetie. You're getting positively grotesque."

Somewhere down at the end of the main hall, a bell started ringing: the bell Daddy used when he was in his study and particularly annoyed or particularly hurried. Anne Marie hesitated—God, how she wanted to give Myra a little of it back; *God* how she wanted to—but not for long. Myra was a pain in the ass. Daddy was something worse.

Sometimes, lying alone in bed and thinking about him down here with his paneling and his books, thinking about his flat black eyes staring at the bulge at her waist or the trunklike roundness of her thighs, Anne Marie had visions. She saw those eyes broken and blood all over his face.

In one thing, Anne Marie and Myra were in perfect agreement. It really was too bad Daddy had done all that with the money. It was even worse there was no one with an excuse to murder him for it.

Almost the first thing Bobby Hannaford did when he realized he'd be alone in the kitchen was take out the half dozen loose pieces of paper he kept his personal accounts on. First he laid them out on the kitchen table in a line. Then he got his calculator from his pocket and put it right beside them. Then he got his fist grip and began to exercise his left hand. It was very quiet in the kitchen, much quieter than it had been at the front of the house. Through the kitchen window, he could see the long line of garages with their swing-out, barnlike doors, every one decorated with silver and gold tinsel wreaths. The kitchen itself was a forest of evergreen and holly. There were the standard Hannaford decorations—the shiny tin balls, bells, angels, and cherubs. Mrs. Washington had even put a miniature crèche on the utility table next to the main stove. Mrs. Washington being Catholic, and there still being forty-two hours to go before Christmas Day, the manger was empty.

Wednesday, December 23.

Bobby looked down at his papers, and his calculator. If he hadn't been so tired, and so floaty, he would probably have been scared. The item that had appeared in last night's paper had been small and buried on a back page, but Bobby had become adept at divining the true nature of the obscure. In the kind of enterprise he was involved in, an early warning system was essential. Now he had his warning—four short lines about a man he'd never met, but knew McAdam had—but no driving need to do anything about it.

In fact, at the moment, he had no driving need to do *anything*. The rational part of his brain kept sending him instructions— he'd seen the item and he had the time; a week of good fast work could get him out of this both rich and untouchable; if he could just get Daddy off his back he'd be fine—but they fell over the rest of him like smoke.

What held his attention was the memory of the Christmas he was ten, the first time he had really understood the way the world worked. He had been hearing about his special status since infancy. He was the Oldest Son, the Hannaford Heir. Sometime in the distant future, he'd be Head of the Family. He'd treated the information the way he'd treated grade-school rumors of high-school algebra classes. He didn't have to worry about it at the moment. When he did have to, he would.

That year, when he was ten, he'd come downstairs before anyone else was up. The tree was in the larger sitting room, a twenty-four-foot Douglas pine weighed down with five generations of Hannaford ornaments. Because he wanted to get a good look at the crystal angel on top, he came at it from the balcony that opened off the west wing. He stood on the balcony for a while, wondering how they got glass to make the dips and swirls of angels' wings. Then he went down the balcony stairs to look at his presents.

He was halfway down the staircase when he realized one pile of presents was larger, much larger, than all the rest. He was stupefied when he reached the tree and found that pile belonged to him. It should have belonged to his father. Back on the stairs, he had assumed it had. His father was the Atlas of his world, part ogre and part god, unassailable and eternal. When Bobby thought of growing up, he saw himself getting taller and stronger year by year and his father getting taller and stronger still.

He opened the three boxes at the top of the pile, wondering if he had so much because the things they'd bought him were cheap and inconsequential. They weren't. He'd asked for a pair of air force binoculars, and he'd got them. He'd asked for a Greenwich gyroscope, and he'd got that, too. He looked across the room at his stocking, hanging from the mantel over the dead ashes of a cold fire and saw the pale blue envelope that should contain a notice saying five thousand dollars had been deposited in his trust account at the First National Bank. Just to make sure it did, he crossed the room and opened it up.

He was stuffing the envelope back into the stocking when he heard the balcony door moving above him. By the time he managed to turn around, his father was coming down the balcony stairs. Bobby backed up a little. He wasn't surprised at the ritual hatred in the old man's eyes—he knew his father hated him; he'd always known it—but there was amusement there, too, and Daddy amused scared Bobby Hannaford to death.

He'd taken a Hershey's Kiss out of his stocking when he'd put the envelope back in. Now he put his fist around it and pumped until the chocolate turned to liquid.

"Things," Daddy said, stopping halfway down the stairs.

"Excuse me?"

"Things," his father said. "That's the only way I know you exist."

"That's why I think you're losing it," Myra said. "You never listen to me anymore."

Bobby came to. He was sitting in the kitchen at Engine House, at some ungodly hour of the morning, looking through the window at a thick and furious fall of snow. He was forty-four.

He caught sight of his papers laid out along the table and started to gather them up. "Sorry," he said.

"*Are* you all right?" Myra said. "I thought you were *comatose.*"

"I'm fine, Myra. I'm just a little tired."

"I suppose you are. Although what got you here at six o'clock in the morning, I don't know."

Bobby let this pass—he always ended up letting a lot of things pass, with Myra—and put his calculator back in its slip case. He was feeling better. The torpor that had paralyzed him for most of the last twelve hours was gone. He could see everything he would have to do in the next week, and he could see himself doing it.

He put his fist grip into the pocket of the jacket he had thrown over the back of his chair and said, "Teddy's here, in case Anne Marie didn't tell you. He called me last night—woke me up from a sound sleep—trying to find out something about Mother. I think he got fired."

"Really?" Myra didn't sound interested. She was fussing with the Dripmaster, making the coffee Bobby had intended to make himself and then forgotten about.

She unhinged the pitcher, carried it to the sink, and started filling it with water. "Listen," she said, "can I tell you a secret? An absolute, dead dark, don't tell anyone secret?"

"Yours or somebody else's?"

"Don't be nasty, Bobby. I've been very good to you, the last couple of years."

"I'm not being nasty, Myra. You're just not very good at keeping secrets."

"I've kept *yours.*"

Myra had kept his secret because it was also hers, and she had no more interest in landing in jail than he did. Bobby didn't tell her that. He just watched her taking the pitcher back to the Dripmaster and pouring the water through the hole at the top.

When she was done and the pitcher was back in place, she came to the kitchen table and took the seat across from him.

"There's going to be a divorce," she said.

"Whose?"

"Mine."

Bobby blinked. "Dickie Van Damm wants to divorce you?" The idea of Dickie, the stuffiest, most pompous, most antediluvian asshole on the Philadelphia Main Line wanting to divorce anybody was like Ronald Reagan joining the struggle for worldwide Communism. Divorced people weren't allowed to attend the Philadelphia Assembly, for God's sake. Dickie mainlined the Philadelphia Assembly.

Bobby groaned inwardly at the awful pun, and Myra started tapping her long glittered nails on the tabletop.

"Of course Dickie doesn't want to divorce me," she said. "I want to divorce Dickie. That's where I have a problem."

"What's the problem?"

"I need money, Bobby. I want to file papers January second, and when I do I have to have enough in the mattress to keep me going until I get what I want."

"What do you want?"

"Half of everything."

"Naturally." Bobby sighed. "I told you last week, Myra. If you can keep Daddy out of my hair until New Year's, I'll have this thing wrapped up and ready to go. You can take your money and abscond to Tahiti, for all I care."

"New Year's."

"That's what I said, Myra."

"And you're sure."

"Of course I'm sure."

"You'd better be more than sure," Myra said. "The divorce laws aren't what they used to be. Dickie can fight this and he probably will. And you know Daddy won't be any help at all."

"Daddy never is."

A current of understanding passed between them, a compound of body language and race memory, made up of the thousand and one horrors they had survived together in this house. Then the water started to come through the Dripmaster, shooting a muddy stream into the pitcher, and Myra got up to get them both coffee.

"Did you say you thought Teddy had been fired?" she asked him.

"That I did."

"That's interesting," Myra said. "I wonder what he got fired for."

3

Upstairs in the west wing, Emma Hannaford was finding it hard to sleep. She was, in fact, finding it impossible to sleep. Unlike her brothers and sisters, she had no consistently terrible memories of Engine House. The one really awful thing that had happened to her here had happened and been done with, except in the minds of the people involved. Emma didn't see what she could do about that. She preferred to forget the incident altogether, whenever she was able. She felt better concentrating on the good things that had happened to her here. Her relationship with her mother, her relationship with Bennis: in a world where parents were distant figures, always on their way in from or out to parties, she had been lucky enough to have two people who put her ahead of everyone and everything else. When Emma thought about her childhood, she always saw it as the One Brief Shining Moment of the *Camelot* song. She even knew the moment it had ended, to the minute.

She looked at the glowing face of the digital clock on her bedside table. 6:15. It was too early to go downstairs. Mrs. Washington wouldn't be in the kitchen for another quarter hour, and she'd be too busy to talk for the half hour after that. It was too early to wake Bennis, too. Bennis had made it quite clear she intended to spend most of the next week conked. Emma sat up and turned on the table lamp, wondering why mornings in winter were always so dark.

(There's a scientific explanation for that, Emma. It's the kind of thing you were supposed to learn in school.)

Emma threw the covers off and hopped to the floor, feeling a little silly in her oversize sleep shirt. The hall outside her door was quiet, but she opened the door a crack and peered out anyway, just to check. The sleep shirt came down only to her knees and was made of a very thin material. She didn't like the idea of being caught in it while she wandered around the house. She'd been living alone so long—and in girls' dormitories for so long before that—she didn't own a robe. Even Bennington, coed and "progressive" as it was, hadn't been able to drag her out of this particular kind of isolation.

She let herself into the hall and headed for the center section of the house. There was a serious library downstairs, full of hardcover editions of Plato and Thomas Aquinas, but there was a smaller one up here, full of what her mother called "diversionary books." Her father had standing accounts at half a dozen bookstores in Philadelphia and New York, and every week a little rainfall of current best-sellers arrived at Engine House, to be unwrapped by Marshall and put up here by whatever maid was available. Emma thought she would get one of these books, bring it back to her room, and read until she could decently go down to breakfast.

She was just edging out of the west wing into the upstairs center hall when she heard the noise. At first, she thought it was birds. It was that kind of noise, faint and fluttery, mutely quarrelsome. Then she realized there couldn't be any birds—Mrs. Washington kept a much cleaner house than *that*—and she began to wonder what someone was doing up here, trying to get away with something in secret.

Aside from the little library, the upstairs center hall held two other small rooms. Emma looked into the tea room first, registering dust-cover covered love seats and shrouded candelabra. She crossed the carpet to the writing room and stood in the door. She saw Anne Marie. She saw the Sargent portrait of Great-Grandmother Eleanor Devereaux Hannaford standing away from the wall and the wall safe open. She stood silent for at least a full minute before she realized what was wrong. There was no reason on earth why Anne Marie should be doing what she was doing in the dark.

Emma wrapped her arms around her body—for some reason, every time Emma had to talk to Anne Marie she had an uncontrollable desire to protect herself—and said,

"Anne Marie? Are you all right? What are you doing?"

Anne Marie's shoulders stiffened—even through the dark, and under all that fat, Emma noticed—but they relaxed almost immediately. She put the papers she was holding into a pile on the mantel under the safe and turned.

"I'm fine," she said. "Mother's up. I'm just getting her some things she asked for."

"In the dark."

"I didn't notice it was dark."

"If Mother's up, can I go in to see her?"

Anne Marie turned around, closed the wall safe, put the picture back into position. Then she folded the papers into a square and put them in her pocket.

"Mother's not in very good shape first thing in the morning," she said. "Why don't you give her about half an hour? She doesn't like to see people when she's—not well."

"What does that mean, not well?"

"I thought Myra told you all about it. Mother has lateral multiple sclerosis." Anne Marie came to the door of the writing room and stepped into the hall, ushering Emma out with her. "Lateral multiple sclerosis is a degenerative disease that results in the loss of control of—"

"She's our mother, for God's sake," Emma said. "Stop sounding like a medical textbook."

"You wanted to know what I meant by 'not well.'"

"I still want to know."

Anne Marie made a face. "Mother sometimes has difficulty lifting objects. Forks, for instance."

"Forks?"

"Forks, knives, spoons. Pens, if they're the metal kind. Glasses."

"Mother has trouble lifting forks?"

"The doctor will be here the day after Christmas, Emma. He'll give you all the information you want."

The hall was drafty and too well lit. All around her, Emma saw globe lamps reflected in the polished surfaces of silvered-shined Christmas bells, balls, angels, and cherubs. She ran a hand through her hair, wondering if she was going crazy. Anne Marie sounded as if she were talking about something else—a cat, maybe, or a case that had come up in a volunteer nursing course.

Anne Marie brushed past her, on her way to the west wing, and Emma put out a hand to stop her.

"Anne Marie, please."

"Please what? Mother's been dying for years, and now she's going to be dead. What did you think was happening?"

"Anne Marie, for God's sake."

But Anne Marie was gone, disappearing through the west wing doors, the solid stack heels of her shoes making an odd thudding noise on the carpet, the tin angel on her chest clacking against the pearls of her necklace. Emma stood staring after her, wondering now if it was Anne Marie who was crazy. God only knew, you had to be crazy to take the death of your mother like that.

Emma thought about going after her, but she had a funny feeling it wouldn't do any good.

4 Half an hour later, Emma got back to her room, climbed into bed, and put the book she'd picked up in the little library on her lap. The book had taken her forever to find, because she hadn't been able to concentrate on looking for it. She kept thinking about Mother and Anne Marie and Bennis. Her dearest wish in the world was that she'd go back to the west wing and find a light under Bennis's door. She desperately needed someone to talk to. Then she reminded herself that if there wasn't a light under Bennis's door, it would be all that much worse if she was stuck in her room without a book.

The book she found was called *The Predators' Ball,* all about insider trading and corporate takeovers. It was reasonably new and shelved toward the front. If she hadn't been so distracted, she would have found it right away. When she did find it, she decided to take it as a godsend. Financial scandal was her absolutely favorite thing, better even than chocolate. She'd once read Ray Dirks's book on the Equity Funding scam twice in one month.

Coming back onto the wing, she found Bennis's room dark. She stood outside the door for a few moments anyway. Bennis had always said Emma should call any time Emma needed her. They were sisters and they would stick together. But Bennis seemed to know all about this thing. She had tried to explain it in the car while they were driving down from New York. If Emma woke her now, what would she say? That the truth had finally sunk in and it had upset her?

Emma went back to her room, got into bed, found her cigarettes, lit up. She couldn't make herself care about Michael Milken. She couldn't make herself care about Ivan Boesky. She couldn't even make herself care about smoking. There were diseases out there that could get you, and the care you had taken with your health wouldn't matter at all.

For Emma, there was something intrinsically wrong with that. It was as if she'd just found out, for certain, that most of the people in jail hadn't done what they were convicted of doing.

FOUR

1 Sometimes, Gregor Demarkian thought the net result of spending a significant part of one's life as a policeman was a kind of mania. No matter what else came along to distract you, including common sense, you kept insisting the world was supposed to be a rational place.

He looked down at the phone, lying off the hook on his bed, and thought about making his call again. He decided against it. It was eleven o'clock on Christmas Eve morning, and he had already made that call twice since he got up. In fact, he'd made it over a dozen times in the last week. The first time had been very satisfactory. Robert Hannaford had picked up himself, and they'd had a short but suggestive discussion of what Gregor was supposed to do to get to Engine House—and what he was supposed to do after he got there.

"I have the money still in the briefcase," Robert Hannaford had said. "You can count it when you get here. You can count it before you leave. Then you can take it with you."

"And what do I do in the meantime?"

"Eat," Robert Hannaford said.

Eat.

One of the things Gregor had been taught, and that he had in turn taught other people, was how to keep someone on the phone when they wanted to get off. He knew two dozen tricks for that purpose, and he had tried them all out on Robert Hannaford. None of them had worked. Like a politician or a surgeon, Hannaford knew how to cut off communication when he wanted it cut off. He knew even better how to say nothing when he wanted to say nothing. Gregor had been left, that first night, with the feeling that he had been snookered—and snookered by a man with a psychopath's voice. He'd ended up so angry he hadn't been able to sleep. He could still see himself, pacing from the kitchen to the living room to the bedroom and back again, feeling more and more certain that what he really wanted to do was break Robert Hannaford's neck.

It was his unaccustomed will to violence, and his feeling that he'd never sleep again if he didn't get some answers, that had made him decide to make the first of the follow-up calls the next morning. Hannaford's voice had had an unexpected effect on him. He was willing to grant Tibor all his nasty suspicions of the man's character. If there was one thing Gregor understood, it was the psychopathic personality—not the brain-diseased delusional-ism of the popular novel's "homicidal maniac," but the core of the men who had no emotions that were not in some way about themselves. And the women, too, Gregor thought. He'd never met a woman like that, but he'd read the files. What mattered here was that there had never been a normal man on earth with a voice like Hannaford's, and there never would be.

He'd called Engine House at eight o'clock, even though he knew it would have been better to wait until nine. He'd been too edgy to wait. He'd been too tired to be alert, too. The phone's ringing had had a different quality than it had the night before, but he hadn't realized it until the call was over. When the phone was picked up, he still expected it to be answered by Robert Hannaford.

Instead, he'd got a woman's voice. It was flat and nasal, with a tinge of resentment in it—the kind of voice he associated with the embittered and divorced. Because he knew none of Hanna-ford's children had ever been divorced—it was amazing what you could find out just by going through the newspapers and *Philadel-phia* magazine, especially when you borrowed the back copies from Lida, who never threw anything away—he'd assumed he was talking to Hannaford's secretary. He gave his name and ex-plained his business and waited to be put through.

There was a sound of papers shuffling on the other end of the line. The nasal voice said, "I'm sorry, Mr. Demarkian. I don't have the authorization to connect you."

"What?"

"I don't have the authorization to connect you," she repeated, sounding firmer. "I am allowed to put through calls only from the people named on this list. You are not named on this list."

"But—"

"It's very early, Mr. Demarkian. I'm sure you'll understand why I have to now get off the line."

There was a click in his ear and then the dial tone. And that was that.

Now he looked down at the mess on his bed—the phone and the newspapers and the magazines and the notes on yellow legal paper—and wondered what he was supposed to do about it all. This last call had been just like the first, and it had left him with the same feeling of residual anger and of residual apprehension. If it hadn't also left him feeling that Elizabeth was closer to him now than she had been at any time since her death, he might have called the whole thing off. He had a precise understanding of just how dangerous it was to get involved with men like Rob-ert Hannaford. Even when they weren't engaged in physical homicide, they were heavily involved in murder.

He'd left a cup of coffee on his night table. He picked it up, took a drink out of it, and winced at the cold flatness of the liquid. Then he put it back. He wanted to get out of the bedroom. The place was full of Hannafords—Bennis in *People* and *Life* and *The New York Times Book Review,* Bobby in *Forbes,* Cordelia Day, Robert's wife, in *The Inquirer* and the city magazines. He'd spent most of the last week collecting this stuff, drawn to it the way cocaine addicts were drawn to street corners, and he was sick of it. Elizabeth or no Elizabeth, he wanted to take the whole mess and shove it down the incinerator.

He had just stood up, and found himself staring at the lines of illness edged all too clearly in Cordelia Day Hannaford's face, when the doorbell rang.

2 Caught in the opening door, Lida Arkmanian looked embarrassed. In fact, she looked devastated. She had a big holly wreath in one hand, a hammer in the other, and a collection of tiny nails sticking out of her mouth. Peeking out of one of the slash pockets of her chinchilla coat she had a card, with his name written across the envelope in Palmer Method script. Gregor found himself biting his lips to prevent a smile. He didn't need The Process, as the Bureau had called it, to figure this one out. Lida had come by, expecting him to be out to lunch or over at Holy Trinity Church, meaning to decorate his life in secret.

Actually, he was just happy to see her. She took his mind off the fact that, the longer he looked at the pictures, the surer he was that Cordelia Day Hannaford was dying. She had an air he knew well, from all the years he had spent taking care of Elizabeth.

Gregor took the hammer and wreath out of Lida's hand and positioned the holly on his door, so that it surrounded the bell. It looked nice there, nice enough to make him wish he'd spent some time decking out the place in the proper Christmas spirit. It shamed him to think he hadn't even considered it. Elizabeth would have started making tinsel balls right after Halloween.

He looked up at Lida and gestured to the wreath. "Nail there," he said. "If you'd brought bigger nails, we'd only have to use one."

Lida was blushing. "I didn't bring the nails for the wreath," she said. "I didn't even bring the wreath. I was just—I mean, I was up—I mean, it was—"

"Donna Moradanyan's idea?"

Lida clucked. "She's a nice child, Gregor. She's very worried about you. Here she has the whole building decorated in satin ribbons and silver bells, and you don't have any decorations to speak of. Not any decorations anyone can see. It's not healthy, Gregor."

"Nail there," Gregor said again.

Lida put the nail through the cluster of lacquered leaves, and Gregor pounded at it with the overlarge hammer. Then she put another nail up, and he pounded on that, too. Pounding made him feel good. Besides, if this was Donna's idea, Gregor felt an obligation. Lida was right. Donna was a nice child, with *child* as the operative word. She was twenty-one and a student at the Art Institute—the top floor apartment, just above Gregor's own, having been bought for her by her father when she had the "crazy" idea of moving into Philadelphia to go to school—but in

Gregor's mind Donna was inevitably a "girl" and not a "woman." She behaved like a girl. She had snow fights with eight year olds in the street. She rode a skateboard to her bus stop in the summer. She seemed sexually as innocent as an Amish virgin. Like a fairy-tale heroine, she had more trust in the benevolence of the universe than she had in the law of gravity. And she had decorated the whole house, or at least the side of it that faced Cavanaugh Street. The building looked like a gigantic Christmas present, wrapped in ribbons and tied with bows.

The last nail was in. Gregor stepped back, nodded at his handiwork, and said, "There. Now Donna Moradanyan won't be disappointed."

Lida stooped down and came back up again with a bowl. She must have left it on the floor while she fiddled with the wreath. Gregor hadn't noticed it.

Lida plucked at the Saran Wrap stretched over the bowl's top and said, "This is for you. That's what I came to bring. It's stuffed vine leaves. I see you all the time, eating at that Ararat restaurant—"

"They have very good food, Lida."

"I'm sure they do. But they're not home, Gregor. I thought you'd like something to eat at night. I know you eat at night. You did that even as a child. And I kept thinking of you coming back to this place, with nothing in the refrigerator but a bottle of diet soda, just like my niece Andrea, and I thought—well, you can guess what I thought."

Gregor could guess. He'd given up eating at night during Elizabeth's last illness, but he thought saying so would make the conversation awkward. He didn't want that. He picked up the bowl and motioned Lida through his door, stepping back to give her room.

"Look at me," he said. "Do I look like I'm starving?"

"You look like you could take off twenty pounds," Lida said, "but that's just heredity, Gregor. My sister's second husband had it. Once he was in the hospital with gallbladder and sick for three months, and he didn't lose an ounce."

"Ummm," Gregor said. He wouldn't ask her why she thought someone could "have" heredity, the way they had a cold. Doing that would just set her off on one of her lectures, and Gregor had been listening to Lida's lectures since they were both four years old. He motioned her into his apartment again.

"Don't you want my vine leaves?" Lida asked him.

"Of course I want them. I just want you to stop worrying about me starving to death. I'm not starving to death."

"You ought to be starving to death," Lida said. Then she smiled a little and passed by him.

For the first time, Gregor was acutely aware that his apartment was not only bare, but eerie. A bad motel room would have had more personality. The foyer was the worst of it—no pictures on the walls, no occasional table for the mail, not even an umbrella stand. Fortunately, Lida seemed to have no interest in spending any time there. She passed through as fast as she could walk, right into the kitchen. Gregor's relief was immense. The kitchen didn't look so much like a place the Bureau would have raided in their search for a serial killer.

Of course, the kitchen wasn't perfect, either. By the time Gregor got there, Lida was rinsing out a pair of coffee cups—but it was obvious, from the way the doors of the cabinets were firmly closed and the papers on the table had changed position, that she had been looking around. And finding him wanting. Now she was making new coffee, in the percolator instead of out of the jar, and scrubbing his cups as if they'd been caked with mud slime instead of just covered with dust. Gregor sat down at the table to watch her work.

"So," he said, "you came up to see Donna Moradanyan."

Lida stopped her scrubbing, stared into the bottom of the cup, and went back to scrubbing again. "Yes, I did. I come to see her every week. Her mother asked me to."

"Her mother's worried about her living in Philadelphia?"

"Oh, she's not worried about Cavanaugh Street." The cup was as clean as it was going to get—cleaner. Lida put it down on the table and picked up the other one. "It's the rest of Philadelphia that bothers Marie. And the Art Institute. It bothers me, too. It's not like it used to be, Gregor."

"No place is."

"Do you remember the dances they used to have, at the church, when we were children? Teenagers, they call them now. In those days, the grandmothers sat in the chairs against the wall and if you talked to a boy your parents knew about it before you got home."

And you hated it, Gregor thought. They had more than hated it. They had spent their high-school lives envying the hell out of their Anglo Saxon classmates, who seemed to live in a world where nobody knew anybody. And everybody necked.

Lida put the fresh coffee and the new clean cup down on the table, and then, as an afterthought, got the milk and sugar. Then she sat down in the seat directly across from him and stared at her spoon.

"Well," she said. "Here we are. After all these years."

"It hasn't been that many years, Lida."

"I think it's been forever," Lida said. She watched him put milk and sugar into his coffee, frowning a little, as if she wanted to give him the same lecture Elizabeth had been so fond of. Then she turned her head away and said, in an oddly abrupt tone, "You think I don't remember. How awful it was. That feeling that we were different, not so shiny and bright as all the rest of them. And you going off to college, nervous all the time, because in those days they were always looking for excuses *not* to give scholarships to 'minority groups.' Oh, I remember. It was terrible. It just wasn't as terrible as this."

"This?"

"Things have changed, Gregor. Oh, I know. Things have changed everywhere. But this isn't everywhere. This is here. This is home. I think we—the older people, you know—I think we thought that if we stayed here, if we didn't move out to the Main Line or Bucks County or someplace else that really belonged to them, that it would be all right. That we could go on being us. But it didn't work."

Gregor threw up his hands. "What do you want? To speak Armenian at home and gain fifty pounds with every baby? To be so afraid of doctors you go to church instead of to the hospital when you're ill, no matter what the priest tells you? Or maybe you want old Karpakian instead of Father Tibor?"

"Don't be ridiculous, Gregor. I'm not senile. I just—I just want the world to make sense."

If Gregor hadn't been thinking the same thing himself, less than half an hour before, he would have smiled. There it was, the one thing everybody wanted, and the one thing nobody got. He felt suddenly sorry for her. She'd lived a life that made the unpleasant truth easy to avoid—and now she must have run into something that made it so clear, she couldn't get around it.

Gregor got up and started to search his cabinets for a plate to put the vine leaves on. It would be polite to offer her something, and he had nothing else. Not even cookies.

"So," he said, when he came back to the table, "is that what this visit is all about? You want me to help you make the world make sense?"

"Don't be silly," Lida said. "I came because—I came because Father Tibor said something, in passing you understand, the other day. You're going into business as a private detective?"

"Of course I'm not," Gregor said, surprised. "Whatever gave him that idea?"

"I don't know," Lida said.

"It would be a mess," Gregor said. "I'd need a license. I could probably get one, but then what would I do? I don't have any interest in adultery and I couldn't care less about insurance fraud."

Lida looked at her hands. "What about missing persons? Would you need to get one of these detective licenses to find a missing person?"

"I suppose anyone could go looking for a missing person, if they didn't charge for it." Gregor was curious. "Who have you got missing? I can't believe your son-in-law would have taken off on that beautiful child of his—"

"No, no." Lida hesitated, then seemed to make up her mind. She reached into the pocket of her coat without the card in it and came up with a small photograph. "Here," she said. "This is the boy. This is the one I want to find."

"Nice-looking boy," Gregor said. He was, too—clean, well dressed, even featured, young. He was not, however, particularly memorable. The photograph had been taken in a studio someplace. It showed a young man with a taste for crewneck sweaters and button-down shirts, posed against a hazy blue background as bland as his clothes.

"Not the sort of young man to stick out in a crowd," Gregor said.

"No," Lida said. "But he stuck out, Gregor. Believe me. At least once, he stuck out much too far."

"Good lord," Gregor said. "You're making a dirty joke."

"I'm making a dirty pun." She took the photograph out of his hand and made a face at it, fierce, like an old woman chasing a raccoon away from her root cellar. "This," she said, "is the nice Armenian boy who came from Boston and got Donna Moradanyan pregnant and just disappeared into thin air."

FIVE

1 It was after five o'clock, full dark, when old Robert Hannaford finally backed his wheelchair away from the niche in the south wall of his study and gave up. In the niche, a black marble bust of Aristotle gleamed with polish and indifference, its base just a little out of true. Just a little. In the old days—no more than a year ago—he had been able to lift that bust straight into the air over his head, never mind the fact that it had to weigh at least forty pounds. Even six months ago he'd been able to get it out and hold it steadily in the air, arms straight to the front of him, for a good five minutes. He was an old man, and a cripple, but he worked at himself. The muscles in his arms and shoulders were massive and solid. From the back, he almost looked young.

From the front, he looked seventy-six, which he was. He drummed impatiently on the arm of his chair. And then, because that hurt, he stopped. His hands were going. The skin on them was slack, and the thickness at the joints was arthritis. Sometimes he woke in the night with pain so bad it reminded him of his accident, all those years ago, when every bone in his body seemed to have been powdered and the powder ground into his nerves.

A lot of things had been reminding him of the accident, lately. Weak or not—and he refused to think of himself as weak, or sick, or old; once you got started in that direction, your life came apart —there was nothing wrong with his mind. Too many things had been odd at Engine House in the last few weeks. It wasn't Myra inviting the rest of them up for Christmas. He could have accepted that as a gesture to Cordelia, and put up with it—as far as he ever put up with anything. His children were a pack of idiots, and dangerous idiots as well. From the time of the accident, he had known that one or the other of them would always be trying to kill him. But Cordelia loved them, and Cordelia loved Christmas. And Christmas, as far as his wife was concerned, was a family holiday. Robert put his trust in truism: his children weren't suicidal. They didn't want to kill themselves, only him. And he'd made sure they knew what precautions he'd taken and just how hard it would be to get out of this house if they did anything stupid. This time.

He wheeled himself to the window and looked out at the drive, clear and wet even though the snow was coming down in sheets. Little things, that was the problem. A pen that moved itself to the living room. A cup of coffee that went from the top of the desk to the top of the mantel. The kind of thing that might be the result of his own forgetfulness, if he were a forgetful man. He wasn't. Once, he'd had an eidetic memory. That had gone—his own father had warned him it would—but he had been left with much better recall than most people started out with. He could no longer flip through a book he had never seen before and then recite it, word perfect. He could tell anyone who wanted to know exactly what he'd done with his day, hour by hour, minute by minute, second by second, inconsequential act by inconsequential act.

A letter that went from the "finished" pile to the "unfinished" one. A sweater left lying on the love seat in front of the fire transposed to the wing chair near the door. Little things.

He leaned back, grabbed the buzzer he had left on the occasional table near his private bar, and jabbed at the button. He was bored, and when he got bored he got angry. He punched the button four or five times, then looked at the red numbers on the digital clock on his desk. If it took Anne Marie at least five minutes to get here, he'd have a perfect excuse to rip into her. What with having to come from the other end of the house, it often took her a good deal more than five minutes. Fat stupid cunt.

This round, it took her no time at all. Robert had barely checked the exact time—5:17:06—when he heard footsteps in the hall. The door swung open, moving on hinges so well oiled they couldn't be heard at all, and Anne Marie was there. Fat stupid cunt, Robert thought again. Trussed up like a *Town and Country* centerpiece in cashmere and tweeds. Vulgarized by one of those crude tin brooches Cordelia had made as a child. The woman was becoming grotesque. She looked gelatinous.

She was also used to his complaints. She shut the door behind her and said, "Are you all right? You sounded frantic."

"Of course I'm all right. Where's that man? It's after five o'clock."

Anne Marie sighed. "Morgan was supposed to pick him up at five o'clock, Daddy. It's only twenty past. You can't get up here from Philadelphia in twenty minutes."

"When he gets here, I want you to bring him straight to me. I have something I want to talk to him about before dinner."

Anne Marie nodded, looking bored—which she probably was. She was not only a fat stupid cunt, but a singularly uncurious one.

"Is that all?" she asked him. "If it is, I'm going to get some work done in the kitchen. We do have a guest for dinner."

Robert rubbed his face, trying the line of the dent where Marshall had nicked him that morning. "How's your mother?" he asked. "She hasn't been down to see me once today."

"She's been tired," Anne Marie said. "She's taken at least two naps. She knows she's going to want to stay up later than usual tonight. I think she just wants to be in good shape."

"Will she be in good shape?"

"She's better than she's been in weeks."

Robert flicked this away, using his hands, as if ideas were physical entities. What Cordelia had been "for weeks" was in a state of collapse. What Anne Marie had just said could mean anything. "What about the rest of them?" he asked. "Have they been in to see her?"

"Haven't they told you? You've had almost every one of them in here for one thing or another today."

"I didn't ask you what they told me. I asked you what you know."

Anne Marie hesitated. "Most of them have," she said finally. "Emma and Bennis—"

"I didn't tell you to get most of them to see her. I told you to get all of them. Jesus God, Anne Marie, what do you want? Emma having hysterics at the dinner table when Cordelia drops a glass?"

"Emma has seen her," Anne Marie said. "She and Bennis went up together right after lunch. And Myra's been in, and Bobby. It's Teddy and Chris I can't seem to find."

"What do you mean, can't seem to find?"

"What does it sound like I mean, Daddy? They've disappeared someplace. I haven't had a call from Baylor at the gate, so I suppose they're still on the property, but I don't know where. They were down for lunch and then they were gone."

"Have you looked for them?"

"Of course I've looked for them. I went to both their rooms and I checked all the common rooms and I even went out to the garage, about half an hour ago, just in case."

"What in the name of hell would they be doing down in the garage?"

"I have no idea," Anne Marie said. "It was just somewhere I hadn't looked."

"Assholes," Robert Hannaford said. "What time's your mother due to come downstairs?"

"Six."

"Try to get them both up to see her before she comes down. Try. I don't want either one of them making a scene while that man's here. And your mother probably wants to see them anyway. She always does."

"Yes," Anne Marie said, "she does."

"Then go look for them. What are you hanging around here for?"

Anne Marie seemed about to say something, but thought better of it. She always did. Robert watched her get the doorknob turned and the door opened, every movement an agony of clumsiness. Fat stupid cunt. At least the rest of them looked all right.

"Fat stupid cunt," Robert Hannaford said aloud.

Anne Marie turned to look at him, her eyes flat. Then she walked into the hall and closed the door behind her.

Robert Hannaford wheeled himself back to the window to keep watch on the drive, burning money by the second in an orgy of electrical heat.

At 5:17:09, only seconds after Anne Marie entered Robert Hannaford's study, Christopher Hannaford lit the fourth of six joints he had brought out to the stables after lunch, took a monumentally huge drag on the slick end of it, and passed it to Teddy. Like the three joints that had come before it, and the two still resting in the breast pocket of Chris's blue cotton workshirt, it was as big as a cigar, and safe. Its safety resided in the fact that Chris had grown the marijuana himself. That was a necessity. Out in California, marijuana dealers tended to deal in other things as well, and because of that they also tended to spray their grass with substances no sane person would want. Heroin. Crack. If you couldn't get your clients hyped by fair means, use foul. It was for that reason—and not just because he liked the stuff so damned much himself—that Chris was in favor of legalizing grass.

Maybe.

At the moment, he was in favor of it because grass had turned out to be the only not-immediately-lethal substance in the known universe capable of calming him down after his interview with his father. He was surprised as hell that it had worked. Actually, he would have been surprised if death had worked. He had this feeling he was going to go into eternity with that scene imprinted on his soul: Daddy in the wheelchair, the papers spread out on the desk, the tapping of the grandfather clock that stood against the west wall and hadn't kept decent time since 1966. It could have been a tableau from a situation comedy about the joys of family life, except that Daddy had seemed so pleased with himself. And Daddy pleased with himself was never an appetizing sight.

"These," Daddy had said, waving his hands over the papers on the desk, "are a communication from a man named Anthony Giacometto. He says you owe him $77,451.22. As of this morning."

On the other side of the loft, Teddy was flailing in the straw, looking happy. On that score, too, this experiment had been a success. Chris had been surprised to find that Teddy had never tried marijuana. He had been delighted that Teddy had taken to it so well. Besides, the dope had made Teddy so spacey, he hadn't been able to continue the conversation he'd started back at the house, which was all about how awful Chris looked. Chris thought he had every right to look awful. The last thing Daddy had said to him, before throwing him out of the study, was:

"Don't forget. Anyone can get through that gate if I want to let them through. Anyone."

Right.

They'd brought a brown paper grocery bag full of goodies from the kitchen when they'd come out. Chris reached into it, found a chocolate chip cookie, and ate the thing whole. Teddy saw him and came scuttling over, looking for dope.

"The thing is," Teddy said, "I thought everybody in California screwed like rabbits. All the time."

Chris took the joint back, inhaled, and blew a cloud of smoke into his nose. "Nobody screws like rabbits any more," he said. "There's AIDS."

"When you came down to lunch today, I thought you had AIDS," Teddy said.

"Jesus Christ," Chris said.

"You look like you haven't eaten for a year."

"I've got an ulcer, Teddy. In fact, I think I've got two."

Teddy nodded sagely and hit on the joint again. Chris had to take it out of his hands to get it back. He did it without rancor. He was by nature a good-hearted man. He hated Daddy, yes—and at the moment, he was scared to death of him—but the way Daddy was, he was practically required to. As for Teddy, Chris had never gotten along with him before and he was getting along with him now—and he thought that was nice.

Or something. He lay back against the hard slat of a broken feed crib and said, "So what do you think? Is Daddy finally going completely around the bend, or what?"

"Daddy?" Teddy jumped.

"Yeah. Daddy. Morgan came and picked me up in Newark, we drive through the gate, there's a guy out there with a Uzi, man."

"It's not a Uzi," Teddy said. "It's a Springfield twenty-two. Anne Marie says she doesn't even think it's loaded."

"If Daddy has some guy out there freezing his nuts doing sentry duty, the gun is loaded. Trust me."

"Well, I don't think that's necessarily crazy. You've got to think about terrorists."

"Terrorists." Chris laughed. "Oh, hell, Teddy. If somebody's going to kill the old goat, it's going to be one of us."

Teddy stiffened. "What for? What would we want to kill him for?"

"Why not? Don't you ever think about it? Just walking into that room of his one day and sticking his penknife in his jugular vein?"

"I wouldn't use a penknife," Teddy said. "I'd use something I could break his legs with. Like a cane."

"Oh," Chris said. His mind skittered to thoughts of thumbs and then away again. "I'm not much for broken bones, to tell you the truth."

"I'm not much for killing Daddy," Teddy said.

Chris looked up at his brother, curious. Teddy hadn't sounded convincing, but Chris hadn't expected him to. What Chris didn't understand was why Teddy wanted to deny what was perfectly clear to—and about—every one of them.

Chris flipped over on his stomach and propped his chin on his hand. In this position, he could see the kitchen yard and windows and one wall of the garages that had once housed Daddy's collection of cars. It was dark, but the overhead safety lights were on. He could see the thick snow slanting in the wind and the gold and silver traces of outdoor decorations. Then the kitchen door opened and a slight figure came onto the porch, looking ridiculous in an overfilled down coat.

"Here comes Bennis," Chris said.

"Bennis?" Teddy sat up straight. "Are you sure?"

"Of course I'm sure. God, she grew up beautiful, didn't she?"

"Mmm," Teddy said.

"Anne Marie's probably looking for us. That's what it's about."

"What time is it?" Teddy said.

Chris looked over his shoulder, confused to find Teddy up and moving around. "You're the one with the watch," he said. "I never wear a watch."

Teddy checked his watch. "Quarter to six. How did it get to be quarter to six?"

"Dope is like that," Chris said.

Teddy brushed away the offered joint. "I've got to get out of here. I had no idea it was this late. I've got to get dressed for dinner. I've got to—"

"Are you all right?"

"I'm fine," Teddy said. "I'm just in a hurry."

"Why? Stay around and talk to Bennis. She—"

Teddy shook him off. "No. The one thing I don't want to do is stay around and talk to Bennis." He found the boot he had lost and got it on. A moment later, he had swung out of sight down the ladder. Chris sat up and stared after him, amazed. Teddy was hopping down to the stable floor. His brace clattered once or twice against the ladder rungs, then landed with a thump in the hay at the bottom.

"Will you just cool out?" Chris said.

Thump. Thump. Drag. Thump. Thump. Drag. Teddy didn't stop moving until he got to the stable door—the back stable door, so he wouldn't even run into Bennis coming in—and then he turned around and said,

"Screw you."

Chris blinked. Teddy was gone. Bennis hadn't arrived. He was alone. He suddenly felt as if he'd been on one of those acid trips he never actually took.

He was beginning to think he ought to give up dope.

3 At 5:59 Bennis Hannaford, fresh from a two-way trek through the wilds of the kitchen yard and an even stranger trek through the wilds of her brother Christopher's mind, came in out of the wind to the warmth and humidity of the kitchen. Mrs. Washington was at the stove,

pulling a tray of hot cheese canapés out of the lower oven. Bennis popped off her boots—nobody in their right mind made a mess of Mrs. Washington's daily-waxed floors—and went over and stole one. She had to snake her thin white hand under Mrs. Washington's broader black one, but this was a game they had been playing since Bennis was three. If Mrs. Washington ever started making it easier for her, Bennis would be wrecked.

Mrs. Washington decided to make it harder by putting the canapé tray on top of the refrigerator. "That man isn't here yet," she said. "Stuck in the snow out there, I guess."

"The snow is awful," Bennis said. "The canapés are good."

Mrs. Washington didn't respond to that one. Her canapés were always good. "Did you find those two?"

"I found Chris. Stoned."

Mrs. Washington took another tray of canapés, ham and cheese this time, and shoved them into the lower oven. "That boy always did have money where he should have had brains. What happened to the other one?"

"I don't know. According to Chris, they were both out there all afternoon, and then just before I came Teddy took off. Actually, what Chris said was that Teddy took off because I came, but that doesn't make any sense, does it?"

"Nobody makes any sense," Mrs. Washington said. "Maybe he went up to see your mother."

"Did he come through here?"

"I haven't seen him yet."

"I saw him at lunch. God, but it's tense around here. I don't know how you stand it."

Mrs. Washington smiled. "Forty-five thousand a year and a

ride to Mass every Sunday. And it's not so tense when the whole pack of you aren't here at once. He's always a nuisance, but your mother and Anne Marie aren't bad."

"I'd rather live with him than Anne Marie," Bennis said. "At least I know what's going on with him."

"There's your brother Teddy now." Mrs. Washington waved her spatula at the wall. "He's going down the east hall. You can hear the brace."

Bennis could quite definitely hear the brace. She'd forgotten what a distinctive sound it made. "I wonder what he's doing over there," she said. "I can't believe he's going to pay a visit to Daddy."

"If he does, your father will beat him to a pulp," Mrs. Washington said. "My, the energy you people waste on hating each other, it's amazing. Myra came through here a little while ago—"

"To give you a lecture on nouvelle cuisine?"

"Wanted to know if I knew where Bobby was. Looked right through the pantry, like he was going to be hiding in the potato bin. Came out and called him an ugly name. Things are tense around here when she shows up."

"Has she been showing up a lot?"

"Once a week or so since your mother got out of the hospital. I'd put it down to worry about Mrs. Hannaford, but she never goes up to see Mrs. Hannaford. Nobody does. Even he waits for her to come down."

"Maybe he doesn't want to impose on her," Bennis said.

Mrs. Washington snorted. "Take one of these ham and cheese things," she said. "Then get out of my kitchen. With all the coming and going around here today, I'm half an hour late."

4

Bennis wandered into the back hall, and then into the foyer, and then—for no reason in particular—into the east wing corridor. She was bone tired. She'd spent most of the day with her muscles tight and her breath coming in hitches, wondering when one or the other of them was going to go too far. It was one thing to moan and wail about your family to strangers, or even nonstrangers, like Michael, who didn't know them. When you did that you just came off like somebody in a sitcom and gave the impression you were Just Too Hip not to be alienated. The truth was, there was nothing sitcom-ish about this place, and never had been. Too much had happened. Too much had gone unresolved and unforgiven. Even elementary conversations about the weather generated currents of history and hate.

There was a door open near the other end of the corridor, a light spilling out into the amber discretion of the hall. Bennis went toward that, unthinking. She wished she knew where Emma was. Bennis had gone looking for her half an hour ago, but Emma hadn't been in her room or the library or Mother's sitting room, her usual places. Then Anne Marie had come roaring out of nowhere, absolutely insisting on having help finding Teddy and Chris. Anne Marie had been looking for those two all day, making everyone's life hell. She would go on making everyone's life hell until she found them. So Bennis, who had seen them slip out the east wing rear door just after lunch, went to collect them.

The open door at the end of the corridor was the door to Daddy's study. Bennis was sure of it. She stopped, confused. From what she remembered, that door was never left open unless Daddy was out and about in the house, and he wouldn't be now.

He'd left instructions with everyone on earth, through Anne Marie, that he wanted that Mr. Demarkian person brought directly to the east wing as soon as he arrived, and that he intended to be there. Bennis thought of the bathroom and rejected it. The study had a bathroom en suite. She advanced down the corridor and stared at the light on the floor.

If she barged in there and there was nothing wrong, he'd have her head. He'd been looking for an excuse to have it, anyway.

On the other hand, he was an old man, and old men had strokes.

Crap.

Bennis Hannaford had never been a ditherer. She had never liked ditherers. She couldn't understand what she was doing here, shifting back and forth on her feet like a grade-school child who needed, but was too embarrassed to ask, to go to the toilet.

Making up her mind, she went down the hall to the door, pushed it open wide, and stepped into the study.

Her father was lying halfway across the room from his wheelchair, sprawled out on the fieldstone overlap of the fireplace base.

Her mother was sitting on the raised hearth, the broad skirt of her blue silk dress wet and heavy with very fresh blood.

Robert Hannaford's head had been crushed into pulp.

SIX

1 At twenty-two minutes past six, Gregor Demarkian, sitting in the back of Robert Hannaford's custom stretch Cadillac limousine, passed through the front gates of Engine House. The main house was so far from the road, he couldn't see it at first. The landscape around him reminded him of stories of the forest primeval. Every once in a while, a hailstone came down in the muck of thick snow falling from the sky. It struck the windshield or the roof of the car and disappeared into the surrounding white.

"This driveway's heated," the driver said, producing the observation in the smooth upbeat rhythm of a tour guide. "That's why we haven't been skidding since we got through the gate."

Gregor said, "Mmmmm." He hadn't noticed they hadn't been skidding since they got through the gate. He hadn't even noticed they had been before they got through it. His mind was on a number of things, all of them anchored back on Cavanaugh Street. Donna. Lida. Those telephone calls. He sat a little forward, trying to see where they were going.

The drive was long and winding, twisting through a stand of trees as dense as a forest. The car did a dip and a turn and another dip and came out at the start of a broad lawn. In the distance, Engine House itself rose like the castle the society writers insisted it was, its stone-facaded wings stretching across the horizon like petrified snakes.

Haunted house, Gregor thought automatically. Just as automatically, he amended it. No house could be haunted when it was so dramatically lit up.

Lit up.

Gregor felt the breath go out of him before his mind had a chance to recognize what it was seeing.

It wasn't Engine House that was lit up. There were lights on the terrace and other lights over the door and one more coming from one of the rooms on the house's east side, but that was all. What was lit up was the ambulance, and the four police cars keeping it company.

He switched into the rumble seat, to be closer to the partition and therefore to the windshield. What he was seeing he had seen many times before. He knew it the way a classical dancer knew the choreography of a ballet. When they got up close enough, there would be a young patrolman guarding the door and a pair of medics waiting with a body bag. Inside the house, there would be a dozen men with nothing to do and one in an ordinary brown suit with a notebook. Somebody would be asking a lot of questions.

At the moment, Gregor Demarkian had only one question he wanted to ask: had old Robert Hannaford finally let loose and killed someone, or had someone decided to kill him?

PART TWO

SATURDAY, DECEMBER 24–TUESDAY, DECEMBER 27

THE SECOND MURDER

ONE

It was something he would never have done, if he had still been with the Bureau. In fact, it was something he instinctively knew was wrong. If there was one thing he had learned in twenty years of federal police work, it was how to respect jurisdiction. He had no jurisdiction here. He didn't even know if he had a technical right to be on the property. If it was Robert Hannaford who was dead, then the invitation to Gregor Demarkian had died with him.

On the other hand, there was no uniformed patrolman at the door, as there should have been. The door was wide open and the foyer was lit—and empty. The place looked deserted, as if a passel of guests had arrived and then gone underground.

You're getting itchy, Gregor told himself. Then he thought he ought to feel guilty, but didn't. For one thing, he was much too curious. For another, he was getting angry. If he had been the chief of police in this town and walked in to find the place in this unsecured state, he would have had somebody's head.

Because there was nobody's head he could have, he left the driver standing at the foot of the terrace and climbed the steps toward the front door. The driver was babbling, going on and on about how poor Mrs. Hannaford must have died of her illness, but Gregor paid no attention. It just proved what Gregor had thought in the car—that the man was singularly unintelligent. If this had been a natural death, there wouldn't have been a whole pile of patrol cars and a medical examiner's van cluttering up the drive.

He stepped into the foyer and looked around. There were

doors to his right and directly in front of him, but they were both closed. The doors to his left were open. He peered down the long hall they opened on and found the first sign of activity: a young patrolman standing in the middle of the carpet at the far end, looking green.

"I'm not going back in there," the patrolman was saying to someone out of sight. "That thing makes me dizzy."

Gregor sighed. "That thing" was probably the corpse. Why did they let these people join police forces when they couldn't stand the sight of an ordinary corpse? Gregor had no doubt this was just an ordinary corpse. If something really strange had been going on here, there would not only have been a patrolman at the door, the entire journalist population of the Philadelphia ADI would have been out there, too.

Fortunately, he had learned a few things besides the etiquette of jurisdiction in the Bureau. He was a middle-aged man beginning to run to fat, not Clint Eastwood, but he could make people think he was the president of the United States if he wanted to.

Gregor squared his shoulders, straightened his spine, and sailed toward the green young man. His strategem must have worked. The green young man came immediately to attention.

"Sir?"

"Gregor Demarkian," Gregor said.

The green young man nodded sagely, as if he'd been hearing the name all his life. Gregor almost felt sorry for him. The boy was scared to death, thinking with fear instead of his brain—and here Gregor was, about to get him in a great deal of trouble.

Another young man came out of a room on the right, not scared this time but sullen and belligerent. He reacted to Gregor's stiff-backed presence like a dog to a mailman. He didn't question Gregor's authority. He assumed it and hated it on sight.

"Oh, Christ," he said. "Another one."

"This is Mr. Gregor Demarkian," the first patrolman said diffidently.

"I don't care who he is," the second one said. "Christ, but I'm tired. Tired to death."

"You're not the one that's dead," the first one said.

"Oh, shut up."

Gregor edged past the two of them, to the door of the room the second young man had come out of. The desertedness of this place was beginning to make him a little nervous. It wasn't right.

He stopped at the door and looked in. He'd half-convinced himself that this wasn't the crime scene after all. The young patrolman had been talking about something else when he'd said he wouldn't go back in this room. The medical examiner and the rest of the patrolmen were wandering around upstairs somewhere, where something serious was going on. But something serious was going on here. There was indeed a corpse, stretched out against the fieldstone hearth of the fireplace, its skull smashed. There was a corpse, but there was nothing else.

Gregor had almost decided he'd followed Alice down the rabbit hole, when he heard steps behind him. They were very forceful steps, nothing that could have belonged to either of the two patrolmen. He turned quickly—and found himself staring into the most physically perfect face he had ever seen.

Male. Black. Furious. Familiar.

And dressed in one of those matte-brown suits bought only by the heads of homicide squads of major suburban police forces.

Gregor Demarkian did not have an exceptional memory for faces, but he remembered this one. It would have been hard to forget it.

"Oh, damn," Gregor said.

"I don't know what you're swearing about," John Henry Newman Jackman said. "I'm the one who ought to be swearing. What the hell are you doing in here?"

Gregor had never thought about the problems of beautiful men—or even their existence—but standing in this hallway with the broken body of Robert Hannaford in the room behind him, it occurred to him that John Henry Newman Jackman had an unfortunate face. It might have been all right if Jackman had been an actor. As a policeman, he was doomed to be an inhabitant of the worst of memories, and with that remarkable bone structure he was further doomed to be unforgettable. Maybe that was part of what was making him so jumpy, although Gregor doubted it. He'd encountered that kind of jumpiness before. It was called FBI Fever, and its most common verbal expression was: Get off of my turf.

Gregor stepped away from the door, to make room, and said, "It's all right, John. I'm retired."

"You're retired?"

"Two years. Over two years."

"But what are you doing here?"

Gregor supposed he could tell the truth, but that seemed less than tactful. He'd met Jackman in Philadelphia during Jackman's rookie year, on a case so gruesome it had given everyone involved in it nightmares for months. From what Gregor remembered, Jackman had been a smart rookie, what the Bureau would have called an automatic rise-through-the-ranks. Now he seemed to have done just that, although Gregor couldn't be sure how he'd landed in Bryn Mawr. Built a reputation in the city and been hired away as a prize, most likely—and that made it all the more important that Gregor not say anything about the patrolman who wasn't at the door and the medical examiner who seemed to have disappeared. God only knew what was going on here.

Instead, he said only, "I was invited to dinner. When I got here there were all the cars parked outside and nobody around, so I came in."

"And straight to the crime scene?"

"It didn't look like a crime scene, John. There were just these two patrolmen. I was looking for anybody at all."

Jackman gave him a long look, angry and exasperated. "Crap," he said. "You're all I need. I mean that, Demarkian. You're all I need."

If you can't fight, feint. That's what they'd taught him in self-defense classes. Gregor remembered it, even though he'd flunked out of every one. He said, "Do you know yet why he was dragged so far across the room? Why somebody didn't just use his wheelchair?"

Jackman stiffened. "What do you mean, dragged across the room?"

"You can see it on the carpet," Gregor said. He went back to the door and pointed inside. "The nap is all flattened. It goes in an arch from the wheelchair—I assume this was Robert Hannaford?"

"Of course it was Robert Hannaford. I thought you knew him. I thought you said you'd been invited to dinner."

"Hannaford was confined to a wheelchair. You can see it in the way his legs have atrophied. He couldn't have walked across the room himself—"

"Why couldn't he have been sitting in the chair?"

The chair was an antique wing back, standing against the hearth about a foot from where the head now rested—but not where the head had rested when it had been smashed. Gregor was sure of that. The raw facts of the case were easy to see, even at a superficial glance. There was the body with its shattered skull. There was the wheelchair in the far corner of the room. There was a large black bust of Aristotle, made of marble and smeared with blood along the base. A great deal of blood.

"The chair," Gregor said, "is what he stood on."

"What?"

"The chair is what he stood on," Gregor insisted. "Or she. You can see it. It was in that corner before, where the indentations are. The bust was what killed him?"

"There has to be an autopsy, Demarkian. You know that."

"Of course I know that. But there's a lot of blood—a lot of blood. His heart must have been beating when his head was smashed. Otherwise, there wouldn't be nearly so much. And look at what you can see of the wound. It's nearly flat."

"So?"

"So, if someone had picked it up and hit him in the normal way, they would have hit with the edge. There'd be an edge line. There isn't one. Try picking up that thing and aiming it at something. See what it makes you do. It must weigh fifty pounds."

"Forty," Jackman said.

"It had to have been dropped right on top of him, John. That's the only way the wound would be flat. Why was he moved?"

Jackman stirred uneasily. "We don't know. The daughter found him—Bennis. She found them both."

"Both?"

"Mrs. Hannaford was in here when Bennis Hannaford came in. She'd picked up her husband's head and was cradling it in her lap. At least, that's what Bennis Hannaford says."

"What does Mrs. Hannaford say?"

"Nothing."

"Nothing?" Gregor raised his eyebrows, but Jackman was turning away, looking back into the room and at the scene. There was so much blood soaked into the rug at the edge of the hearth that even from a distance that spot looked wet. Robert Hannaford didn't bear looking at. Gregor put his hand on John Jackman's arm and said, "He'd have been drugged. He'd have had to have been."

"Drugged," John Jackman repeated.

"As I said, I'd never met him. But I've talked to people who knew him, and I've talked to him. He was a vigorous old man. He wasn't senile and he had a temper. Nobody could have dragged him out of that wheelchair and across the room if he wasn't drugged."

"Nobody around here looks like they're on drugs," Jackman said. "One of them looks like he has AIDS, but that's not the same thing."

"This is a house full of rich people, John."

"Meaning they all go to psychiatrists and get Valium? Maybe."

"And there are two invalids," Gregor pointed out, "or were.

There may be painkillers around. I don't know the nature of Mr. Hannaford's disability."

"As far as I'm concerned," Jackman said, "you know entirely too much. Is there anything else, Mr. Demarkian? Mrs. Peacock in the conservatory with the candlestick? Anything?"

"Did you find a briefcase?" Gregor asked.

"No," Jackman said.

Gregor almost hated to do it. He could only remember one case like it, in Yellowstone Park in 1971. It shamed him a little to remember how excited it had made him: not potential spies or low-rent drug dealers or even homicidal maniacs, but real people pushed to the edge and over. Pushing themselves over, to be honest. That was how it happened.

In this case, Robert Hannaford himself may have done the pushing. He sounded to Gregor like a man who played dangerous games on a regular basis. But whoever had done the pushing, here they were.

He pointed across the room toward the body and said, "Do you see that thing on the floor? That flat metal thing?"

"What thing?"

"It's buried in the carpet to our side of the patch of blood."

Jackman gave Gregor an odd look, but he put on a pair of white cotton gloves, crossed the room, and knelt where Gregor was pointing. A moment later, he stood up again, holding a piece of tin about the size of his palm. It was a very flimsy piece of tin, and old. It had begun to crumble around the edges.

"What is this?" he said.

"I don't know," Gregor said. "I know what it looks like. There are Christmas decorations on the walls outside. Old-fashioned bells and angels. They're made of that kind of tin. But they're the wrong shape."

"A Christmas decoration."

"There aren't any in here," Gregor said. "In fact, from the look of this room, I think Mr. Hannaford may have belonged to the bah, humbug school of holiday celebrations."

Jackman let the piece of tin drop. "I think it's time I got you out of here," he said. "You're beginning to make me feel weird. You always made me feel weird."

"Why? I'm just—"

"Don't," Jackman said. "I've heard your lecture on internal consistency. I've memorized your lecture on internal consistency. I don't want to hear it now."

"I wasn't going to deliver a lecture," Gregor said.

"You aren't going to get the chance." Jackman took off the gloves and put them in the pocket of his jacket. They made a bulge that reminded Gregor of the bulges guns made.

"Mr. Demarkian," Jackman said, "you are a suspect in this case. As a suspect in this case, I think you ought to meet the other suspects in this case."

"You mean you think I ought to get out of your hair."

"Interpret it any way you want to. You're going to get out of here. Now."

TWO

1 Cordelia Day Hannaford was sitting in a yellow wing chair next to the fireplace, directly in line with the open door. She was the first thing Gregor saw when he came into the room. She was the only thing he saw for many minutes afterward. She had her arms propped up on the arms of the chair, her back propped up by its back, and her feet flat on the floor. In repose, she was perfect, a Lady of the Manor as imagined by Turner. Her bones were fine and delicate. Her eyes were large and widely spaced and deeply blue. Her hair was white, but thick and glossy, as if it had turned early. It was only when she moved that Gregor realized something was wrong. She tried to turn her head when he came into the room. Her effort was not only slow and painful, but completely without control. First she jerked right. Then she jerked left. Then her hands and arms began to shake. Once they started, she couldn't make them stop. It was like watching that terrible old movie, *Lost Horizon*. Cordelia Day Hannaford was physically disintegrating in front of his eyes.

With Elizabeth, until the last year, reality had been less obvious. In fact, it hadn't been obvious at all. In the early days, living with Elizabeth's dying had been an almost hallucinatory experience. She looked well. She almost always felt well. Every once in a while, she went off to the hospital for chemotherapy—and then she was sick. Gregor had come to hate the chemotherapy with a fine hot passion he'd never been able to work up for serial murderers. Or presidential assassins. Elizabeth looked terrible when she came back from the hospital and felt worse. He would leave for work in the morning and hear her vomiting in the bathroom, vomiting and vomiting, like someone who had swallowed poison. When he got drunk enough—and there had been nights; he hadn't been able to help himself—he started to think they *were* giving her poison. Then the chemotherapy would be over, and she would be fine again. So fine, he might as well have imagined the whole thing.

Elizabeth's last year had been a shock. After five years of sick-and-well, well-and-sick, he hadn't been prepared for it. Cordelia Day Hannaford's children would have no such problem. Gregor didn't know what she had, but looking at Cordelia Day he was sure it had been a progressive disease. Muscles didn't melt into Silly Putty overnight—and if they did, their owner didn't accept the change without a lot of panic and denial. Cordelia Day was in pain, but she was at peace, at least about herself.

The room was very hot. The fire was blazing. Gregor became suddenly aware of a number of unpleasant things. He was still wearing his heavy winter coat over his best winter wool suit. All those layers of insulation were making rivers of sweat run down his back. Then there was Cordelia Day. She was staring at him and he was staring at her—and her children were staring at both of them. Now the movie all this reminded him of wasn't *Lost Horizon,* but something by Antonioni, or maybe Bergman, one of those endless black-and-white productions with very little dialogue and a lot of long silences.

He tried to pull himself back emotionally, and in the process noticed a few things he should have noticed right off. Cordelia Day Hannaford was covered with blood. There was so much of it soaked into the skirt of her pale blue dress, it had probably been wet when Jackman first saw her. Now it was drying. Thick, stiff clots of it were webbed across the material that covered her knees. They made the dress look embroidered.

The other people in the room, the children, were not as hostile as he'd expected them to be. Bennis he recognized from her author photos. She was almost too cordial. The tall, lanky young man with the weak mouth and the frightened eyes wasn't frightened of Gregor. The very young woman who looked so much like Bennis, but wasn't as pretty, barely registered his existence. What animosity there was, and it was palpable, came from the man with his left leg in a brace and the stout middle-aged woman who stood behind Cordelia Day Hannaford's chair.

He looked around the room. There were holly bows everywhere, and candles and ribbons, and clusters of the same kind of decorations he had seen near the study, the ones that were too small to account for the piece of tin on Robert Hannaford's study floor. There were miniature Christmas trees and miniature Santa Clauses. There was even a miniature crèche, with the Christ child missing from the manger. Tibor would have approved.

He turned his attention back to the Hannafords, shrugging off his coat as he did so. The two people in the room he hadn't paid attention to before—a man who epitomized the Complete Corporate Yuppie and a woman dressed like a thirties movie star playing a tramp—were just shell-shocked. Gregor turned to the stout middle-aged woman. Her manner said he'd have to deal with her first. He thought he'd give her what she wanted. Besides, he felt a little sorry for her. She was a mess. Her tweed skirt was wrinkled. Her cashmere sweater was stained and out of true. Even her pearl necklace was hanging out-of-kilter. She didn't look like the kind of woman who usually allowed herself to look out of control.

He got his coat as far as his wrists, and Bennis came to life.

"Oh, God," she said. "I didn't even take your coat. Nobody took your coat."

"Why should anyone take his coat?" the Movie Star said. "Who is he? Why is he staying?"

Bennis sighed. "I'm Bennis Hannaford," she told Gregor. "That's my sister Myra Hannaford Van Damm. Mrs. Richard Van Damm. Can I put that somewhere for you?"

Gregor handed her the coat. Bennis folded it over her arm, looked around the room, and finally settled on laying it out across a vacant chair. There were a lot of vacant chairs. The room was enormous, and stuffed as full of furniture as an exhibit in a sec-ond-rate museum.

"This must be Gregor Demarkian," Bennis said. Gregor nod-ded, and she smiled. When the rest of them looked blank, she added, "Daddy's dinner guest, remember? In all the confusion, we forgot to head him off at the pass."

"Of course," the Yuppie said. "Anne Marie strikes again. Effi-ciency in action."

"Oh, shut up," the stout woman said. "I'm as efficient as you've got any right to expect me to be. It's not as if I had any help."

Bennis shot Gregor an apologetic look, then stepped into the middle of them and started pointing. "That's my brother Bobby," she said, indicating the Yuppie, "and you and Myra have already been introduced. The man on the floor is Theodore," (the brace, Gregor thought) "and the woman behind Mother is

Anne Marie. You probably guessed. The person who looks like he just came back from a Grateful Dead concert is Christopher. And this," she waved her hand over the very young woman's head, "is Emma."

"Every time you introduce me to anyone," Emma said, "you always make it sound as if I'm Sarah Bernhardt."

"Well, you are Sarah Bernhardt, sweetie. It's just that nobody knows it yet but me."

Emma had been sitting on the floor, with her back against the legs of a Victorian sofa. Now she stood up, in a single fluid dancer's motion, and went to Cordelia Day Hannaford's chair.

"This is our Mother," she said. "Mrs. Robert Hannaford. She—"

"She's very ill," Anne Marie said.

Emma flushed. "He can see that she's very ill," she said angrily. "Anyone could see it. I was just trying—"

"She's only trying to be polite," Myra said. "God, Anne Marie. Sometimes I wonder what goes on in your head. You know how Mother feels about manners."

"Stop talking about her as if she can't hear," Emma said. "There's nothing wrong with her ears, and there's nothing wrong with her mind, either."

"Oh, Christ," Chris said.

In her chair, Cordelia Day Hannaford stirred. Her movement stopped all other movement in the room. The pain of it was a tangible thing. Gregor had to go rigid to keep himself from rushing to her aid. Her children knew her far better than he did. If she liked help, they would help her.

Surprisingly, when she began to talk her voice was clear, almost steady. "Mr. De*mark*-ian," she said. Her hesitation was so slight, Gregor wouldn't have caught it if he hadn't been listening for it. "My husband—was look-ing—for-ward—to—your—vis-it."

"Thank you," Gregor said.

"You must—have—a—seat."

"Yes," Gregor said. "Thank you again. I think I need one."

Cordelia raised her hand, very slowly, and touched Anne Marie's arm where it rested against the back of her chair. "Ring for Marsh-all," she said. "We must—have the—the *cart.*"

"The cart," Anne Marie repeated.

"It's only right," Emma said. "We have a guest. We can't just let him sit there like—"

"What are you talking about?" Anne Marie said. "We've got a corpse, that's what we've got, lying not a thousand feet from this room—"

Cordelia Day Hannaford jerked her hand away. Anne Marie jerked in response, frightened. "Oh, God. Oh, Mother. Oh, I'm sorry. I didn't mean—"

"Marsh-all," Cordelia said.

"Yes," Anne Marie said. "I'll go get Marshall. I'll go get the cart. Just—just rest, please. I won't be a moment."

"You could ring," Christopher said.

"Don't be an ass," Anne Marie said. She hurried out of the room, taking a door at the back Gregor hadn't noticed before.

Once she was gone, the rest of them relaxed a little, but not much. If Gregor read them right, they were more concerned with their mother than they were with each other, or with the fact that their father was dead in another room. Their principal reason for being so angry at Anne Marie was her insistence on referring to the "corpse." They wanted it safely out of sight, in another universe.

He turned his attention back to Cordelia, and decided—sentimentally—that she'd come to the same conclusions he had. It would be odd if she hadn't. Most people overreacted to violent death, and when they were past that they overreacted to their connection to it. He'd have understood if they'd talked obsessively about the murder, or about the father they hadn't liked very much. It was worse than strange to find them like this.

Cordelia was drooping. Her head had fallen forward. Her eyes had closed. Her hands had curled in on themselves, like the hands of a quadriplegic. Bennis got up and went over to her, checking her out carefully, as if she were a baby.

"Asleep," she said.

"Thank God," Myra said. "What's that idiot policeman thinking of? She should have been medicated hours ago."

"I told him that," Bennis said. She moved her mother's head so that it was resting more comfortably on the back of the chair. "I wonder how much of a horse's ass he really was. Does she have medical insurance? Does she have survivorship? Did he consider for one single moment that he might get run over by a truck?"

"Well, I'm sure he didn't think he was going to end up murdered," the man in the brace said. "Although he should have."

"Shut up, Teddy," Myra said.

"Why?"

"She's got a survivorship." This came from Bobby, the Complete Yuppie. He was sitting straight up like the rest of them now, but Gregor was interested to note that only the mention of money had gotten him that way. A dead father, a dying mother —none of that had moved him to action. "She hasn't got medical insurance, because she was diagnosed before he bought his policies. But she gets the annuity incomes as long as she lives, and that should take care of medical expenses. And running the house. Hell, he put everything he had into those annuities."

"No he didn't," Myra said.

Bobby ignored her. "There's a life insurance policy, too," he said. "A million dollars worth. I don't know if it has a double indemnity clause for murder. But she can use that money any way she wants to. She isn't going to need it."

"She isn't going to use it, either," Bennis said. "She isn't going to last till New Year's."

"I don't see what good a million dollars would have done her, anyway," Bobby said. "That won't pay the taxes on this place."

Bennis looked ready to hit Bobby with something serious, but at that moment Cordelia's head slipped, and she was closest. She got it into position again and stroked her mother's hair. Then she looked up at Gregor.

"I heard them talking," she said. "He was killed with that statue of his. I don't see why they're bothering her. She couldn't have done that—"

"I'm surprised anybody could do that," Teddy said.

"He used to be able to do that," Christopher said. "When he was younger, anyway. He used to keep his arms in shape with it. Lifting it. Putting it down. Lifting it again."

"That was *years* ago," Bennis said, "and the point is, Mother couldn't have done it. And if Mother couldn't have done it, there's no reason to keep her here like *this.*"

They all looked at their mother, asleep in her chair like *this.*

"They're only doing this because she's the only one with any motive they can think of," Bennis said, "but anyone with any brains and any decency could see it isn't a motive at all."

"Wait." Gregor couldn't stop himself. "Why is she the only one of you with a motive? He was a rich man. You're all a rich man's children."

The rich man's children looked at each other, and then at the floor, and then at each other again. Gregor saw Bennis shake her head, almost imperceptibly. Then Teddy got up and started pacing around the room, thumping his brace against the hardwood floor for a diversion.

"Maybe it'll turn out to have been an accident," he said. "Chris is right. He did used to use that thing to keep his arms in shape. Maybe he made a huge effort, and got it over his head again, and then lost control and let the thing fall on him."

"Oh," Emma said, "I hope so."

"Hope but don't expect," Bobby said. "Something tells me, if there was any possibility of that, we'd have heard about it already. Aren't I right, Mr. Demarkian?"

Gregor nodded. He knew better than to give them any particulars, but he could answer this. "Very right. The last thing Mr. Jackman wants to do is to investigate a family like yours in a town like Bryn Mawr. If he had any reason to hope for an accident, he'd be hoping out loud."

"There," Bobby said.

"Don't look so damn satisfied," Myra said.

"I'm not looking satisfied. I'm just being realistic."

Myra shot Bobby a look that was very much like the one Bennis had given him before. He was saved this time by the arrival of Anne Marie, complete with drinks cart. She saw her mother as soon as she came into the room and bit her lip. God only knew what she was stopping herself from saying.

Away from the family, Anne Marie had acquired a determination Gregor was surprised to see in her. She wheeled the drinks tray to his side, waved her hands over the collection of bottles on the top shelf, and plastered a determined social smile across her face.

"There," she said. "Vodka, whiskey, bourbon, gin, and four kinds of Scotch. We're ready for anything."

What she was really saying, of course, was that she was ready for him. Gregor decided to give in to that gracefully. It wasn't his investigation, after all, and he'd get better information out of Jackman when Jackman questioned him than he could ever get from the younger Hannafords.

Gregor asked Anne Marie for a Scotch and water, and settled back for a long boring evening of social inanity.

2 Exactly one half hour later, a young patrolman came to the living room door and asked Gregor to come into the hall with him. Gregor came, and supplied the boy with his name, address, and telephone number. Then he shut up and waited to be invited into the presence of the great John Henry Newman Jackman.

He wasn't.

"Detective Jackman," the boy said, "thinks it's about time you went home."

THREE

If Anne Marie Hannaford had had any sleep, she might have decided to skip Christmas Day altogether. Skipping it was what she had wanted to do right from the beginning, when Myra had first talked Mother into this silly project. Now she had an excuse. Mother was in no shape to come down to dinner—although she was going to insist on doing it. The rest of them were in no shape for anything, and even less use. It had snowed all night. If the police hadn't left when they did, and sent that Demarkian man home before them, the house would be full of strangers. According to the latest weather reports, there was a foot and a half of snow out there. There would be more, later. Mrs. Washington was never going to make it in from Philadelphia.

The police had given Mrs. Washington a ride to her sister's. Otherwise, she would have spent the night, and Anne Marie wouldn't be stuck with a twenty-two pound turkey she had no idea how to cook. Never mind fresh corn, flown in from Mexico, to be stripped from the cob before it was creamed. And potatoes to be mashed. And stuffing. Anne Marie had been taught to run a house, not to keep it. Fortunately, she was a Hannaford. Hannafords either got filthy rich or they died in the gutter.

Bag ladies.

Out in the hall, the clock struck ten. Anne Marie smoothed hair from her face and decided she couldn't get away with canned vegetables. There were cases and cases of canned vegetables in the pantry, but they must have been there forever, laid on in case of fire and flood and thermonuclear war. They'd certainly never been served to Robert Hannaford V at his table.

She put the can of Niblets brand corn on its shelf and backed out of the pantry. She was tired, that was all. When she got tired she got trite. And confused. And even a little frightened. It was odd. Yesterday morning, if she'd been asked what she most wanted for Christmas—and decided to answer honestly—she would have said, Daddy dying suddenly. Now, instead of being more relaxed than she'd been the past few months, she was less. First there had been all those police in the house, going back and forth, asking stupid questions. She'd heard them talking in the halls, and some of the things they'd said had been terrifying. Then there had been that charade in the living room with Mr. Demarkian. Mother acting like the perfect Main Line hostess. Herself pretending not to know who that damnable man was. The rest of them—but it wasn't the rest of them who bothered her. She hadn't expected to be able to count on them. She had expected to be able to count on herself, and instead she'd been jerky and impulsive, almost obsessive, all evening long. Every time she looked at Mother's dress, she thought about Daddy on the floor of the study, bloody and dead. The deadness of him seemed to be in the room with her, stalking her, so that every time she turned around she expected to see his corpse risen and walking at her side.

By the time she'd gotten the strangers out of the house and Mother settled and the rest of them packed off to bed, she'd been so tired she'd thought she was going to pass out in her clothes. She hadn't. She'd never gotten to sleep at all. As soon as the light was out, she stared at the ceiling, and once the light was on again she stared at her hands. It was impossible. The corpse was still walking, but there were nightmares waiting for her on the other side of consciousness. She wanted nothing to do with them. Bloody and dead, bloody and dead, bloody and dead. It was odd how you could hate someone so much when he was alive, and then be so—upset—when he was dead.

She stepped out of the pantry hall into the kitchen to find Bennis standing at the counter next to the sink, throwing what looked like raw mushrooms into a mixing bowl. She bit her lip. Bennis was dressed in her hanging-around-home uniform—jeans, turtleneck, knee socks, baggy flannel shirt—and it was so damn inappropriate for Engine House. On the other hand, Bennis also seemed to be doing something about dinner, and Anne Marie didn't want to get in the way of that.

Bennis saw her, looked up, and waved her over. "Celery," she said. "I can't finish this without celery."

"Celery," Anne Marie repeated.

Bennis sighed. She looked as tired as Anne Marie felt. "Is that the only refrigerator we have? Is there cold storage someplace else? It takes six or seven hours to cook a turkey this size. If we don't get our acts together, we're not going to be able to eat until New Year's."

"Oh," Anne Marie said. She turned around and headed back to the pantry hall—ran, really, losing her cool all over again. There were a lot of extra refrigerators at Engine House. There was a whole wall of them, built in, opposite the pantry closet. Anne Marie rummaged around in the carrots and parsnips and green beans, found two stalks of celery—or was it heads?—and grabbed them. Myra always claimed not to know one vegetable from another in its undoctored state, but Anne Marie thought that was a lie. Myra was always on a diet.

Back in the kitchen, Bennis took the celery, laid it down next to a pile of onions, and said, "Mrs. Washington called. She can't get in today. She's got half a foot of snow in front of her door."

"I was expecting that," Anne Marie said.

"And I went in to see Mother," Bennis said. "She was practically coherent. I still think it was shitty of that doctor to refuse to come out last night."

Anne Marie shrugged. "It isn't as if Mother hasn't been in that state before. And he wouldn't be negligent, Bennis. He'd be too afraid of getting sued."

"If anything happens to her, he is going to get sued. That's one of the nice things about having a lot of money you've made yourself. You can spend it any way you want to." She threw the last of the mushrooms into the bowl and reached for the onions. "Look," she said, "there's something we have to talk about."

Anne Marie stepped away from the counter. Quickly. "I know what you want to talk about. I'm not going to do it. I don't want to hear a thing."

"Anne Marie, you're going to have to hear about it. Believe me—to cop an attitude out of the latest private-eye fiction—you'd much rather hear it from me than from the police."

"I don't know what you're talking about."

"Oh, yes, you do."

"No, I don't," Anne Marie said. "Teddy might be right. It might have been an accident. That policeman could just be grandstanding or something. Trying to get his name in the papers."

"It's Bobby who was right. And that Gregor Demarkian. The Bryn Mawr police don't want to investigate people like us. It's a pain in the ass. It would be like the Boston police going after somebody named Cabot. There had to be something in that scene last night that made murder the inevitable conclusion, and it had to be something obvious, because they hit it right away. And that means we're in big trouble."

"I don't see why we have to be in any trouble at all. Somebody got in from the outside—"

"Oh, for Christ's *sake.*" Bennis threw chopped onion into the bowl and reached for the celery. "Look, the police may not know it yet, but you've been around Daddy for years. You know what the security is like at Engine House. There's a seven-foot wall around this property, and the top of it's electrified. There are guys patrolling the gate. I was still living here when the police tried to make Daddy stop arming them. The old man was a paranoid nut. Nobody got in or out of here yesterday without being signed, timed, stamped, and dated."

"So?"

"So there's going to be a list, and there's going to be nobody on it but us. One of us killed him, all right?"

Anne Marie turned away. She was so tired, the room seemed to be swimming. "You shouldn't say that. Not out loud where people can hear you."

"If I don't say it, maybe it will go away?"

"Maybe."

"Anne Marie, I called Michael last night."

Anne Marie turned around just in time to see Bennis throw chopped celery into the bowl and reach for a bag of commercially packaged croutons. God only knew where they had come from. "Am I supposed to know who Michael is?" she said.

"He's the man I've been seeing the last couple of years."

"And?"

"He happens to be a lawyer. With the Boston DA's office. I got him out of bed at three o'clock in the morning because I wanted to cry on his shoulder, and I ended up getting a lot of information instead."

"I can't believe you wanted to cry on anybody's shoulder," Anne Marie said. "Not about Daddy."

"Never mind what I wanted to cry about. Michael spent half an hour giving me chapter and verse on one Mr. Gregor Demarkian. Get the turkey. If you hold it up for me, I'll be able to stuff it faster."

Anne Marie looked at the turkey. The idea of touching its cold, wet skin made her physically ill. She never touched raw meat. She never touched anything slimy. She never even looked at the cuts she got in her hands when she was gardening.

Bennis had poured a large measuring cup of water into the mixing bowl, and now she was staring at her. Anne Marie grabbed the turkey around its thickest part and held it as far away from her as she could.

"I didn't like Mr. Gregor Demarkian," Anne Marie said.

"I did," Bennis said. That was only half true. Sometimes, he made her very nervous. Anne Marie could tell. "But that's not the point. Do you know why Daddy invited him to dinner?"

"No."

"You're not just saying that because you promised to keep it secret?"

"No. He never told me anything, Bennis, except what it was he wanted me to do, when he wanted me to do something. I spent a week arguing with him about Demarkian. Mother's so damn sick. I couldn't imagine her surviving a full-scale dinner party. It was like talking to a deaf mute."

"Was it Daddy's idea to have us all here for Christmas?"

"It was Myra's."

"Could he have asked Myra to make it look like her idea?"

"The only word Daddy has addressed to Myra in the last three years is 'cunt.' Scratch that. Sometimes he said 'stupid cunt.'"

"Marvelous."

"Daddy was a marvelous man."

Bennis flipped back the flap of skin at the turkey's neck and started filling the cavity with soft brown mush. "The thing is," she said, "Mr. Demarkian is not your ordinary retired FBI agent. Michael says he's famous. He was the best man they had at investigating murders for twenty years. Apparently the FBI investigates murders that take place on federally owned land and in kidnapping cases and things. When I mentioned his name, Michael practically croaked."

"So?"

"So why did Daddy invite a murder expert to dinner on Christmas Eve?"

Anne Marie sighed. "Daddy wasn't rational, Bennis. You know that. He put up a good front for the lawyers, but if he hadn't had so much money he'd have been institutionalized years ago."

"Look at it from that Detective Jackman's point of view. Daddy invited Demarkian for dinner, and the night Demarkian is supposed to show up, Daddy got himself killed. A murder expert *and* a murder."

"Bennis, what are you talking about?"

"If I were Detective Jackman, I'd be sitting at home right now, doing a lot of thinking about premeditation. Anne Marie, on the surface of this, right now, it looks like Daddy knew somebody was trying to murder him."

The turkey was very slippery. It was so slippery, it fell right out of her hands and crashed into the pan she'd been holding it steady in, scattering pieces of brown mush all over the counter. "But that's ridiculous," Anne Marie said, wondering what had gone wrong with her head. Her ears seemed to be ringing. "If Daddy thought somebody was trying to kill him, he'd never have everybody here. He'd throw us all out until he calmed down."

"Anne Marie, I knew Daddy. You knew Daddy. Jackman didn't know Daddy."

"But—"

"And there are a couple of other things. If Jackman doesn't get happy very soon, he's going to investigate everything. If he investigates everything, he's going to start looking into the money. When he starts looking into the money, he isn't going to stop with where it went, he's going to want to know why it went that way, and then—"

"Bennis, please."

"—then we're really up shit creek."

Anne Marie swallowed, very carefully, making sure there was room in her throat. "Bennis, he couldn't possibly find out about that. There wasn't any evidence. There wasn't anything. He was just—"

"Myra will talk," Bennis said. "She'll get a couple of martinis under her belt some afternoon while Jackman's here and she'll talk her head off."

"Oh, God."

Bennis picked up the turkey and shoved it back into her hands.

"As long as you're having a nervous breakdown about that, I've got something else for you. Mr. Demarkian spent at least half an hour alone with us last night."

"I know."

"So does Jackman."

This time, Anne Marie almost thought she could squeeze the turkey and have her hands go straight through.

She put it down carefully, not wanting to see any more pieces of brown mush. Mush and brains. Blood and skin and bone. Everybody standing in the door of the study last night, Bennis holding them back, saying over and over again that somebody had to call the police. Everybody sitting in the living room later, pretending it hadn't happened.

Bennis had taken a pack of cigarettes out of the pocket of her flannel shirt and was lighting up. "Anne Marie?"

"I'm all right," Anne Marie said.

"No, you're not. I bet you never got any sleep last night at all."

Of course, Anne Marie thought, Bennis did sleep. Bennis would sleep. Bennis always knew everything, always did everything, always thought of everything. But then, Bennis hadn't been living here in the house with him, all these years.

Am I making sense? Anne Marie wondered. She decided she wasn't, but it didn't matter much. She wasn't afraid anymore.

Just sick.

2 On that Christmas Eve, Teddy Hannaford got the best sleep he'd had since he was ten years old. He slept until noon, as unconscious as a rock, and as soon as he woke up he vaulted out of bed. His bad leg hurt a little when it hit the floor, his brace cut into his knee, and he slid about half a foot, but he didn't care. He barely noticed. He felt *good*. The grief reaction he'd been dreading hadn't materialized. There was no reason why it should have—he'd hated his father without a break for two decades—but Teddy knew that reason rarely cut much ice with the human psyche. He'd carried his hate around for so long, he'd been a little worried he'd start mourning for it. Instead, he was free, happy, and at peace. He wanted to sing about the wicked old witch being dead, except that he couldn't remember the words and witches were supposed to be girls.

Actually, he was a little feverish. He recognized that. The fever had started the night before, when it had finally sunk in that the old man was gone, and was heating up now, because there was so much about that situation he didn't know. He was surprised he cared, but there it was. Obviously, that policeman thought one of them had killed him. Teddy knew all of them had wanted to, except maybe Emma. He'd never been able to get a real fix on Emma. Right now, he couldn't even get a real fix on himself. It was as if he had two different songs playing in his head, unrelated but not discordant. He didn't want to listen to either of them, but he couldn't seem to shut the music off. What he could do was concentrate on one and then the other. It made him feel like an audition master of nightmares.

Daddy was dead, and everything was not all right. That was the problem.

Teddy stared at his hands.

Daddy was dead—and now what? From where he was sitting, on the edge of the bed, he could see the neat stack of "professional papers" he had put out on the writing table the night he arrived. He hadn't looked at them since, hadn't even thought about them, because they were mostly for show, in case Bennis came into his room. Now he needed to think of them. They summed up his predicament as nothing else could. Greer College was still up there in Maine. The chairman of the English department was still planted solidly in his corner office on the second floor of Adrian Hall. The photocopy of Susan Carpenter's paper was still sitting in a file somewhere, waiting to do him in. No matter how he looked at it, it turned out that Daddy's dying hadn't changed his life at all, and wasn't going to. It scared the hell out of him.

He slipped out of bed, found a pile of fresh clothes in the larger of his two suitcases, and started to get dressed. He hated to admit it, but he didn't want to give up teaching. He didn't like it, but he didn't want to give it up. He was going to have to do something to make a living. The income from his trust came to only $22,286.37 a year. That was it. Even with his teaching income added in, he was always in hock to his credit cards. What kind of work could he get, if he went looking for work? And how would he survive it? All those rigid hours, those great five-day blocks of time where you weren't allowed to be anywhere else. All that worrying about getting fired. Teddy was convinced that people who worked jobs worried about getting fired all the time. Even Chris must do that, because he spent so much of his time doing that radio program and writing poetry brought in so little money. Teaching had it all over that kind of thing. Besides, there was one thing about teaching he did like. The ego trip.

You stood up there in front of a lot of good-looking eighteen year olds, and every time you opened your mouth they took notes.

His leg was stiffer than usual this morning, probably because he'd been up late last night and moving around so much. He sat on the bed and held it straight, the only way he could get his jeans on over the brace. He was very cold. If he didn't do something soon, he was going to be utterly, irrevocably screwed. He wouldn't be able to keep it from them, either, and especially not from Bennis. There were too many links between academia and publishing. The first student he'd ever stolen a paper from was now writing mystery novels. Bennis probably knew him.

In his head, the two strains of music began to merge and complement each other. The backbeat was clear and driving, irresistible: it's not fair it's not fair it's not fair. It was the simple truth. It wasn't fair. Daddy was dead. Once that happened, everything was supposed to be all right.

Jeans on, he limped out into the hall and down to the landing. He took the stairs slowly, one at a time, dragging his bad leg after his good one like a boxer's dummy that had been inexplicably attached to his hip. In the foyer, he stopped and listened, but heard nothing. Christ, but this was a quiet house. He thumped over to the door that led to the wing where the study was and looked through it down the dark hall. Nothing.

And no one. That wasn't right. There was a whole ritual for opening Christmas presents. It should be going on right now.

He thumped back across the foyer and went into the main drawing room, where the tree was set up and the presents laid out. The tree was lit up, but the presents seemed to be untouched. Teddy wondered what that was about. Why wasn't Mother in her chair, handing out packages like Lady Bountiful? Why wasn't the audio system blasting out Christmas carols? Maybe they thought there was something wrong with opening presents the day after there'd been a murder in the house. Teddy looked around for a box with his name on it, found three, and took the biggest one.

He was just deciding that pink velour pajamas were the most idiotic present he'd ever received, from anyone—what had Chris been thinking? The damn things were off the rack. They'd never fit over his brace—when the drawing room door opened and Myra came in. She was shoeless and makeupless, so unlike her normal self he almost didn't recognize her. He banished the twinge of guilt he'd been feeling since he'd seen Chris's name on the "from" end of the tag—Chris had brought presents; Teddy had not—and blinked.

"Good God," he said. "You look almost human."

Myra got a glass from a shelf under the bar and started filling it with ice cubes. "Go stuff yourself," she said.

"I will if anybody ever gives me dinner. What time is Dickie supposed to arrive?"

"Dickie's at his mother's."

"And you're here?"

"I was supposed to go over at three o'clock. Not going to. It's snowing again."

"Well, Dickie ought to love that. Dickie's mother ought to love it even more. Do you intend to be married after New Year's?"

There was a bottle of vodka on the bar, opened and out. Myra filled her glass from it, dispensing with side issues like tonic and water. Then she threw a slice of brown, dried-up lime over the top. Teddy thought things must really have gone to hell here last night, what with the police in the house and everything. Limes were never allowed to sit around until the morning.

Myra threw herself into the chair next to the fireplace—where the fire hadn't been lit; curiouser and curiouser—and said, "I was in the kitchen for a while. I couldn't stand it any more. Bennis is cooking, and Emma is following her around like a puppy dog, asking what all the terms mean."

"Bennis is cooking? Where's Mrs. Washington?"

"Snowed in, in Philadelphia."

"Can Bennis cook?"

"I really wouldn't know."

There didn't seem to be anything to say to that. Bennis being Bennis, she probably could cook, but that was a can of worms Teddy definitely didn't want to open. Not when he was feeling so awful. He went back to the tree and got the other two boxes, and then two more he found behind them. By the time he got resettled in his chair, his leg was aching like a son of a bitch.

"So," he said, "what has you drinking at fifteen minutes past noon?"

"I'm not drinking, Teddy. I'm just relaxing. I have a right to relax."

"Right," Teddy said.

"Besides," Myra said. "I've been thinking."

"God help us all."

Myra swigged. "Do you really think Daddy's dying was an accident?"

"Let's just say I think we ought to think so. If you know what I mean."

"I know what you mean. I want to know what you think. Do you think it was an accident?"

"No."

"Neither do I," Myra said. She stared into her drink. "If it had to be one of us who killed him, and you could pick anyone you wanted to be it, who would it be?"

The second box had gloves in it. Black leather gloves. Teddy already had six pairs. "Are we assuming this person is going to get caught?" he said.

"Would it make a difference?"

"Well," Teddy said, "if there was no danger of getting caught, I wish it had been me."

"Ah," Myra said.

Teddy threw the gloves on the floor. They were from Emma. Emma had given him the other six pairs. "Assuming a trial and a conviction and God knows what else, then I'd want it to be Bennis."

"Bennis?" Myra looked startled. "Whatever for?"

"Balance, I guess," Teddy said. "She's the one who's had the perfect life."

"Bennis?"

"Just look at her, Myra. She's rich as shit. She's famous. She's beautiful. She's even got a man who wants to marry her."

"Well, yes," Myra said, "but even so. She's had to work for all that. And the man—" Myra made another face. "Greek," she said, as if it were an explanation.

"Now, now," Teddy said, "don't be a snob."

"Anybody could marry a Greek," Myra said.

"Who would you want it to be?"

"Oh, Bobby. Definitely," Myra said. "He's the one who's had

the really perfect life. I know he works like a dog, but he doesn't have to. It's just some macho kick he's on. He's got that huge trust fund, and that house in Chestnut Hill, and he goes running off to Europe every two and a half seconds. Besides, at the moment I want to kill him, and I'd much rather have the state of Pennsylvania do it for me."

Teddy tried to remember if Pennsylvania had the death penalty, and couldn't. "Why do you want to kill him? I didn't think you even saw him much."

Myra went back to staring into her drink. It seemed to fascinate her. "He's just such a horse's ass," she said.

Teddy shook his head. "If someone was going to kill him for that, they'd have done it years ago."

"I know. But you see—shit. I wish I hadn't given up smoking. Bennis is out there puffing away, and every time I see her I want to mug her for a butt."

"It *has* been a little tense around here."

"Tense," Myra said. "Yes. Teddy—"

"Yes?"

"If you did know something, something strange, that might get one of us arrested, would you tell the police about it?"

"I don't know," Teddy said. "That would depend."

"On what?"

Teddy laughed. "On whether or not it was about Bennis."

"Sometimes you're just as much of a horse's ass as Bobby is." Myra looked into her drink again, saw that it was empty, and stood. "I'd better go get dressed. If Anne Marie sees me like this, she'll have a fit. And I really can't put up with one of Anne Marie's fits today."

"You're not going to tell me what it was?"

"What what was?"

"What you saw," Teddy said patiently. "The something strange."

"Oh. That. Well, it wasn't something I saw, exactly. It was something I didn't see. Something that was in the study last night when we were all looking at—at Daddy's body, and then it wasn't in there today."

"Maybe the police took it."

"Maybe. But I don't see why. It wasn't anything personal."

"You shouldn't have been in the study today anyway. That Jackman person practically put a curse on the place to keep us out of there."

"Well, he put a seal on it, and that's all that matters." She put her empty glass on the bar. "I'm going upstairs. Open my presents if you want. I can't bear to see the horrors they've perpetrated on me this year."

She swished through the doors to the foyer and slammed them behind her.

Teddy looked into his third box and found a pair of ear muffs, bright orange. He checked the tag and found, "From Anne Marie."

3

Up on the second floor, Emma Hannaford walked into her bedroom, shut the door behind her, and locked it. Her mouth was as dry as sand. Her heart felt like a thin-skinned balloon being attacked by a sledgehammer. She kept telling herself to hurry, because Bennis was down in the kitchen and thought she'd just gone to the bathroom and would expect her back any minute. It was one of those internal lectures that had no practical effect whatsoever.

She reached under her sweater and pulled out the small cardboard accordion folder she'd taken off her father's desk. It looked perfectly innocent, there was nothing in it but a lot of newspaper clippings about charity balls and fund drives, but it felt like a snake in her hands.

She put it down on the bed.

Daddy was dead. Dead, dead, dead. And unlike the rest of them, she had never hated him, not even for a minute.

She picked the folder up again and shoved it between her mattress and her boxspring. It caught on something sharp she couldn't see.

With any luck, it would be ripped to shreds.

FOUR

On the day after Christmas, Gregor Demarkian bought Father Tibor a very expensive lunch at a restaurant called Leitmotif in Liberty Square. The lunch was a kind of apology. Gregor hadn't been at church on Christmas morning, and he hadn't been at Lida Arkmanian's in the afternoon. After all the trouble these people had gone to to provide him with a real Christmas, he hadn't been anywhere on Cavanaugh Street. Donna Moradanyan had been standing at her front windows when he left the building at six o'clock. His upstairs neighbor told Tibor and Lida he hadn't been stuck on the Main Line overnight, and that he hadn't—as yet—killed himself. For the rest of the day, the three of them worried. Gregor was a missing person. He could have been smoke.

Where he had gone, of course, was out to the cemetery where his mother and Elizabeth were buried. He'd done that every Christmas of his life since his mother had died, and for the last two since Elizabeth had died, and it seemed perfectly natural to him. It even seemed natural that he hadn't visited Cavanaugh Street when he was in town. He bought flowers three or four days ahead of time and put them in the refrigerator. He knew from experience that the closer you got to Christmas, the fewer flowers there were to buy. By Christmas Eve, all the good ones had disappeared from the shops, leaving nothing but wilted poinsettias and poisonous mistletoe. His mother had always loved carnations. Elizabeth had always wanted roses. He was good and got them early.

At the cemetery, he made hollows in the snow next to the

headstones and put the flowers in, knowing they would keep longer in the cold than they would have in the summer. Then he looked around and wondered why he bothered with this at all. Gregor knew most people considered cemeteries morbid, but it was an attitude he'd never understood. The places were so damn impersonal. All they said to him was the obvious—that we die, that we have always died, that we are always going to die. Mute testimony to the course of human destiny, a friend of his had called it—and been dead drunk at the time, if Gregor remembered correctly. Maybe you had to get dead drunk if you spent your life worrying about the course of human destiny.

Gregor had spent his worrying about Elizabeth, and his mother, and the few people who'd been either close to him or important to him because of his job. Cemeteries were blank places for him. He never felt less close to Elizabeth than when he was putting flowers on her grave. He never remembered his mother so badly as when he was staring at her name etched into the granite of her tombstone. Here were the two people who had been most central to his life, the two he heard and saw and smelled better than anyone living, and when he came out to play his conventional tribute to them he lost them completely.

After a while—it was two hours, let's be honest here—he realized he was cold. He walked back to the cemetery gate and south along the sidewalk that hugged its outer wall. It was eight-thirty on Christmas morning. The sky was dark. The snow was going to start falling again any minute. The streets were deserted. He started to think he was going to have to make it back to Cavanaugh Street on foot.

Ten minutes later, he got smart and found a bus stop. Ten minutes after that, he got smarter and realized he couldn't go back to Cavanaugh Street. He wasn't half as depressed as they thought he was—although Cordelia Day Hannaford had thrown him; *that* was something he didn't want to think about—but he wasn't ready to spend the day with somebody else's children. What he really wanted to do was to be by himself in his apartment. Barring that, he wanted to hole up in the main branch of the public library. His apartment was across the street from Lida Arkmanian's town house and the library was closed.

He got off the bus in central Philadelphia and went looking for a newsstand. Eleven hours later—when he knew Lida's family would have gone back to Bucks County and Radnor and Chestnut Hill—he found a cab and went back to Cavanaugh Street. He felt like a total, unregenerate fool. His insides were collapsing from the assault of gallons of bad coffee. His eyes hurt from hours of trying to read in the bad lights of a dozen second-rate diners. His head was so full of the Hannaford murder, he thought it was going to split open. If he hadn't been depressed when he left his apartment in the morning, he was most surely depressed now.

For the most part, he was depressed because it had finally hit him that the Hannaford murder was a local sensation. At least. For all he knew, the news would hit the New York *Post* and the Boston *Globe* within hours, and go from there to network television. There would be no way to escape it. Leaving Engine House, he had cooled his annoyance at being told nothing about what had happened—beyond what he had been able to see for himself—by telling himself he was just going to walk away from it. He was going to go back to his apartment, involve himself in the not-so-mysterious disappearance of Donna Moradanyan's boyfriend, and pretend the Hannafords had never existed. With the headline on the Philadelphia *Star* reading SOCIETY

KILLER STRIKES BRYN MAWR, he had a feeling that wasn't going to work.

He got out of the cab, overtipped the driver, let himself into his building, and climbed the stairs to his apartment. The building smelled of food. He wondered what Cordelia Hannaford had done with her day. Then he told himself he was crazy, and on his way to getting crazier. The whole damn thing bothered him. It was also none of his business. He had to let it go.

He was standing in the middle of his bedroom when the phone rang, and he picked it up, and it was Tibor. He was thinking about Robert Hannaford's suitcase full of $100 bills and the very short list of uses it might have had.

Which was when he decided to invite Father Tibor to lunch.

There was an elegance to that solution Elizabeth would have appreciated.

2 There were at least five people in Leitmotif stoked to the gills on dope, including the headwaiter. Once, that would have upset Gregor endlessly. Now, he barely noticed it. He was much too interested in the reactions of one Father Tibor Kasparian. Tibor had lived long stretches of his life in the great capitals of Europe, but this was the first time he would ever eat in a restaurant where the bill came to more than the price of the cab fare home.

The idea of a restaurant away from Cavanaugh Street had been Tibor's. He wanted to discuss Donna Moradanyan's problem, and it was better to do that as far from the interested parties as possible. In this case, the interested parties included every woman over sixty in the neighborhood. They knew Donna was pregnant. They knew the father had abandoned her. They were on the warpath—against the boy. Gregor wondered how the younger woman felt. The older ones had never heard of "options," and wouldn't consider "just having the baby and keeping it" as a solution that made any sense. The younger ones all seemed to be in law school.

Tibor frowned at the headwaiter's back all the way to their table, but paid no attention at all to the homosexual couple holding hands in the corner booth. He was wearing his newest, brightest, cleanest day robes for the occasion, marking himself as a priest, but when the headwaiter called him "Father" he frowned all the harder. Gregor decided not to say anything about what Tibor probably didn't know. This was a heavily Roman Catholic city. The headwaiter thought Tibor was a monsignor.

The headwaiter seated them, made a lot of cooing noises in bad French, and disappeared. He was replaced by an ordinary waiter, who passed out a pair of oversize menus and disappeared, too. Then the wine steward came up, and Gregor ordered a bottle of chardonnay, mostly for the hell of it. He had the impression that Tibor didn't drink much.

Leitmotif was one of those restaurants that had been meticulously coordinated. The linen tablecloths were pink. The linen napkins were pink. The mirrors that lined three of the four walls were tinted with pink. Even the Christmas tree was pink. Tibor checked this all out very carefully, then stared for a moment at the gigantic fern hanging from a ceramic planter above his head, as if he were afraid it was going to fall on him. Then he shook his head.

"That waiter," he said. Gregor knew he meant the headwaiter.

"That waiter is another one. I can't understand it. Sometimes I think people are very, very stupid."

"People are often very, very stupid," Gregor said.

Tibor waved this away. "You say that like that because you've spent so much of your life dealing with criminals. And criminals are the stupidest people alive. Thank the good Lord God. But Gregor, I spend my life with normal people. And I'm telling you, they're often stupider than the criminals."

"Are you back on Donna Moradanyan already?"

"No, no," Tibor said. "That wasn't stupid. That was only natural."

"Right."

"A young girl in love and using a little bad judgment, that is an understandable thing. If the mother keeps her head, there doesn't need to be a tragedy. But drugs, Gregor. Anybody with any sense can see what happens with drugs. What do these people think they're doing?"

"Maybe they don't think."

"Don't be ridiculous," Tibor said. "Thinking is more natural to human beings than sex."

Fortunately, at that moment the wine steward came back with the chardonnay. Gregor didn't know what he would have done with that last comment—or with a discussion about drugs, either. It got a little complicated, trying to explain that he had ended up investigating serial murders because he hadn't wanted to end up investigating drugs. Most Americans seemed to think the Great Drug War was the most exciting, most noble, most glorious crusade the Republic had ever engaged in. Witness all the time they spent watching movies about it, reading novels about it, even setting up educational programs to combat it. Maybe only law enforcement officers realized how truly boring it all was. To Gregor's mind, a thirty-year-old lawyer getting himself hooked on cocaine wasn't "not thinking." He was brain dead.

The wine steward wanted to go through the whole elaborate ritual of smelling and tasting. Gregor let him do it, to buy time, even though he had the distinct feeling that neither one of them knew what he was doing. When the charade had been played out to its inevitable conclusion—polite murmurs of appreciation all around—the wine steward filled both glasses on the table halfway up and left.

Gregor picked up the bottle and topped Tibor off. "So," he said, "Donna Moradanyan."

"Donna Moradanyan," Tibor agreed.

"Do you mind if I tell you something? I haven't talked to Donna yet, and the situation may be very different after I do, but at the moment, I'm very confused about this."

Tibor was surprised. "Confused? What's there to be confused about? The girl's pregnant."

"Yes, Tibor, I know."

"And the boy ran," Tibor said. "Panic. Is that unusual, in your experience?"

"Not at all. It isn't Donna and her boy I'm thinking of. It's Cavanaugh Street."

Tibor had already finished half his wine. Now he finished the other half and reached for the bottle. "Are you going to give me one of those lectures like Lida's daughter does? About time warps? Because if you are—"

"No, no," Gregor smiled. "Look. When I was with the Bureau, I had a young woman working under me, as a technician.

This is the mid-sixties. She was a very smart woman, and there wasn't much chance of promotion for women in those days, so she quit and went to graduate school. She got a doctorate in sociology and wrote a book. Which I read. I wouldn't have read it, but I knew her—"

"I know how that is," Tibor said. "I always read books when I've met the people who wrote them. Sometimes this means I read very bad books."

"Well, this wasn't a very bad book. It was a little dry, but it was her dissertation. I'd guess that was normal. It was a book about community responses to illegitimate pregnancies. Maybe it was 'cultural' responses. Whatever. According to this woman, it's the pregnant girl who gets ostracized, not the boy. And now I have a lot of old women telling me they want to—"

"Ah," Tibor said.

"You can't just say 'ah,' Tibor. You have to elaborate."

Tibor nodded slowly. "Were you born here? In the United States?"

"In the United States, in Philadelphia, and about half a block from here. There used to be a hospital in this neighborhood called Philadelphia Lying-In."

"You had no sisters?"

"I had one brother. Much older. He died fighting at Anjou."

"That explains it, then," Tibor said. "The trouble with you, Gregor, is that you're a middle-class man. A middle-class American man."

"By the criteria you're using, Lida Arkmanian is a middle-class American woman."

"Mothers keep daughters closer to them than they keep sons,"

Tibor said. "Or they used to. The women of Lida's generation on Cavanaugh Street were brought up by peasant women. The very old women there are peasant women."

"So?"

"So, peasants don't have the same sort of attitude to these things the middle and upper classes have. The initial reaction of these women to a pregnant and unmarried daughter will be negative, of course, but after the anger is out they'll get very practical. It's the practical that matters. Would you say Donna Moradanyan was a nice girl?"

"She's a very nice girl."

"Yes," Tibor said, "nice, and not very bright. No—drive? Ambition is what I mean. She's respectful of older people. She comes to church. She doesn't swear. She likes going to school, but she doesn't really know what she's doing there, and she doesn't really care. If she didn't think people would laugh at her —people like Lida's daughter Karen—she'd probably tell you what she wants to do with her life is be a wife and mother."

"And Cavanaugh Street likes that," Gregor said.

"Well, Cavanaugh Street likes Karen Arkmanian, too. Brilliant. Ambitious. Successful. That's fine. What wouldn't be fine would be a lot of men. Do you think Donna Moradanyan has known a lot of men?"

"I still can't get used to the fact that she's known one."

"Exactly. So here we have a very nice Armenian-American girl, a sweet girl, a vulnerable girl, a girl who is twenty-one but still a child. Karen Arkmanian is the same age. You'd never call *her* a girl. Do you see what I mean?"

"Maybe."

"Of course you do," Tibor said. "The old women on Cavanaugh Street admire Karen Arkmanian. They're proud of her. They don't understand her. But Donna Moradanyan. Here she is, what you would call old-fashioned, and one morning she wakes up with a very old-fashioned problem. And the boy ran away, Gregor. There is that."

"Meaning that by running away he makes himself the villain?"

"Exactly. But right now what we have here is practicality. When a peasant girl gets pregnant, her mother makes sure she also gets married. That solves everything. Then, soon, there is a grandchild, and everybody's happy."

"It sounds like a fairy tale," Gregor said drily.

Tibor wagged his finger. "Now, now. You are talking like an American. Use your imagination, Gregor."

Gregor used his hands, to pick up the wine bottle and refill both their glasses. The wine was nearly gone. They were both getting pleasantly tipsy in the middle of the afternoon. Gregor put the bottle back in its bucket—chardonnay was a room-temperature wine, but at Leitmotif it came in a bucket anyway—and watched Tibor light a Marlboro cigarette. In deference to American prejudices about smoking, he'd left his Egyptian specials at home.

"Have you talked to Donna Moradanyan about this?" he asked Tibor. "Does she want this boy of hers found?"

Tibor sighed. "I have talked to Donna Moradanyan, yes. She doesn't want her mother to know—but her mother already knows, because Lida Arkmanian told her."

"Lida Arkmanian would," Gregor said.

"Also, she does not want to have an abortion or give the baby up for adoption. Both of which are very good decisions, because to have decided the other way in either case would have made her mother crazy. And Donna is very close to her mother. Do you see what I mean?"

Gregor saw what Tibor meant. This was a grandchild. Donna's mother wouldn't want to lose it, no matter how she had acquired it. As for abortion—well. People thought the Roman Catholic Church was fanatically opposed to abortion. People thought that because they knew nothing about the Eastern Churches, which gave new meaning to the word "fanaticism" any time they decided to get serious.

Which, fortunately, was almost never.

Gregor stretched his legs and poured himself still more wine. "In the first place," he said, "you've got to understand that finding this boy is going to be easy, unless Donna picked him up in a singles bar. I take it she didn't."

"She met him at a dance at the Assumption Church. The one that calls itself American Orthodox."

"All right. So he's connected. People know him. Donna probably has his right name. She knows where his parents live?"

"In Boston," Tibor nodded.

"Well, that could mean Boston or any one of a dozen suburbs. Still, it won't be hard. Did she know him long?"

"Eight months."

"Not a drifter, then. And not a one-night stand—"

"Gregor," Tibor winced.

"You have to consider these things, Tibor. But not a one-night stand, meaning not a man who went on the prowl one night and maybe lied about half a dozen things to get what he wanted. Which doesn't mean he didn't lie about something, but we'll cross that bridge when we get to it. In the meantime, we have what appears to be a perfectly ordinary boy. Did you ever meet him?"

"Once. Donna brought him to a—a pot luck supper? It was Sheila Kashinian's idea. To raise money for the Sunday school."

"What was he like?"

"He wasn't like anything," Tibor said. "He was in a pair of blue jeans and a sweater, like they always are. And he was very polite."

"No alarm bells going off in your head?"

"Oh, no," Tibor said. "I remember thinking it was nice she had found such a nice boy."

"What about the older women? Any alarm bells going off there?"

Tibor bit back a smile. "Lida met him, and I thought she was going to have the engagement announced then and there. Even though there was no engagement."

"Fine," Gregor said. "Now. Do you know what he was doing in Philadelphia? Did he have a job?"

"He was taking a course in archaeology at the university. He was very interested in Greek ruins."

"When was the course supposed to be over?"

Tibor thought about it. "It *was* over," he said finally. "At the end of the summer, I think. You will have to ask Donna about this, Gregor. From what I heard, I had the impression he had stayed in Philadelphia to be with Donna, after his course was over. But I'm not certain."

"All right, I'll ask Donna," Gregor said. "Assuming she wants to talk to me."

"She wants to talk to you."

"The point is, nothing about this sounds as if there was anything strange about the boy. Fine. But that brings me back to the problem I had with this in the first place."

"Problem? But Gregor, I don't understand. I thought you just said there wasn't going to be any problem."

"There may not be any problem finding the boy," Gregor said. "There may be a problem about whether or not we want him found."

"But Donna—"

"Even if Donna wants me to find him, it may be a better idea if I didn't do it. Shotgun weddings aren't such a good idea, Tibor. I don't care if they're all the rage back in the old country. In this country, they far too often end up with a wife who gets her bones broken once a week."

"*Gregor.*"

"Don't tell me you've never heard of such a thing," Gregor said. "And don't tell me you don't think it could happen to Donna."

"In America," Tibor hesitated.

"People are the same in America as they are everyplace else."

Tibor looked away. His face was flushed. The restaurant suddenly seemed much too warm. Gregor wondered what was going through his mind. Maybe he'd spent so much of his life dealing with big evils, the little ones had escaped his notice. Persecution, torture, genocide—in the middle of all that, a little wife beating or an everyday rape might not seem very important, if they registered at all. But the little evils were important. Gregor was sure of that. Out of them, everything else flowed. In them, the very essence of being human was fully and irrevocably destroyed.

Genocide was impersonal. Child abuse made the worst sort of paranoid delusion look like a badly managed Halloween party.

Tibor was fussing with his cigarette lighter and his cigarettes, like a boy who had never used either. Finally, he pushed them away and folded his hands on top of the tablecloth. He looked like he was about to deliver a lecture, maybe on those verses in Paul's second letter to the Corinthians where wives are admonished to be dutiful to their husbands.

Instead he said, "Gregor, does this mean you won't look for the boy at all?"

Gregor felt immensely relieved, although he couldn't have said why. "Of course not," he told Tibor. "I'll be happy to look for him. Given one or two conditions."

"Yes?"

"In the first place, I want to talk to Donna Moradanyan alone. I want her to tell me she wants the boy found."

"Yes," Tibor said. "Yes, yes. That is very sensible."

"In the second place, when I do find him, the only person who's going to know I've found him will be Donna. I'll give her a name, an address, a phone number. Whatever she needs. She can do what she wants with them. Including not tell the rest of you that she has them."

Tibor's eyebrows climbed up his forehead, as slowly and evenly as if they'd been raised by hydraulic drift. "Not even Donna's mother?" he said.

"Especially not Donna's mother."

"You're a very intelligent man, Gregor."

Gregor didn't know how intelligent he was, but he thought he'd at least been rational, in this case. He picked up the bottle of wine, found that it was empty, and waved for the wine steward. First the Hannaford murder, then Elizabeth's grave, then Donna Moradanyan's little problem. The world seemed to be full of depressing situations.

The wine steward was doing his best to indicate, without actually saying anything, that chardonnay was not the sort of thing one should use to get definitively drunk on in the daytime. Gregor ignored him. He'd never had a strong taste for alcohol, but there were times it was absolutely necessary for medicinal purposes. This was one of them.

The wine steward came back with a fresh bottle, went through his little dance, and departed. Gregor filled both the wineglasses and got Tibor started on the happiest topic he could think of.

Meaning the traffic in Jerusalem.

FIVE

1 In the Eastern churches and in Orthodox countries, Christmas is not as heavily celebrated a holiday as Epiphany. Children get their presents on Epiphany. Adults get their liquor on Epiphany. Priests get to say one of the most beautiful eucharistic liturgies ever written on Epiphany. Gregor had never lived in an Orthodox country—and wouldn't have wanted to—but he had grown up in an Armenian household. He was geared to Epiphany. Downtown Philadelphia, with its stores full of after-Christmas sales and its streets full of shoppers and pickpockets, disoriented him.

Either that, or his headache was even worse than he thought it was. This was why he hadn't become an alcoholic after Elizabeth's death. Not willpower, not strength of character, not common sense, not any of the things he prided himself on—just the simple fact that liquor always gave him a wicked headache, and soon. Some people could drink and feel high and happy for hours. For Gregor, the hangover always started in the middle of the third glass of wine.

On the sidewalk in front of Independence Hall, Gregor hailed a cab and put Tibor and himself into it. Tibor was happy. The wine seemed to have gone right through him, making him cheerful but not drunk, and he was stuffed full of something called a hot fudge crepe. He was also entranced by the American Christmas spirit, Philadelphia style. To Tibor, after-Christmas sales, overstuffed Christmas stockings, straining credit card limits and mountains of discarded silver foil paper were not vulgar. They were miracles.

"It's a good thing I'm not a Puritan," Tibor said. "I have never understood the Puritans. I understand them intellectually, of course. But I don't understand them."

"Well," Gregor said, "they always sounded to me like a very unpleasant group of people."

"Illogical," Tibor said. He had lit a cigarette, rolled down his window, and stuck his head into traffic. Now he pulled back again. "What these Puritans did, Gregor, their theology, it was not Christian. Fate and money, that was all. And no enjoyment of the money."

"I thought money was the root of all evil."

"Gregor, Gregor. It is the love of money that is the root of all evil, and love in that passage means—means—obsession? Yes, obsession. Lust, like with people who are insane with sex and think of nothing else. It doesn't mean being happy you can buy a microwave oven."

"Do you have a microwave oven?"

"I have two. Anna Halamanian gave them to me. She thinks I never eat."

The cab turned onto Cavanaugh Street at the north end, onto that block that was only nominally part of the neighborhood, where the Armenian-American families were interspersed with student artists and student writers and student actors. From here, they could see the painted dome of Holy Trinity Church, glittering gold even in the half-hearted sun. The cab began to slow down.

"Do you think he'll miss the church?" Tibor said. "All the cabdrivers, they always miss the church."

"They do?" Holy Trinity wasn't an especially large church, but it was large enough. And it didn't look like anything else in the neighborhood.

"You tell them church and they think of spires," Tibor said. "They get to Cavanaugh Street and there are no spires and they go right past."

"Oh."

"I'm very disappointed in you," Tibor said. "Money is the root of all evil. That is trite, Gregor. That is the kind of thing American college students say when they think they can show how intelligent they are by letting you know how much contempt they have for their fathers."

The cab had pulled to a stop in front of the church, a perfect landing. Gregor got out his wallet, paid the fare, and gave the driver an extra-large tip, because of Tibor's cigarette. Gregor had no way of knowing if the driver minded, or if it was legal to smoke in cabs in Philadelphia. He did know that no one ever challenged Tibor's right to smoke. With priests and foreigners, people never did.

Out on the sidewalk, Tibor was pulling up the collar of his coat against a new onslaught of snow. Gregor, who felt as if he'd been snowed insensible over the last few days, didn't bother with his own.

"Maybe the college students have a point," he told Tibor, searching through his pockets for the gloves he never remembered to bring with him. "We were in Liberty Square. You must have noticed people sleeping in the street."

"Of course I saw them."

"But what did you think of them?"

Tibor shook his head. "Gregor, Gregor. Christ said, 'Feed the hungry, clothe the naked, shelter the homeless.' Not, 'Be sure to vote for the congressman who promises to build the most low-income housing.' "

"Meaning what?"

"Meaning, Gregor, that if the people who called themselves Christians behaved like Christians, there wouldn't be any people sleeping in the street." Tibor smiled shyly. "You should come to visit me, Gregor, in my apartment. I have given you an invitation. And you might like to meet my houseguests."

Houseguests, Gregor thought. He felt struck dumb.

Could Tibor really be picking up strangers off the street and filling his apartment with them? Gregor opened his mouth to argue against this craziness—to argue against it in the same way and for the same reasons he would have argued against Tibor's taking a pleasure hike on the West Bank—but when he looked down, Tibor had disappeared. Gregor saw no sign of him when he looked up, either. The man had dematerialized.

Gregor turned away from the church and headed down Cava-naugh Street toward his apartment. Christianity was all well and good, but a third of the homeless were supposed to be mentally ill, outpatients who should never have been let out. Another third were supposed to be addicts of one kind or another, alcoholics and junkies. Tibor was going to end up getting his throat cut. Or worse.

Gregor had never been the kind of person who saw blood in his dreams. If he had been, he would never have survived in Behavioral Sciences. Now he was having technicolor visions of carnage. Tibor dead. Tibor murdered. Tibor slaughtered, and all because the man was some kind of idiot saint—

He had his eyes on the ground and his mind on another world, so preoccupied he almost missed the entrance to his building. He would have missed it, except that the man who had been sitting there stood up as he approached, and came down to the sidewalk, and stopped him.

"Mr. Demarkian? Excuse me. I think maybe I ought to start with an apology."

An apology.

Gregor blinked.

It took him nearly a full minute to realize he was looking at John Henry Newman Jackman.

John Henry Newman Jackman didn't like Gregor Demarkian's apartment. Because nobody ever liked it, Gregor decided not to apologize for it. He ushered Jackman through his foyer into his living room, sat him down on one of the two chairs, and headed for the kitchen to make coffee. He heard Jackman get up almost as soon as he was out of the room. Pacing.

They had gone through it all on the stoop, and again on the stairs, but Gregor knew they would go through it once again, in here. That was the way things were turning out to be between Jackman and himself. It was too bad. From what Gregor could make out, Jackman had done a remarkable job in the less than forty-eight hours since Robert Hannaford's death. Jackman had certainly done a remarkable job on him, and he was both the least important and most difficult of the subjects Jackman had to deal with. If Jackman had been half as good with the rest of his case, he must have broken the Hannafords into molecules by now.

The truth of it was, you never got over having been the subordinate of a man you truly respected. Gregor had been that way with his first superior in the Bureau. Jackman was that way with him now—even though they'd only worked together that one time, and under conditions that kept them apart more often than threw them together. Gregor was worried. With the wrong kind of man—and he didn't know Jackman well enough to know if he was wrong or not—a situation like this quickly became infantilizing, and finally generated resentment. The last thing Gregor wanted was John Henry Newman Jackman nursing a resentment. Jackman had brought the Hannafords back to him. After a dismal Christmas Day and an even more dismal afternoon spent trying to get drunk enough to feel happy, Gregor was rejuvenated.

Maybe I am going crazy, he thought. I'm beginning to have emotions I don't even recognize until four or five hours later.

It hadn't been four or five hours. It had been barely two.

Gregor put the coffee and everything else he could think of on a tray and carried it out to the living room.

Jackman, caught pacing, blushed. He sat down again, quickly. "I'm sorry," he said, for what must have been the fiftieth time. "I didn't mean to be a son of a bitch. I really didn't."

"You weren't."

"You were making me nervous," Jackman said. "I mean, I walked into that room and there you were, looking over the scene, and I thought—what was I supposed to think?"

"I told you I was retired," Gregor said.

"I know you did. But this is the federal government I thought I was dealing with here."

"You thought I was lying?"

"Never mind," Jackman said.

"I'm very retired."

"Yeah," Jackman said, "so they tell me. But I couldn't be sure about that. And you said all those things, about the murder—"

"I kept trying not to. I didn't want to interfere. No," Gregor amended, "that's not true. I wanted very badly to interfere. I couldn't keep my mouth shut."

"It got to you, did it?"

"Oh, yes."

"It got to me, too. I stood around in that house thinking I could have taken my vacation this week. Last week. Whatever. I could have taken my vacation and been in the Bahamas when this call came, and instead there I was, stuck with it."

"Stuck?"

Jackman laughed. "Look at me. I should have stayed in Philadelphia. I went out there because they offered me a lot of money. I have a good rep and I'm the right color—and don't think it doesn't matter. Everybody on earth is trying to make their quotas. Don't ask me what I think of it, because I don't know. I do have a good rep."

"I'd think you would," Gregor said. "You were only a rookie when I met you. You did exceptionally well."

"For a rookie? For a black man?"

"For a cop."

"Fine." Jackman sighed. "So here I am," he said, "or there I am, in Bryn Mawr, investigating one of the founding families of the Philadelphia Main Line. Did you know that's what they were?"

"I'd have suspected it. I knew they were railroad money."

"Railroad money. Oil money. Banking money. Do you know how much Hannaford was worth? Four hundred million dollars."

"Four *hundred?*"

"That's what I said."

"You are in a lot of trouble," Gregor said.

Jackman stood up. Gregor was beginning to think it was just as well he hadn't noticed the coffee. Jackman's restlessness was almost a mania. And it seemed to be getting worse by the second.

"Look," Jackman said, "Myra Hannaford told me you were some kind of private detective, but I checked into that. You aren't, are you?"

"No," Gregor said.

"Do you want to be?"

"I don't know what you mean."

Jackman draped himself over the fireplace mantel.

"What it means, depends," he said. "Mostly, it depends on what you were doing in Hannaford's house the night he was murdered."

"Ah," Gregor said.

"If you were a good friend of his, it wouldn't work out."

"I wasn't a good friend of his," Gregor said. "Believe it or not, I was doing a favor for my priest."

"Your priest?"

Gregor poured himself a cup of coffee. It was as thick and black as that awful Turkish stuff no one was ever allowed to mention in an Armenian neighborhood, but he didn't care.

This was going to be good.

3 The story of how Gregor Demarkian had ended up at Robert Hannaford's house on Christmas Eve was not a long one, but it was an impossible one, and because of that it took an interminable time to tell. Jackman had comments, especially about that briefcase full of money. Jackman had questions. He had the same questions Gregor had. He kept going back to them, over and over again, as if if he asked them one more time he'd get the answers. Gregor didn't have the answers. As far as he knew, only one person had ever had those. And he was dead.

Even so, the conversation had its uses. By the time Gregor had gone over the few facts he had half a dozen times, Jackman was on the floor of the living room—shoes off, legs crossed, hands behind his head—at ease, if not relaxed. His face had taken on a faraway quality. This was insane. This was absurd. This was the kind of thing he saw in the movies that made him think nobody in the whole city of Los Angeles, California had ever met a crime in his life.

Gregor knew that feeling. He'd had it once or twice himself.

Gregor poured himself another cup of coffee and waited in silence for Jackman to do something.

What Jackman did was throw himself down on his stomach and say, "Shit. These people are crazy. These people are nuts."

"I did get that impression," Gregor said. "Will you answer a question for me?"

"Maybe."

"In all logic, we know that, no matter how crazy it seems, there must be internal consistency—"

"Oh, no," Jackman said.

"But internal consistency is important," Gregor insisted. "You

realize that with psychopaths. A psychopath starts with an irrational premise—that he's the Archangel Michael, say, or that all
the women in the world have come together in a great conspiracy to destroy him. It makes no sense, but everything that follows
from it does make sense. Once you know his premise, everything
he does is strictly logical, entirely consistent. You just—"

"We're not dealing with psychopaths here."

"We're dealing with at least one person who must justify to
himself, or herself, something that cannot be justified in the ordinary way. This was a particularly deliberate murder, John. It
wasn't the kind of thing you could excuse yourself for afterward
as having been done in the heat of the moment. If half my specu-
lations the night of the crime were correct—"

"Half of them weren't," Jackman said wryly. "All of them
were. Or all of them we could check out."

"He was drugged before he was hit?"

Jackman sighed. "He had about a hundred fifty milligrams of
Demerol in him, his prescription, came out of a bottle in one of
his desk drawers. We found traces of it in a cup of hot chocolate
he had on the table next to the fireplace. I asked one of the
daughters, the fat one—"

"Anne Marie," Gregor said.

"Anne Marie. She said the only way she ever saw him take
Demerol was by chewing them, straight, not even water to wash
them down. And she said he only took one at a time, and that
maybe once a month."

"Meaning he hadn't built up a tolerance to them," Gregor
said. "A hundred fifty milligrams. It's remarkable he wasn't in a
coma."

"Maybe he was."

"True." Gregor sat back, thinking. "Do you see what I mean?" he said finally. "This is a murder that was meant to look like a murder. Somebody went to a great deal of trouble to make sure there was no ambiguity. Why not just put three hundred milligrams of Demerol in the hot chocolate? That would have muddied the issue just enough. We might have suspected accident. We might have suspected suicide—" Gregor stopped. "That's interesting," he said.

"What's interesting?" Jackman was suspicious.

"Suicide. Something I heard while I was waiting in that suspects' room of yours. Robert Hannaford had an insurance policy."

"That's right." Jackman nodded. "It was a small one for somebody like him. About a million dollars. But it was made five years ago. The restrictions are history. The insurance company would have paid off even if it had been suicide."

"What about murder? Was there double indemnity for murder?"

"Yes," Jackman said, suddenly thoughtful. "Yes, there was."

"Accident?"

Jackman's face fell. "Yeah. There was double indemnity for accident, too."

"Don't look so depressed," Gregor said. "You have to find out something about the man's habits, that's all. It's possible that an accident, an incontrovertible accident, would have been impossible to arrange. Certainly it couldn't have been done by feeding the man Demerol. The insurance companies don't operate like the courts. The only thing they need not to pay off is a reasonable excuse for being suspicious."

"And Demerol would have given them a reasonable excuse for claiming suicide? I can see that."

"So, if there's no way to arrange a solid, bulletproof accident, the only alternative is to make the murder look like a murder. And I'll tell you something else."

"What?"

"There are laws in this state, in every state, preventing a murderer from profiting directly from his crime. Do you know who the beneficiary of that insurance policy is? If it's one of the children—"

"It's not one of the children. It's Cordelia Day Hannaford."

Gregor stopped. "Ah," he said.

"The only one in the house who couldn't have committed that crime," Jackman said. "I know I was being a pain in the butt that night, but I never even suspected her. She's—"

"I know," Gregor said. "Physically incapable."

"I don't think I've ever seen you look frustrated before. Christ, I'm frustrated all the time. Maybe people aren't always internally consistent."

"I didn't say people were. I said criminals were. And lunatics."

"Whatever. Do you want to hear what I really came here about?"

"Not the murder?"

"Oh, it's about the murder, all right. Over the past couple of days I've had a really brilliant idea. I want to hire you."

"As what?"

"A consultant. Why not? That jerk out in Oregon or whatever hired himself a phony psychic. I should be able to hire myself a nationally known murder expert, a guy who's had his picture—"

"Jackman."

"Well, I should. And you're interested. And you're bored stiff with being retired. I saw that as soon as I walked into this apartment. You're living like a monk and you've got a pile of puzzle magazines in your bathroom that looks like delivery day at the local newsstand. You'd love to have me hire you."

"I don't have a detective's license," Gregor pointed out. "I have no intention of getting a detective's license."

"So who says you have to be a detective? Like I said, you could be a consultant."

"Do you know what that is?"

"No," Jackman said, "but that's not the point. Neither does anyone else."

Gregor poured himself another cup of coffee. He was being set up. He knew he was being set up. He just didn't care. He hadn't felt this good—this invigorated—since Elizabeth had gone into remission in 1982. He got his lonely bottle of Scotch off the bookshelf, poured a finger into his coffee, and handed the bottle to John Henry Newman Jackman.

"You have an ulterior motive for all of this?" he asked.

"Of course I do," Jackman said. "You seen the newspapers lately?"

"Mmm." Gregor didn't know how "lately" Jackman meant.

"This is big-time publicity," Jackman said. "It's making the networks, for Christ's sake. Do you know what happens when there's big-time publicity?"

"Intimately," Gregor said.

"Yeah," Jackman said. "You would. Well, I'm taking a lot of heat. Be practical, Gregor. If you do this, the publicity will be terrific. I'll look like an effing hero. And if I look like an effing hero, the bozos will stay off my back."

"I see. So, which is it? Am I supposed to consult or am I only supposed to pretend to consult?"

"Oh, you're supposed to consult." Jackman looked alarmed. "If you've got any more ideas like the ones you had on the night, I want to hear about them."

"Fine." Gregor sat down again. "I have this idea. I think you'd better get yourself ready for another death."

SIX

1

The trouble with Engine House, Bennis Hannaford thought, is that it's just like a self-winding watch. If you don't do something in particular to stop it, it goes on and on and on and on and on.

She looked down at the old-fashioned telephone she'd just hung up. It was eight o'clock in the morning, two days after Christmas, Tuesday, December 27. Back in Boston, it was a workday. Michael had just been getting out of the shower when she called. It bothered her he'd been so damn annoyed to hear from her, especially because he'd been expecting to. Eight o'clock was the time they'd agreed on, to get around the little problem of the telephones at Engine House. Cordelia Day Hannaford was an old-fashioned woman. She didn't want phones in most of the rooms of her house. There was one in the kitchen, because Mrs. Washington would have quit without it. There was one in the study, because Daddy had insisted on it. There was one in Anne Marie's room, in case of emergency. Other than that, there was this one small telephone stall off the sitting room on the first floor. Engine House was an enormous place, with wings spread out over the landscape. To make a call here, you sometimes had to hike through half a mile of corridors.

You're exaggerating, Bennis told herself. It wasn't the hiking she minded as much as the possibility of being overheard—or the certainty of it. She kept getting these urges to restrict her phoning to business calls, even though she had no business to call about. The new book was in the stores. The new tour was over. The radio and print interviews had been wrapped up months ago. She had nothing to do with her life but read other people's novels and concentrate on Michael—except all this had come up, and she couldn't concentrate on anything. She put her cigarette out in the ashtray she'd brought along from the kitchen and then put the ashtray on the upper shelf, where the maid was sure to see it.

This morning, Bennis thought Daddy's dying was a lot like the ache you get after riding a horse for the first time. You ride. You feel fine. You think everything is going to be all right. Then, long after you have any reason to expect it, it gets you. They'd been cool enough the night it happened, and they'd been cool enough on Christmas Day—if you could call the way they were when they were together "cool." Even yesterday hadn't been too bad. Myra and Teddy had played chess, which they did every Christmas. They'd ended the chess with an argument, which they also did every Christmas. The rest of them had wandered aimlessly around, eating too much and talking about the Flyers.

Now, with the holiday over and the snow under control, the servants were back in force, and Engine House was having the Christmas Mother had planned for it. Sort of. Through the door of the telephone room, Bennis had seen silver serving tray after silver serving tray being delivered to the dining room. They would be set out on the sideboard and provided with silver serving spoons. The result would be something like the breakfast scene in Daphne du Maurier's *Rebecca,* elaborate and barren. Even when Mother was in fine form and nothing out of the ordinary had happened and they were all on their best behavior— say once every ten years—that scene was barren. Today—

The prospect of today was so daunting, Bennis was almost ready to go back upstairs and hide herself in bed. She would have done it, but she knew she would never get back to sleep. Bennis was an early riser, when she wanted to be, and sometimes when she didn't. Long, long ago—not so long, really; it just seemed like it—she'd trained herself to get up at four o'clock in the morning and get moving as soon as her feet hit the floor. That was when she was writing her first book and working as a secretary at First Boston Financial. If she'd been an ordinary typing-pool secretary, she might have been able to write when she got home, at six o'clock, like everybody else in her writers' group. Instead, she was assistant to the second-highest officer in the corporation. She never got home before nine. By then, she was usually just this side of catatonic. Her boss was a full-fledged, manic-depressive, paranoid psychopath.

On the other hand, it might be just as well she hadn't been able to write after work. None of the other members of her writers' group had published as much as a short story.

Somehow, all this mental nattering about her career felt, well, disloyal to Daddy. Bennis had no idea how she could be disloyal to a man who had spent more than thirty years letting her know how much happier he'd have been if she'd never existed, but there it was.

She pushed through the green baize door to the dining room and looked at the overloaded sideboard, the overextended table, the huge poinsettia centerpieces with their chokers of holly and mistletoe. Then she looked at Emma, who was standing next to the coffee urn.

"You look terrible," she said.

"It's the music," Emma said. "I want them to stop the music."

Music was so much a part of Christmas at Engine House, Bennis hadn't noticed it before. Ten years ago, Mother had made a single concession to modernity. She'd had all the common rooms in the house wired into a stereo system. At the moment, that system was pumping out an organ rendition of "Silent Night."

"Idiot," Bennis said. "He's got to know there's been a death in the house. What does he think he's doing?"

"Who?"

"Marshall," Bennis said. Marshall was the butler. Sometimes Bennis got the strangest feeling, just realizing her mother had a butler.

Emma looked into her empty coffee cup. "He's just doing what he was told to do. Anne Marie wrote all the instructions on a piece of paper. I saw it hanging in the pantry."

Bennis took Emma's coffee cup, filled it from the urn, and put it on the table. "Sit," she said. "You look ready to collapse."

"I *am* ready to collapse," Emma said.

The tea was set out in two large pots. One had brew so strong it looked black when it was poured. The other had plain hot water. You were supposed to mix the two. Bennis didn't bother.

She shoved enough sugar into her tea to turn it into syrup and set the cup next to Emma's on the table. "Silent Night" had become "Noel," played on a harpsichord. The instrument sounded tinny, as if it had been discovered after being long abandoned, and played without being retuned.

Mother used to play the harpsichord.

Bennis got out her cigarettes, extracted a crystal ashtray from under the largest of the centerpieces, and lit up.

"You ought to get some sleep," she said. "You're not doing anybody any good staying awake in the night."

Emma shrugged. "You're not getting any sleep either. The rest of them walk around all night, too, you know. I heard them from my room. Bobby—"

"Bobby? Bobby stayed here again all night?"

"Myra says he's going to stay all week. That's not such a bad idea, Bennis. The weather's been really terrible. And the news last night said there was going to be snow again tomorrow morning."

"What was Bobby doing walking around?"

"I don't know." Emma took a tentative sip of her coffee and made a face. "I went to the upstairs library about two and he was there, working with his calculator. It was weird. He just kept punching buttons and punching buttons, but he didn't have papers or anything to work with. It was like he knew all the numbers by heart. It made me wonder."

"About what?"

"Well," Emma said. She blushed and looked into her coffee cup again.

Overhead, "Silent Night" became "The Holly and the Ivy"— played on a virginal. Mother used to play the virginal, too. For all Bennis knew, Mother had played the music she was hearing now, and recorded it, against the time she would no longer be able to make the carols herself.

The idea was so depressing, Bennis could hardly stand it. She lit another cigarette, realizing too late that the one she'd lit before had hardly been smoked. She put them both out.

"I just talked to Michael," she said. "He says that now the holiday's officially over, the police will get in gear. Things will start to happen—"

"Things have already happened," Emma said. "All that questioning."

"Well, yes. He meant the wider investigation. Talking to the lawyers and the bank and the insurance company, that kind of thing. Looking for motives."

"They don't have to talk to all those people to get motives," Emma said. "They just have to talk to us."

"I don't think they see it that way, Emma."

Emma finished her coffee and got up to get some more. She fumbled with the spigot on the urn, then filled her cup until it was slopping over. Bennis frowned. That fumbling motion had made her think of something, but she couldn't figure out what. She tried to see it again, replay it in her mind, but couldn't make it happen.

Emma came back to the table. "I'd feel better if they acted as if they cared," she said. "He was our father. It doesn't matter if we loved him or hated him, does it?"

"It matters to the police," Bennis pointed out.

"Oh, the *police*." Emma waved a hand in the air. "Chris was walking around last night, too, you know. I found him in the hall, where the portraits are, with the candles under them, and he started talking to me about poetry. I mean, poetry. Hell. It's like it never happened."

"I don't think that's true," Bennis said.

"We should be sitting around in a bunch, trying to figure out which one of us did it. That's what people do in books."

"Maybe we don't want to know which one of us did it." Bennis lit yet a third cigarette, promising herself to actually smoke it this time. "I don't think *care* is the word I'd use, but I think it matters to them. Matters that he's dead. It's just taken a little time to sink in, that's all. It's not like he was around all the time. Even when we were all home together, he spent most of his time hiding out in his study. He only emerged for meals and fights, and he didn't always emerge for meals. His not being around isn't all that strange, Emma."

"It's strange to me."

"Maybe you're more sensitive than the rest of us."

Emma sighed. "I don't like the way the house feels since he's died. Bobby and Chris. And Myra—"

"Myra?"

"When I got up this morning, she was rummaging around in the cedar closet, looking for a pair of long johns. Can you imagine Myra in long johns?"

"No," Bennis said.

"And she was wearing jeans," Emma went on. "Jeans and a great big oversize sweater. When I first saw her, I thought she was you. Except not for long, you know. Because she's dyed her hair that peculiar color."

"I think she gets tired of all the dressing up she has to do. I think Dickie insists on it, and it annoys her."

"Don't be ridiculous, Bennis. Myra was born in spike heels."

Emma took a cigarette out of Bennis's pack and lit up herself. She was beginning to look haggard again. With those huge black bags under her eyes and the skin of her face gone slack, Emma looked fifty. It was a shock to realize it, but it was true.

Jesus Christ, Bennis thought. She's younger than I am.

"Bennis?" Emma said. "I know what you're thinking. I know what you're all thinking. You have to understand it isn't true."

2 If there was one thing Christopher Hannaford was sure of, it was that, once he got beyond the gates of Engine House, he was going to be scared out of his mind. He'd been anticipating it all morning—all night, really. He'd gone into the hall and taken the candlesticks from under the picture of old Robert Hannaford II. He'd gone back to his room and hidden the candlesticks in his blue nylon backpack. He'd told himself he was a complete fool. Once he was in the car and on his way to Philadelphia, he was going to be so terrified, he wouldn't be able to do anything at all.

As it turned out, he was nothing of the sort. Maybe he was too tired to summon the energy for fear. Christ only knew he hadn't slept in days. First there was that long stretch in California, playing and replaying that phone call about his thumbs. Then there was that even longer stretch getting across the country, renting cars under assumed names, sleeping in motels so bug-ridden they should have declared themselves flea circuses. Then there was Engine House, with all its security, and one good night's rest—and then, of course, there was the murder.

Maybe the murder had knocked all the imagination out of him, so he could no longer make threats to his thumbs seem real. At the moment, nothing seemed real, except the drumming restlessness in his arms and head. He was so tired, he was nearly blind. The last time he'd been this whacked, he'd pulled three all nighters in a row his junior year exam week at Yale. What had happened then was happening now. The air in front of his eyes was full of tiny points of light.

In the seat next to him, Bobby was going through one of those accordion-sheet computer printouts, checking things off with a gold Mark Cross pen. It was ten o'clock in the morning, late by the world's standards, but Bobby was going to work. He looked it—white shirt, black tie, grey pin-striped suit. Away from Bobby, Chris was never sure people really dressed like that. Looking at Bobby always made Chris feel stoned.

It also made him wonder.

Chris rolled his window down and stuck his head into the cold, wet air. They were nearing downtown Philadelphia, site of the Laedemon Building, where Bobby had moved the offices of Hannaford Financial less than three years ago. It was a monied part of town. The sidewalks were crowded. The store windows were full of decorations that looked expensive by virtue of also looking as if they'd cost a lot of work. Gigantic foil snowflakes, hand-cut in varying patterns. Tableaux of Victorian Christmas scenes, complete with authentically crafted miniature furniture and dolls dressed in velvet and bustles. Did people like doing this sort of thing?

A robed choir had begun to assemble itself on the steps of one of the churches. Because Chris had never liked Christmas carols —they were either sentimental or bloody—he pulled his head back into the car and rolled his window up again. Bobby was staring at him. He had taken his coat off as soon as he got into the car, probably to keep his suit from wrinkling. The open window had frozen his face into a mass of goose bumps.

"You could at least think of Morgan," he said. "Just because your relatives put up with your nonsense doesn't mean the servants will."

"Sorry," Chris said.

"You're always sorry. Jesus Christ Almighty, Chris. Didn't Mother teach you anything?"

Mother had taught him a lot of things, but Chris didn't want to go into them at the moment. Once Bobby got started on an argument like this, he could go on for hours—and it wouldn't make any more sense when he'd finished than it had when he'd started. Chris wondered what Bobby did for excitement. His own restlessness had just jacked itself up another notch, making him feel really wild. Wild and invincible. That was what it was about betting, what betting had that nothing else did. When you got on a real roll, you could do anything. You really could. It wasn't an illusion. You picked up the dice and you threw them against the board and you saw them in the back of your mind, saw them turning. You made them turn just the way you wanted them to. It was better than being God and better than magic, too. It was even better than being stoned. You got going and the world changed color. Your head exploded. Your skin merged with the air and your nerves plugged right into the great river of cosmic energy and you—

And you stole your mother's best pair of sterling silver candlesticks.

Chris looked down at his backpack. The doubt was creeping up his spine, spreading across his back like a nasty attack of boils.

He jerked his head away and stared determinedly up at the ceiling, breathing in and out, in and out, in long whooshing streams of air that just might calm him down.

Beside him, Bobby folded the computer printout into some semblance of its original shape and put it away in his briefcase. Bobby's movements were prissy and awkward, as if he had lost the knack of moving the way he normally moved, and was now trying to reproduce the effect by rote.

"Are you all right?" he asked.

"I'm fine," Chris told him.

"You don't look fine." Bobby dumped the briefcase on the floor. They were moving very slowly through heavy traffic, in a scene that seemed to Chris to be entirely unreal. A stretch limousine with tinted windows. A uniformed driver. A telephone and television and a fully stocked bar, all built into a cabinet between the regular passenger seat and the rumble. What had Daddy been thinking of?

Bobby put his pen away, in a little pocket in his wallet that had been designed for the purpose. "You look like death," he said. "I know you say you haven't got AIDS, but—"

"I haven't got AIDS," Chris said.

"You ought to get it checked out. You look ready to collapse. You've got to be thirty pounds underweight. If you haven't got AIDS, you're killing yourself some other way, and let me tell you—"

"Don't tell me. For Christ's sake, Bobby, don't tell me."

"Somebody has to tell you."

"Bennis tells me," Chris said. "She appointed herself my surrogate mother years ago. Emma tells me—"

"There's something wrong with Emma, too. I saw her in the foyer when I was coming out. She looks—I don't know how she looks. I don't like the way this family is disintegrating."

"Right," Chris said.

"There's something else. The police seals have been broken. The ones on the door in the study. I was down in that hall this morning, and—"

Bobby was going on and on, trying to explain his way out of what it was impossible to explain his way out of, but Chris wasn't listening to him. Chris had been looking at the car ceiling all this time. Now he pulled his head down, caught sight of the backpack, picked up no bad vibrations, and turned his attention to Bobby. Bobby was sweating as heavily as a construction worker pounding rivets on a hot August day, and that was very odd.

"Wait a minute," Chris said. "What do you mean, the police seals have been broken?"

Bobby got a handkerchief out and wiped his face. "They've been broken. It's like I said. I went into that hall to—"

"Don't tell me why you went into that hall."

"But it's important."

"No it isn't," Chris said. "The police seals are important."

"Chris, there's nothing to say about the police seals. They were broken, that's all. Somebody's gone into the study. I noticed it right away. You know how they were, strips of paper stretched across the door like they do with toilets in bad hotels?"

"I know."

"Well, they'd been ripped. Very carefully, so that the tears were straight. And then the ripped parts had been taped back together again. If you were standing at the end of the hall, you wouldn't necessarily notice it. But when you got right up to the door, there it was."

Chris thought about it. "Which side had they been ripped on?" he asked finally. "The side with the knob or the other one?"

"Why is that important?"

"It shows what kind of trouble whoever it was went to," Chris said. "If they're ripped on the knob side, whoever it was just did it and wasn't thinking clearly. You know the police are going to notice if they've been ripped on that side. But if they were ripped on the other—"

"It was the side with the knob," Bobby said.

"Interesting."

Bobby turned away. "I don't see what's so interesting about it. This is a serious business. You don't seem to realize. None of you seem to realize. The police are going to want to arrest somebody for this murder, and if we don't watch out—"

"What?"

Bobby stared down at his black, polished, archaic wing-tip shoes. "It was Myra," he said. "I saw her coming out of that hall. Just before I went in."

"Today?"

"Yesterday."

"When?"

"Around three o'clock. In the afternoon, I mean."

"I thought you said you went into that hall today."

"Well, I did. I noticed the police seals today. But I was there yesterday, too, I wanted something from the supplies closet, and Myra was just coming out as I was going in. And you know where the supplies closet is. It's way up at the foyer end of the hall. I couldn't see anything from there. But this morning—"

"Bobby," Chris said, "you're talking about seventeen, eighteen hours. Or more. If you don't even know if the seals were broken when you went into the hall yesterday—"

"They weren't broken at one o'clock," Bobby said.

Chris raised an eyebrow. *"One* o'clock?"

Bobby turned away. "Don't look at me like that. I didn't do anything. I just went down and looked at the door. I couldn't help myself."

"Grief for dear old Dad," Chris said.

Bobby got his briefcase off the floor and put it in his lap. "Just go screw yourself. Just turn right around and stuff it up your own—"

"My own what?"

"Asshole. This is my office, Chris. I have to get out."

Bobby's office was half a block up—half a block of slush and grit, the kind of thing Chris was sure Bobby never walked into, no matter what. Even so, Bobby was putting on his coat and rearranging the pieces of his suit. His suit seemed to need a lot of rearranging.

"You sit out in California," Bobby said, "and you don't realize what's happening out here. You don't realize. Some of our dear bosom relatives have been losing their marbles for years."

"Like Myra?"

"For one," Bobby said.

"You know what's really interesting?" Chris said. "You, trying to implicate Myra in Daddy's murder. That's interesting."

"I don't know what you're talking about."

"You ought to. Myra had the watch yesterday afternoon. She was in Mother's suite from one until six. I was with her from one-thirty to four. The only way you could have seen her coming out of the study hall door at three was if she'd gone into a trance and thought transferred herself there. And believe me, she never went into a trance. She was beating my pants off at gin."

The car was still inching through traffic, but Bobby popped his door, swung his legs into the gutter and hopped out onto the pavement. He landed in a puddle, sending up a spray of mud that splattered his pants up to his knees.

Chris transferred himself to the rumble seat, opened the privacy window, and told Morgan where he wanted to go. He felt good again. Oh, yes. He felt excellent. He was at one with the cosmic consciousness, at home in the sea of chance, in love with the spinning of the universe. He was going to hock the hell out of these goddamned candlesticks and then he was going to make himself a killing, the kind of killing you only made once or twice in a lifetime.

The kind of killing that would solve everything. The way killings always did.

He was so hot, he was running a fever.

It was 10:24 A.M.

3 Out in Chestnut Hill, Myra Hannaford Van Damm had just finished going through the papers she'd found in Bobby's desk drawers. She was putting them back again, haphazardly, not really caring whether she got them into the right places or not. If Bobby came back and found his desk a mess and his papers rifled and got himself spooked, all well and good. The stupid little bastard deserved to be spooked.

She stood up, went over to the makeshift bar Bobby had set up on one of the bookshelves and poured herself a Perrier and lime. Most of her family thought she was stupid, but that wasn't strictly true. In some ways, she was enormously stupid. In others, she had a touch of genius. She couldn't have understood three lines of *War and Peace*. She could, however, read a financial report better than a bank examiner, an IRS auditor, or a computer.

She dropped into a leather wing chair and considered her present problem. It wasn't the fact that Bobby had been embezzling from Hannaford Financial that bothered her. She'd been embezzling from Dickie Van Damm for ages. Over the past three years, she'd relieved her darling and thoroughly obtuse husband of well over half a million dollars—and got it right out of his checking account, too, where he should have noticed it. Because Dickie hadn't the faintest idea of how to balance his checkbook, he never would. If Daddy hadn't discovered what she was doing, she could have gone on with it for another three years. By then, she'd have had enough in secret bank accounts to walk out on her marriage. She wouldn't have had to worry about settlements or delaying tactics or Pennsylvania's quaint little custom of allowing for contested divorce.

She got up again and went back to the bar, watching her face in the mirrored surface of the bottle tray as she poured another Perrier. She was beginning to worry about Bobby's mental health. She really was. What he had done—well, she could hardly believe it. Fake customer orders. Fake stock certificates. Fake bonds. Fake everything—and it all looked fake, too, as phony as a Main Line accent on a Brooklyn-born real estate developer. It was as if Bobby was *trying* to get himself caught.

She squinted at her reflection in the bottle tray and rubbed at a smudge on the tip of her nose. No matter how crazy he made her, Bobby the Embezzler was not her problem. He could embezzle himself right into Leavenworth and she wouldn't bat an eye. She wouldn't go with him, either. She'd always been considered much too empty-headed to have anything to do with the business. With the way she'd set things up, if Bobby tried to implicate her, it would be his word against hers.

Her problem was these huge, unexplained waves of cash, these mountains and mountains of cash, that came rolling through the records at unpredictable intervals.

She did not, of course, have anything to do with this cash.

She had not, of course, even known anything about this cash. If she had, she would have put a stop to it, right away.

The investigation of an embezzlement was one thing. The investigation of stock fraud manipulation was something else altogether. That could go very deep, and get very sticky.

She finished her Perrier and put the glass down on the bookshelf, still full of ice. Then she wandered out of the room and into Bobby's front hall. Cash. It bugged the hell out of her that she was going to have to save that little asshole's neck just to save her own.

She had left her coat lying over the banister at the bottom of the stairs. She picked it up, put it on, and went out the front door. The door snicked closed behind her, locking automatically.

What could you do with a man who didn't even notice his keys were missing when he left for the office in the morning?

She stepped onto the sidewalk, raised her hand for a cab, and had a very troublesome thought.

That Gregor Demarkian person was an FBI man.

The FBI worked on federal bank and stock investigations.

What if Daddy had known about this, too?

SEVEN

1 There was a grandfather clock in the hall outside her bedroom. When it began striking, Cordelia Day Hannaford began counting the notes. It was easier to do that than to get up and look at the bedside clock, or even lift her arm and look at the watch on her wrist. She had tried to do both those things when Emma left the room. She had succeeded with the watch, but the effort had left her nauseated and mentally fogged. And it had taken a very long time. She had no idea how many minutes it had been from the moment Emma left to get the tea tray to the moment she had got her wrist up high enough, and her mind cleared long enough, to see that it was 10:36.

It was now eleven o'clock. She had been at rest for twenty-four minutes, more time than she needed to make the sick feeling go away. As always when she felt well these days, her mind seemed to be detached from her body, floating and free, in her skull but not of it. She had felt much the same way on those mornings, long ago, when she had woken after a night of too many champagne cocktails. Champagne cocktails. She wished Anne Marie weren't so conscientious about doctors' orders. She was going to be dead before New Year's. They weren't telling her, but she knew. What she would like between now and then was a day on the chaise in the sitting room, listening to Cole Porter on the stereo and drinking champagne cocktails.

What she would like between now and then was to be at ease.

She stirred in bed, involuntarily, just enough to dislodge the blanket and send it puddling around her waist. She knew they wondered about it, all of them, not only the children but the people she met outside. They wanted to know why she had married Robert Hannaford. Some of them wanted to know why she had stayed with him. He could be an evil man. Some of the things that had happened in this house would scare the skin off a mercenary soldier. But the scenarios they invented for her were all wrong. She had been poor, yes—but she hadn't married him for his money or stayed with him for it. By the time she had met him, she had had her life all planned. She would go through with the ridiculous charade of a debutante year, eating other people's food, dancing in other people's ballrooms, wearing hand-me-down Balenciagas that had graced the backs of the richest heiresses in town. Coming out could cost a quarter of a million dollars or nothing at all, depending. She was the last living representative of a great old Philadelphia name. She had the right connections, the right background and the right tale of woe. People wanted to do things for her, and she let them. She felt she owed it to herself—and to her mother, who had cared so painfully much about all that sort of thing. When it was over, she had every intention of turning her back on it, coming up to Penn State, and getting sensible.

Instead, she met Robert Hannaford, at a dinner for a hundred and six given by a Rockefeller connection with ambitions. The dinner was idiotic: too much food, too many people, too little planning. Robert was seated beside her for no good reason either of them could tell. Because she was "horsey" and he was not, most hostesses would have assumed they had nothing to say to each other. Well, she had had nothing to say to him, but he had had a great deal to say to her—and she had recognized in him, right at the beginning, a quality she had encountered before only in her father. Robert Hannaford was a man who could attach himself to *one* person. If he never met that person, he would attach himself to no one at all.

She had let herself be attached. She had let herself stay attached. She had even been happy. Robert could be a good man, if he wanted to be—and he always wanted to be, with her. He bought her things. He took her places. He did everything but settle money on her, and she didn't mind that. That was the measure of his fear. He was sure that if he ever gave her the chance, she would run away.

It was the children who changed everything. He had hated them from the beginning, even hated her pregnancies, always disappearing for the last four months before the births so that he didn't have to witness either her agony or her joy. She had loved them more than she expected to. Sometimes she thought she should have stopped at one, or maybe two, as soon as she knew how they were affecting him. She couldn't have done it. She'd had seven and she would have had more, if her body had held out. Even now, old and sick and almost dead, what would have made her happiest was to hear that she was pregnant.

By the time things started going seriously wrong, there was nothing she could do about any of it, except kill the man herself. That one of the children was going to kill him had been obvious for years—either that, or they were going to start killing each other. That was why she had been so relieved to find him dead.

Outside, the clock struck the quarter hour, a single bass-note chime that sounded like a dinner gong.

It was 11:15.

Cordelia Day Hannaford closed her eyes and told herself not to panic.

In the bedroom across the hall and three doors down from Cordelia's, Emma Hannaford sat on the edge of a grey princess chair and watched a pool of her own vomit spread across the oak floor. It was an immense pool, bigger than an ocean, and the dimmer her sight got the bigger it seemed to become. She was seconds away from passing out. Once she passed out, she would be dead.

I should be afraid, she thought, and then she thought of all the things people did in situations like this in the books she read. Leave a dying message. Leave a dying clue. She ought to do something to warn the rest of them, but she couldn't. She knew what had happened to her. That replayed itself, like a movie on a loop tape, over and over again in her mind. The teacup. The spoon. The back turned and the elbows moving oddly, in the wrong directions, for what was supposed to be going on. It must have been Demerol that got put into the tea. She was allergic to it, although she was the only one here who knew that. When they had given her a prescription for it in New York after she broke her leg, it had made her sick, then, too.

If she could get out of her chair and across the room, she could ring for a maid and the maid might be able to help her. She couldn't get out of her chair. The room was very dark and very long, darker and longer than it had ever been before. She was having a hard time holding up her head. This must be what it was like to be Mother. Muscles that wouldn't obey you. Nerves that had gone on strike. A mind that drifted from one thing to another, never catching hold of anything. That much had started back in the city, coming on her every month or two like a sudden chill. That much had frightened her, until she had seen Mother—and what was happening to her was instantly clear.

But that had nothing to do with this.

This was—

She fell back into her chair, feeling black.

She should do something to warn them. She should, she should, she should. She should do something heroic and very, very wise.

It was the middle of the afternoon and it was snowing and it was dark and she was dying. And she didn't want to die.

She really didn't.

PART THREE

TUESDAY, DECEMBER 27–WEDNESDAY, DECEMBER 28

THE THIRD MURDER

ONE

1 Until the telephone call came, Gregor Demarkian had been thinking about something else. That was odd, because for days he had been thinking of nothing but the Hannafords, even when he was ostensibly concentrating on something else. But it had been an interesting day, and an illuminating one. Ordinary things had crept up on him and finally taken him over. For once, his apartment seemed neither alien nor cold. It was just a place he was utterly incapable of taking care of.

It was two o'clock on the afternoon of Tuesday, December 27. Gregor had spent the morning talking to Donna Moradanyan, a soothing exercise if there ever was one. Unlike Tibor and Lida and everyone else on the street, the girl was not panicking. She wasn't depressed, either. She'd knocked on his door just after he'd finished his breakfast, fresh from a snowball fight on the sidewalk, glowing and cold and happy in spite of everything. For the five hundredth time, Gregor told himself she was the least Armenian-looking woman he had ever seen. Tall and fair and athletic, she reminded him of the Swedish girls in 1930s movies.

She stood on his mat, stamping snow off her L. L. Bean's Maine Hunting Shoes, her hands balled into fists in the pockets of an oversize army flak jacket.

"I feel like I should whisper," she told him. "You know, just to keep the spy motif going."

"Spy motif?"

"Like the way it is with Mrs. Arkmanian. Every time I bring this up, she practically starts talking in code."

Gregor let her in. Because she'd been in before, she spent no time looking over the apartment and wasted no breath telling him how bad it was for him. She just went straight to the kitchen and started fussing with the stove, the way some women will with men they think can't cook. Gregor supposed this was a ritual that was now out of fashion. He thought that was too bad. Assuming the man involved was not a complete jerk—which was assuming a lot in some cases, he would grant that—fussing like this could be a great comfort to both parties.

Donna threw her coat over the back of one of his kitchen chairs and went to work on his dishes, few as they were. "So," she said, "are you going to find Peter for me?"

"Is that his name?" Gregor said. "Just Peter?"

"Peter Desarian. It might have been Bagdesarian originally. I don't know why I think that. Armenians don't usually change their names unless they're going to be actors. Like Mike Connors."

"Mike Connors?"

"He was Krekor Ohanian. Originally." She looked into the sink. He really hadn't had a lot of dishes, just some coffee cups and some spoons and the chipped, dessert-size plate he put his toast on. These were now stacked neatly in his dish drainer, dripping small beads of water. "You know what bothers me about all this? How it happened. That's what bothers me."

Gregor had visions of arcane sexual practices, black magic rituals, God knew what. "I don't think I understand," he said.

Donna threw herself into an empty chair. "I don't mean the mechanics of it. That was simple enough. Everything was simple enough, really, except the other thing was so stupid. Really stupid."

"What other thing?"

"Being ashamed of being a virgin."

Gregor's astonishment must have shown on his face. Donna blushed furiously and looked away. "Maybe we should talk in code. You might find it easier."

"No, no." Gregor recovered himself, took a deep breath, and counted to ten.

"I know it wasn't the same when you were young," Donna was going on. "I mean, everybody was a virgin then, right? Until they got married. Either that or they were bad. But, Mr. Demarkian, I'm twenty-one. Until I met Peter, I was the only person in the whole Art Institute who'd never had sex."

"I know it may have seemed that way," Gregor said.

"Karen Arkmanian's been on the pill since she was sixteen," Donna said. "And most of the girls I knew in high school took the plunge before the end of senior year. Except me."

"Why not you?"

Donna shrugged. "I don't know. I had a boyfriend then. This was out in Ardmore. About a month before our prom, when everybody was buying tickets and looking for dresses, he gave me an 'or else.' And I just got so mad. I got so *mad*. It just seemed like the worst thing anybody had ever done to me. So I told him—"

"To go stuff it," Gregor said.

"Exactly," Donna said.

"Maybe that was common sense. If all your friends really were having, ah, making love, maybe that wasn't common sense. Not everybody is ready for the same things at the same time."

Donna sighed. "I don't know about common sense, Mr. Demarkian, but I was getting really scared. Especially after I got to the Art Institute. Everybody there is so sophisticated. That was one of the reasons I got Daddy to buy me the apartment. I shared an apartment for a while, a rented one, with a girl from school. She was very nice, but she was always going to bars and bringing home men. And I started to feel, well—"

"Unpopular?"

"Repressed," Donna said. "That was the other thing. I took this psychology course in the summer. And it was, like, I hadn't even ever really felt the urge. If you see what I mean. It wasn't just that I was a virgin. It was that I didn't care I was a virgin."

"Did you feel the urge with this Peter?"

"No. I just didn't mind the whole idea. With most boys, you know, I'd get really turned off. I was beginning to think I was a lesbian."

"Were you attracted to women?"

"I wasn't attracted to anybody."

"Fine," Gregor said. "I don't think you're a lesbian. For that, you have to be attracted to women. I don't think you're repressed, either, whatever that means. Excuse me. I don't have a lot of respect for psychology."

Donna laughed. "Right now, I don't have *any*. I can't believe I did this. I can't believe it. And for what?"

"Did you at least enjoy yourself?"

"With the sex, you mean? I don't know. It was all right, I guess. Kind of an anticlimax."

"My wife used to tell me it often is. For women."

"Not for men?"

"Not that I've ever heard of."

"If men weren't so crazy, I'd wish I was one." Donna went back to the sink. There was a dish towel hooked over one of the knobs on the cabinet next to the window. She picked it up and started drying coffee cups. "Mrs. Arkmanian said you could find him for me," she said. "Peter, I mean. She said you could find him and maybe get him to talk to you."

Gregor nodded. "I can probably find him, if you'll give me some information I need to get started. But right now I'm very confused. Why do you want to find him? You sound as if you don't even like him."

"I like him well enough," Donna said. "He's a nice person, really. A little young, you know, and maybe a little weak, but nice. I don't want to marry him, if that's what you mean."

"If you don't want to marry him, what are you going to do with him when I find him?"

"Talk to him. Just to get a few things straight in my mind. And tell him about the baby, of course, because he's the father and I'm going to have it and he ought to know. And. Well. Ask him to do something for me. Something important."

"What?"

"Oh," Donna said. "You know. It's a brave new world."

"I'm sorry. I just don't—"

"The AIDS test," Donna said. "I want him to have the AIDS test. I mean, I thought he was all right, when I first met him, but now, with all of this, how can I know? He's so irresponsible. He could have been doing anything before I met him."

"I suppose he could have," Gregor said.

"I think it's a lot of crap," Donna said. "All that stuff about how everybody wants sex all the time and just pretends they don't or stuffs it down in their unconscious or something. I think some people do and some people don't. And I don't see why it has to be bad if you're one of the people who don't."

"Of course it's not bad," Gregor said.

"Everybody always tells you it is," Donna said. "Especially boys. Men. Whoever. Do you want to see a picture of him? I've got a good one."

Gregor held out his hand. "First the picture, then everything he ever told you about his family, his life, his schooling—everything."

"He told me a lot about his life." Donna sat down at the table again. She looked very earnest and very young and very, very angry. "The problem is, Mr. Demarkian, I think most of it might have been lies."

"Lies?"

"Lying was something he did, wasn't it? He's the one who was talking about marriage for eight months. I never brought up the subject. And it's not like you have to say those things just to get yourself laid these days."

She reached into her jacket, came up with a wallet and threw the wallet on the table.

"There," she said. "Everything there is to know about Peter Desarian and Donna Moradanyan, Couple."

2

Out on Cavanaugh Street, the snow was coming down again, thick and hard—the start of another blizzard. After Donna Moradanyan had left his apartment, he'd spent some time making calls—checking information for Boston and five of its suburbs; talking to a friend of his in the Boston city government; talking to another friend of his who was still at the Bureau—and then he'd stretched out on the couch, feeling vaguely disturbed. Donna Moradanyan was such a nice, ordinary girl. He couldn't believe she was also a crazy, although she'd sounded like one. He wished he watched more television, or read more popular fiction. Maybe the things she had described to him were perfectly normal now, as mundane as war movies and John Wayne westerns had been when he was younger. He had no way of knowing.

After a while, he got up and started to wander around the apartment. It was a useless exercise. The only popular fiction he owned was a copy of one of Bennis Hannaford's books, and that wasn't going to be much help to him. For one thing, the damned novel took place in fairy land, or wherever it was unicorns were commonplace. For another, he'd got the impression, from reading the first few chapters, that Bennis Hannaford had an unusual sensibility. She would never have been taken in by "psychology." Assuming she knew it existed.

He sat back down on the couch, stretched out again, and folded his hands over his stomach. The last two calls he had made would bear fruit in a very few hours. People would get back to him, and the things they had to tell him would point him in the right direction. If the boy was an habitual liar—and so many people were; it never ceased to surprise him—he'd have to start again from the beginning, but he didn't think he'd mind that. What he minded was Donna Moradanyan, so confused she didn't know what she thought or felt any more—so much in love and not even knowing it.

Love, he decided, had been a lot easier in the old days, when he and Elizabeth had met. Then courting had been a dance, engraved in stone, and everyone had known the steps. He could remember sitting alone in the tiny one-room apartment he h⸴

rented when he was a graduate student at Harvard, counting out quarters and dimes and trying to come up with enough for half a dozen red roses. Roses were the universal language, practically a proposal of marriage—especially if you were poor and the girl you were seeing knew you couldn't afford them. People might not have had so much sex in those days, but they'd had assurances.

He closed his eyes, dreaming of hole-in-the-wall restaurants and tightly packed cafés and little dance places with postage-stamp floors where you had to dance cheek-to-cheek or not at all. Elizabeth's perfume: Chanel No. 5, bought once a year in minuscule bottles after much frantic saving, applied sparingly and only on very special occasions. Elizabeth's clothes: silk and wool hiding an infinity of mysterious rustles. Elizabeth's shoes: high-heeled but sturdy, making her seem taller and thinner than he wanted her to be. Gregor had to remind himself that those days hadn't actually taken place in black and white.

He started drifting into sleep, and the dreams changed, in color and intensity. Elizabeth, Elizabeth, Elizabeth, he thought, and saw her growing older, into the woman he was married to. But not growing sick. In dreams like this, Elizabeth never got sick. She just got lovelier and lovelier, more and more perfect. Her hair got white and the skin on her face got impossibly soft. The polish she wore on her fingernails got paler.

He was just slipping into the best dream of all, when the phone rang. The phone was in the bedroom, but he had turned the ringer on high, to make sure he heard it no matter where he was in the apartment. When ringing, it sounded as shrill and crazy as a police whistle under his ear.

He sat up, brushed the hair out of his face, and waited. It rang on and on and on. He got off the couch and went into the bedroom.

"Stupid," he said.

Then he picked up the receiver and listened to the sound of police sirens, whirring and screaming and choking in somebody else's endless night.

3 "Gregor," Jackman said, as soon as the noise had fallen off enough for him to say anything. "Listen. I'm at Engine House. I've sent a police car for you."

Gregor sat down on the bed and ran his hands through his hair again and made another stab at counting to ten. "What do you mean, you sent a police car? You can't send a police car for me here. Everybody on the street will think I'm being arrested."

"I'm not arresting you, Gregor."

"I know that," Gregor said.

"I'm just in a goddamned hurry. I told them to put the siren on. When they get there, just climb in back and let them bring your ass out to me."

There was the sound of someone talking in the background, an urgent, excited voice just a little too indistinct for Gregor to hear. Jackman said, "Just a sec," and stopped breathing into the phone. A moment later, he was back, swearing.

"Goddamned idiots," he said. "Christ, Gregor, you can't get anything done right any more. Not anything. They say it's black people they've lowered the standards for, but let me tell you. They're hiring white idiots, Gregor. They're taking white people on this police force with IQs of twenty-nine."

"Mr. Jackman," Gregor said.

"Oh, stop with the Mr. Jackman. Come on out. The car'll be there any minute."

"Why?"

"Why do you think?" Jackman said. "You were right. I've got another body. She wasn't a body when we came through the door, but she sure as hell is a body now."

"Cordelia Hannaford?"

"Emma Hannaford," Jackman said. "And you were right about something else. I'm being set up to believe she committed suicide out of remorse. And I do mean set up."

"How?"

"For one thing, I've got a suicide note that's not a suicide note."

"John—"

"Gotta go," Jackman said.

The connection was broken with a slam, making Gregor wince. He looked down at the slippers on his feet and sighed.

He wasn't dressed. He wasn't ready. He wasn't even awake.

And there was a police siren out there someplace, getting closer.

TWO

1 For some reason—maybe because this was the second death—Gregor had expected the scene at Engine House to be more garish, more lurid, more melodramatic than the one he had walked into Christmas Eve. Instead, it was less. The day was dark, its sky carpeted in black storm clouds, its air full of snow and grit—but there was still enough light to see by. None of the vehicles parked on the circular turnaround at the bottom of the terrace steps had its lights on. Stacked together there, wearing none of their ordinary badges of emergency, they made Gregor think of the commuter lots that had sprung up all along the Main Line.

The car Jackman had sent for him had turned out not to be a regular police car, but a "transportation vehicle" meant to bring accused but possibly dangerous prisoners from jail to courthouse during a trial. There was a cage in the back, but only a single man in front. Gregor was able to ride in the passenger seat, like a normal person. After a while, he'd even managed to convince the driver to turn off the siren. Like most of Jackman's lowest level footmen, this one was very young and scared to death of his boss. To make him see reason, Gregor had had to make the boy just as scared of *him*.

The car slowed. Gregor opened his door and jumped out, hitting the ground just as the boy hit the brakes. *Hit* was the operative word. Gregor slipped a little on the ice that had formed between the fieldstone edge of the terrace and the heated gravel of the drive. In fact, he almost fell on his ass.

Above him, the great double front doors of Engine House

opened and Bennis Hannaford came out. She had put a pair of clogs on her feet, but aside from that she was dressed as Gregor remembered her. Jeans, turtleneck, oversize flannel shirt with the shirttails hanging down to her knees. In her author photographs, Bennis Hannaford always looked city-sophisticated, rich, and successful. In person, she looked like a college student with a paper three days late.

She found him, nodded to him, and came across the terrace and down the steps. She had been crying, hard enough and recently enough so that the skin around her eyes was puffy and red. Her manner commanded him to ignore that.

"Mr. Demarkian?" she said as she came up to him, holding out her hand. "I'm Bennis Hannaford."

"I know. You introduced yourself the other night." Gregor took her hand and gave it a little shake. "I'm surprised to see you. From the phone call I got, I expected John Jackman to be waiting for me with a fishnet."

"A fishnet?"

"To make sure I didn't get away."

Bennis sighed and turned to look at the house. "Mr. Jackman is up in Emma's room, pacing around and swearing a lot. He's driving my sister Anne Marie crazy. She doesn't like to hear people say *hell* in the house."

Gregor turned to look at the berry-strewn wreath on Engine House's front door.

"If all Jackman is saying is *hell,* your sister is getting off lightly."

"All Mr. Jackman is saying is not *hell,*" Bennis said. "I'm supposed to bring you up there. Do you want to come?"

"Of course."

Bennis shrugged at the "of course," and then started back up the steps to the terrace and the doors. Gregor followed her. It was remarkable what a difference a heated surface made. The terrace was wet but not slippery, and its warmth radiated up his legs and under his coat. By the time they got to the doors, he was feeling almost comfortable.

Bennis let him in, to be met by a small man in a black day suit and a heavily starched shirt. Gregor searched his memory and came up with a name and a designation: Marshall, the butler. He shook off his coat and handed it over.

Bennis shut the doors. "We have to go up the stairs and to the right," she said. "I'd give you directions and let you go by yourself, but it's a long hall, and it's full of people now."

"Police," Gregor said.

Bennis nodded. "Police and people connected to the police. Before all this started, I'd had no idea how many people showed up when you had a murder in the family."

"Do you agree with Jackman, then? That your sister didn't kill herself? That she was murdered?"

Bennis was halfway up the stairs. She stopped and turned back to him. "Can you tell me something? Were you working for the police the night you came here, Christmas Eve?"

"No," Gregor said.

"But you're working for them now," Bennis said.

"I've been asked to, yes. I don't know what the legalities are in a situation like this, Miss Hannaford. If you don't want me here, you can probably get John Jackman to send me home. He isn't going to want to compromise his evidence."

"Would you compromise his evidence?"

"I don't know."

"I don't want him to send you home," Bennis said. "I can talk to you better than I can talk to him. I knew that the other night. I kept hoping you'd be the one to handle things, but then you went home."

"I got thrown out," Gregor said drily.

"You left the room and it was Mr. Jackman who came back, at any rate," Bennis said. "Were you working for Daddy then?"

"Not exactly. Your father approached a friend of mine, who approached me, about my having dinner here that night. If he had approached me directly, I probably wouldn't have come."

"Daddy didn't hire you?"

"No. He didn't even offer to pay me."

Bennis smiled faintly. "That's typical. Daddy didn't offer to pay anybody, most of the time. He didn't pay the dentist until the fourth dunning letter came in. That's rich people's behavior. Other people have to worry about their credit ratings."

"I take care of that by never having a credit card."

"Daddy never had credit cards, either. He had accounts." She started up the stairs again, dragging her hand along the banister. "It's been terrible here the last few days. Really terrible. I always used to think things would be better when he died, but they weren't. We all sat around wondering who did it and thinking we knew."

"I think that's fairly normal."

"Do you? I don't think it was normal at all. And it was worse because of the alibis, or the lack of them, or whatever. We were all wandering around the house. And now this."

"Now this," Gregor agreed. "Was this sister the one you were closest to?"

"Of the sisters, yes. Not of the family. Emma was too much younger than me for that."

"She looked up to you," Gregor said.

"Oh, definitely. She looked up to Mother, too. She was a hero-worshiping kind of person. I don't think I ever took her seriously, except once, and now I'm beginning to wonder about the once."

"What happened that once?"

They had reached the top of the stairs and come out on a great, sweeping landing that reminded Gregor of the balconies at opera houses. It was that large and that formal. A waist-high railing ran across one edge of it, on either side of the stairs, decked out with clusters of bells and balls, cherubs, and full-grown angels. To the left and right and center there were doors. The one on the left was closed. The one on the right was open, but blocked off by a sawhorse and guarded by another young patrolman.

Gregor would have had no trouble finding his way to Jackman without a guide. He saw Bennis notice him notice and decided not to call her on it. He had a feeling it had happened not because she was practiced at deception, but because she was no good at it whatsoever.

She stood back to let him pass and said, "Maybe, when you're done with Mr. Jackman, you should let me take you out and buy you a drink. Someplace away from the house."

"And away from the police?"

"I don't really care about the police, at the moment. I'm more worried about being overheard by the Lollipop Brigade. There isn't one of them that's going to have sense enough to realize everything's changed."

"I'm going to have to tell John Jackman anything you tell me," Gregor said. "You must realize that."

"I do and I still don't care. I'm not trying to hand you information I don't want the police to have. It's just what I said. I'd find it easier talking to you than talking to him. And I don't think what I have to say is unimportant."

"It's about this one time you took your sister Emma seriously?"

Bennis grimaced. "It's about why I thought Emma killed Daddy," she said. "It's about why I was convinced of it. When Anne Marie came down today and told me she'd committed suicide, I thought it made perfect sense."

John Jackman was standing in the middle of Emma Hannaford's bedroom, waving his arms and delivering a lecture about Why Fingerprints Weren't Going to Be Important in This Case. He had come in a good wool three-piece suit, but two of the pieces—vest and jacket—were now hanging on one of the posters of the bed. His tie was undone. His shirt was open at the collar and rolled up at the sleeves. He looked like a politician in a campaign commercial about "excellence."

Gregor made a few pleasantries with the man at the door and slipped inside. The room was huge, an immense cavern of a space with a fireplace at one end. One wall was taken up with oversize windows, each double-curtained in damask and net. The bed was dwarfed, even though it was queen-size and postered and made of thick mahogany. There were half a dozen people in the room, but they didn't come close to filling it.

"Check with what's-his-name," Jackman was saying, "you know, the lawyer guy, Evers. And check with the security people, too. I don't want some prosecutor on the phone, making this sound like something out of Mickey Spillane. And bag that cup, for Christ's sake. I've told you three times. And—" He saw Gregor and stopped. "You. I thought you'd had an accident. Why didn't I hear the siren?"

"Because there was no siren to hear," Gregor said. "I made your patrolman turn it off."

"I'll have that kid's head."

"If you do, I'll have yours." Gregor gave the dark back corners of the room another look, but they were just as empty as they'd seemed when he was standing at the door. He sighed. "It's a lot like being with the Bureau. By the time you get to the scene, it isn't really a scene anymore."

"It wouldn't have been in any case, this time," Jackman said. "It's like I told you on the phone. She wasn't dead when we got here. Close, but not done. The ambulance guys worked her over for nearly half an hour."

"They didn't take her to the hospital?"

"They said it was too dangerous to move her. If I'd found her by myself, I wouldn't have known she was breathing. I don't know how long she'd been in here—"

"Where? On the bed?"

"That chair." Jackman gestured across the room, toward the fireplace, where a chair had been pulled away from the rug and left standing on the hardwood. "Before you ask, nobody moved the chair. That's where we found her. We've had a lot of luck this time. Starting with the fact that we got here at all."

Gregor checked out the chair. Next to it was a side table, bare except for a large shiny cherub brooch.

"Since she wasn't dead, I'm surprised you did get here," Gregor said. "I was just talking to Bennis Hannaford. She said Anne Marie thought it was a suicide attempt, and she thought it was a suicide attempt, until you started saying otherwise. Why on earth did they call you?"

"They didn't," Jackman said. "I was listening to the police band. I do that sometimes. Believe it or not, it puts me to sleep. I told you we've had a lot of luck. In case you haven't noticed, the weather's turned nasty again."

"I noticed."

"The ambulance had trouble getting through. There was a traffic call. When I heard where it was for, I came running."

"And found what?"

"This." Jackman reached into his shirt pocket and came up with a small folded sheet of notepaper, the stiff kind sold by jewelry stores and overpriced gift shops. "It was lying over there on the night table next to the bed, weighted down by the alarm clock."

Gregor unfolded it. *"Dear Bennis,"* it said. *"By now you must know this was all my fault, all of it, and the more I think about it the worse it makes me feel. I can't understand why I cause all this trouble, or what I'm supposed to do about it afterward. Right now I'd rather be dead than alive. Sometimes I just get so confused. If I was dead, would it matter to you? Emma."*

Gregor folded it up again. "It's a very credible note. More like what suicides actually write than most people would think. Fake notes tend to be—more direct."

"I know. That's because this isn't a fake note."

"I thought you said on the phone—"

"I did. I said I had a suicide note that wasn't a suicide note. And that's true. Emma Hannaford wrote that"—Jackman gestured at the note again—"to Bennis Hannaford as a letter, about three months ago. It worried the hell out of Bennis, so she kept it. She says she's been meaning to talk to Emma about it ever since they all got to Engine House, but she hasn't had the chance. And this morning, that note was sitting in her pocketbook, on her bed, in her bedroom, just where she's been keeping it since the day she got it. She says she saw it there at ten-forty-five."

"I take it there's some significance to ten-forty-five," Gregor said.

Jackman shrugged. "Not as much as I'd like, but enough." He looked around until he found his notebook, discarded absent-mindedly on top of the windowseat. He picked it up and flipped through the pages. "I took some time and made out a table, as far as I could, from the little questioning I've been able to do since I got here. It's not complete, but it's got some interesting points. You want to hear them?"

"Of course I do."

"Good," Jackman said. "In the first place, Teddy Hannaford saw Emma coming out of their mother's room—that's just down the hall here—at a little after ten-thirty. He was going to his own room, and she was going to the stairs. A few minutes after that, Bennis passed her in the foyer. According to Bennis, Emma looked 'woozy and distracted'—and she should have. You didn't see the body, or the not-quite-body, but I did. We're talking about a drug overdose here, not a standard poisoning. Whatever killed her, she must have taken at least an hour before she died. Maybe longer."

"Can you be sure of that before you get the medical examiner's report?"

"I can't be take-it-into-court sure even then," Jackman said. "But you and I both know that doesn't matter. You take into court what you can. You figure out what happened with a lot of things you'll never use at a trial. The M.E.'ll tell me what kind of drug it was. Under the circumstances, I'm betting Demerol."

"I would, too."

"Yeah. At any rate, Bennis passed Emma in the foyer, and then Emma went to the kitchen. She talked to"—Jackman consulted his notes—"Mrs. Washington. The cook. She asked for some tea for her mother. She said she felt sick. She sat in the kitchen for a while. In the middle of all this, Bennis got to her own room, locked herself in and went looking through her pocketbook for a fresh pack of cigarettes. That's when she saw the note. She says she even took it out and read it."

"What was Emma doing?"

"Going back to her own room," Jackman said. "Mrs. Washington says she sent her to bed. The Hannaford children are taking turns watching their mother. With the weather and the short notice, they haven't been able to get a nurse. Or maybe Cordelia Day Hannaford doesn't want them to. She's supposed to have refused nurses before. The Hannaford children are taking a day each, sitting with Cordelia and getting her what she needs. This was supposed to be Emma's day. Mrs. Washington says she told

Emma to go to bed and she'd get one of the others to take over. And Emma went. Anne Marie says she saw Emma in the upstairs hall at about ten to eleven, and they talked. Emma said something about wanting to lie down and Anne Marie came downstairs to see if the mail had come in."

"And Bennis?"

"Still in *her* own room. Now, at about eleven fifteen, Cordelia Hannaford buzzed the kitchen. She has a little button thing, electric, not the pull cords the rest of them have. Mrs. Washington hadn't been able to get in touch with any of the others, and she'd just finished putting together the tea. She buzzed Anne Marie and asked her to look in on Cordelia—"

"Why hadn't she buzzed Bennis, first?" Gregor said. "If she was looking for someone to take care of Mrs. Hannaford—"

Jackman shook his head. "Anne Marie's the only one with a two-way intercom in her room. Her and her mother, that is. Those were put in specially when Mrs. Hannaford got so sick. With the other rooms, there are those pull cords, and if you want to get in touch from downstairs you have to come all the way up."

"Why hadn't she buzzed Anne Marie before?"

"Mrs. Washington? She says she had. No answer."

"Where does Anne Marie say she was?"

"That, I haven't got around to yet," Jackman said. "It isn't the relevant time."

"It might be the relevant time if someone stole that note out of Bennis Hannaford's pocketbook," Gregor said. "If Emma didn't do it herself—"

"Emma didn't do it herself, and neither did anybody else, not then. Bennis was still in her room. In fact, she stayed in her room until eleven-twenty, when Anne Marie knocked on her door and told her something was wrong with Emma."

"Eleven-twenty?"

"According to Anne Marie, she went into her mother's room and found Cordelia very worried about Emma. She then went into Emma's room and found Emma, sick all over the floor and nearly unconscious."

"And all this time, Bennis was in her own room, and the note was in there with her."

"Exactly."

Gregor thought it over. "When I was talking to Bennis on the stairs," he said, "she told me Anne Marie had told her that Emma had committed suicide. And she believed Emma had committed suicide. Why would Anne Marie think Emma had committed suicide, if the note wasn't there?"

"According to Anne Marie, a note was there, but not the same note."

"Better and better," Gregor said.

"You mean more and more impossible," Jackman said. "And don't forget, we've got the three still unaccounted for, Bobby, Christopher and Myra Van Damm. They're all supposed to have left the house around ten o'clock, but that doesn't let any of them out of having drugged Emma Hannaford's—whatever."

"Does it let them out of stealing that note? Or both notes?"

"It seems to let Bobby and Christopher out," Jackman said, "as far as I can tell, the way things stand now. Myra Van Damm was definitely back at Engine House in time to do that much."

"Why would somebody start out with one note and replace it with another?"

"To suppress evidence in the note?" Jackman suggested. "There might have been something in the original somebody doesn't want us to know about, even if it had nothing to do with Robert Hannaford's murder. Or Emma's death. Some mistake, maybe. On the other hand, there may have been no such note."

Gregor nodded. "You like that," he said. "I don't blame you."

"I'd have liked a real suicide even more," Jackman said. "But here we are, and it doesn't look like we're going to get one."

"Maybe we ought to talk to the Hannafords before we decide what we're going to get," Gregor said. "They may even start making sense."

Jackman sighed. "I believe in the tooth fairy, too," he said. He started to leave the room, but stopped at the door.

"Just one more thing."

"What more could there be?"

"Something we found in the room. I'd show it to you, but it's been bagged for evidence. I think you ought to get a copy."

"Why?"

Jackman was grinning. "It's called *The Predator's Ball*. It's all about stock fraud and insider trading."

THREE

1 What he wanted, Gregor decided, was a mystery worthy of this house—or people worthy of it. That was the problem with the ancestral rich. No matter what the founding father had been like—and Gregor thought Robert I must have been remarkable, you had to have something to build a railroad 3,000 miles across the wilderness—the descendants always seemed to be wimps, weaklings, liars, and dilettantes. Maybe that was what Thomas Jefferson had in mind when he'd come out so strongly against inherited wealth. Someone with enough money to buy and sell the government would have seemed like a fantasy in 1776. The liars and the wimps would have been present in force.

Politics. If he got onto politics, he'd start sounding like Tibor, and Tibor was an anarchist. He followed Jackman down the second floor hall, glancing right and left at the portraits that lined it. Somebody in this family had had a dynasty complex. The portraits were all framed in gilt and positioned over Queen Anne chests. The chests were covered by lace runner cloths and the cloths were anchored by pairs of candles in sterling silver candlesticks. In the dark, the chests looked like altars.

"I've got half a mind to declare this whole damn hall a crime scene," Jackman was saying. He was swinging along, five paces ahead, as briskly and self-confidently as a CEO in absolute control of his company. Jackman was like that: contradictory internally and externally. One minute, he was playing stupid and honestly feeling inadequate. The next, he was bright and unshakably self-assured. Gregor wondered what went through the man's mind when he was alone.

"I would declare it all a crime scene," Jackman said, "if I thought I could get away with it, which I don't. Technically, I don't need a search warrant to go through a house where a murder's been done, but I know what would happen if I tried that here. The place is so damned big."

"It is that," Gregor said.

"Fortunately, the Hannafords are either stupid or really in a mood to help. I got Cordelia Day to sign a waiver and then I got what's her name, Anne Marie, to countersign it. Just in case. It may be a useless precaution, but if one of the boys turns up that other note—"

"You still wouldn't have a suicide, John."

They were coming near the end of the hall, Jackman droning on and on, the portraits getting more and more elaborate. The people in the portraits were getting more and more elaborate, too, and much less modern. The men in the pictures that had hung near Emma Hannaford's room had been dressed in ordinary business suits or, at most, tuxedo jackets. The man in the picture that hung just inside the hall door was in full traditional white tie and tails. Gregor stopped in front of him and read the brass tag screwed into the bottom of the frame: *Robert Hannaford II.*

"Wait," he said.

Jackman was already out of the hall onto the landing. He had to come back to answer. "Now what?" he said. "I've got a temporary office set up down in the study. I've had people looking over it, too. When I sent my guy down there today, he found the police seals broken."

"Did he?" Gregor said.

"Breaking police seals isn't a minor matter, Gregor."

"It's an inevitable matter," Gregor said. "What did you expect? They've probably all been in there once, just to look around. The only way you could have prevented that was to stake a man at the door. Since you didn't do it, I'd guess you didn't think there was anything left there to find."

"Okay," Jackman said. "It was mainly a precaution."

"Look at this. What do you see?"

Jackman stepped back from the portrait and looked up into Robert II's face. "Well, it's a fat old white man with a really evil face and sideburns long enough to braid."

"What's under it?"

"A chest. With a little lace thing on top."

"And no candlesticks," Gregor said.

"Candlesticks?"

Gregor gestured back along the hall. "Look at them. One portrait between each pair of doors, on both sides of the hall. Each portrait is in a gilt frame. Each is above a chest. Each chest has a piece of lace on it and two candlesticks. Except for this one. This one doesn't have any candlesticks."

Jackman walked back along the hall, turned around, and came back to Gregor. "You're right," he said. "Does it matter? Maybe they didn't have enough for this one here. Or maybe the ones that belong here have been taken somewhere to be cleaned."

Gregor shook his head. "If they were going to leave one portrait without candlesticks, they'd have chosen one of the ones at the end of the hall. Look at them. The most important ones are at this end. By the time you get down to Emma Hannaford's room, you're looking at minor members of the family. But they wouldn't have left a set out in any case. They'd have bought a pair to complete the effect."

"What about cleaning?"

"In a house like this, silver wouldn't be taken someplace else to be cleaned. If you have a butler, he's in charge of the sterling. Once a week, once a month if the house is understaffed, he'll come up here with an assistant or two and polish the candlesticks where they stand. He'll do the same with the table silver downstairs. Just take it out of his drawers, put it on the nearest countertop, and wipe it down."

Jackman rubbed his face. "Are you telling me the damn things have been stolen? Are they worth anything? Who would take them? If you're implying that some servant—"

"No, no," Gregor said. "Look at the hall, John. The minor portraits are down there, and so are the minor candlesticks. There's a picture of a pretty, vacuous woman next to Bennis Hannaford's door, and what's under it is a pair of perfectly good but not very interesting Tiffany candlesticks, close to brand new. Now look at the candlesticks as you get closer to this door. Each set is more and more ornate, more and more individual, heavier and heavier. And older."

"So?"

"So the candlesticks that belong under Robert Hannaford II must be very ornate, very heavy and very old. We're probably talking a pair of antique Georgian sticks. John, a pair of antique Georgian candlesticks went at auction at Sotheby's two years ago for over twelve thousand dollars."

"A pair of *candlesticks?*" Jackman said.

Gregor smiled. "You don't have to worry about the servants, either. If a servant was going to steal a pair, it would be one of the ones at the other end. Georgian silver was made to order, almost always in a design created especially for the lady of the house. It was as good as a signature. Better."

"If they were heavy enough, they could have been sold to someone to melt down—"

"Would you want to turn something worth twelve thousand into something worth fifteen hundred?"

"Maybe nobody involved knew it was worth twelve thousand."

"A professional fence would have guessed," Gregor said. "He wouldn't touch it. It would be asking to land in jail."

Jackman sighed. "Gregor, this is the crack age. The world is different now. People do the damnedest things these days. You wouldn't believe it—"

"I wouldn't believe a servant on crack lasting half an hour around Anne Marie Hannaford," Gregor said. "And Anne Marie Hannaford, from what you've told me, is the person who runs this house."

"True," Jackman said.

"If somebody took these candlesticks, and somebody must have, that somebody was one of the family. Only a member of the family had a hope in hell of taking them and not getting prosecuted for it. And that brings up a number of very interesting possibilities."

Jackman nodded. "One of them could be very strapped for money," he said. "From what the Hannafords told me the other night, the estate goes to Cordelia Day on Robert Hannaford's death, but Cordelia has to be a much softer touch than old Robert ever was."

"There's also the possibility that this isn't the first theft,"

Gregor said, "and that Robert Hannaford knew about the others. Or even about this one. We should talk to that man, Marshall, and find out when he last saw the candlesticks here. But there has to be some explanation of Robert Hannaford's inviting me to dinner in that strange way. Maybe this is it."

"You think this was worth a hundred thousand in cash to Robert Hannaford?"

"No," Gregor said, "but then, that may have been a hoax. You never did find the briefcase. Anything is possible if the man was eccentric enough. And the way they talk about him, he sounds eccentric enough for anything. Then there's the third—"

Gregor never got to the third. There was a thudding on the stairs, then a clatter and an echoing panting on the landing. Gregor and Jackman turned together toward the hall door. A uniformed patrolman was standing there, looking flushed, sweaty, and out of breath.

"Excuse me," he said. "There's a man downstairs. A Mr. Evers. He's pacing around the study and insisting on seeing you, and I think he's about to lose control."

2

Floyd Evers turned out to be a short man in good shape with sparse hair, dressed in the kind of suit Gregor always thought must be ordered from a lawyers' uniform supply house. He was not, however, anywhere near losing control. When Gregor and Jackman came into the study, he was sitting in the chair behind Robert Hannaford's desk, looking exasperated.

Unlike most of the lawyers Gregor had met, Evers gave off

neither a fog of evasion nor a bristle of self-importance. He didn't even have many papers. There was a briefcase in front of him on the desk, but it was neither too thick nor too thin. It contained a small sheaf of typed, legal-size pages bound together with a paper clip. Gregor pegged him instantly as *married, children, Bucks County.* It was a stereotype, but not necessarily an inaccurate stereotype. There were two kinds of lawyers in major cities like Philadelphia. Evers didn't come off as a man who would do anything for money.

In Gregor's experience, the kind of man who did had a job in a firm with too many names on the masthead, a condominium in Radnor, and two mistresses.

Evers stood up as soon as they came into the room and extended his hand. It was a mistake. Jackman was in a combative mood.

"You," he said. "I've been looking for you for a week."

Evers sat down again. Now Gregor saw what the patrolman might have meant by saying Evers was about to lose control. At the moment, the man's good humor was only tenuously pasted on. Underneath the self-disciplined politeness, he was very angry about something.

He crossed his arms over his chest. "You've been looking for me for a week," he said. "That's just fine. You've been leaving messages for me all over creation, mostly at my office. That's just fine, too. You've made my partners think I'm about to be indicted for child murder at the least. That's just fine, fine, fine. In the meantime, Mr.—"

"Jackman," Jackman said.

"Jackman," Evers repeated. "It's Christmas, in case you haven't noticed. If you'd taken any time at all to think the thing through, you'd have known I was where everybody else is who can get the time off."

"Where?"

"Visiting relatives, Mr. Jackman. In my case, visiting relatives in Vermont, where my wife has family, and in Connecticut, where she also has family. It is not a suspicious circumstance when someone isn't spending Christmas in his own damned house."

"Don't you leave a contact number with your office?"

"Not if I can help it."

"Tsk, tsk," Jackman said.

"And on top of it all, I can't for the life of me see what you need me for." Evers turned to Gregor. "Who are you?"

Gregor introduced himself. Evers nodded, pleased. "That's good. I've read about you. Are you working for the family or the police?"

"The police," Gregor said.

"Well, it couldn't hurt." Evers unfolded his arms from across his chest and put his hands flat on the desk. He looked ready for action, but there didn't seem to be any action he wanted to take. He had, however, calmed down. He glanced around the study, not lighting on any one thing, looking puzzled.

"It's like I told you," he said. "You don't really need me for anything. The Hannaford situation being what it is, the only one who needs me is Mrs. Hannaford. She's the one I've got to explain things to."

"I was hoping you'd explain a few things to us," Jackman said. Gregor was glad to see he'd calmed down, too, or at least decided to abandon his hostility. He dropped into the chair next to the window and said, "There's been a murder here, you know.

There may have been two. If it's at all possible, we need to know everything there is to know about Robert Hannaford's will, his—"

"But that's the point," Floyd Evers said. "There isn't any will."

Jackman blinked. "The man was worth four hundred million dollars and there isn't any will?"

Evers sighed. "Obviously, you don't read the newspapers," he said, "or you weren't reading them in 1980, when all this happened. There isn't any will because there doesn't need to be any will. Robert Hannaford was worth four hundred million dollars, yes, but not when he died. When he died, all he had was the income from most of that. Not the capital."

"I don't get it," Jackman said.

"I think I do." The last empty chair was stuck way off in a corner, facing the wall. Gregor dragged it into the center of the room, sat down, and turned to John Jackman. "There is something called a living trust," he said, "for very rich people who want to leave their money to institutions. Foundations for diseases, universities, that kind of thing. Instead of putting those provisions in a will and making the institution wait until you die, you give the money while you're still alive. The institution then guarantees to pay you an annuity from that money for life."

Evers brightened. "Right. The foundations like it a lot better than money left in a will. Wills can be challenged. A man can do anything he wants with his money while he's still alive."

Jackman looked incredulous. "Hannaford did this with all his money? Every cent of it?"

"Almost," Evers said. "Also the house, some other property

he's got scattered here and there, whatever. He put about ten million dollars into trusts for his sons—"

"Just his sons?" Gregor asked.

"Just his sons," Evers said. "Not a dime to any of the girls. And not much for the sons, either, if you want to know the truth. Robert, the oldest son, got a fair amount—I think it comes to about a hundred thousand a year. The other two got less, much less. You don't make all that much money on ten million, if ten million is all you've got—"

"I'd make plenty of money on ten million," Jackman said.

"You might not think so if you'd been used to all this," Evers said. "And Hannaford's children were definitely used to it. Horses, schools, fifty-thousand-dollar birthday parties. He brought them up like heirs to an Arab sheikdom. They didn't like this one bit, let me tell you."

"They didn't see it coming?" Gregor said. "He'd given no indication, beforehand—"

"Hell, no. That's why it made the papers." Evers grinned. "That's why I can talk like this and not have to worry about confidentiality. With the Hannafords, there's no such thing as confidentiality. Before 1980, old Robert H. was the typical rich old man. First he loved them, then he hated them. First he made a will one way, then he made it the other. And since Hannaford Financial was a privately owned company at the time—"

"What happened to it?" Jackman said.

"It went public, also in 1980. But you see how it was. Hannaford's nuttiness was business news, not just society news. It made its way into the tabloids and the straight papers. Once in a while, it even made it onto local television. That was why it was such a big deal when he decided to settle the situation once and for all."

Gregor closed his eyes, thinking. "Were you Hannaford's lawyer at the time?" he asked.

"I wasn't any kind of lawyer at the time," Floyd Evers said. "I hadn't passed the bar exam. I took the Hannafords over after Tom Wanderman died. He was the founder of my firm. He and Hannaford had known each other forever."

"Why you?" Gregor said.

"I was Wanderman's assistant. And Robert Hannaford liked me, don't ask me why."

Jackman stirred uneasily. "I don't get this. Nobody benefits from Robert Hannaford's death? Nobody?"

"Cordelia Day Hannaford has right of survivorship," Evers said. "She goes on getting the annuities as long as she lives. And the foundations benefit a little. The contents of this house, for instance. Technically, they belong to Yale University, to be sold at auction when both the senior Hannafords are dead. And, of course, there's the insurance policy."

"One million dollars," Jackman said.

"Two, in case of murder. To Cordelia Day Hannaford." Evers nodded.

Jackman was persistent—or persistently obtuse. "But none of the children benefit. None of them gets anything because their father's dead."

"Right." Evers nodded again.

"I wonder why the girls were cut off so completely." Gregor had been silent for so long, they'd forgotten he was there. They turned to stare at him. He shrugged at their incomprehension. "It's not that strange a question. Rich old men tend to get on better with their daughters than their sons. You'd think he'd have gotten on with at least one of them. And Cordelia Day Hannaford must have been already ill in 1980."

"So?" Jackman said.

"So, Anne Marie Hannaford has given up her life to take care of her mother, a woman Robert Hannaford was supposed to have loved. You'd think he'd make some provision for Anne Marie, at least, in gratitude if nothing else."

"You'd think he'd make better provision for the boys," Floyd Evers said. "If there's one thing I've learned about the Hannafords, especially old Robert Hannaford, it's that they're family proud. Family *nuts,* if you ask me."

Gregor thought about the portraits in the upstairs hall. "Yes, there is that. I wonder what *happened* in 1980."

"Why would anything have to have happened?" Jackman said. "Maybe he just got tired of making wills and unmaking them again."

This time, Floyd Evers actually laughed. "Whoo," he said. "You don't know rich old men. Half my clients do nothing but. And the rich old women are worse."

"They want to hang onto power, that's the important thing," Gregor said. "They always want to hang on to power. I've known men in my life who've given up smoking, who've given up heroin, who've given up sex. I've never known one who voluntarily gave up power."

"He didn't give up all the power," Evers said. "He wasn't that stupid. When Hannaford Financial went public, some shares were sold, some shares went to Robert, but the biggest block went into another of those living trusts. Hannaford didn't get money from those. He got the voting rights."

"And these voting rights also pass to Cordelia Day Hannaford until her death?" Gregor said.

"That they do," Evers said.

Jackman had been pacing back and forth in front of the fireplace, restless and upset. Now he stopped, leaned back, and began to look happier.

"That's it, then," he said. "We've got to check into Hannaford Financial. Obviously, nobody killed Robert Hannaford for his money. And it would explain Emma, too, that book. She probably knew something. No one got any money, except for Cordelia, and she wasn't hauling furniture around this room in her condition. But if something's wrong at Hannaford Financial—now that, that would provide us with a motive."

"It would provide you with a great motive," Evers said cheerfully. "They're sending all those idiots to jail."

Gregor wasn't feeling so cheerful. He was thinking about a pair of silver candlesticks and about the dead-white face of an emaciated young man who was much too frightened for any explanation that made sense.

The more he thought about those things, the more incomprehensible they seemed to get.

Half an hour later—after Floyd Evers had gone up to Cordelia's room and Anne Marie had gone over her story five times, by rote—the young patrolman who had met Gregor and Jackman on the stairs emerged from the second floor hall, triumphant. In his hands was a piece of blue notepaper, the kind supplied for every writing table in every bedroom of the house. It was crumpled and torn, but not illegible.

"*Dear Bennis,*" it said. "*You'll know what I mean when I say I can't stand it any longer. I've got to put a stop to this one way or the other. Now. Love, Emma.*"

The original suicide note.

Found in the wastebasket in Bobby Hannaford's room.

Along with four $100 bills.

Jackman stared at the money and said, "It wasn't a hoax. There was a briefcase full of money."

"We always knew there was one at Tibor's," Gregor pointed out. "Now we know there was one where Hannaford said it would be. In his study Christmas Eve night. Something tells me, if we look around now, all we're going to find is the briefcase."

"What?"

Gregor had been fingering the bills. He handed them to Jackman. "Find out if there's a service dump here. Someplace they put trash from gardening and lawn work. Houses of this size usually have them, placed pretty far from the house itself. If there is something like that, our briefcase will be at the bottom of it."

"But not our money."

"Of course not," Gregor said.

FOUR

1 By the time Cordelia's doctor arrived, the police were gone, Bobby and Chris had received the most brutal account possible of Emma's death, and Anne Marie Hannaford was beginning to think she was having a nervous breakdown. She always did think so, in situations like this, when Mother had been very bad and then started to get better when she should have gotten worse. Anne Marie wanted to believe the world was an inevitable place. If she did certain things—kept Mother quiet, gave Mother all her medicines, transmitted an unwavering message of Disneyland hope—Mother would be well. If she did other things—got Mother excited, let Mother stay awake too long, admitted for one moment that there was anything wrong at Engine House—Mother would be sick. With Mother's disease, things were not so simple. Cordelia had reacted the way Anne Marie expected her to at Daddy's death. The shock had been profound, devastating. Anne Marie had thought it was all over. The woman was going to implode, collapse in on herself like a building with a ruined foundation. The death of Emma should have finished her off. Instead, she was getting better. Anne Marie had picked it up right away. This time, when she called the doctor, she was adamant. Yes, it was snowing, but the streets were passable and would be for hours yet. He could damn well get his ass up to Engine House.

Now she sat in a chair in the hall outside her mother's door and listened to Bobby and Christopher arguing in the foyer, their voices sharper than usual against the interminable carols. She was very tired. Since Christmas Eve, her fear had been absolute—that

Mother would die before she had a chance to get ready for it, that Mother would die before she managed to get a grip on herself, that Mother would die. God only knew she ought to be used to the idea. Mother had been dying for years. Maybe that was the problem. Mother had been dying for years, but not in any danger of being dead, until that attack in November that had brought them all running home for Christmas. Anne Marie had to admit it. That was the first time she had really believed it was going to happen.

Somewhere inside Mother's room, a chair scraped against hardwood. The doctor was getting up, getting ready to leave. Anne Marie stood up herself, trying to force an expression on her face, the one the doctor was expecting to see. She didn't do a very good job of it. She hadn't known Emma very well, that was the problem. With all the worry about money, with all the strain of keeping the house going when Daddy was still alive and likely to go crazy at least once a day, Anne Marie hadn't had the emotional energy to care about a sister she had never really known and very rarely saw. Bobby was the same way. She had seen it in his face when she told him. Christopher's reaction had come as a complete surprise. Such a complete surprise, in fact, that Anne Marie had almost thought he must be faking.

The chair scraped again—back into position, probably. Then there was the sound of metal things being tossed against each other, followed by a sharp snap. A moment later, the door opened. Anne Marie looked up to find Dr. Borra's sour young face glaring at her over the velvet collar of a Chesterfield coat. Dr. Borra's face was always sour. Years ago, on the day he'd been taken into the Rittenhouse Square practice where he was now a full partner, he'd been apprised of the "special circumstances" under which that practice served the Hannafords. He still didn't like them. To Dr. Borra, neither $400 million nor family connections going back to six generations gave anybody a right to house calls.

Anne Marie smoothed her skirt, stared at the floor, and said, "Well?"

"Well what?" Dr. Borra said.

Anne Marie looked up angrily. "Well, how is she, for one thing," she said. "You've been in there for forty-five minutes. You must have found out something."

"Found out what?" Dr. Borra said. "Miss Hannaford, I don't know how many times I have to tell you this—an infinity of times, as far as I can see—but people don't die of adult onset lateral multiple sclerosis. Not these days. They get weak. They become prone to opportunistic infections. They don't die of—"

"You should have been here a few days ago," Anne Marie said. "She certainly looked like she was going to die *of* it."

"Shock." Dr. Borra shrugged. "I told you when you called on Christmas Eve. She should have come in to the hospital."

"She doesn't want to go to the hospital."

"I know what she doesn't want, Miss Hannaford. I'm merely telling you what she should have. All I can do is make suggestions. If the patient won't take them, I can't force her."

"Meaning if I want to indulge her, you can't force me."

"Well, Miss Hannaford, she's hardly competent, is she? I could go to any medical review board in the country and make a good case for total mental breakdown."

"That's because you don't live with her," Anne Marie said. "Believe me, she's perfectly competent. She just has a little trouble expressing herself."

Dr. Borra shrugged, again. Anne Marie looked away, down the hall, to where the yellow plastic strips of the police seals gleamed falsely under the dim hallway lights. The police seals annoyed her unreasonably. There they sat, a great big boulder in the middle of an already rocky road, one more obstacle to be gotten around on her way to—what? Anne Marie didn't know what she was on her way to, anymore. She was just furious at Emma, for causing all this trouble.

"Tell me," she said, "have you got any idea, now that you've seen her, how long she's going to be able to last? Should I expect her to die tomorrow? Should I expect her to live to 1995?"

"Yes," Dr. Borra said.

"Don't be juvenile. This isn't an anxious relative question. My father is dead, in case you don't remember—"

"It would be hard to forget. It made the front page of *The Inquirer*."

"It also made *The Wall Street Journal*," Anne Marie said. "That's not the point. There's a large estate involved here, a lot of complicated legal questions. Mother and I spent an hour and a half with the lawyer today. Today, Dr. Borra, with my sister dead in a room down the hall and God knows what else going on around here. You've got to understand—"

"I do understand. You're the one who doesn't. I can't make the kind of predictions you're asking for. Your mother has an unsteady heart—"

"What's that supposed to mean?"

"It means I don't like the way it sounds, that's what it means. I'm not saying I've found any evidence of heart disease. I haven't. I'm just hearing some irregularity. It could mean everything and nothing."

"Wonderful," Anne Marie said.

"If you want my instinct, I'd say she was good for another three months. At least."

"Oh."

"On the other hand—"

"Don't spoil it," Anne Marie said. She turned away from him and started down the hall toward the landing, listening to be sure he followed her. He did. "I'll let you out now," she told him. "I suppose you're busy with something. But I wish you'd remember—"

"That I'm supposed to come any time you call? If I did that, I wouldn't get anything else done."

"That's the most ridiculous lie I've ever heard. We don't call you every hour. We don't call you every day. We don't even call you every week. Mother wouldn't have it."

"Nevertheless, you always call at the most inconvenient possible time."

They were out on the landing now, going down the stairs to the foyer. Anne Marie stared at the black-and-white checkerboard marble floor and saw it start to swim before her eyes. She was boiling.

"Do you believe in euthanasia?" she asked him.

Dr. Borra said, "What?"

"Euthanasia," Anne Marie repeated. "There are so many people these days, young doctors mostly, from what I read in *Time,* who think old people who have lost their faculties are simply being irrational when they want to go on living. Who think—"

Downstairs, the front door opened and Teddy came in, limping painfully. Anne Marie bit her lip. She was very good at what she had just started to do to Dr. Borra, very good. Aside from the satisfaction it would have given her—sometimes she just wanted to smash this man's face—it might have had its uses, in the long run. Now she was stopped, by Teddy planting himself down there at the bottom of the stairs. She marched past him, not looking at him, and pulled open the front doors.

"Good night," she said to Dr. Borra.

Dr. Borra pulled up the collar of his coat and shrugged.

"Christ," Teddy said. "What did you do to him?"

Anne Marie slammed the front doors and headed back up the stairs. "Mother's better," she said. "I have to go up and make sure she stays that way."

Then she went on up to the second floor, stomping all the way, making the central well of the house reverberate as if it were being attacked by a wrecking ball.

2

For Teddy, the day had been futile and frantic. Worse, it had been insubstantial. Everything that had happened—from the phone calls he had made to "friends" in Boston and New York, to the searching he had done through the papers he had brought with him from Greer, to the candles nestled in evergreen boughs on every surface in the house, to Emma's dying—had seemed less and less real. By the time he'd decided to go out for a walk, he had managed to convince himself he was wandering through a dream. It had to be a dream. Only in a dream would he have decided to go wallowing through the snow, especially on a day when his leg had been aching since the moment he woke up. It was aching even more now, going beyond dull throbbing to the dreaded territory of sharp, shooting pains. Teddy's doctors always said those pains were imaginary, but they seemed real enough to him. And they made him angry. It was like Prometheus and the eagle, or whatever it was. Constant pain, constant torture, constant punishment —and for what? He'd never done a thing in his life to hurt another person. Even stealing his students' papers hadn't hurt the students. The little idiots had no use for the damn things once they'd been handed in—and Susan Carpenter was a fool for thinking otherwise. Why he'd ever decided to make an issue of his libido in her case, he'd never know. She wasn't even all that attractive. She always had a big cluster of pimples on her butt.

He watched Anne Marie go upstairs, wrapped in the cocoon of her habitual bad temper, then headed for the living room. He liked it in the drawing room. The Christmas decorations were thicker there than anywhere else at Engine House, and with the fire going he could almost get into the holiday spirit. He thought about Emma and wondered why she hadn't meant more to him. That didn't seem to have an answer, so he gave it up. He'd never been close to any of his brothers and sisters, never liked them much, never wanted to know them well. They existed for him very much the way the characters existed in the novels he taught —as archetypes. Bennis The Golden One. Christopher The Tortured Poet. Anne Marie The Frustrated Spinster. He just wished one of them was a Knight in Shining Armor, so he'd have a hope in hell of being rescued from this mess.

What his "friends" had told him, evasively but firmly, was that there wasn't a thing they could do for him. That was when he'd started putting quotation marks around that word. What they were handing him was a lot of nonsense. One of them was dean of faculty at a small college outside Albany. The place was always hard up for professors and never particular about the men it took. One of them was chairman of the English department at an even smaller place in Dedham, Massachusetts. *That* was a junior college where students weren't even required to submit SAT scores for admission, because no one would have dared to ask for them. Listening to these two blither on for twenty minutes apiece about "standards" and "professional responsibility" had made Teddy sick—but not half as sick as he'd been when he'd realized they both already knew what was going on at Greer. The academic grapevine was efficient, but this was nothing short of paranormal. The Pregnant Frog must have been on the phone all Christmas week.

Teddy opened the living room door and stepped inside. The Christmas tree had been lit. Some servant must have done it automatically, not realizing how bad it would look to outsiders, shining away like that in a house where there had been two deaths in a little more than three days. On the other hand, the outsiders were all gone. The police had packed up their evidence cases and headed for the glories of downtown Bryn Mawr, and Mr. Gregor Demarkian had gone with them. The drawing room was fragrant with evergreen and wax, the picture of a Victorian dream Christmas. Teddy wanted it that way.

His glance stopped for a moment on the little collection of family photographs in Tiffany silver frames his mother kept on an occasional table and then passed on. The pictures would only get him started again. He liked looking at the harpsichord better. Someone had uncovered it, dusted it off, and propped back the shield that protected the keyboard. It looked ready to play.

He moved into the room. He wanted to find the family copy of *The Complete Sherlock Holmes* and settle down in a chair for a nice long read. Logic and gaslight, that's what he needed. He'd ring for Marshall and get himself a nice hot buttered rum. The rest of them—living, dead, and dying—could just go to hell.

He was making his way through the overcrowded cluster of furniture in the corner between the windows and the bookcase when he stepped on something he didn't like the feel of at all. It was both too hard and too soft, too giving and too intractable. He looked down. His foot seemed to have landed on a long piece of green chamois cloth. If he followed that cloth toward the windows, it ended in a pale white hand.

He stepped away, shaking slightly. Then he leaned sideways a little to get a look over the back of a royal blue velvet love seat.

"Jesus Christ," he said. "Christopher?"

Christopher was lying on the rug, flat on his back, with one of Mother's Steuben glass ashtrays sitting in the middle of his chest. His eyes were closed, but the ashtray held a burning joint, rolled in pink-and-blue paper. His hair was a mess. Teddy couldn't understand it. The room was so damn cold, even with the fire going. Christopher was oozing sweat like a glass of iced tea in high summer.

"Christopher," Teddy said again.

"I'm fine," Christopher said. "Go away."

"I'm not going to go away." Teddy sat down on the love seat. "It's my house as much as yours. I want a book and a drink."

"Have a joint instead."

"You must be out of your mind. There are police all over this place. You're going to get arrested."

Christopher sighed, a sound like the wind rushing out of an overfilled balloon. Then he opened his eyes and sat up. "Teddy, the police left hours ago. And even if they were here, they wouldn't care."

"Of course they would care," Teddy said. "This isn't California."

"It isn't Wyoming, either. A kid with a joint in his high-school locker, they might care. A grown man smoking a little dope in his own living room, they wouldn't even notice. The jails are full of hopheads, Teddy. Crack has made marijuana de facto legal in half the states in the Union."

"You look terrible," Teddy said.

Christopher lay back down. "I feel terrible. You should feel terrible, too. Emma was a little sweetheart, and now she's dead."

The joint had been smoked to a nothing-but-paper wedge. Eyes closed, still flat on his back, Christopher rolled another one. It was astonishing to watch. Like a high-wire artist or a professional bicyclist, like an athlete doing a routine he had trained for every day for a decade, Chris went through the motions as perfectly as if he'd been sitting up and cold straight.

Teddy got off the love seat and went to the bookcase. The Sherlock Holmes was where it was supposed to be, on the third shelf from the top, in the middle. Teddy took it out and stared at its plain brown cover.

"Chris?" he said. He tried to think of some way to word the question he wanted to ask without sounding like a jerk. There wasn't one. He took a deep breath and asked it anyway. "Does it really bother you?" he said. "Emma's dying, I mean. Do you really care?"

"Don't you?"

The reaction was milder than Teddy had expected. Thank God

for marijuana. "I hardly knew her," he said. "She was around when we were children, and then I went off to college, and I almost never saw her again. You're older than I am. It must have been the same for you."

"Not exactly." The joint rolled, Christopher lit it. He did that with his eyes closed, too. "I saw a lot of her in the last five years. She used to come and visit me in California, when she had the chance and the money. Or when Bennis had the money and would lend it to her. Maybe once a year."

"And you got along?"

"Of course we got along. Why shouldn't we? She really was a sweetheart."

Teddy put the Holmes back in its place on the shelf. "That's not what everybody said, you know. There was all that business, back when Daddy changed his mind about the money, that got us all in trouble. And everybody said—"

"That Emma was responsible for it?"

"Yes," Teddy said. "That Emma was responsible for it."

Christopher blew a stream of smoke into the air. "I asked her about it once. She said she had nothing to do with it. I believed her."

"Bennis thinks—"

Christopher sat up. "So what's this? Bennis thinks and it must be so?"

"Something like that."

"Bullshit. Especially coming from you."

"I just think Bennis knew Emma," Teddy said. "Better than the rest of us. She may have gone out to visit you once a year, but she went to Boston once a month. Bennis was with her all the time."

"So?"

"So Bennis should know," Teddy insisted.

Chris took a monumental drag on the joint, held it in for interminable minutes, then let it out again. His eyes were getting very red, in a dry, cracked way that was different from what they were like when he'd been crying.

"Look," he said, "if you think Emma was responsible for that, how do you explain all this? How do you explain Daddy? How do you explain Emma herself? Emma got herself murdered."

"Maybe she did and maybe she didn't."

"The police have already been here, Teddy. They say it was murder."

Teddy shook his head stubbornly. "They're going by those notes. But there are lots of explanations for those notes. The one they found in Bobby's room could be real—"

"Then why was it in Bobby's room?"

"Bennis put it there," Teddy said. "Bennis didn't want anyone to think Emma had committed suicide. You know how protective Bennis always was of Emma. She saw that note and she took it, and later she got rid of it and substituted her own letter. Then she acted like the letter was the only thing she'd ever seen."

"To make the police and everybody else believe Emma hadn't committed suicide."

"Right."

"To make them believe Emma had been murdered."

"Right again."

"Crap," Christopher said. "Bennis is the most straightforward person I know. And the most sane. She'd have known doing something like that would get one of the rest of us in trouble. She wouldn't have done it."

"She wouldn't have done it to you maybe." Teddy came back to the love seat. Now that Chris was sitting up, it was easier to look at him while talking to him. It was less like having a conversation with a hyperanimated dead body. "I know you and Bennis have always been friends, but she isn't the same way with the rest of us as she is with you. Especially not with me."

"The note wasn't found in your room, Teddy."

"I know it wasn't. I was just trying to point out—"

"And you can't complain about the way she treats you, either. For God's sake. She loans you money. She lets you sleep on her floor—"

"Does she tell you everything we talk about?" Teddy said. "Does she call California and report every time she gets off the phone to me?"

"Of course she doesn't. Teddy, be reasonable. You've got nothing at all to make you think Bennis is running around Engine House tampering with evidence in a murder case. Two murder cases. You've got everything to make you think otherwise. And in case you haven't thought it out, the otherwise is much more interesting than the junk you're handing me."

"What 'otherwise'?"

Christopher took another drag. Outside, it was getting late, growing darker. Teddy watched the snow come down, illuminated by the lights on the back terrace. He loved Engine House. If he could have cleared it of his family, exorcised it, he could have lived there forever. That was the one strong feeling he'd ever had for his sister Emma. If she hadn't done what she'd done, he just might have been able to live there forever. Even now, thinking about this place as a haven instead of a threat, he wanted to break her neck.

Christopher said, "Think of this. We all hated Daddy. Somebody killed him. So what? Any one of us can understand why any of the others would have done it. Right?"

"Right," Teddy said.

"Now," Christopher said, "think about Emma. Emma never did anything to hurt anybody, not to hurt any of us, at any rate. Emma was a nice, sweet little girl. And somebody killed her."

"Maybe," Teddy said.

"If somebody did, we're all in a lot of trouble. Somebody's going around killing people for no reason at all. If somebody did it once, somebody's going to do it again."

Teddy sat straight up. "Don't be ridiculous," he said. "That's—"

"Crazy?"

"Of course it's crazy."

"Maybe somebody around here is crazy," Christopher said. "That's the otherwise, and that's what worries me."

Teddy looked down at the bag of grass now sitting in Christopher's lap. Obviously, marijuana, like all other drugs, must make people paranoid.

3 Up in his bedroom, Bobby Hannaford looked down at the stacks of money laid out on his bedspread, counted through them one more time, and reached for his briefcase. In his briefcase, he had a cellular phone. He needed it.

Ever since the police had come to him with the story of the note and the money, he had been worrying. Ever since the police had left, he had been locked in his room, counting. He had bolted the door. He had pulled the Klee watercolor off the wall and dumped it on the writing table. He had left the safe standing open. Right from the beginning, he had found it hard to think. Now, with the money all counted and not a bill of it missing, he couldn't think at all.

It kept coming to him, the worst case scenario, a worse worst case scenario than any he'd imagined in all these months of terror and exhilaration. Hundred dollar bills in the wastebasket. That was good. That was incredible. Who had put them there? If he could only believe it was Myra, he could relax. But Myra wouldn't do that. If Myra found out what he was up to, and wanted to do something about it, she'd be much more direct. She already knew the combination to this safe. She'd told him she did. If she wanted to scare the shit out of him, she'd just walk in here one day while he was at work and clean the damn thing out.

Somebody knew what he was doing and he didn't know who. That was the kicker. He didn't know who.

And because he didn't know who, he didn't know what that someone would do.

McAdam's phone was ringing. It sounded far away and fuzzy, the way everything did on cellular phones. Once the conversation started, it would be like talking through water.

The ringing stopped. Someone had picked up on the other end.

"Hello?" McAdam said.

"Don't hang up," Bobby said.

There was a long silence. Then McAdam said, "Jesus H.

Christ. Of course I'm going to hang up. What do you think you're doing?"

"Don't hang up," Bobby said again. "I've got to talk to you."

"Now?"

"Soon."

"Here?"

"Anywhere you want. But soon."

"Where are you calling from?"

Bobby put stacks of money onto other stacks, clearing a place for himself on the bed. "I'm on a cellular," he said. "I'm calling from Engine House. But that's not the important thing. I've got to see you. Not next week. Not next month. Not next Tuesday. I want you to be at the place tomorrow at seven."

"Seven? In the morning?"

"In the morning."

"Bobby, there won't be anybody there at seven in the morning. We'll stick out like bag ladies at the April-in-Paris Ball."

"I don't give a shit."

"Bobby—"

"Be there," Bobby said. He shoved his thumb against the power switch and turned the phone off. It wasn't as satisfying as really hanging up, but it had something. He shoved the antenna down and threw the phone back into the briefcase.

He had money all over the bed, and he had to put it back.

There was a digital clock on his bedside table, the kind that told the seconds as well as the minutes and the hours. It reminded him of a cliché he'd thought of when he first met McAdam, but hadn't allowed himself to dwell on since. *It's only a matter of time.* How true. How true, how true, how true.

And now was the time.

Someone knocked on his door. He stood up and started shoving money back into the safe.

"Who is it?" he said.

"Myra."

"Just a minute."

Crap, he thought. Shit shit shit shit crap.

Daddy was dead. Daddy was out of the picture. Once Daddy was out of the picture, everything was supposed to be fine.

And it wasn't.

Myra knocked on his door again. He took a huge fist full of cash and threw it at the open mouth of the safe. It hit the side and scattered bills everywhere.

Emma was dead, but he didn't think about it. To Bobby Hannaford, Emma dead seemed like the least important thing in the world.

FIVE

1 Gregor Demarkian didn't want to go home.

He was riding in Jackman's unmarked police car, at six o'clock in the evening, through the center of Philadelphia—and he felt good. That was what he was trying not to admit to himself. The Hannaford case was like an adrenalated narcotic. The first few doses had energized him, but left him substantially free. Now he was as addicted to it as the monkeys he had heard about, who had become so enamored of being high that they'd chosen cocaine over food. He couldn't remember the last time his mind had worked so well. Long before Elizabeth had fallen sick, he had fallen shell-shocked. Too many years of too many crazies too mindlessly obsessed with brutality had numbed his brain. There was nothing numb about it now. It was working away, sorting through bits and pieces of information, snagging on inconsistencies, and it felt good, too. Thinking had become a physical pleasure.

If he had been a different kind of man, he would have worried about his insensitivity. That poor girl was dead. From what he'd seen, she'd been as innocent and undeserving of execution as Donna Moradanyan. Somebody should grieve for her. Gregor knew too much about the world to think that someone ought to be him. It was a damn good thing there were people who could think without becoming sentimental, who could divorce themselves from the emotional to concentrate on the objective truth. Without them, the human race would still be living in caves.

Jackman turned onto a side street, taking some shortcut through the rush hour traffic Gregor didn't want to understand.

"I don't understand why you don't like the financial angle," he said. "I don't believe Bobby Hannaford is straight. You don't either. If he's fooling around, he's got a real motive. Now that the old man is dead—"

"Hundred-dollar bills are showing up in wastebaskets," Gregor said. "And you should have found the briefcase."

"I did, Gregor. It was right where you said it would be."

"That briefcase started out in Robert Hannaford's study. He told me it would be there."

"There's too damn much manipulation in this case," Jackman said. "And it's weird manipulation, too. It's like something out of an Agatha Christie novel. It's not real."

"What's real—a couple of idiot nineteen year olds blowing each other away with Uzis over a quarter of a pound of crack?"

"That does tend to be more usual."

"That also has all the reality of a Kafka nightmare."

Jackman laughed. Gregor went back to looking out the window. They were in a part of Philadelphia he knew, but he didn't know why he knew. They weren't near Cavanaugh Street, and they weren't near the library, either. He stared at the solid, undistinguished office buildings and wondered what they meant to him.

"You okay?" Jackman asked him.

"I'm fine. Where are we?"

"Out behind the Dick Building."

Gregor sat up a little straighter. Of course. It had been years, but he should have remembered. He checked the numbers on the buildings they were passing and saw they were going in the right direction. Slowly, but in the right direction.

"John," he said, "not this block coming up, but the one after that. Pull up to the curb in the middle and let me get out for a second."

"Get out?"

"There's something I want to see."

Jackman looked at him like he'd just announced he was going to take LSD, but he slowed the car even further, and in the middle of the block in question pulled up to the pavement. Gregor got out, scanned the building numbers until he found 1227, and went up to its front door.

The front door was two mammoth pieces of plate glass, locked. Through it, Gregor could see the call board, rows of little steel buttons next to white-on-black company names arranged in alphabetical order. The first of those names, at the top of the list, was Aardvark Construction, Inc. The fifth was Federal Bureau of Investigation, Philadelphia Office.

Gregor stepped back. There was a call button on the outside of the building, so that people with late meetings could get far enough into the lobby to buzz up to whoever was waiting for them. Somewhere in the basement there was probably a janitor with access to a television security system. Gregor scanned the door frame and found the camera.

"Fine," he said, to the snow falling on his head.

He went back to the car, stuck his head in Jackman's window, and announced, "You can leave me here. I've got something I want to do."

This time, Jackman looked sure Gregor needed a psychiatrist—but he went.

2 The man at the front desk was a stranger. Gregor had expected that. For one thing, he had been retired long enough for a new crop of recruits to go professional. Those recruits almost always ended up at front desks or on information lines for the first six months or so. For another thing, once he'd made it to the call board and announced himself, it had taken at least three minutes before he was buzzed through the inner doors. That meant the deskman hadn't known his name. It also meant somebody else had.

That somebody else must have been impressed with him. The deskman nearly leapt to his feet when Gregor came into the office. Then he sat down again, reached for his intercom, and said,

"Mr. Demarkian? Mr. Flanagan will be out right away. Please. Why don't you just sit down?"

Flanagan. Gregor smiled. He'd been sure there'd be someone he knew up here, even this late at night, but Jim Flanagan was a piece of very good luck. Flanagan had been at Behavioral Sciences for three years, and they'd gotten along. Gregor took off his coat, laid it across one chair, and sat down in another. He felt a little guilty about being so amused. The deskman meant well. He was just too wet behind the ears to realize there was no need to be this formal after normal business hours.

Seconds later, the inner door opened and Jim Flanagan stuck his head out. His face was mottled and mournful. His hair was still bright, electric red. His eyes were a deep, clear blue. He looked so much like the stereotypical Irishman, he could have been invented by a turn-of-the-century anti-Papist.

"Gregor," he said. "It is you. I thought I was hearing things."

"I still think I'm seeing things," Gregor said. "Can't you afford to get someone in here to paint?"

"No," Flanagan said. "Dope."

"Dope?" Gregor said. "Not Miller?"

"I don't even want to think about Miller," Flanagan said. "Go in the back there and say Miller, four men will probably try to kill you."

"Just four?"

"Four is all we've got, besides me and Steve here." Flanagan stepped back. "Come into my office and have some coffee. I'm supposed to be working out the details of a coordinated drug bust. I'm bored stiff."

Gregor knew all about being bored stiff. He also knew Flanagan's work wouldn't suffer for it. He gathered up his coat and followed Flanagan through the inner door.

3 Flanagan's office was a cubbyhole oversupplied with paper, file cabinets, and manila folders. It had been painted even less recently than the outer office and in a shade of particularly unattractive green. The only indication that Flanagan was head man here was on the door. There was a placard screwed into that, with Flanagan's name on it in letters the size of a *National Enquirer* headline.

Flanagan cleared off a chair, reminding Gregor of Tibor that first day in the church. Then he dropped into the chair behind the desk and shoved a Pyrex pot of primal ooze onto the hot plate on the shelf behind him.

"So," he said, "what brings you here? If you've just dropped in for a talk, I won't mind. I'd do just about anything not to have to think about timetables any more."

"It's late," Gregor said gently. "And you're not exactly in a prime shopping area."

"True. But you could have been in the area. I tried to call you, you know, after they did that piece about you in *The Inquirer*. Your number's unlisted."

"I unlisted it because of *The Inquirer* piece."

"Nuts," Flanagan said wisely. The primal ooze began to bubble, and he took it off the plate. In the harsh light of the fluorescent lamps that lined the ceiling, his face looked even more mottled and more mournful than it had in the outer room. It also looked infinitely tired, with that bone-crushing weariness that comes of digging through slime for centuries without getting any nearer to cleaning up the mess. Gregor felt suddenly very sorry for the man.

"I don't suppose it's been much of a picnic around here since I left. I'm sorry I didn't think about how beat you'd be at this time of day. I saw where I was and I just came in."

"You *were* in the neighborhood," Flanagan said.

"I was driving through. Or rather, a friend was driving me through."

"That's good. You were never much of a driver." Flanagan had found his coffee mugs. He put them on the desk and filled them. "But I meant what I said. I'm glad to see you, as long as you're not involved in some drug thing. I can't take the drug thing any more. It's one of those days. Sometimes it doesn't faze me. Sometimes I get very attracted to the Gordian knot solution. I just want to get hold of an AK-47 of my own and blow these jerks to kingdom come."

"I'm not involved in any drug thing," Gregor said. "I never was."

Flanagan shrugged. "So? You had ax murderers and people who ate their mothers for breakfast. Literally. Also other people's mothers. It doesn't sound much better."

"It wasn't. But the past tense is important, Jim. I'm retired."

"Funny," Flanagan said. "You don't look retired."

Gregor took the mug of coffee Flanagan had pushed in his direction and gave it a try. It was worse than his own. Much worse.

"I'll tell you something," he said. "I'm glad I came in. I've been sitting around the last couple of months, wondering if I'd have felt better if I hadn't retired. Not that I could have done anything about that. I'm fifty-five. I've hit the age limit—"

"I was sorry to hear about Elizabeth, Gregor."

"I know. You sent a card. I appreciated it, even if I didn't answer it. But Jim, I'm glad I'm not still in it."

"I'm fifty-two," Flanagan said. "Some mornings, I count the time. It's not the same. Drugs changed everything, Gregor, drugs and this weird attitude they've all got now."

"I know what you mean. They don't know the difference between fact and opinion. To them, the law of gravitation isn't even a theory. It's a biosociologically determined concept."

"It's the laws of morality I'm worried about. I don't care about the sex so much. People have been sleeping with people they shouldn't be sleeping with forever. But the other things. Catch this, Gregor. We've got petty theft problems in the office."

"Here?"

"Here. Pencils. Pens. Paper clips. Junk. Theft for the sake of theft."

"I think I liked it better when guilt was in fashion," Gregor said. "I also think we're getting old. Listen to us. We're talking about the young as 'them.' "

"The young are 'them.' " Flanagan said it firmly.

Gregor took another sip of his coffee, decided he was not feeling suicidal enough to try to finish it, and pushed the mug away across the desk. "The thing is," he told Flanagan, "I didn't just come to talk. I need some information I don't even know if you have."

"Really? What did you do? Decide to go private?"

"Not exactly." Gregor explained his arrangement with Jackman and his involvement in the Hannaford case. He was gratified to see that Flanagan was impressed. "The problem with it all," he said, "is that I'm sure Jackman is right. Bobby Hannaford is not straight: Bobby Hannaford is in trouble up to his eyeballs. It's the easiest thing in the world to see."

"Is it?"

"Of course it is. And from the look on your face, Flanagan, I'd say you think so, too."

"I know so," Flanagan admitted. "I want to know why you know so."

"Because he spends more money than he has, but he doesn't have that—that look people get when they're in serious debt. I was thinking about it today when I was out at Engine House. One of the other brothers, Christopher, he has that look. Kind of an adrenaline worry and a paralysis at the same time. Bobby Hannaford looks like a man who thinks he can do something about his problems. Do you see what I mean?"

"No," Flanagan said.

"It figures," Gregor said.

"I never could see what you meant," Flanagan pointed out. "I don't know how many times you gave me that lecture of yours about internal constituency—"

"Internal consistency."

"Whatever. I could never figure out how to do it. Nobody could but you. The younger guys used to finish working on a case with you and walk around for weeks, talking like they'd been present at a miracle. I don't think you do miracles, but I don't usually think you're wrong."

"Am I right this time?"

"Spell it out for me," Flanagan said. "Give me a laugh."

Against his better judgment, Gregor tried the coffee again. His throat was dry, and he needed something. Unfortunately, Flanagan's coffee was not it. He put the mug down again.

"If you ask me, there's two things going on. One of them definitely involves the oldest sister, Myra—"

"Myra?"

"Myra Hannaford Van Damm. If you haven't turned her up, I'd check on her. There's something going on between those two. You can feel it when you see them together. And I think Mrs. Van Damm may need money. Her father didn't give her any. She's married to a rich man, but that's not the same as having her own."

"Ah," Flanagan said.

"But I think there's something else. Bobby Hannaford is a neurotic. He's addicted to possessions, yes, you can see that, but he doesn't really care about them. He cares about his father. I think he hated the man. But I don't think he killed him."

"Internal consistency again?"

"It wouldn't be internally consistent to leave a lot of hundred-dollar bills in a wastebasket with what's supposed to be a suicide note. It wouldn't be internally consistent to stage a murder that looks like a murder when what you wanted was to avoid discovery of financial manipulation. Tell me that for a start: Do you know anything about Robert Hannaford doing anything whatsoever in the last six months to indicate he might suspect his son of embezzling? Stock fraud? Insider trading? Anything?"

Flanagan had a pipe. He got it out, lit it up, and watched it die. He didn't try to get it going again. "On the first of November of this year," he said, "Robert Hannaford used his voting stock to force the board of Hannaford Financial into scheduling a directors' audit. It's supposed to commence right after the first of the year."

"All right."

"Will you tell me something? If you're so sure Bobby has nothing to do with the death of his father, why are you also so sure he really had a motive?"

"Think."

"I've done too damn much thinking in my life."

"First we have a supposed suicide," Gregor said. "Then Jackman shows up and refuses to buy it. Then we find a suicide note —not genuine, almost certainly—in a wastebasket with a lot of money in it. If the crime is going to be internally consistent, Flanagan, we know two things. One, there must be some reason somewhere, as yet undiscovered, why we could be led to believe that Emma Hannaford would make a credible murderer. There must also be some reason why Bobby Hannaford would make one. No motive, no sense."

"Maybe there's something else going on altogether. Maybe you're right about your Mrs. Van Damm. Maybe neither of them had anything to do with it, and she wants to do her brother in for some reason of her own."

"Maybe. Am I right about Bobby Hannaford? Did he have good reasons for wanting the old man dead?"

Flanagan stood up. "He had the best reasons in the world and none at all."

"Meaning," Gregor said, "you're already onto him, but he doesn't know it yet."

Flanagan went to his file cabinet, opened the top drawer, and drew out a thick manila file. He tossed it on the desk in front of Gregor. "Here. It's insider trading, by the way. It's not mine and it's sensitive, but you might as well know. Hell, you already do know, practically. I wish to hell I knew how to do that."

"Internal consistency," Gregor said.

"Right." Flanagan dropped down into his chair again, looking old and tired and grim. "Let me tell you all about a man named Donald George McAdam," he said.

An hour later, Gregor was on the street again. He knew more than he really wanted to about Donald McAdam. He knew all he could about insider trading, considering the fact that he knew nothing about stocks and even less about the operations of the market. He had what he had gone to get, confirmation of just how Bobby Hannaford's neuroses had played themselves out in real life.

Unfortunately, he also had a problem. He could see a way to make the killings of Robert and Emma Hannaford make sense.

He could devise an internally consistent scenario for what had been going on at Engine House with no trouble at all. But if that scenario was right, then the framing of Bobby Hannaford could not be happening.

"So maybe it isn't," he said to the wind and the rain.

Then the cab Flanagan had called for him drew up at the curb, and he got in. He leaned back in his seat, closed his eyes, and started to worry. He worried all the way home, through a Philadelphia still locked in an orgy of Christmas celebration and a wariness about the weather.

He only stopped worrying after he'd gotten out of the cab on Cavanaugh Street, tipped and paid the driver, and started walking up the steep stone steps to his vestibule. That was when he saw Bennis Hannaford, leaning out old George Tekamanian's front window.

She looked very Christmasy, in a bright red sweater with a large shiny tin bell brooch spread across the shoulder.

SIX

1 Bennis opened the door for him. George was enthroned in his very best easy chair, wedged between a drinks cart and a pile of hardcover books, wearing an emerald green sweater someone must have given him for Christmas and a pair of reindeer socks. The socks were noticeable because George wasn't wearing shoes. A pair of tasseled Gucci loafers had been abandoned unceremoniously in the middle of his carpet. Gregor could hardly believe his eyes. George looked deliriously happy. Bennis looked bemused.

She ought to look bemused, Gregor thought. She had drunk her way through half of one of George's Yerevan Specials, a time bomb that consisted of vodka and just enough lime soda to make you think you had nothing but a nonalcoholic punch. Gregor had been ambushed by one of those himself, the first week he knew George. He recognized the glass.

He shut the door behind him, shrugged off his coat, and hung it up on George's coatrack. Bennis wasn't wearing any shoes either. Hers, a pair of L. L. Bean's Maine Hunting Shoes just like Donna Moradanyan's, were lying on the fireplace hearth.

At least she wasn't wearing reindeer socks.

She went to sit on the floor at George's feet and took a book off the hardcover stack.

"Look, Krekor," George said, "Martin brings me all the books in real hard covers for Christmas, and now Bennis, she signs them for me."

"All nine of them," Bennis said.

"Are either one of you sober?" Gregor said.

Bennis made a face at him and bent over the book in her lap, writing. She wrote for a long time. Gregor wondered what she could be finding to say.

He took a chair from the edge of the room and dragged it to the center. They looked comfortable together, these two—and he was surprised to find he was *not* surprised at that. He didn't put much credence in the evidence of novels. Elizabeth had told him, over and over again, that a great many men who had written wonderful things had been terrible people in their private lives. It was the Bennis Hannaford of the stairs at Engine House whom Gregor had known would do so well on Cavanaugh Street. Now she finished with the book in her lap, put it aside, and picked up another one. All the books looked impossibly long.

"Would you like me to get you a drink, Krekor?" George said. "I'm so tired, I keep forgetting myself."

"That's all right," Gregor said. "I don't need a drink right now. Miss Hannaford here has offered to buy me one."

Bennis stopped writing. "Was everybody terribly angry at me for bugging out? I mean, I know I should have hung around for the police—"

"It is customary in a murder investigation," Gregor said.

"—but everybody was getting crazy, and I knew it was just going to get crazier when Bobby got home, so I got out. I just did some shopping and then came over here as fast as I could. I wasn't trying to avoid you."

"No," Gregor said, "you were just trying to avoid John Jackman."

"I make it a policy to avoid men who are prettier than I am," Bennis said. "If you were a woman, you would too."

"She was just standing out there in the cold," old George said. "And I recognized her from her pictures."

"He's been very nice," Bennis said.

Old George sighed. "We called Tibor, Krekor, but he was not home. He was not at the church, either. Somebody must be feeding him dinner."

"Did you try Lida's?" Gregor said.

"Is that Mrs. Arkmanian?" Bennis asked. "We did try her. She wasn't home either."

Old George sighed again. "He will be very disappointed, Krekor. And I will be disappointed, too. I try and try, I can't make her tell me what happens to Rogan le Bourne. Tibor, he could make her."

"No he couldn't," Bennis said. "I don't know what happens to Rogan le Bourne. And stop worrying about your friend Tibor. I'll come back and sign his books for him if he wants me to."

"I think he only has the paperbacks," Gregor said.

"I've got a supply of the others." Bennis snapped shut the cover of the book she was writing in, abandoned it, and took another. "You are angry at me, aren't you? I know I should have stuck around. And I know I shouldn't be flip. Not about Emma. Emma—well, I don't want to get into Emma."

"She's told me all about it," old George said. "This is a terrible thing, Krekor."

"This is a dangerous thing," Bennis said. "That's what worries me. And I did come here."

"It was dangerous from the beginning," Gregor said.

"No it wasn't." Bennis shook her head vigorously. "Not if what was going on was what I thought was going on. But now it can't have been, and I just don't know—" She threw up her hands.

Gregor sat back and looked her over, curious. She had been crying again, recently enough so that her eyes were as red and puffy here as they'd been back at Engine House this afternoon. He would never have called her flip. Even when she tried to be sarcastic, the sarcasm didn't come off. He had a feeling that Bennis and Donna Moradanyan might have more in common than hunting boots. Bennis was prettier, of course, and more intelligent and more accomplished and more sophisticated and more of everything else. Unlike Donna, she had developed a rock-hard foundation of self-confidence that the mere opinions of other people could not shatter. What was similar was that air of innocence. In Donna, Gregor had thought it was sexual innocence, and been wrong. Now he put another definition to it. Bennis Hannaford and Donna Moradanyan were two young women who believed, at the core, that the world was a good and righteous place where virtue triumphed and evil failed, where people always wanted to do the right thing and only did wrong out of ignorance or confusion. And no matter how much evidence they got to the contrary, they would go on believing it.

Gregor watched as Bennis finished the last of the books and restacked the whole mess next to old George's chair.

"There," she said, "finished. When I have the next one, I'll send you a copy."

"No, no," George said. "Send Father Tibor a copy. He can't afford to buy them. I have Martin."

"Martin is his grandson," Gregor said.

"He told me. Electric carrot crinklers." She stretched out her legs. "Do you still want that drink? I was thinking, under the circumstances, it might make more sense if I bought you a whole dinner."

"Under what circumstances?"

"Well," Bennis said, "for one thing, I'm hungry."

"I'm hungry, too," Gregor said. "I've been living on coffee all day."

Bennis waved her Yerevan Special in the air. "I'm also a little drunk," she said.

"True," Gregor nodded.

"But the real reason, of course, is that this story is going to take a little time. It may take quite a lot of time."

"What story?"

"Ah," Bennis said. "Well. Mostly, it's the story of how Emma tried to do it once before—or how we all thought she did."

"Tried to do what?" old George asked.

"Tried to kill our father, of course." Bennis looked into her Yerevan Special, took a deep breath, and swallowed half of what was left.

2 Gregor didn't know if taking Bennis to Ararat was foolishness or incitement to riot. It was certainly an experience. As soon as they had been seated in one of the back booths, heads began popping out of the swinging doors that led to the kitchen. Old and young, the women of Ararat wanted to get a look at Gregor and his presumed "date." The news—that Gregor was having dinner with a woman, and a much younger woman at that—would be all up and down the street in no time. Their only hope for an uninterrupted meal was

the possibility that Lida was out because she'd gone to visit her grandchildren in Paoli. Even without Lida, they were going to have to suffer through better than average service.

Still, Gregor liked the comparisons he could make between this and the last time he had eaten in a restaurant. Then, he had taken a poor man to an expensive place. Now, he was sitting with a rich woman in a relatively cheap one. The two experiences were a lot alike. Like Tibor, Bennis Hannaford was fearless when it came to food. Having told him she'd never eaten Armenian before, she then proceeded to order everything she liked the sound of on the menu, including a main course that must have been a mystery to her. Ethnic restaurants in tourist centers explained their food in plain English, but Ararat wasn't in a tourist center. It was in an Armenian neighborhood, and its usual patrons had been eating the dishes it served since childhood. Bennis ordered cheerfully and without hesitation even so, then handed the menu to their waitress and asked for a cup of black coffee.

"Goodness," she said, when the waitress left. "I think that woman's going to have us married within the hour."

"Within the week, at any rate." Gregor smiled. "That's Linda Melajian, youngest daughter of the house. They sent her over because she has the best memory."

"The best memory?"

"The rumor is she's better than a distance mike with a tape recorder attached. She can pick up conversations three miles away and repeat them verbatim."

"It must be nice," Bennis said, "to live in a place where everybody knows who you are."

Linda Melajian came back with Bennis's coffee, and Bennis drew the cup to her and started doctoring it with sugar. She put in a lot of sugar, as if she wanted to be not only awake but hyperactive.

"So," she said, "on to the important part, the story of Emma and Daddy and how it all happened with the money. Do you know about the money?"

"About the living trusts?" Gregor said. "Yes, we know about that."

"I thought you might. You were in there with Floyd Evers for a long time. Didn't you think that was strange?"

"I thought it was very strange," Gregor said.

"In case you aren't used to dealing with people like us, let me tell you it isn't the done thing to cut your daughters out of your estate. It wasn't even in the old days—when the money was made, I mean. Conventional wisdom on the Main Line is that you provide your sons with opportunities and your daughters with escape routes. Husbands being what they are, that is."

"Didn't that lead to a lot of daughters being married for their money?"

"Nope," Bennis said. "The Main Line rich have always had very good lawyers. The daughters got incomes outright and the capital was entailed. That's what we thought was going to happen, Anne Marie and Myra and Emma and I. Daddy was a very old-fashioned man."

"What about divorce?"

Bennis took a sip of her coffee and shuddered. "God, I hate it this sweet. But it's the only thing that wakes me up. Look, Mr. Demarkian. The Main Line—the old Main Line—doesn't get divorced. That's as true today as it was in 1910. Oh, there have always been exceptions, women who ditched their husbands and went to live in the South of France or whatever. But there are at least four clubs in this city that won't accept divorced people, and the Philadelphia Assembly won't accept them, either. One of the girls my coming-out year had a mother who'd been married before, and she wasn't allowed to attend her own daughter's debut. And that was in—what?—1972? It's even worse now. People are getting more conservative, not less."

"That doesn't sound like money would be much of an escape route."

"You don't have to get divorced to leave your husband, Mr. Demarkian. The Main Line is full of married-but-separated ladies."

Gregor raised his eyebrows. This was like listening to a recap of a novel by Henry James. The odd thing was how real it sounded. He had no trouble at all imagining the old Main Line as just what Bennis said it was.

"But," he said, "you and your sisters don't have an escape route. Your brothers don't have many opportunities, either."

"That was just spite," Bennis said. "Daddy was just as spiteful as he was old-fashioned. He thought the boys were a lot of mush-headed wimps. With us, with the girls, it was very different. And the thing is, I could hardly blame him. I mean, he did think one of us had tried to kill him."

"Emma," Gregor said.

"He didn't know it was Emma. And maybe we didn't either, but I'll get to that. I think Anne Marie tried to tell him once, but he wasn't about to listen. He just went out and bought fifteen editions of *King Lear* and put them up all over his study. And did all that with the money, of course. But if he'd been sure it was Emma, he would only have cut out Emma. He'd have loved that, really."

"Not a nice man," Gregor said.

"No," Bennis agreed. "Daddy was not a nice man."

"This was in 1980?" Gregor said. "Was that when he was confined to the wheelchair?"

"This was in 1980," Bennis said, "but by then he'd been confined to the wheelchair for years. Since Teddy was ten, as a matter of fact. I was in Paris at the time. I remember, though, because Daddy ended up in the wheelchair and Teddy ended up in the leg brace because of the same accident. Of course, Teddy always claimed Daddy had tried to kill him."

"Of course?"

Bennis smiled. "Teddy's like that. One of those people who's always being done to, if you know what I mean—and never by accident, either. No matter what happens in Teddy's life, it's not just somebody else's fault, but somebody else's plan. Mostly mine."

"Your brother thinks you're out to get him?"

"My brother thinks I've written and published nine fantasy novels—and landed them all on *The New York Times* best-seller list—in a deliberate attempt to keep him from getting a job in the Harvard University English department."

"Why do I have this terrible feeling that you think what you just said is supposed to make sense?"

Bennis laughed. "It doesn't make sense. None of the Hannafords makes sense, except maybe Mother. Teddy is sure Daddy tried to kill him. You couldn't convince him that it isn't true. But then, he's convinced that the only reason he hasn't had a brilliant academic career—he teaches in a small college in Maine —is because he's being done out of it by nefarious plots. He likes to think I'm behind those plots because I do have a brilliant career, or what passes for one in popular literature. It would never occur to him it might have something to do with the fact that I work my butt off and he doesn't. And if it did, he wouldn't believe it."

Linda Melajian came back to the table, her arms laden down with plates of stuffed vine leaves and sautéed eggplant. She laid the plates out between them, then took a moment to stare at them each in turn. The verdict of the street was in. Bennis Hannaford was too young for him and probably up to no good. Gregor wondered what the good ladies of Cavanaugh Street were going to do about it—and then reminded himself that they were only looking out for him, trying to protect him from himself. Awash in the atomized peculiarities of Hannaford family life, he didn't know if he liked that or not.

Linda rearranged the plates, rearranged the salt and pepper shakers, and then, reluctantly, turned to go. Bennis and Gregor both watched her retreat, amused for different reasons.

"I should have worn my city clothes," Bennis said. "I'd really have looked like a scarlet woman."

"She doesn't think you're a scarlet woman," Gregor said. "Just a fortune hunter."

"Wonderful," Bennis said.

Gregor speared a piece of eggplant. "Go back to this murder attempt. Are you sure it was a murder attempt? It couldn't have been another accident?"

"It was reported as an accident," Bennis said. "That goes without saying. If it had been reported any other way, Emma would have had to stand trial. She was over eighteen at the time. Mother wouldn't have put up with that. But knowing the circumstances, I'd say it wasn't possible. For it to be an accident, I mean."

"What were the circumstances?"

Bennis speared a piece of eggplant of her own. "Well, this is early 1980, you understand. January. Usually the middle of miserable weather in Philadelphia. But that year, we had an exceptionally warm January thaw, and temperatures in the high sixties for about a week. The snow melted. Flowers started to come up. False spring."

"I've lived through a few false springs," Gregor said.

"Yes. Well. Daddy's doctor was always telling him to get out into the air, so in the middle of this false spring he decided he wanted to sit out by the bluff. That's to the back of our property, way to the south. There's a place where the land just stops, a kind of dirt cliff. It's not tremendously high, but it is straight down and there are a lot of jagged rocks at the bottom. Very jagged rocks. At any rate, Daddy decided he wanted to go sit out there, and Mother decided she wanted to have us all together for a family barbecue or something. Mother was always trying to get us together for something or the other. And we were all home—"

"Was that unusual?"

"Very unusual," Bennis said. "It wasn't a pleasant house to live in and none of us got along with Daddy. But this was Emma's coming-out year. Mother wanted us around to give her a send-off, so we were there. All seven of us. Mother got this picnic together and told us all she wanted us to be there. Anne Marie and Emma and Myra and I gave in immediately. We always do when Mother asks us for something. The boys—"

"Somehow," Gregor said, "I can't believe the boys defied your mother."

"They didn't defy her. They just found excuses. Lots and lots of excuses. Good ones, too."

"And they didn't come?"

"They didn't come."

"I was wondering why your father was sure it was one of his daughters," Gregor said. "I was imagining lipstick on his collar."

"If there'd been lipstick on his collar, he'd have known it was Myra," Bennis laughed. "She's the only one who wears enough of it to have it smear off. No, it was just that the boys were other places."

"As far as you know."

"Excuse me?"

"As far as you know," Gregor repeated. "It seems to me that no matter where they said they were, any one of them could have followed you out there and been hiding in the bushes."

"I suppose they could have," Bennis said. "I know we never checked up on them later. But it's like I said. We thought—Anne Marie and Myra and I thought—we thought we knew what had happened."

"What did happen?"

"We had lunch. And when that was finished we cleaned up, and Daddy said he wanted to sit out on the bluff, close, where he could see over. Anne Marie and I wheeled him as close as we liked, which wasn't very close at all. We told the police later we'd put him right up to the edge, but it wasn't true. We stopped the chair a good ten feet back. The ground there is flat, and before you get to the drop it goes up a little."

"Meaning he couldn't have just rolled off."

"He would have had to have been pushed. And he would have had to have been pushed hard. And long. Anne Marie and I put him out there, and we put on the brakes—I saw the brakes on, Mr. Demarkian, and I didn't make a mistake—and then he asked for a hot chocolate. So Anne Marie and I went back to the fire—"

"Could you see your father from the fire?"

"No. There's a stand of trees out there. He was on the other side of it from where the rest of us were. We got back to the fire and told Mother he wanted some hot chocolate, and then Emma offered to bring it to him. So we let her."

"You sound as if you don't think you should have let her."

"We shouldn't have," Bennis said, "even if it turns out she didn't try to kill him, that time. They'd had a tremendous fight the night before. Emma was always very protective of Mother, and in those days, before Mother got seriously sick, Daddy could be very abusive to her. Not as abusive as he was with the rest of us, and not on purpose. If Daddy had known the effect the things he was saying were having on her, he'd never have said them. That's one thing you have to give him. He did love Mother. But he was a cruel man, Mr. Demarkian, naturally cruel, so naturally he often didn't know he was being cruel. And the night before this happened, he'd said something to Mother that Emma objected to, and Emma just lit into him. Then he lit into her, and they had a screaming match that lasted over two hours. At the end of which, by the way, Emma told him she thought he should be dead."

"Ah," Gregor said.

"Ah, indeed. Emma brought him his hot chocolate. Then she came back. Then we cleaned up around the fire. After a while, we all started to drift off. I know that sounds strange, in January. But it was a really warm day. I remember I was wearing a cotton turtleneck and a cotton sweater and no coat, and I felt over-dressed."

"Did you fall asleep?"

"We all did. Or we thought we all did."

"And then?"

Bennis coughed. "I woke up. I'd been lying on a blanket, right next to the fire, and when I looked up I saw Emma's place was empty. A few seconds later, Emma came out of the stand of trees."

"Where did she say she'd been?"

"Where do you think? Taking care of necessary business, of course. It was a perfectly sensible explanation, and I didn't think anything of it. We talked for a while. I gave her a lecture on diplomatic relations with Daddy. She was so much younger than the rest of us, she hadn't lived through the very bad years, she had no idea how to handle him when he got out of hand. Then Mother got up, and looked at her watch, and said we'd better go tell Daddy what time it was. Because it was getting late."

"Who went?"

"Anne Marie and I. Together."

Gregor nodded. "And your father had been pushed over the bluff."

"Very recently pushed, Mr. Demarkian. That's a big part of it. If we'd been much later on the scene, he would have died. The doctor told us that, afterward."

"Your father was unconscious?"

"In more ways than one. He was full of Demerol."

Gregor was surprised. "How do you know? You say there wasn't a criminal investigation—"

"I know because I asked the doctor to check," Bennis said. "We were behind the trees, but we weren't far away from him. We would have heard him if he'd cried out. And he should have cried out, attempted murder or not. Even if he'd gone over that bluff accidentally, and been asleep when he started moving, the drop should have woken him up."

"Miss Hannaford, did you tell the police about this Demerol?"

Bennis picked up a grape leaf and studied it. "We told them he'd taken some, yes. Daddy was always taking some painkiller or the other. He was paralyzed, but the nerves in his lower body weren't entirely dead. They hurt him, often."

Gregor got a grape leaf of his own, but he ate his. It was good. Everything at Ararat was always good.

Across the table, Bennis Hannaford was looking tired and sad. She kept picking up food and putting it down again, as if she'd forgotten what it was for.

"I asked her about it," she said finally. "I confronted her with it, really, that same week. After we knew Daddy was going to live. She said she hadn't done it."

"You didn't believe her?" Gregor asked.

"No. Emma was always—sketchy, sort of. Not too stable, I suppose you'd say. When she was a child, she'd have terrible tantrums, hold her breath until she passed out, I don't know what. Anne Marie and Myra and I were all so—practical, I guess."

"Was that what the note was about? The one the police found in her room? About the fact that she knew you suspected her?"

"Yes."

"What about the other note?" Gregor said. "The one Anne Marie found originally?"

"I don't know. I never saw it." Bennis blushed. "I didn't go into the room. The room where Emma was. I didn't want to see her—"

"It's all right. I understand that. You weren't in the house when the note was finally discovered?"

"I left about half an hour after you started talking to Evers. Do you remember what it said?"

Gregor sighed. "Let's just say I found it less convincing, as a suicide note, than the one that had been sent to you."

"Which wasn't a suicide note at all," Bennis pointed out.

"I know that." Gregor slapped his hand against the table. Simplicity. That was what this pointed to. Simplicity. Somewhere, in all this mess of motives and secrets and plots, there was a perfectly straightforward course of action, a person who killed or tried to kill, over and over again, always in much the same way. And that meant there was also a perfectly straightforward reason for it all. Not Hannaford Financial and a complex embezzling scheme. Not Teddy's baroque fantasies of persecution. Something else, something simple, something obvious—but not obvious enough for him to see what it was.

Linda Melajian came to clear the appetizer and put out the salads. Gregor sat back while she wiped the table in front of him. She scrubbed too long and too vigorously, but he had been expecting that.

When she was gone, he leaned across his salad bowl and said, "Would you do me a favor? I'd like to come to Engine House, on my own, without John Jackman. Would you invite me?"

"Of course I will," Bennis said. "When do you want to come?"

Gregor thought about it. "Tomorrow morning. We might as well not waste time. I don't think you want to waste time, either."

"Mr. Demarkian, for ten years, I thought Emma had tried to kill Daddy. When Daddy died the way he did, I thought she'd tried again and succeeded. I had nothing to worry about as long as I thought that was true. Emma wasn't dangerous to the rest of us. And she wasn't dangerous to Mother."

"And you're worried that whoever is really doing these things is dangerous to your mother?"

"I don't know. But she's the most vulnerable one. And she's helpless."

Gregor understood. But he had something much more immediate to worry about, immediate and frightening. He saw the swish of skirts. He saw the glint of lights on hair. He heard the rustling of a fur coat.

"Krekor!" Lida Arkmanian trilled. "It is *you!* And a friend of yours I haven't *met!*"

Which took care of what the good ladies of Cavanaugh Street were going to do about his dinner with Bennis Day Hannaford.

SEVEN

1 At six o'clock on the morning of Wednesday, December 28, Christopher Hannaford woke up on the floor of his bedroom. He turned over onto his back, looked up at his bed, and decided it might not be such a bad idea to get stoned again right away. Then he realized that, bad idea or good one, it was impossible. He had finished the dope he'd brought from California. He was dead broke. And after his experiences yesterday afternoon, he had no damn intention of leaving Engine House again for any reason whatsoever.

He sat up, looked around, and touched his hair. It was stiff with dried sweat and very clammy. Through his bedroom windows, he could see the glow of security lamps on the back terrace and chart the passage of a heavily falling snow. He didn't bother looking in the other direction. Over there was the writing desk, with the top left drawer sitting slightly ajar, where he'd tried to close it and hadn't been able to. In that drawer were Mother's candlesticks. Every once in a while, it would hit him: what he had done and what he had tried to do, first in attempting to sell them and then when he knew he wouldn't be able to do it. The picture that came to him most clearly was of the pavement just outside the main doors of Pennsylvania Station. The derelict with the mud in his beard. The crazy lady with the vest and no shirt. The fake veteran with the American flag sewn across his chest. Most of all, the people going in and out with the trains, so different from what they would have been like if this were Los Angeles. Out there you got a lot of kids, teenage and stupid. Here it was mostly well-dressed men in middle age, with somewhere in particular to go. He hadn't been able to classify himself, although he had tried. He had tried again last night, in the wake of Emma's dying, nearly catatonic with dope and guilt. Now he decided not to bother again, not yet. It was too much. He didn't have the energy and he didn't have the courage.

He got up, crossed the room, turned on his night-table lamp, and sat down on the edge of his bed. Down the hall, a door opened and closed, letting padded footsteps into the corridor. He got up, stuck his head out the door, and caught Anne Marie just as she was disappearing into the bathroom. She looked terrible, her hair snarled, her body—much fatter than he'd realized, seeing her in clothes—squeezed into a yellow velour bathrobe that made her look like a stuffed canary covered in Saran Wrap. Her face was as sour as he'd ever seen anybody's. Looking at it, he realized sour wasn't an expression he had much experience with, these days. Menacing, yes. Seductive, certainly. Exasperated, every day. But sour—that was an emotional territory confined exclusively to Engine House.

He shut the door of his room again and then, on impulse, went to check the writing desk. The candlesticks were still there, wrapped in a thin plastic bag from a Pathmark in the Jersey town where he had spent half an hour getting gas and lunch. He took them out, felt their weight, and thought about putting them back where they belonged. Then he wrapped them in the plastic bag again and pitched them into the drawer.

Last night, wallowing in the precursor to this condition, he had promised himself that as soon as he got up this morning, he would talk to Bennis. As soon as. Now he was up, and it wasn't even dawn yet. Bennis was on vacation. Did it make sense to wake a woman from a sound sleep when you wanted to ask for her help?

He got off the bed again, opened his door again, stuck his head into the hall again. He felt like one of those souvenir gooney birds they sold in the Stuckey's off southern highways, going up and down, up and down, in a senseless imitation of perpetual motion. He stepped into the hall and closed his bedroom door behind him.

All around, between all the candlesticks on all the chests in the hall, there were holly baskets: Mother's traditional first preparation for Twelfth Night. He squinted into the distance and saw there was a holly basket on the chest without candlesticks, too—but of course, there would be. Christmas decorations at Engine House were orchestrated with all the battlefield solemnity the manager of Rockefeller Center brought to the lighting of the giant tree. Now someone knew those candlesticks were gone, and he only had to worry about who.

He crossed the hall and started counting doors, until he came to the fourth to the north of his. He raised his hand to knock, then thought better of it. No use waking Bennis the way the volunteer firemen would. Christ only knew what she'd think was going on, before he had a chance to tell her it was only him. He opened the door very slowly and stuck his head in.

Bennis's bed was empty. It had been slept in—or wrestled in, from the look of it—but it was empty. He opened the door wider and tried to search the room.

"Bennis?"

"Here," she said.

The voice came from behind him, and he jumped. Just like a bad actor in an even worse comedy.

"Jesus *Christ*," he said.

Bennis slipped under his arm—she was small enough and he was tall enough so she hardly had to stoop—and went to turn on the night-table lamp.

"I was in the bathroom," she said. She picked up her cigarettes and started fumbling with the paraphernalia: lighter, ashtray, butt. "I couldn't sleep. I take it you couldn't sleep either."

"I slept like a log, I just didn't do it long enough. I guess it was mostly the dope."

"Are you still smoking dope?"

"I have to do something, Bennis. I don't smoke anything else. I don't drink. Last couple of months or so, I don't even get laid."

"Shut the door," Bennis said. "If Anne Marie sees us, she'll want us to do something."

Chris shut the door. Behind him, Bennis was sitting cross-legged on her bed, draped in a man's red football jersey, her hair pinned to the top of her head in a haphazard way that told him she'd stuck it up there to get it out of the way, without looking in a mirror to be sure she got it right. She was unbelievably beautiful—and that made him feel even guiltier than being here. It was the kind of thing he ought to remember about Bennis, but never did.

He came over and sat at the foot of her bed. "So," he said. "So. Hell. Why do I have this terrible feeling you know why I'm here?"

"You look terrible, Christopher."

"I could look terrible because Daddy died. And Emma. Especially Emma."

"You looked terrible before any of that happened. I remember seeing you when you first came in. I thought what Teddy thought. I thought you had AIDS."

"I don't have AIDS."

"I could ask you how you're sure you know, under the circumstances. But I won't."

"Good. And if you want to get technical about it, I don't know. I just know I've got an ulcer—same one I had at Yale—and it's acting up and I can't eat. There's a lot of reasons I can't eat."

"How much?" Bennis said gently.

"Seventy-five thousand dollars."

"Ouch."

He stood up. "Believe it or not, I'm not asking you for it. I came in here to ask you for money, but not for that money."

Bennis brushed stray hair off her neck, impatient. "Don't be idiotic," she said. "The problem with you and money for that is that you always start out borrowing it from the wrong people. And I asked Michael about it—round about, don't worry, I didn't tell him it was you. He says they really do the things people say they do in novels."

"I wouldn't know about that," Chris said. "They threaten to do them."

"Somebody has been threatening to kill you?"

"Somebody's been threatening to cut off my thumbs. Why would they want to kill me? How could they get paid back out of that?"

Bennis took a long drag on her cigarette. "It's funny," she said. "I took this course in college, introduction to psych or something like that, and when we got to all the nature-nurture theories I thought the whole argument was silly. Especially the nurture part. But look at us. The children of a psychopath—"

"You're not a psychopath, Bennis."

"Neither are you."

"I'm something." He sighed. It was getting harder and harder to talk to her. He went to the windows and looked out. It was snowing out there again. Hard. "I don't think I'm crazy because I got Daddy's genes," he said, "and I don't think I'm crazy because Daddy warped my mind, either. I think I'm crazy because I'm a jerk."

"I don't think that kind of attitude is going to get us anywhere."

"I think it's going to get us a hell of a lot farther than the attitude I've been taking, which is that I just can't help myself, no explanations necessary."

"Oh," Bennis said.

"Let me tell you what I did yesterday," he said. "Just so you get the picture."

Bennis took another drag. He could hear it. "I know about the candlesticks," she said quickly. "I saw you take them."

"I still have them. I tried to sell them, but I couldn't do it. They're some kind of custom antique."

Bennis laughed. "They're that, at least. They're great-grandmother Eleanor's Georgian wedding silver. I'm surprised a pawnbroker knew that."

"Pawnbrokers are not dumb. That's how they stay out of jail. It's what I did after I couldn't sell them that bothers me. You want to hear about my day?"

"Of course."

He leaned close to the window, letting his forehead touch the glass. "I had about twenty-five dollars on me at the beginning. I went to a house I knew of, a gambling place—"

"This was in the morning?"

"These places never shut down. Anyway, this was a place I knew about from someone else, but not a place that knew me. So I went there and I played my twenty-five dollars and I lost it. When it was gone, I didn't dare ask for credit. I've got too bad a rep, all across the country. If I'd given my name, they'd have made a phone call, and—well, you know the and. So I left."

"And?"

Deep breath, ten count, deep breath again. It was so hard to keep going. "I wanted to play," he said. "I didn't have any money, but I wanted to play. So I went to Penn Station, and I stood outside the front doors, and I tried to panhandle—"

"Oh, dear *Lord.*"

He turned around. "Bennis, what do you think I do? How do you think I live? This isn't the first time—"

"But they let you borrow so much money—"

"They let me borrow until they get nervous and then they don't let me borrow any more. But I still want to play. I still have to play. Bennis, I want to go out and play now."

"Stress," Bennis said.

"I don't care if it's astrology. I thought about it last night. If Daddy hadn't done all that with the money, and I'd come in for —what would it have been? Fifty million dollars? I could have gone through it in five years."

Bennis looked down at her cigarette. It was smoked to the filter. She dropped it into the ashtray. "I think we should deal with the seventy-five thousand," she said. "For the moment."

"Deal with it, if you want. I'll be grateful. But it's really not what I came here for."

"What did you come for?"

"Bennis, I want to borrow the money for a shrink. Don't—I know how you feel about shrinks. I don't mean some Viennese guy in an office in Beverly Hills. There's a place in Vermont. For people who do what I do."

"A sanatorium?"

"I guess you could call it that. A former friend of mine—former because he doesn't play anymore, he goes to Gamblers Anonymous—this former friend went there. He calls it Camp Boredom."

"Would it be any good to you, if it made you bored?"

"I don't know. Maybe I could use some boredom. The last five years or so, all I've been is scared. And stoned. This place is expensive, Bennis."

"I'm not worried about expensive." She got out a new cigarette and lit up again. She always chain-smoked when she was tense. Christopher thought she'd probably been chain-smoking since the moment she walked into Engine House. She took a deep drag and blew the smoke into the air. "Let's clean up the seventy-five thousand first," she said again. "Let's do that today —or at least let me make the phone calls today. I've got a couple of things on, but I can make time to call my bank."

"I don't want to tap you out, Bennis."

"You won't tap me out. I just signed a new contract." She smiled. "Three million dollars a book, after agents' commissions. Michael says I'm bound and determined to make as much as Daddy would have left me and then come back and thumb my nose at him. Or Michael used to say that. I don't know what he'd say, now that Daddy's dead."

"I'm impressed," Chris said. "I had no idea so many people wanted to read about unicorns."

"I think it's the sex, myself."

"Will you loan me the money to go to Camp Boredom?"

"Yes," Bennis said. "But thumbs first, okay?"

"Okay."

"I know you think what you're doing is terrible," Bennis said, "but we can fix it, Chris. At least we can fix this part of it. I was up all night, thinking about Emma. That was what got to me. That there was no way to fix it."

"Maybe your Mr. Demarkian can fix it," Chris said. He stood up. For the first time since he'd woken, he felt as dirty as he probably was—sweaty, sticky, foul. He had to take a shower.

"Let me go throw myself under some water," he said. "Then we can meet in the hall and go down to breakfast together. That ought to scare Anne Marie off."

Bennis's face lit up for the first time in days. "Let's go down and pretend I'm going to become a Rastafarian," she said. "Let's drive Anne Marie straight into cardiac arrest."

2 Myra Hannaford Van Damm wanted to do something drastic.

Of course, Myra always wanted to do something drastic—and she didn't mean breaking into Bobby's house, or taking a lover, or even divorcing Dickie Van Damm. She certainly didn't mean smoking one of Bennis's cigarettes when she had Dickie on the phone. That was what she had been doing for the past half hour, from seven-thirty to eight. Actually, she had smoked five of Bennis's cigarettes, one right after the other. The first had been an act of defiance. Smoking was the one thing Dickie could get himself worked up about. He literally screamed when he saw a cigarette in her hand. The other four had been simple, addictive need. Like a woman who has been starving long enough to lose her appetite and is given a little food, hunger was suddenly the only thing in her life—nicotine hunger, in her case. Sometimes Myra thought hunger was the defining emotion of her existence. Sometimes she thought Teddy had had a point, the other day, when he'd said Bennis's life was perfect. Whatever was going on with Bennis, she certainly seemed to be at peace.

At peace.

Myra tapped the phone with the tips of her long fingernails, almost breaking one. What she wanted to do this morning was go into Bobby's room and get the money out of his safe. That was what she'd decided to do, last night, after they'd had their little talk. She didn't know how much he had in there, but she thought it must be a lot. It might even be enough to cover her losses, although she doubted it. Her losses were going to be huge. It made her crazy. Her plan was simple, and foolproof, but once it was blown it was blown. There could be no starting over again after a disaster.

First, she and Bobby bought stock in Hannaford Financial under assumed names.

Then they held it, for a year.

Then Bobby started a very discreet rumor that Hannaford Financial was going to be the target of a takeover.

Then the stock went up.

Then they sold it.

Perfect.

Unfortunately, Bobby had been a much bigger fool than Myra had ever suspected. Instead of using his own money to buy secret stock, he'd embezzled it from the company. Instead of being content to wait and make a single killing, he'd gotten involved with that man McAdam. As soon as Myra had heard that name come floating through Bobby's door, she had wanted to slit her throat. Business gossip wasn't restricted to the dusty caverns of old-line men's clubs. It was thrown around freely in the women's clubs, too, and in the country clubs everyone on the Main Line belonged to. Rumors about McAdam were where Myra had gotten her idea in the first place. He was supposed to be doing what she was doing, but on a much bigger scale, and not with family. He was just paying people off, delivering thousands of dollars in $100 bills to confederates here, there and everywhere, delivering it in cash and in briefcases.

There was all that cash in the safe in Bobby's room.

There was all that cash washing inexplicably through the accounts of Hannaford Financial over the past two years.

There was no reason to forget, now, that this was exactly what had gotten Ivan Boesky arrested.

Myra Hannaford Van Damm was not a hypocrite. The legal name for what she and Bobby were doing—and for what Bobby and McAdam were doing—was "insider trading," but what it really was was simple fraud. She had no qualms about engaging in simple fraud. Or complicated fraud, for that matter. As far as she was concerned, Daddy had asked for it, by taking a fit and cutting her out of what should have been hers. She did have something against getting caught. That was why she had finally decided not to take the money out of Bobby's safe. Bobby was asking to get caught. He'd been running around flashing warning lights at federal regulators for two years. They had to know what he was doing by now. He'd gone out to meet McAdam again this morning. If he didn't manage to get himself arrested today, he'd do it next week, or next month. She had no way of knowing what the time frame was.

Just in case it was very, very short—hours instead of weeks—she thought it would be a good idea not to have a lot of unexplained cash wandering around her life. She also thought it would be a good idea not to try to sell her Hannaford Financial stock right now. The price was going to be in the toilet as soon as Bobby's little party hit the papers. She was going to be out almost a quarter of a million dollars. It didn't matter. She would much rather be poor than arrested.

She left the telephone room and looked into the kitchen, where Mrs. Washington was having a "baking day." There was flour everywhere, and no sign of any of the family. Mrs. Washington never liked company on baking days. Myra turned around and went down the hall in the other direction, to the dining room. That was where the family was, or what of it was awake and moving around and still in the house. Bobby, of course, was absent. The rest of them—Bennis, Teddy, Anne Marie, Chris— all looked depressed. The poinsettia centerpiece, decked out for Twelfth Night in candles and foil, looked lunatic.

She came in, sat down at the table, and said, "Does somebody over there want to hand me some coffee?"

Bennis, standing at the coffee urn with a cup and saucer in her hand, turned around. "Oh," she said. "Myra."

"I see you got the music off," Myra said. "God, it was driving me nuts. All that tinny harpsichord music."

"Mother loves harpsichord music," Anne Marie said. She was standing at the coffee urn, too, or right beside it. Right beside her was Teddy, looking pained. Chris was the only one, besides Myra herself, sitting down. Myra thought he hardly looked capable of standing up.

She took the cup Bennis passed to her and put it squarely in front of her on the table. "Just because Mother loves harpsichord music doesn't mean I have to. And it was eerie, all those Christmas carols and everybody in mourning."

"Nobody was in mourning for Daddy," Teddy said. He got his act together and sat down, too, right next to Chris. "It's Emma who's gumming up the works around here."

"I wouldn't call it 'gumming up the works,' " Bennis said.

"Don't you start," Teddy said. "I don't want to hear one more word about one of us being some kind of homicidal maniac. Daddy was the only homicidal maniac. And he's dead."

Bennis put her coffee down on Chris's other side. "I don't think a homicidal maniac is what we have to worry about." She turned to Myra. "That's what we were talking about. We were trying to get a hold on what was going on here."

"You really don't think Emma committed suicide?" Myra said.

"No," Bennis said. "I don't. And Gregor Demarkian doesn't, either."

"I think that's just sentimentality," Anne Marie said. "You liked Emma. You think suicide is a terrible thing. You're just trying to make it easier on yourself, emotionally."

"I think she feels guilty," Teddy said. "Emma wrote her that letter, and she didn't do enough about it right away, and she thinks that if she had Emma wouldn't have committed suicide at all."

"Don't psychoanalyze," Anne Marie said.

Myra took out the pack of cigarettes she had borrowed from Bennis, got a cigarette, and lit up. "No matter what the police think, a suicide makes sense. After all, Emma tried to kill Daddy once before—"

"Did she?" Bennis said.

Myra was surprised. "Well, of course she did. Who else could it have been? I know I didn't do it. And the boys weren't even there."

"The boys could have been there," Bennis said. "It's not like they have iron-clad alibis, or whatever they'd have to have."

"Alibis?"

"I know what this is," Teddy said. "Demarkian again. Alibis, for Christ's sake."

"That's what they called them," Bennis said, "last time I checked."

Anne Marie stirred uneasily in her chair. "I don't think we should talk like this. If it wasn't Emma—if somebody else killed Daddy and then somebody killed Emma—I don't think—isn't that what happens in books? Someone starts nosing around and finds out too much, and the next thing you know he's dead."

Myra tapped impatiently against the side of her coffee cup. If she wasn't careful, she really would break that nail. Honestly, Anne Marie was such a dork. "This isn't a book. In real life, people don't go around killing other people just because they know too much, or just because they suspect something, or whatever. In real life, people kill for money."

"Money," Anne Marie said. "Nobody killed Daddy for money."

Myra could think of at least one person who could have killed Daddy for money, but she didn't want to bring that up right now. It wouldn't explain Emma's dying, anyway. As to what would—she looked down at her coffee and pushed it away from her.

She was being silly. After this debacle with Bobby, she had a good idea just how competent her family was at making and executing plots. She had a fair idea how most of the world was, at that. That was why she could never get behind conspiracy theories. Most people were much too stupid, and much too shortsighted, to work their way through the long haul. And for what she'd been thinking to be true, somebody would have had to be working a very long haul indeed.

Still.

She picked up her coffee cup, took it back to the sideboard, and poured the coffee in it into the utility urn. Then she poured herself another cup and went back to her place at the table.

"Was there something wrong with the coffee?" Anne Marie said.

"I put too much sugar in it." She hadn't put any sugar in it at all. She thought Anne Marie probably knew that. She could see Bennis did. She reached for the sugar bowl and carefully poured half a teaspoon into this cup, just to cover herself. "Are you sure you didn't take that first note?" she said to Bennis.

"Of course I'm sure," Bennis said.

"What about you?" This to Anne Marie.

Anne Marie flushed. "I didn't take anything. I got out of the room as fast as I could. There was vomit on the floor and the place stank."

"Well," Myra said, "there's probably a simple explanation for it. Maybe Emma didn't leave a note. Maybe the one they found in Bobby's wastebasket was on the floor somewhere, and a maid picked it up and threw it out without ever knowing what it was."

"That's a thought," Teddy said.

"It's a dumb one," Bennis said.

Myra shrugged. "Look at it this way. If Emma didn't kill Daddy and then kill herself, this is just like *Alice in Wonderland*. One of us has to be crazy as a loon."

"Maybe Mrs. Washington's crazy as a loon," Teddy said. "I'd opt for Marshall, but I can't see how he'd get to the hot chocolate. Mrs. Washington is always hanging around the food."

Myra sighed. The rest of them were taking him seriously and getting all worked up. She knew there was no reason to take any of them seriously. As to what she'd been thinking before . . .

She looked back into her cup. Nonsense, really. Total nonsense. It would take too much intelligence, too much planning, and too much nerve. Daddy was the only one of them who had ever had all of that.

Besides, she had nothing to worry about. She'd poured this coffee herself. She knew with absolute certainty that no one had had a chance to doctor it.

It was 8:32.

At 9:35, Bobby Hannaford, white with cold and fear, walked into a Mercedes dealership off Route 9 outside Wayne. He had his car parked at the curb, and his briefcase locked inside the trunk of the car. The briefcase was full of money. His meeting with McAdam had not gone the way he'd expected it to. An out, that was what he'd been looking for. Instead, he seemed to have found a way further in, and he didn't even know how. The briefcase had at least $50,000 in it. He didn't want anything to do with it.

The main building of the dealership was a huge concrete block warehouse with a facade wall of plate glass windows. Through them, Bobby could see SEs and SLs and SELs of every possible color and description, including one exactly the make, model, and color of his own. The similarities should have been exact, because Bobby had bought his car only four months before, at the beginning of the new product year. He had settled on a maroony red-purple. It wasn't red enough to raise his insurance rates, but it wasn't really any other color. He stopped at the main doors and looked back at it, rapidly being hidden under a fresh fall of heavy snow. The weather was god-awful.

He went inside, looked around, and found a saleswoman at the back. She was dressed like an international banker. She looked like she was going to be just as hard to convince. He told himself she was in business to sell cars and went up to the counter anyway. Even international bankers got talked into nonsense sometimes. Look at all the bad loans they'd made to South America.

"Excuse me," he said. "There's a car over there, a sort of maroon car? I'd like to buy it. I'd like to pay for it by check and drive it off the lot today."

EIGHT

1 At 10:22, Bennis Hannaford took a telephone call in the kitchen. She had spent the last twenty minutes in there, getting Gregor Demarkian supplied with coffee, cookies, and rolls and delivering an endless monologue on just how awful her morning had been. She had been talking too much, because Gregor always made her nervous. He seemed to see so much, and say so little. Fortunately, Mrs. Washington had finished the mix-and-match part of her baking early. By the time the dining room had been cleared at nine, the kitchen had been more or less clean and ready for an onslaught of leftover food and dirty dishes. At ten, when Bennis brought Gregor in, there was nothing to be seen but dough molded into bread pans on the counter next to the stove and piles of hot fresh rolls in wicker baskets on the table. The wicker baskets were lined with linen napkins, red and green in honor of the season. The crèche on the other side of the room had been supplied with an infant Jesus, too. Murders or no murders, Mrs. Washington wasn't about to lose her grip on Christmas.

Bennis almost felt as if she were regaining her grip on Christmas. Emma was still at the back of her mind, and maybe always would be, but being around Gregor sometimes made her feel better. She wished she could be less ambivalent about him. He was, she thought, a very solid man. There was something about him that was steady, like a well-built house, something she had never come across in any other human being. Not even Michael. She pushed Michael into the well where she had trapped Emma and concentrated on finding the butter dish in the puzzle that was the "everyday" refrigerator. Her call to Michael this morning had been even worse than the one yesterday, which had been worse than the one the day before that. Their relationship was disintegrating rapidly. Bennis thought she knew why that was. In the first place, up-and-coming assistant DAs didn't like being intimately connected with the suspects in a highly visible murder investigation—and the murders at Engine House were certainly highly visible. Bennis had caught a good two minutes of them on last night's eleven o'clock news. In the second place, she wasn't in Boston to tell him what a creep he was. Sometimes Michael needed to be reminded of the most commonplace things, like whether or not he was living up to the code of behavior he kept trying to impose on everybody else.

She had just gotten to the part where Myra was sitting at breakfast, insisting people only murdered other people for money, when the phone rang. She picked it up, expecting it to be her bank, saying the money she had asked to have transferred from her money market account to her checking account had come through. Instead, she got a high-pitched, whining litany of complaint that made her grit her teeth. In the middle of it, she put her hand over the mouthpiece and told Gregor,

"It's Dickie. Doing his usual thing."

"Dickie?" Gregor said.

"Dickie Van Damm. Myra's husband." She took her hand off the mouthpiece. "Dickie? This is Bennis, not Myra. . . . Yes, I thought you knew. . . . Well, it doesn't do any good telling me, does it? Why don't I go get . . . yes, of course she's awake, she was at breakfast. . . . Yes, I understand your mother's very ill. . . . Yes . . . but . . . I sympathize with you about the publicity, I really do. . . . I don't think that's likely, Dickie.

. . . No . . . no . . . I know we're in the middle of another blizzard. . . . Yes . . . yes . . . why don't I just go get Myra and you can tell her yourself?"

She put the receiver down on the table and motioned Gregor to follow her, out of the kitchen and into the hall. When the kitchen door swung closed behind them, she rolled her eyes.

"He's always like that," she said. "He thinks there's nobody in the universe but the Van Damms, and he's such a bore he never has anybody to talk to, so when he gets you on the phone he refuses to shut up."

"I'm surprised your sister stays married to him," Gregor said.

"He's got a lot of money. And it's like I told you the other day. The Van Damms are very, very, very old Main Line."

Bennis led him down the hall into the living room. "Myra will be in the television room, listening to soap operas," she said.

"I don't think there are soap operas on this early in the morning," Gregor said.

Bennis smiled. "Myra won't be listening to today's soap operas, she'll be listening to yesterday's. On tape. Soap operas are on at the wrong time of day for Myra."

She opened the door on the other side of the living room, ushered Gregor into another hall, and snaked around him so she could lead. "This is where Anne Marie went, to get the drinks tray, that first night you were here. If you go through that door," she pointed to a large mahogany swing on their right, "you end up in a small butler's pantry. One of four. My great-grandfather was a flaming alcoholic."

She came to the end of the hall, opened the door there, and entered another hall. The hall they had just come through was visibly a service space. This was just as visibly a family one. The runner rug was custom cut and thick. The walls were hung with cloth instead of paper. Bennis was so unused to wallpaper, she still couldn't make herself live with it, even after all these years away from Engine House. On her walls at home, she had paint.

She stopped in front of the last door on the left and listened. "There," she said. "Can't you hear it? *Days of Our Lives.*"

"I can hear it," Gregor said.

Bennis opened the door, walked in, and stopped. She stopped so quickly, Gregor Demarkian plowed into the back of her, nearly tipping her over.

Days of Our Lives was playing on the television, casting its strained portents of Sturm und Drang throughout the room.

It didn't need to. The television room had enough Sturm und Drang of its own.

Gregor grabbed her by the shoulders. She could feel him pushing her toward the door.

"Get out of here," he was saying. "Get out of this room *now.*"

But she couldn't get out, she really couldn't. She had to look at it and look at it, just to make sure it was there.

Myra's body, lying on the floor, her face battered out of shape into gore. Myra's big shiny-tin ball brooch, smeared so thickly with blood it looked like it had been painted red.

At Myra's feet, a heavy cylinder of metal winked and glittered, in the thousands of tiny places where it hadn't been smeared.

One of great-grandmother Eleanor's Georgian silver candlesticks from the upstairs hall.

PART FOUR

WEDNESDAY, DECEMBER 28

THE SOLUTION

ONE

1 If there was one thing Gregor Demarkian understood, it was what to do when he was first at the scene of the crime. He could go through that drill on automatic pilot, and he did. God only knew he couldn't have done it any other way. His mind was caught in the vision of the television room and the mistakes he had made that had allowed this murder to happen. Mistakes. God, how he hated mistakes. That was why he had walked off that last case of his. It wasn't just that Elizabeth had been dying and he'd wanted to concentrate his energies on her. Both of those things were true, but there had been something else. He had been distracted. And, in his distraction, he had started to make mistakes. That was the last thing you wanted to do when faced with a man who was murdering five-year-old boys.

Women.

Gregor shut it out of his mind. Now was not the time. He had to figure out where he'd gone wrong, in this place, with these people. His fundamental discovery was not a mistake. He was convinced of that. Too much—the evidence of the money, the evidence of the notes, the evidence of the book in Emma Hannaford's room—pointed in that direction. But somewhere along the line, he had made an error. If he hadn't, Myra Hannaford's face wouldn't have been smashed. There would have been nothing about the death that pointed to murder.

The whole thing was making him distinctly jumpy. The only way he could make sense of this particular murder was to assume there was going to be another. That was bad enough, that was god-awful, but he kept getting stuck on the why. He knew what had happened. He even had a guess—and only a guess—as to who had made it happen. But a motive for this mess was beyond him.

Now he stood in the foyer, watching John Henry Newman Jackman getting out of an unmarked car in front of Engine House. Gregor hadn't thought about it before, but he found Jackman's personal response to this case very odd. He'd known cops who were intense, and cops who were scared, and cops who didn't give a damn. Jackman was none of those things. He seemed to be operating on another plane altogether. Gregor had seen him exasperated, puzzled, annoyed, and impatient. He had never seen him angry, shocked, or appalled. Maybe Jackman found it hard to accept people like the Hannafords as real. Gregor had had that problem himself the first time he'd been forced to deal with someone who didn't have to work for a living.

Outside, the snow was falling with all the force of hurricane rain. They were in for a world-class blizzard. Even moving swiftly, Jackman couldn't avoid snow piling up on his shoulders and coating his chest. Every once in a while it hit him in the face, and he blanched.

Gregor moved away from the foyer windows and opened the front doors. He'd had as much of servants as he could take in one day. Every time he turned around there was someone there, in uniform, looking studiously blank. And then there was Anne Marie. She drifted through the house, an omnipresent spirit. He didn't like it. Lida Arkmanian knew everything there was to know about her cleaning lady: name, age, marital status, and medical history. Gregor Demarkian thought Anne Marie Hannaford knew no more about her maids than what she had to pay them.

The wind was blowing straight at his face, getting snow all over his suit and the foyer floor, so he stood back a little. Jackman came across the terrace to him, shivering.

"Christ," Jackman said, "can't these people ever have a murder in good weather?"

Gregor raised his eyebrows, but Jackman didn't see him do it. He was too busy looking at the chandelier.

"I read a murder mystery once where someone got killed with one of those," Jackman said. "It was held up with a chain and the chain had been cut through, and just at the right moment—"

"Do you think that's really possible?" Gregor said.

"Hell, no. But things don't have to be possible in murder mysteries. They just have to be weird."

The terrace was electrically heated, but the snow was coming down so fast it didn't matter much. The uniforms and lab men coming up behind Jackman were plowing through minor drifts. Jackman stepped aside to give them room to enter. They stopped, each and every one of them, to wipe their feet on the mat.

"I think you ought to give me a minute," Jackman said to a tall man in an overcoat so outsize it would have made him look like a Skid Row bum if it hadn't been so new. "I want to get a look at the scene before you guys mess it up."

The tall man shrugged. "Anything you say. You take long enough, we'll be stuck here for the night. Or maybe the week."

Jackman turned back to Gregor. "This is what it's like out here. They worry about the weather. They worry about their clothes. They don't worry about anything important. Which one was it?"

Gregor hadn't been able to get through to Jackman directly when he called, but he had left a very detailed message. He found it hard to believe Jackman hadn't gotten it in full.

He said, "It's Mrs. Van Damm. Myra Hannaford Van Damm. And it's more like the first one than the second one."

"What do you mean, more like the first one?"

"Debris," Gregor said. "Stage sets. Props. A lot of nonsense strewn all over the landscape."

"To make it look like murder?" Jackman was interested.

"I think at this point, whoever it is knows we're going to know it's murder," Gregor said. "The impression I got was that there was a lot of care being taken to give us clues about motive, say, and suspects. You'll have to see the body, John."

"I'm going to see the body. Where are the Hannafords?"

"Cordelia Day Hannaford is in her room. Anne Marie Hannaford is with her. Bennis and Christopher are in what they like to call the 'living room.' It's got a tree worthy of Rockefeller Center in the middle of it. Teddy was asleep, last I heard. I don't know where Bobby is. Bennis told me he'd left for work early this morning."

Jackman frowned. "I don't think we should leave them wandering around the house like this. On their own. Where's the body?"

"In a room called the television room. It's at the back of the house, down a little hall. It's not on a main thoroughfare."

"Still," Jackman said.

Gregor smiled. "They could be running in and out of the scene, messing up everything, is that it? I say let them."

"What?"

"Let them," Gregor said. "Come on, Mr. Jackman. There are a few things I'd like to show you."

Jackman started to look mutinous. Gregor turned his back on him and walked away.

He must, he thought, be feeling better. A week ago, Jackman's attitude would have made him depressed. Now, it made him want to break the idiot's neck.

2

Gregor could have worked up a police seal for the television room. A tape, some string—there were a hundred ways to do it. He hadn't used any of them. It was like he'd told Jackman when they'd found the seals broken on Robert Hannaford's study. In a situation like this, you had two choices. You could post a man outside the door. Or you could accept the fact that the seals were going to be broken eventually. That was it. Because Gregor hadn't wanted to spend his morning standing outside the writing room door—and because he didn't see any point to sealing the scene anyway—he'd let it go. The only thing the Hannafords could do to really ruin things was take the body away and dispose of it. Anybody who tried that would get caught at it.

He led the whole crowd of them through the three back halls that were the only route he knew of, feeling all the time like a character in that Shirley Jackson novel about Hill House. You needed a map to find your way to the bathroom in this place, or maybe bread crumbs. Every time he moved around by himself he worried about getting lost. He was a little proud of himself for not, this time. He'd only been back here once before.

He found the door of the writing room, and opened up to look inside.

She was still there, exactly where he had left her, stretched out across the floor like a damaged carpet. Gregor went in and held the door open for John Jackman. Jackman stepped in, looked at Myra Van Damm's face, and winced.

"Ouch," he said.

"Not as much of an ouch as it could have been," Gregor pointed out. "Look at her."

Jackman looked. It was his job to look. He just didn't like it.

"The face got worked over after she was dead," he said finally. "There's not enough blood."

"Not enough blood and not the right kind of blood," Gregor said. "It's all flecks, no wash. Look at the candlestick."

"Is that what was used to work her over?"

Gregor shook his head. "There's not enough blood on that, either. It looks gory, but then you realize it's too dry. If that had been used on her face, even after she was dead, there would be blood and flesh all over it. All it's got is that little stain on the felt at the base and some clotted matter in one of the crevices. It was used later, after the real work had been done. Just rolled around in the muck to get it dirty."

"Ouch," Jackman said again. He crossed the room and knelt down next to Myra Van Damm's body, getting much closer than Gregor had allowed himself to. Gregor hadn't wanted to disturb anything. Jackman leaned forward as far as he could and searched Myra's face. Gregor could see Jackman liked this even less than he'd liked looking at the body from a distance. He was going a little green around the jawbone.

Jackman stood up, wiped the palms of his hands against his pants as if he'd gotten something on them—which he hadn't—and took a deep breath.

"Poker," he said. "I'd almost bet my career on it."

"I was thinking poker myself," Gregor admitted. "The problem is, the pokers are over there," he pointed to a cast-iron stand beside the fireplace, "and they're all clean."

"Someone could have used a poker and taken it away," Jackman said.

"I'm sure they could have. How would we know?"

"What do you mean, how would we know?"

Gregor sighed. "John, this house has what? Forty rooms? Fifty? Every one I've been in has had a fireplace, including the bedrooms and the kitchen. Every one of them has a poker stand full of pokers. There have to be hundreds of pokers in this place. I wouldn't know how to begin to find out if one of them were missing. And if whoever did this was smart enough to wash what he used immediately—"

"Washing won't do it," Jackman said sharply. "There are tests. It's almost impossible to get blood off a surface entirely."

"Fine, John. Which surface? Do you want to test a couple of hundred pokers for bloodstains?"

"If I have to."

"Then do it," Gregor said. "In the long run, you may even have to. But think about this situation, John. Just think about it. Doesn't anything seem odd to you?"

Jackman had been backing away from the body ever since he'd made the remark about the poker. Now he backed all the way out of the room, taking Gregor with him. The uniforms and lab men were crowding the hall. Jackman nodded to the tall man in the too-large overcoat, and they surged inside, ready to do all the technical things they were paid to do.

Jackman looked over the hall, pausing briefly on the runner carpet, the paintings, the ceiling. Gregor didn't blame him. This was a back hall, a secondary part of the house, and it would have cost three or four times Jackman's salary to buy the things that furnished it. Then there were the Christmas decorations. Jackman seemed especially taken with those. Red velvet ribbons and little silver bells. In this house, at this time, they had the effect of a casket dressed up as a birthday cake.

There was a bench under one of the paintings on the far wall. Jackman sat down on it and stretched his legs.

"Gregor," he said, "everything about this situation is weird. I was talking it over with my wife last night, and she put her finger on it exactly. It's like something out of a Hercule Poirot novel. Do you read Hercule Poirot novels?"

"No," Gregor said. "I probably ought to. *The Inquirer* called me an 'Armenian-American Hercule Poirot.' "

"You're too fat," Jackman said, "and you don't have face hair. Seriously. A murderer who wants me to know he's committed a murder. Suicide notes that appear and disappear and reappear. And now this—"

"A candlestick smeared with blood to make it look like it was used to batter a face?"

"Right," Jackman said. "Count on it, that candlestick is going to belong to somebody. The note in Bobby's wastebasket. The candlestick—"

"Do you remember, the day Emma Hannaford died, we had a

discussion about candlesticks?" Gregor said. "In the upstairs hall?"

"Where a pair of them was missing," Jackman said. "Yeah. I suppose you're trying to tell me that's one of them."

"Well, it's antique Georgian. It's old and it's heavy. The pair upstairs are the only candlesticks I know of that are missing. And there's this, too. If you search Christopher Hannaford's room, you'll probably find the other one."

Jackman stared at him. *"Christopher* Hannaford? What would Christopher Hannaford be doing with twelve-thousand-dollar candlesticks?"

There was another bench, next to the writing room door, opposite the one Jackman was sitting on. Gregor's feet hurt and his legs were heavy. He sat down and put his hands on his knees.

"This is just conjecture," he said, "but I think I'm right, and you can check on it. I think that sometime on the day Emma Hannaford was killed, or before, Christopher took that pair of candlesticks and tried to pawn them."

"I thought you said nobody in his right mind would pawn them. Christopher Hannaford may be a long-haired weirdo, but he isn't that kind of nuts."

"I said no one who knew anything about silver would try to pawn them," Gregor said. "That includes most of the servants. The butler would have instructed anyone who worked here in what was valuable and what was not, to make sure they didn't damage anything important. It includes most of the family, too. Cordelia Day would have taught her daughters about those things. Upper-class mothers do. Bobby would have known because Bobby makes it a point to know about *things*. That leaves Teddy and Chris."

"Why not pick on Teddy?" Jackman grinned. "I'd like to pick on Teddy. Man makes my teeth grind."

"Teddy was in the house all day the day Emma Hannaford died, for one thing," Gregor said, "or around the house, anyway. I know, I know. The candlesticks might have been stolen earlier. But look at the two of them. Teddy Hannaford seems to be scrambling a little, and he's definitely worried about something. Christopher Hannaford is in desperate need of money."

Jackman's head came up quickly. "Did you check that out? The information you got us on Bobby Hannaford was wonderful. Does the FBI know something—"

"No, no. You can see it, that's all. A certain kind of rich person dresses poor these days, but Chris Hannaford's clothes are worn to shreds. He stopped taking care of himself in the most fundamental ways. He doesn't eat. He doesn't sleep. I don't think he's brushed his hair in weeks."

"That could be dope."

"I don't think Christopher Hannaford takes serious drugs," Gregor said. "The indications aren't there. He isn't jumpy and paranoid. That rules out cocaine. He's not glazed over and he's not shaking. That rules out heroin. The psychedelics aren't addictive, just bad for you. Maybe he smokes a little marijuana. He has the smell clinging to him."

"But if he isn't taking dope, what would he need money for?" Jackman asked. "He's got a regular job. It doesn't pay Lee Iacocca's salary, but it does pay a living wage. And he's got that trust fund. That pays just about a living wage, too. What would he need money for?"

"I don't know."

"But you definitely think he needs it," Jackman said.

Gregor nodded. "I think he took the candlesticks to pawn. I think he found no pawnbroker would take them. I think he brought them back and left them in his room."

"Why didn't he put them back in the hallway?"

Gregor shrugged. "Lethargy. Fear. Lack of opportunity. Who knows? That young man is not thinking straight. But if I'm right about all this, that," Gregor jerked his head toward the writing room door, "makes a lot more sense than it might."

"I'm glad it makes sense to you," Jackman said. "I'm beginning to think we have an upper-class Charlie Manson on our hands."

"If we had an upper-class Charlie Manson, we'd have a lot less of this kind of strangeness and a lot more of the messy kind. If there's one thing I've learned about psychopathic serial killers, it's that they love rituals. And there's nothing ritualized about this. The murders have been planned, John, but the settings haven't been."

"The settings," Jackman repeated.

Gregor stood up, restless. "Always, always, the murderer is using whatever is at hand. The Demerol. It's all over this house. There's a stock of it in almost every medicine cabinet. The death of Robert Hannaford. The statue was in the study. The murderer didn't bring in something to crush his head with. The death of Emma Hannaford. The second note was in Bennis Hannaford's handbag. The murderer didn't write a new one."

"What about the first note?"

"I don't know yet, but I think we'll find it had been left around the house, too. Assuming it wasn't a real suicide note."

Jackman rubbed his jaw. "I was thinking about something, last night after you called me about Hannaford Financial. We keep forgetting about that book we found in Emma Hannaford's room. *The Predator's Ball*."

"I haven't forgotten about it," Gregor said.

"It's about the junk bond business. Ivan Boesky and Dennis Levine and all those people. Insider trading. I was thinking Robert Hannaford might have been killed because he'd found out what Bobby was up to at Hannaford Financial, and Emma Hannaford might have been killed because reading this book had given her ideas—"

"John, whatever the reason for those murders, they have nothing to do with Hannaford Financial."

"Why not?" Jackman said. "It fits, doesn't it? The mess at Hannaford Financial is the best motive we've got, for Christ's sake. And there doesn't seem to be any other motive. Cordelia Day Hannaford gets the insurance, but she's in no shape to go running around this house dropping statues on people."

"What about the death of Mrs. Van Damm?"

"I say we go looking for a link with Hannaford Financial," Jackman said. "I'll say we'll find one."

"Maybe you will," Gregor said, "but if you do you have *another* problem. At least theoretically, Bobby Hannaford wasn't here when this was done to Mrs. Van Damm."

"The theoretical isn't the actual," Jackman said. "You told me that when I was twenty-two years old."

"I'm glad you remembered it. But John, if Bobby Hannaford did this, he'd have had to get into the house and stay in it for over an hour without anyone seeing him. It took that long for the Demerol to kill Myra Van Damm."

"Maybe Bobby fed it to her early this morning, before he left for 'work.' "

"And came back," Gregor pointed out, "and got in unnoticed —remember the guard at the gate. There'll be a record, and there's no way to sneak onto this property. That was the first thing you checked out. If Bobby left, there will be a record. If he came back, there will be a record. If he was in the house, he had to get around, use a poker on Mrs. Van Damm, hide the poker or wash it or whatever, get the candlestick out of Christopher's room—"

"Assuming that's where it was."

"Assuming that's where it was," Gregor agreed. "But my objection stands. This house is full of servants. It's better staffed than a hotel. Somebody would have seen him."

"Crap," Jackman said. He slumped. "Now what are we going to do? I can't buy hate as a motive in this case. To kill three people out of hate you have to be certifiable. And besides—"

"You don't think people kill other people out of hate?" Gregor smiled. "I don't either. At least, I don't think they kill in this way."

"Right. Pick up a poker and bash somebody's head in in a fit of pique, that's hate. Run around exchanging suicide notes, that's premeditation. And premeditation means a practical motive."

"Which we don't have." Gregor stopped pacing and leaned against the wall. "I'll tell you what we do have. Three people dead. Three very particular people dead. And three people involved in attempted frames."

"This is not news, Gregor."

"I know it's not. But it's the answer, John. It came to me as soon as I saw her in there. It can't be Hannaford Financial, because everything possible has been done to point us to Hannaford Financial. It's what we're being pointed away from that we have to consider."

"Gregor, there isn't anything we're being pointed away from. There isn't anything to be pointed away from. There's just Hannaford Financial."

"There is something," Gregor said. "And not only is there something, but it's got to be something so obvious we're going to kill ourselves when we find it. That's the only way all this trash makes sense. There's only one reason for strewing all these clues around the landscape, and that's to make sure we don't see what would otherwise be all too easy for us to see."

"Crap," Jackman said.

Gregor looked up at the hallway wall, to the picture niche where a Braque etching had been decorated, beyond all reason, with a cluster of Hannaford family ornaments. A cherub, a bell, a ball, an angel. Tin. Gregor sighed.

"That's the only thing that doesn't fit," he said. "That's the only thing that must be a mistake. That piece of tin on the floor of Robert Hannaford's study. I wish it had been smaller. Then it could have been one of these decorations."

"Well, it wasn't smaller," Jackman said. "And it probably was a decoration. The damn things are everywhere."

"I know."

Down at the end of the hall, a door opened. Gregor and Jackman raised their heads together, to see Anne Marie Hannaford walking slowly toward them, looking shaken and angry at once. Gregor knew all about the mood she was in. She was frightened at what was going on in her house and angry because it had been going on long enough so that she could no longer count on what they would do. Gregor didn't blame her. If he was right—and he was right; Jackman's skepticism notwithstanding—there would have to be another death in this house.

Anne Marie covered half the distance to them and stopped, reluctant to come any closer.

"Excuse me," she said. "Mr. Demarkian? My mother—my mother would like to see you."

TWO

1 Gregor spent more time thinking about Cordelia Day Hannaford than anyone else in this case, but he didn't like to. That was inevitable, given Elizabeth, but it had a few kicks to it he wouldn't have expected. Until he had seen her that first time, on the night Robert Hannaford died, Gregor hadn't thought he was a numb man. If he felt less than he used to, it was because he had less to feel. All the drama and emotion of a protracted dying: it was like living through a monsoon season. When the season was over, normal weather was bound to feel like no weather at all.

Then he had walked into the living room. Gregor could still see that: Cordelia in her chair, her dress covered with blood and her head held steady by act of will; the rest of them stretched out around her, like dangerous kittens protecting a mother cat. Gregor had felt made of eggshell, irreparably cracked. It was silly to tell himself that seeing her had "changed everything." It hadn't. It had simply changed him back.

Now he stood in front of Cordelia's door, as reluctant to go in as Anne Marie was to let him in. If Anne Marie had her way, Gregor thought, he'd be packed up and sent back to Philadelphia without another word.

Because she couldn't do that—sick or not, Cordelia Day got what she wanted from her daughters—Anne Marie made do with standing directly in front of the door, crossing her arms across her chest, and glaring. It didn't quite come off. Anne Marie was a very shaky young woman at the moment. She twitched.

"My mother," she said, "is a very sick woman. And she's very tired."

Gregor hesitated. It was always hard to know what to say to someone who was overstating the obvious.

"I'm not forcing myself on your mother," he pointed out. "You said she asked for me."

"She did ask for you."

"So?"

Anne Marie wrapped her arms more tightly around herself, making herself look less angry than cold. "She doesn't like to believe she's sick. She never has. That's why we've almost never had a professional nurse in the house, why it's always been me. If it's me, she can pretend it isn't real."

"I don't think she pretends it isn't real, Miss Hannaford."

"She pretends it makes no difference. She's been knocking herself out on charities for years. Visiting. Chairing meetings. Going to parties. And then coming home to collapse."

"And then you had to take care of her."

"I don't mind taking care of her," Anne Marie said. "I mind her trying to kill herself. Nobody wants to keep her alive more than me."

Gregor nodded. He thought that might be literally true. Anne Marie probably wanted to keep Cordelia alive more than Cordelia wanted to stay alive.

"I don't want you to go in there and upset her," Anne Marie said. "She was better than she was. Now she's looking worse. Up and down, up and down. This morning—"

"Yes?"

"Last night she was much better. Then this morning when I

came in to bring her her tea, she was worse again. Much worse. I could see it. And now—"

"Now?"

"I should have called the doctor," Anne Marie said. "That's what I'm supposed to do. But he's no help and I'm sick and tired of him, and I know what's going on. I know it."

"What is going on?"

"She isn't going to last past New Year's." Anne Marie looked away, up the hall, even though there wasn't anyone there. "I'd like her to last to New Year's. I'd like it very much if you didn't upset her."

"I'll try not to."

Anne Marie stepped away from the door. "She thinks she wants to know all about it," she said bitterly. "All about the murders and the investigation. She wants to take an interest. It's going to kill her."

"Miss Hannaford—"

Anne Marie shook her head. "Never mind. She'll do what she wants to do. She always does. You wouldn't know it to look at her, but she was a great beauty once. One of the most beautiful women in Philadelphia. And Myra was always asking me why I didn't take care of myself."

She stepped around him and began backing away. "Go on in. Just be careful. One death in the house a day is all I can stand."

She turned around and went pumping off toward the doors to the balcony, a fat woman who seemed to get fatter as he watched her walk.

Gregor didn't blame her for not "taking care" of herself. Under the circumstances, he couldn't have put much energy into it himself.

Anne Marie had said her mother was "much worse." Going into Cordelia's room, Gregor expected to see a woman in a state of total collapse. That was the only thing he could think of that would be "much worse" than the last time he had seen her. It wasn't like that. Cordelia was sitting in a wide wing chair, her legs stretched out on a matching ottoman. Her hair was "dressed," in the old-fashioned meaning of the term: off her neck, and pinned around her head in an intricate pattern, fastened with four tin combs that echoed the decorations in the rest of the house: an angel, a cherub, a ball and a bell. Her nails were done and her makeup was on. Her body was covered from neck to ankles in a bright brocaded house dress. The house dress had Christmas trees and Santa Clauses on it, an expensive version of old George Telkamanian's reindeer socks.

Gregor walked across the room to her and took the empty chair beside her, watching her watch him. Her eyes moved quickly, but her head didn't move at all. Suddenly, Gregor realized she was much worse. She looked better, but with her disease what she looked like didn't mean anything. On the night of her husband's death, she had been able to move her head and talk clearly in almost-sentences. Now her head seemed fixed, and Gregor knew sentences were too much to hope for.

He leaned forward. He didn't know if multiple sclerosis affected the hearing, but he didn't want to take any chances. "Mrs. Hannaford," he said, "I know you sent for me, but if you're not feeling up to it—"

"Stay."

It was one word, but it was clear enough. Gregor relaxed a

little. "I'm very happy to stay. I know this must be frightening for you. If I can do anything at all to help you—"

Cordelia's head jerked, back and forth. The movement was so swift and violent, Gregor thought at first it had been involuntary. It wasn't. Cordelia was shaking her head no.

She closed her eyes and sat very still. She sat that way for a long time, second after second going by with no sound in the room but her labored breathing. Then she sucked in as much breath as she could, stiffened her arms against the arms of her chair, and said,

"Help—*you.*"

"You want to help me?" Gregor said. "Do you mean you want to help the police? Because of the—the deaths?"

There really wasn't anything wrong with Cordelia's eyes. She shot him a look as imperious as that of any able-bodied duchess.

"Murder," she said.

Gregor nodded an apology, embarrassed. After Elizabeth, he should have known better. Especially because this woman reminded him so much of Elizabeth.

"That's right," he told her, "murder. Three murders, to be exact."

"Yessss."

"If you think you know something that will help, I'll be glad to hear it. We'll all be glad to hear it. Your children are very disturbed."

Cordelia seemed to smile, although it was hard to tell for sure. She didn't have much control of the muscles around her mouth. She let her beautiful eyes wander around the room and then stop.

"Table," she said.

Gregor followed her gaze. This was a sitting room, not a bed-room—Cordelia had a suite—but on the other side of it, under a window, was a writing table much like the one in Emma's room. Its surface was clean and polished, its drawers were tightly shut. It looked as if it hadn't been used in decades.

"Draw-er," Cordelia said.

"There's something in the writing table drawer?"

"Yessss."

"All right."

Gregor got up and went over to it, shivering a little in the draft from the window above it. It had four drawers, one in the center under the writing surface and three down the side, like a desk—but no one in his right mind would have called it a desk. It didn't look like one. Gregor opened the center drawer first, because it seemed the easiest one to get to. It was empty.

He tried the first of the smaller drawers on the side, but it was empty, too. He tried the center one. Empty. He looked at the one on the bottom and then up at Cordelia, questioning.

"Yessss," she said.

Gregor tried not to wonder how she'd managed to get what-ever it was into that bottom drawer, in her condition. Anne Marie could have put it there for her—but if Anne Marie had, it would make more sense for Cordelia to get Anne Marie to bring it to him. He opened the drawer. Inside, there was a small brown accordion folder and a manila file. He took them out.

"A folder and a file," he said. "Which one?"

"Both."

Both. Gregor shut the drawer and went back to his chair. Cordelia had lost much of her anxiousness. She was still watching him, but without the urgency she'd brought to it when he first came into the room. Whatever she wanted to tell him must be substantially contained in what he now had.

The manila file was flat, the accordion folder thick. Gregor thought the file would take less time to get through. He wedged the folder between his leg and the chair to get it out of the way.

The file was full of small blue sheets of note paper, the kind supplied to all the writing tables at Engine House, each scribbled over in dark blue ink. He picked up the first one and read:

Dear Bennis: I keep starting this letter and starting this letter, and just not knowing how to go on.

That was it. He dropped it back into the file and looked up at Cordelia. She seemed to be trying to smile again.

"Emma," she said.

"Emma wrote these?"

"Yessss." She thought about it. "False—starts," she said.

"False starts." Gregor looked at the note again. "False starts of suicide notes?"

"No."

"Of letters to Bennis? About something else?"

"Yes." This time she made an effort, and bit off the "s" before it could become a hiss.

Gregor nodded. "You're saying the first suicide note wasn't a suicide note at all. It came from this file."

"Yesss." The attempt at control didn't work.

"Was this file here, in your room, the day Emma died?"

"Yessss."

"Was the note we found in the file then?"

Cordelia closed her eyes. "Don't—know."

"No," Gregor said, "I don't suppose you would. You must sleep a great deal."

"Yesss." She smiled her smile again. *"Em*ma," she said. "Sick."

Gregor was startled. "Emma was sick?"

"This," Cordelia said. The urgency was back in her voice. *"This."*

Gregor blinked. "Emma had what you have? She had multiple sclerosis?"

"Yesss. Check—au—au—"

"We should check the autopsy?"

"Yesss."

"Mrs. Hannaford, are you trying to say Emma did commit suicide? Because she knew she was sick?"

"No. No. Didn't—did *not*—know—"

"Emma didn't know she was sick," Gregor said. "But you knew."

"Yesss. May-be."

"Meaning you don't know if she knew or not."

"Yesss. Not—not—"

"Not suicide," Gregor said.

"Not." Cordelia closed her eyes again.

Gregor stood up, agitated. This was getting worse and worse by the second, and what it made him think of was worse still.

"Mrs. Hannaford," he said, "do you know who's committing these murders? Do you know for sure?"

She opened her eyes and stared at him. She had very blue eyes, big and widely spaced. Her mouth worked and worked, and finally produced a real smile. It was a smile with an infinity of ambiguity in it.

"Yesss," she said.

"Will you tell me who it is?" Gregor said.

"No. My—child."

"You won't say because it's one of your children."

"Yesss."

"Was Emma killed because she knew who had tried to kill your husband the first time?"

Cordelia looked surprised. "Told—you?" she asked.

"Bennis told me," Gregor said.

"No," Cordelia said. It took Gregor a moment to understand she was saying no to his original question, not denying it had been Bennis who told him about the day on the bluff.

Gregor turned away and looked up at the picture over the fireplace mantel, a portrait of Cordelia Day Hannaford when young. Anne Marie was right. Cordelia had been a great beauty. She still was one, when she didn't move. He wished she was anything but sick the way she was. Even if she'd been on her deathbed with cancer, he could have applied a little pressure. She must realize that not only was one of her children committing these crimes, but her other children were dying from them. She must know it made no sense to protect the dangerous one. In fact, Gregor was so convinced of her intelligence, and her stability of mind, he was also convinced she must have a compelling reason for doing what she was doing. He couldn't imagine what it might be.

He couldn't pressure her, either. If he tried, he would get nowhere. She would simply retreat behind her illness, and he would look like a monster. Most people didn't understand the terminally ill. They thought the dying were incompetent at worst and emotionally unstable at best. Even Jackman treated Cordelia as if her brains had melted along with her triceps.

He turned back to her. "Will you tell me why you think Emma was killed?"

Cordelia's eyes were closed again. "Yesss," she said. "Money."

"Money?"

"Mon-ey." The word came out harsh, the best she could do to make it firm.

"That isn't a great deal of help to me," Gregor said gently.

Cordelia seemed to be slipping away from him, drifting into sleep. "Fold-er," she said softly.

Gregor got the folder from the chair. "There's something in the folder?"

"Answer," Cordelia said.

Gregor opened the folder and looked inside. It was thick with newspaper clippings, some old, some new. He pulled them out and thumbed through them. Cordelia and her daughters all dressed up in evening gowns at a charity ball. Cordelia and her daughters all dressed up in velvet party dresses, in a fashion spread from an ancient copy of *Vogue*. Cordelia and her daughters, all dressed up in riding clothes and standing in front of a little clutch of horses. He looked up, confused.

Her gaze was intent again, urgent. "Rob-ert," she said.

"Robert had these? Your husband had them?"

"Yesss. *Emma—Em*—got—"

"Emma got them for you?" Gregor thought of the police seals, broken. "Emma got them for you from the study, after Mr. Hannaford was killed."

"Yesss."

"Why? Why did you want them?"

"An-swer," Cordelia said stubbornly.

"The answer to what?" Gregor asked her.

But it was useless to ask Cordelia anything. In the space of seconds, she had melted away. Her eyes were closed. Her arms were limp. Her skin seemed to have gone slack. He couldn't have brought her back to consciousness from that even if he'd wanted to. He didn't want to.

Gregor got the file and the folder both and tucked them under his arm. He'd go down and give these things to Jackman. Maybe the Greatest American Policeman could make more of them than he could.

He just wished Cordelia Day Hannaford didn't look so dead, when she was only asleep.

THREE

1

This was the third time Bennis Hannaford had seen the police take a body out of Engine House, and she wasn't used to it yet. She was beginning to wonder if anyone ever got used to it, even ambulance men or soldiers in a war, who got to see body bags as a matter of course. She shifted the telephone receiver from her left ear to her right, pulled at the cord—it was snaking back across the hall, into the telephone stall—and wiped fog off the narrow utility window with the flat of her hand. Outside, it was snowing harder than ever. The police cars already looked buried. The ambulance van looked marooned. On the terrace, the bag with Myra's body in it was strapped to a stretcher, and four men instead of two were trying to get it down the steps. Poor, stupid, complicated Myra. Four decades of plots and machinations, and it all came down to this.

She got out a cigarette, lit up, and tapped imaginary ash into the ashtray she'd left on the window sill. Then she said, "Richard, I know seventy-five thousand dollars is a lot of money. I can count, for God's sake. I don't want you to lecture me about it. I want you to wire—"

Richard interrupted—again—and the door at the far end of the hall opened. Bennis tuned Richard out and watched Gregor Demarkian coming toward her. He looked tired, which didn't surprise her. Talking to mother always left her exhausted, no matter how little time she spent doing it. If he'd come straight here from there, he'd been in Mother's room for over an hour. He made hand motions asking if she wanted him to leave her in privacy. She shook her head, and motioned for him to wait.

On the other end of the line, Richard seemed to have run out of breath. Temporarily. Bennis gave it another try.

"What I want you to do," she said, "is wire seventy-five thousand dollars to my account here, from my money market account there. It's not that difficult. You wire me money all the time. When I was out in Texas last year—"

"That was only five thousand dollars," Richard said.

"What does the amount have to do with it? I can't believe your fax machine won't take a five figure transfer—"

"We don't use fax machines, Miss Hannaford. We—"

"I don't care if you use carrier pigeons," Bennis said. "Will you stop all this nonsense and wire that money to me?"

"I just need to ask a few questions."

"Why?"

"It's my responsibility to protect you—"

"Richard." Bennis took a long drag on her cigarette, counted to ten and waited. "Richard," she started again, "I'm not a fuzzy geriatric widow who doesn't know her checkbook from her laundry list. If I need your advice, I'll ask for it."

"An investment that requires a cash delivery of this size—"

"I'm not making an investment, Richard."

"Oh." Pause. "If you're in some kind of trouble—"

"I'm not in any kind of trouble. I'm not being blackmailed and I haven't become secretly addicted to cocaine. I simply want to take available funds from my money market account, where they're supposed to be deposited on a demand basis, and have them transferred to Philadelphia, where I can get at them. I do have seventy-five thousand dollars?"

"Yes," Richard said. "In fact—"

"In fact," Bennis rolled over him, "I have something in excess of three hundred thousand dollars in that account—"

"It's a very irresponsible use of money, Miss Hannaford," Richard said. "If you had reinvested it as I advised you to do last month—"

"Let's not bring last month into it," Bennis said. "Just wire the money, Richard. Wire it now. Because if it isn't in my Philadelphia bank tomorrow morning, I'm going to cause you a hell of a lot of trouble." She started to hang up, realized she was still in the hall, and stalked back to the telephone stall. There, she did hang up, hard.

She came back into the hall to find Gregor Demarkian waiting for her, looking amused. "I thought your friend in Boston was named Michael," he said.

Bennis sighed. "Richard is what's called my 'personal banker.' It's code for 'interfering old snoop.'"

"He's trying to protect you from yourself," Gregor said. "He probably has a dozen women coming into his bank every day, trying to invest in bogus gold mines."

"Just women?"

"Men invest in bogus oil wells," Gregor said.

"All I want to do is lend some money to Chris." Bennis looked out the window again. "There goes the ambulance now. There goes Myra."

They stood together, trying to see through the narrow pane of glass. The ambulance bumped along until it got to the stand of trees, and then disappeared. The rest of the cars stayed where they were, big white lumps, like snow-dusted dinosaur bones. Bennis turned away and leaned against the wall. She didn't want to watch that. It made her flesh creep.

She looked down, saw the cigarette still burning in her hand, picked up the ashtray and put it out. "Were you up with Mother all this time?" she asked. "It must have been difficult."

But Gregor was shaking his head. "I was with your mother about ten minutes. I've been talking to Detective Jackman. And to your brother with the brace. Teddy?"

"Teddy," Bennis confirmed. "Theodore, of course. That must have been almost as difficult as talking to Mother."

"You said you didn't like your brother."

Bennis thought about it. "I don't dislike him," she said, "the way I dislike Anne Marie, say, or Bobby. I don't think he's a bad man. He just—lies."

"Does he?"

"Don't go all detectivey on me," Bennis said. "Of course he lies. You must know that. He's the kind of person who lies about silly things. He says he went to Woodstock, when he didn't. He says he's a full professor when he's only an associate. He tells people we're very close—which I wouldn't mind being, if he didn't resent me so much. He aggrandizes himself."

"Yes," Gregor said, sounding thoughtful. "I got that impression. Did you know he was in danger of being fired from his job?"

"Fired? But how could he be? He has tenure."

"Some things can get you fired even if you have tenure. Plagiarizing from your students, for instance."

"Oh, dear." Bennis winced. "Poor Teddy."

"Poor Teddy?"

Bennis looked into Gregor's flat, impassive face. She'd never realized just how flat and just how impassive it was.

"Of course, poor Teddy," she said. "He's just so—he wants it so badly. Wants to be important. Wants to be someone. If Daddy hadn't done all that with the money—"

"But Teddy got money," Gregor protested.

"Teddy got about twenty-five thousand a year. Maybe less. He should have been a rich man. He'd always expected to be. And being a rich man would have been enough, you know. He'd have joined a lot of committees and made a lot of pompous speeches about the social responsibility of the rich and he'd have been fine. A flaming bore, but fine."

"I think you have a very strange way of looking at things."

Bennis turned away again. "Maybe. I don't like to see people's lives ruined for no good reason whatsoever. And that was Daddy's stock in trade."

"Always," Gregor said, "we come back to your father."

Bennis said "Mmm," and stared at the walls and ceiling of the hall. This was not one of her good days with Gregor. He was making her uncomfortable.

She caught a movement out of the corner of her eye and turned back to him just in time to see him taking a thick accordion file out of his jacket.

"What's that?" she said.

Gregor handed it to her. "Your mother gave it to me. She says it was in your father's study when he died. She had Emma go down and get it out after the police were gone. Open it up and look inside."

Bennis opened it. She pulled out the *Vogue* spread and smiled at her twelve-year-old self. She remembered sitting for that spread. The photographer kept telling them to sit still, and she kept pinching Anne Marie on the ass.

She tried to hand the folder back, but Gregor wouldn't take it.

"I know what's in here," she said. "Mother's pictures. Or copies of the pictures, anyway. When we were children, we used to be photographed together a lot."

"It was your mother's idea?"

"Well, it certainly wasn't mine. I used to hate it. So did Anne Marie. I think Myra enjoyed it after a while. And Emma, of course, was usually too young to know what was going on."

"In the picture you're holding, she's almost an infant."

"About two. I think. I think I was twelve. She was a very sweet looking baby, wasn't she? She was a very sweet person, all her life. I wonder why Daddy had this. It wasn't as if he ever cared."

"I looked through all the photographs in that folder," Gregor said, "and one thing struck me. They're all pictures of your mother and her daughters. There are never any pictures of the boys."

"But there wouldn't be," Bennis said. "There's nothing strange about that. The society pages and the magazines are always doing mother-daughter stories. It's a kind of cliché."

"And that was the only reason? Your mother had nothing—against the boys?"

"The way Daddy had something against his daughters?" Bennis smiled. "No. Mother liked having daughters. Some women get more involved with their sons, but Mother always enjoyed girls. She liked clothes, and she could dress us up. The boys wouldn't have stood for that, and she wouldn't have wanted to—to feminize them, anyway. She paid a little more attention to us than she did to them, mostly to counteract Daddy, I think. He didn't pay any attention to us at all. Unless he was being cruel. I think Mother felt she had to make up to us for the way he was."

"She seems to have a great sense of obligation, your mother."

"Oh," Bennis said. "Yes. An incredible sense of obligation. I don't think she could have been a modern mother, the kind that works. She would have felt she was depriving us of something. And a lot of women in her position just hire nannies and never see their children at all."

"Your mother brought you up herself?"

"Very much herself. But she's the same with people outside the family. Servants, you know, and people who work under her on committees. She's got a very highly developed sense of the relative importance of things."

"But not much faith in the relativity of other things?"

"I don't understand," Bennis said.

Gregor leaned forward, intent. So intent, Bennis found herself wanting to back away. "You said just now your mother wouldn't have been the kind who worked, because she thought she would be depriving you of something. Is she also the kind who believes something like that is binding on her, no matter what else is going on in her life? She wouldn't, for instance, think it all through and try to balance what she wanted with what you wanted? She'd think there were things she should do, whether she wanted to do them or not?"

Light dawned. "I see what you mean," Bennis said. "To tell you the truth, I don't think 'I want' is a big factor in my mother's life. 'I should' is much more important. And she's the kind of woman who always knows what she should do."

"Always?"

"Yes. I think I could say always. I don't know what her marriage was like, Mr. Demarkian. Living with Daddy might have caused a few moral dilemmas. But on the whole, I'd say always."

Gregor nodded. "She's a remarkable personality, your mother. One of the strongest I have ever known."

"You wouldn't be able to say that if you'd met Daddy. It always looked to me like she was scrambling around, trying to repair the damage right after Daddy did it. Like all that business with Teddy and his leg."

"Excuse me?"

"Well," Bennis said, "Teddy's leg was ruined in an automobile accident. You know that. And Daddy was driving. And Daddy was not sympathetic or supportive or any of the rest of that seventies nonsense when it was over. He just turned on Teddy. And Mother has been making it up to Teddy ever since."

"Teddy," Gregor said. He frowned and seemed to sink into thought. Bennis stared at him curiously. He was—different, now that Myra was dead. She couldn't put her finger on how, or why, but there it was. She looked around the hall again and wondered if she should be doing something polite. No matter how hard Mother had tried, she'd never managed to turn Bennis into a natural hostess.

She got out another cigarette, lit up again, and then stared at the burning tip. At the rate she was smoking on this trip, she was going to have to quit for at least three months when she got back to Boston, just to be able to go on breathing.

"Maybe we should go someplace else," she said. "Out of the hall. We could go into the living room and have some coffee."

Gregor came to. "Coffee? No, no. I'm sorry, Miss Hannaford. I meant to tell you when I first came in. We're leaving."

"We?" Bennis said.

"Detective Jackman and I. We've done everything we can do

here. There are some small details to clear up, but they're the crime unit's business. It's after three o'clock. I have to get back to Philadelphia."

"I keep forgetting you have a life away from us," Bennis said. "Did you find what you came here looking for, before all this started?"

"I don't know."

"I hope you did."

Gregor took the accordion folder from her. Bennis watched it disappear into his jacket.

"We'll be out again," he said. "Try to take care of yourself."

He turned away and went walking down the hall the way he'd come in.

Bennis stood where she was, watching him. It was true. He had definitely changed. And she didn't like it.

She was beginning to think she'd made a mistake. She had had it all worked out, when she'd first gone to speak to him—but now . . .

She watched him lumbering off down the hall, and told herself she wasn't frightened. Then the phone started ringing, and she nearly jumped out of her skin.

2 In a perfectly ordinary police station in central Philadelphia, Bobby Hannaford stood leaning against a wall next to a pay phone, listening to the ringing on the other end of the line. The fact that he was in a perfectly ordinary police station bothered him. What he had committed

was a federal crime. He ought to be at the FBI, or in the U.S. Marshall's office. He ought to be taken seriously. Being in a perfectly ordinary police station put a complexion on things he didn't like at all.

He kept his back to the squadroom, so he didn't have to look at McAdam. McAdam was handcuffed to a chair.

"Listen," one of the detectives back there was saying, "what he did was, he had this money in the back of his car. A kind of maroon Mercedes. It was in the trunk."

"Fifty thousand dollars in one-hundred-dollar bills," one of the patrolmen said.

Bobby knew who was who, because they'd been having this conversation repeatedly for most of the last three hours.

"So anyway," the detective said, "the money is in a briefcase. In the trunk, like I said. He drives into this Mercedes dealership, and he goes in, and he finds a car just like the one he's driving—"

"Another sort of maroon Mercedes."

"Right. And he buys this car that looks just like the car he's driving, and he turns the car he's driving in for the trade-in. But he leaves the money in the first car."

"This is what I don't get. He was going to walk away from fifty thousand in cash?"

"That's what it looks like."

"But that's nuts."

"These aren't your ordinary criminals here. These are rich guys. Rich guys are nuts."

"Didn't the dealer think he was nuts?"

"Nah. The dealer's used to working with rich guys. So anyway, Hannaford here, he leaves the money in the first car, and he starts to drive away in the second car. Then the Feds come in behind him and stop him, and they search the car he's driving, but it's the second car, and the money isn't in that—"

"This must have taken forever. Dealers don't like to let cars drive off like that."

"You go into some dealer some time, put a guaranteed check down on the table, see what happens."

"So the Feds pick him up and he's in this second car—"

Bobby put his head down against the phone and closed his eyes. He just wished he could shut out sound the way he could shut out sight. When the detectives told it, the whole damn thing sounded impossibly, unforgivably stupid. In fact, it sounded impossible and unforgivable, period. Briefcases full of cash. Switched cars. Dawn meetings in tenth-rate cafés where the waitresses spoke only Arabic. Or whatever. He'd seen television movies that made more sense than this.

But here he was, and there they were, and on the other end of the line the phone was ringing at Engine House. Bobby wondered if Marshall was drunk. Somebody should have picked up by now. If he had real luck, he'd get Myra herself right away, and not have to explain anything to anybody else. For the moment.

Not too far down the road, there were going to be newspaper headlines, and legal formalities, and other things he'd rather not think about. For all the Keystone Kops aspects of this morning, this was serious. Eventually, he'd make himself believe that. In the meantime—

The phone on the other end picked up. Bobby heard a clear, high voice say,

"Engine House. Who's calling please?"

He sighed. It was Bennis, of course. That's the way his luck was running today.

Now that Daddy was dead, the person he least wanted to hear about his little secret was Bennis.

Even though she was the only one with enough money to loan him the bail.

FOUR

Getting out of Jackman's car in front of his apartment, Gregor felt like the Complete Television Daddy. Here he was home from work, and everyone in the world was waiting for him. Of course, Television Daddies had wives and children, not priests and pregnant neighbors, but in his cold and weariness the analogy seemed apt. Maybe any analogy would have seemed apt. He couldn't remember being this cold, or this tired. It was hard enough getting frustrated with God and the universe. At least they were bigger than you were. Getting frustrated with a two-bit idiot who had killed three people and not even been intelligent about it was something else again. In the Bureau, life had never been like this. Once he knew, he did something about what he knew. Now all he could do was explain the whole thing to Jackman, and try not to get physically violent when Jackman said, "No evidence, no motive, no point."

Jackman's car rattled and shuddered to a stop. Gregor rolled down his window and twisted his neck until he could see his living room windows. Yes, he had been right, even from a block and a half away. The lights up there were lit, and the two people walking around in front of the windows were Donna and Tibor. He wondered if Lida was up there too, in the kitchen, getting ready to make sure he ate a decent meal for once.

He pulled his head back into the car and got his gloves off the dashboard. He never wore gloves, but he always carried them. Elizabeth had told him to.

Jackman was fiddling with the dangling end of his key chain.

Actually, it was the department's key chain. It had a little tag on it with an address that could be used to mail it back to the Bryn Mawr police.

"Don't tell me," Jackman said, "you're still on your Favorite Suspect."

"You make it sound like we're reading a murder mystery and we've lost the last chapter."

"We might as well be."

"It's nothing so vague."

Jackman drummed his fingers against the steering wheel. "Look, I don't know how long you've been harboring this particular suspicion—"

"I told you that. Since just about the time we left Engine House. It occurred to me when I was talking to Cordelia Day. Then I checked it out by talking to the rest of them."

"God," Jackman said, "we both say *them* like we're talking about giant ants. Gregor, I'm not saying you're wrong, you understand me? If anything, I'm inclined to think you're right. Psychologically, it fits. But you could write me the greatest shrink study since the death of Freud and it wouldn't do me any good. I've got to have something solid."

"Opportunity," Gregor said.

"They all had opportunity."

"Means," Gregor said.

"They all had the means, too. I've got half a mind to turn that idiot doctor of theirs in to the drug squad. He prescribes Demerol the way a Jewish grandmother prescribes chicken soup. Now come out and say *motive* and give me something to hang it on. It would also be nice to have one piece of physical evidence."

"That piece of tin," Gregor said.

"We don't know what it is," Jackman said. "And it's probably nothing."

"We should be sure."

Jackman sighed. "Gregor, I'll check it out. I'll start tomorrow morning and I'll check into the ground. But you've got to understand, I've got no more reason to suspect who you want me to suspect than I have to suspect any of the others."

"Yes, you do."

"No, I don't," Jackman said. "Not the kind of reasons I need."

Gregor shoved his gloves into his pockets, opened his door, and got out. His foot went into a white mountain that was all give and no resistance. He pulled it out to find his pants caked with white.

"Listen," Jackman said, just before Gregor slammed the door shut and cut off conversation, "go to sleep. Get a good rest. We'll start tomorrow."

Gregor chinked the door shut and stood on the sidewalk, watching Jackman drive away.

The character of Cordelia Day Hannaford.

That accordion folder full of clippings.

The people who were dead and the sequence they had died in.

It seemed perfectly clear to him.

He turned around, went up the steps, and let himself into the building. Old George Tekamanian's apartment was dark, so he didn't knock. He just picked up his meager collection of mail and stuffed it into his coat.

He was already on his way up the stairs when he saw the Federal Express envelope lying on the hall table near the door. Just in case, he came down again and checked it out.

It was, surprisingly enough, addressed to him. It was return-addressed to a friend of his in Boston, who had left the Bureau and gone into business as a private detective. Gregor opened the envelope and found a single sheet of paper.

Gregor—
  Called and called but could never get in touch. Didn't know how fast you needed this.

                              Keep in touch.
                              Timmy

Underneath there was a name and address.

Gregor sighed. He'd give this to Donna Moradanyan and let her do what she wanted with it. At least somebody was going to get what they were after today.

He let himself into his apartment to find that not only were Tibor and Donna in his living room, not only was Lida in his kitchen, but old George Tekamanian was ensconced in one of the living room chairs, drinking rum he'd brought up from downstairs and looking very pleased with himself. It was a kind of party, staged entirely for his benefit, complete with food. He could smell the food. Lida was in there with his pots and pans—and probably some of her own pots and pans—cooking. He stuck his head into the kitchen and mumbled a few courtesies, just so he could tell himself he wasn't being as rude as he felt like being. Maybe Lida was feeling ruder.

She shooed him out without really looking at him and went on with her cups of flour and folds of dough.

Gregor hung his coat and jacket on the coatrack, loosened his tie, and rolled up his sleeves. Then he tucked the Federal Express envelope under his arm and went into the living room.

The television was on in there, blaring out the story of Bobby Hannaford's arrest. Donna looked up as he came in and smiled.

"This is incredible," she said. "This guy must have been nuts."

"A corporate raider," old George said solemnly. "I told you that, Krekor."

Tibor unwound himself from his place on the couch. "Is this the answer to your case, Gregor? We have been talking, Donna and George and Lida and I. We think, perhaps, this young man has done dishonest things with his father's company, his father is an evil and unforgiving man, so—*pfft.*"

"*Pfft,*" Gregor said. He looked at Bobby Hannaford's face on the television. The news had reached Engine House before he and Jackman left, so he knew all about it—more, in fact, than the television reporters possibly could. The story had been so bizarre, he'd called Flanagan and checked on it. Now Bobby Hannaford looked mulish, silly, and thoroughly frightened, like a small boy used to getting in trouble, but not this much trouble.

"So," Tibor said. "What do you think of our theory?"

"I think it's wonderful," Gregor said, "except for the candle-stick."

"Candlestick?" George said.

Gregor explained about the candlestick. Then he explained about the notes that had appeared and disappeared after Emma Hannaford died. Then he explained about pointers, the kind that went the wrong way.

"The money in the wastebasket," he told them, "must have come from the briefcase Robert Hannaford showed Father Tibor. Hannaford told me he'd have it with him and I could count the money before I ate my dinner. It must have been in the study when he was killed. It must have been removed by his murderer. And when it became increasingly obvious that Jackman wasn't going to buy suicide in Emma Hannaford's death, some of the bills from it were planted in Bobby Hannaford's wastebasket to point us at Hannaford Financial."

"But where's the rest of it?" Donna asked, confused. "Where's the briefcase?"

"The briefcase is where I thought it would be," Gregor said. "In the utility dump used for the lawn and garden garbage. That was luck, in a way. I've had the luck to be introduced to large, formal houses. They always have something of that kind. And that was the only place for it, really. Those dumps are always far from the house, much too far to be searched immediately. It could have been months before the police got around to it. If ever."

"And the money?" George prompted.

"Oh, that," Gregor said. "Well, our murderer is very practical. That'll be stashed somewhere for use at a later time. When things die down."

"Couldn't you get one of those warrants and search the house?" Donna said. "Then, when you find the money, you'll have the evidence."

"Maybe," Gregor conceded, "but I'd bet on one thing. That money isn't the only stash of hundred-dollar bills in the house. Assuming the briefcase money is even in the house. The other stash—Bobby Hannaford's payoff money from McAdam—now that, definitely, is there. And easily discoverable in a not-too-improbable place."

"Oh," Donna said.

"That's why the money was used," Gregor said. "There were other ways to point us to Hannaford Financial. The note itself being put in Bobby Hannaford's wastebasket was enough. Bobby has to have money, in hundred-dollar bills, somewhere in Engine House. And our murderer has to know it. If he didn't, there'd be no reason to put these—you see what I mean."

"Are murderers always so careful?" Tibor asked.

"Thank God, no," Gregor said. "But this one is."

"I think this is depressing," Donna Moradanyan said. "There ought to be something you can do. Don't you have any idea who did it?"

"I know who did it," Gregor said. "The problem is, I don't know why and without knowing why I can't prove it. And the Bryn Mawr police department is not about to arrest a member of one of the founding families of the Main Line on evidence that could apply to five other people on my say so."

"Oh," Donna said.

Gregor dropped onto the couch. He caught Donna's eye and pointed to the Federal Express envelope he was still carrying. She bit her lip and nodded. It hurt him to see the hope in her face. He put the envelope on the sofa cushion, so she could pick it up when nobody was looking.

"What I need," he said, "is a link."

They all stared back at him, confused. Even Tibor wasn't ready to say anything, or even ready to want to. Gregor got off the couch again and started pacing, back and forth, back and forth, in front of his living room window.

"A link, a link, a link," he said. "Given the people who were murdered, given the nature of that family, there are only two of them who could be doing this and still have it make sense. Of those two, one has no motive I can figure out, and one has no motive, period. I'm sure of it. The first one has to kill the second one, to make it come out right. Why, I don't know. When, I don't know. Add something here—only one of the two of them could be responsible for the dust."

"Dust?" Tibor said.

"That's how I think of it, all the extra clues that keep getting thrown at us. Stir up enough dust, and you can blind people to anything. I knew a faith healer like that once. He was about to go down for sexual misconduct, so he created a big brouhaha about his being the victim of racism, which wasn't true, by the way, and then—"

"I love this," George said. "Agatha Christie."

Donna Moradanyan was shaking her head and looking stubborn. She had also stuck the Federal Express envelope out of sight under her jacket on the floor. "I don't understand how it eliminates anybody," she said. "It didn't have to be the killer stirring up the dust, did it? Anybody could have stirred up the dust. Maybe one of them knows who did it, too. Maybe all of them do. They're all brothers and sisters. Maybe they're protecting someone."

"Not in that family," Gregor said.

"But Gregor," Tibor said, "if all the clues are false, how can you know who is doing the killing?"

Gregor shrugged. "It was something Cordelia Day Hannaford told me, and then I talked to Bennis and Teddy and they confirmed it. You'd like Mrs. Hannaford, Tibor. She's an old-fash-

ioned woman. She has a tremendous sense of family, of obligation. Like the grandmothers you're always talking about."

"What are you saying about grandmothers?" Lida had come in
from the kitchen, covered with flour, holding a pan full of stuffed
grape leaves. Gregor bit back a smile. The grape leaves were as
neat and organized as Lida herself was messy. Elizabeth's sister
was just the same way. She went into the kitchen, cooked like a
maniac, and made sure she was a total wreck by the time she was
done. It let her family know how much *work* she did.

Gregor turned slightly, so that he was facing Lida, and said,
"We weren't saying awful things about grandmothers. We were
talking about Cordelia Day Hannaford."

"Ah," Lida said. "The mother. The poor woman."

"Yes," Tibor said. "I think she is a poor woman."

"Tcha," Lida said. "It's bad enough to have one of your children go bad. It's bad enough to have two of your children killed.
It's bad enough to lose a husband. But to have all that happen at
the same time, and when you're so near death yourself, with no
time to wipe away the bad memories and replace them with
good—"

Gregor snapped to attention. He couldn't have been more
shocked if Lida had thrown a pail of ice water over his head. He
couldn't have felt more stupid if—he had nothing to follow that
if. He felt like Pinocchio, a man with a head made of wood.
When he'd first entered the Bureau, one of his training officers
had told him, "You always forget something, and the something
you forget is always the obvious." But it had never happened to
him before now.

Lida had veered off her original subject and was into a monologue on the sorry life of mothers everywhere. She was tearful.

She was pleading. She was speaking with her hands as eloquently as if she were a deaf person using sign language.

"Wait," Gregor told her. "Stop for a minute. Go back and say that again."

"Say what again?" Lida looked offended.

"What you just said," Gregor insisted. "About Cordelia Hannaford not having time."

"Well, Gregor. You've told me over and over again. The poor woman has a disease. She gets better sometimes but mostly she gets worse. She will die maybe before the year is out. And I tell you, if she dies that soon—"

"Oh, dear *sweet* lord Jesus Christ," Gregor said. "Cordelia Day Hannaford's heir." He stood up. They were all staring at him, and he didn't blame them. He must look like a lunatic. In a minute, he was going to *sound* like a lunatic. He couldn't help it. He didn't have time to explain it to them. If he were right—and he knew he was right, it was the only way it all made sense, all of it, even old Robert Hannaford and his $100,000—if he were right, there was going to be another death and it was going to happen soon.

He turned to Donna. "Get me your car," he said. "Go take it out of the garage and get it warmed up and ready to go. I'll be ready as soon as I make a phone call."

"Car?" Tibor said. "Gregor, look out the window. It's snowing again."

Gregor was moving too fast to pay attention. He moved right out of the living room into his bedroom, shut the door, and sat down on his bed. Then he picked up the phone.

Early this morning—so early now it almost felt like another day—he had told Jackman that the deaths of these three particular people must have changed something. He just hadn't been able to think of what. Even after he knew who his murderer was, he hadn't been able to think of what. That was the problem with the obvious. It never seemed to be important, but it always was.

He flipped through his address book until he found the name of the man he always thought of as "that lawyer." Floyd Evers. There it was.

He was going to ask Floyd Evers what he should have asked him in the beginning. He was going to ask if *Cordelia* Hannaford had made a will.

FIVE

1 Anne Marie Hannaford had never thought of Engine House as haunted before, but tonight she couldn't think of it any other way. The place was so big, and so dark, and so quiet. With the weather as bad as it was, she had been forced to let the servants go early. They had packed up and gone back to Philadelphia right after the police had left. Things were so much easier in the old days, when servants lived in. Now they all wanted their own houses. Only Morgan lived on the grounds, and that was because the driver's apartment was over the garages and well separated from the main building. There was no loyalty anymore, that was the problem. Servants wanted to take your money, but they didn't want to live with you. They didn't want to know you. It all came down to an exchange of cash.

She looked into her mother's face and sighed. It had been a bad evening. Only yesterday, Cordelia had been so much better. Even the doctor had said she might last three months or even a year. Now she was wondering if Cordelia would last the night. She ought to send for an ambulance. An hour ago, they had sat in this room—Chris, Teddy, Bennis, and herself—keeping a death watch. If it hadn't been for Bennis, she would have called the hospital then. But Bennis had been insistent, and when Bennis insisted—

Bennis.

Anne Marie put her hands up to her hair and began to fix it, automatically. In all the crisis and confusion, it had come down around her neck. She was being stupid, she knew. She had no reason whatsoever to be afraid of Bennis.

She went to the side of her mother's bed and switched on the intercom. It had special speakers that picked up the smallest sound in this room and amplified it through the rest of the house. When she left here, the *house* would seem to be breathing.

She fixed the blankets, plumped the pillows, touched her mother's forehead. Everything was as all right as it could be, meaning just all right enough for her to go down and have some dinner. Meaning awful. She left the lamp on and went into the hall.

Long hall. Dark hall. Cold hall. Down there, Emma had died.

Anne Marie went to the balcony, moving as fast as she could. The lights were dim there, too, but at least it wasn't so closed in. Sometimes she thought the house was shrinking, closing in around her the way plastic did on cheap toys, cutting off her air.

She left the hall door open and started down the stairs. Teddy and Chris were in the foyer. She hadn't seen them before because they were sitting at opposite ends of the bottom step. She hadn't heard them because they were talking quietly, and she couldn't hear anything over the sound of Mother's breathing. She kept telling herself everything would be all right as long as Mother didn't stop breathing. Listening to that rasp and hitch was like listening to her own heartbeat. No matter how awful it sounded, it was better than no sound at all.

Six o'clock. Maybe five after. The foyer was in shadow. It was hard to see the face of the clock.

She got to the step where Teddy and Chris were sitting and stopped.

"Maybe you ought to come in to supper," she said. "I think Bennis is making something."

Chris stretched his legs. He looked better now than he had

earlier in the day, when that Detective Jackman had found the other candlestick in his room. He had been called in to talk to Jackman and Mr. Gregor Demarkian, and when he had come out he'd looked better than Anne Marie remembered seeing him in years. It made her wonder. Now he seemed to have taken a bath and trimmed his hair and put on a better set of clothes—clothes that looked suspiciously like Bobby's. They hung on Chris.

"I'm not hungry," he said.

"I don't know how anybody can be hungry," Teddy said.

Anne Marie turned to him. He looked no different than he ever did, but maybe a little self-satisfied. What could he possibly have to be satisfied about, with Mother dying upstairs?

As if answering her question, Chris said, "Teddy's changing jobs. He got the news this evening."

"Changing jobs?" Anne Marie said.

Teddy smirked. "I'm going to Landon College. It's in Hudson, New York. Just about an hour from the city by train. Much better."

"Teddy has a friend on the faculty," Chris said blandly. "A friend who owes him something."

"He doesn't owe me anything," Teddy said angrily. "He just appreciates me."

Chris smiled. "Teddy's going to start right after Christmas. It's not like when you and I were in school. They don't hold the first semester over until after Christmas vacation any more."

"The semester starts January sixth," Teddy said sullenly. "I'm going to have a lot to do between now and then."

Including attending your mother's funeral, Anne Marie thought. She didn't say it. The two of them seemed totally unreal to her, sitting here discussing job changes, sitting here in the dark with that ragged breathing all around them, not noticing it at all. She moved off the step into the foyer, wishing she wasn't so cold.

"I'm going to have supper," she said. "I'm starving, and I'm probably going to be up all night. If you two have any decency, you'll be up all night, too."

"Wouldn't it make sense if some of us slept and one of us sat with mother?" Chris said. "I'll go up and sit with mother now, if you want."

"I don't know how you could sleep," Anne Marie said.

"He'll smoke marijuana," Teddy said. "That's how he always sleeps."

Chris stood up. "I'll go sit with Mother, Anne Marie. If you want, I'll turn that thing off, so you don't have to listen to it while you eat."

"No," Anne Marie said. "Don't turn it off."

"Isn't it driving you crazy?"

"It means she's breathing," Anne Marie said.

Chris nodded and went up the stairs. Teddy said, "If I were breathing like that, I'd want myself to stop."

Anne Marie left him where he was sitting and let herself into the hall.

2

She had expected to find Bennis in the kitchen. When instead she found the kitchen empty—and clean; Bennis cleaned like a servant, when she was done the house looked as if nobody had ever lived in it at all—she went down the back hall to the dining room. She didn't like being in the back hall. It really was a small space, narrow and low ceilinged. With the sound of Mother's breathing, the walls seemed to suck in and out.

She let herself through the baize door and found Bennis standing at the sideboard, small and thin and beautiful, the only one of them who had ever made sense. She had poured herself a cup of coffee and was putting too much sugar in it.

"There you are," she said. "I was beginning to think I'd made all this for myself."

"All this" was soup and a cold platter for sandwiches. Anne Marie looked at the soup and bit her lip.

Bennis put her coffee cup on the table and sat down. "I've been thinking," she said. "About things—you know? About Daddy and Emma."

"I wish you'd turned the lights on," Anne Marie said.

"I turned some of the lights on. I didn't want it to be too light. It didn't fit, somehow."

"Nothing fits." Anne Marie got a cup of coffee for herself and took the seat next to Bennis. Then she put the coffee down on her far side and stared at it. "I haven't been able to think of anything but Mother. Maybe that's all I ever think about. Mother."

"Maybe that's true."

"It sounds terrible, listening to the breathing on the intercom. It sounds like something from a horror movie. Do you remember when you made me take you to that horror movie, when we were children?"

"The old Empire Theater in Philadelphia. We went to see *The Tingler*. But you weren't such a child."

"I was child enough. I can still remember that movie. Where the man scares his wife to death."

"You take things like that too seriously." Bennis stood up and went to the sideboard again. She filled a bowl of soup and then another one, two immense bowls full of split pea Anne Marie didn't think anyone could eat. Bennis put them on the table and went back for spoons. "Eat," she said, handing Anne Marie a spoon. "You look terrible."

Anne Marie put the spoon down next to her bowl. The breathing seemed to be getting louder and louder. The house seemed to be getting smaller and smaller. She was so very tired, she didn't understand how she was staying awake at all. She wished she could be Bennis, always ready for anything.

"When she's like this and I sit with her I talk to her. I tell her —things. About when we were children, you know, and about our coming out. You never liked coming out."

"I hated it," Bennis said.

"You never liked anything here," Anne Marie said. "I never understood that. It's the most wonderful life in the world."

Bennis stirred more sugar into her coffee. It had to be syrup by now. "I didn't have any control over it. It had nothing to do with me. It wasn't something I'd earned. It wasn't something I'd invented. It was just a dance made up a million years ago by people I didn't know and probably wouldn't have liked very much."

"There's nothing wrong with being rich, Bennis."

"I never said there was anything wrong with being rich. I like money."

"Just money?"

"I like a man in Boston, but that probably won't last very long."

"I don't like men at all," Anne Marie said, "but I don't like women, either. That way."

"I know."

"I wish I knew what you thought about," Anne Marie said. "I watch you walk around here and it's—it's like you came from Mars. And it shouldn't be. You're more like Daddy than any of the rest of us."

"I know," Bennis said again.

Anne Marie looked up. She had been staring at her plate of soup, thinking how thick and impenetrable it was. There could be rocks or ground glass in it, and she would never know. She wished Bennis would eat some. She wished Bennis would stop staring at her—except that Bennis wasn't staring at her. Bennis was looking in the other direction entirely, fussing with her cigarettes and her green Bic lighter. A flame went up, too high, and Bennis jumped back. She didn't turn around.

"Do you like it," Anne Marie said, "being like Daddy?"

"I like the single-mindedness. It gets me a lot of things I couldn't live without."

"Funny, I never thought of him as single-minded. He always seemed to have his hand in everything, to be everywhere. He always seemed to be spread out and spread thin."

Another flame went up. This time Bennis caught it, leaned close to it, sucked. Anne Marie watched. Bennis's face was lit up more than her cigarette was. The flame shuddered and licked. Bennis's cheekbones went in and out of shadow. She looked Slavic, or like a vampire.

Yes, Anne Marie thought. That's what they're both like. Vampires. They suck people up.

Except that Daddy was dead.

Bennis put the cigarette lighter down. "Are you all right?" she said.

"I'm fine," Anne Marie said.

Bennis got up and went back to the sideboard. Anne Marie could hear her putting together a sandwich, scraping a knife against the edge of the mayonnaise pot. The breathing got softer suddenly and louder suddenly, making them both jump.

"She's dying," Anne Marie said.

And Bennis said, again, "I know."

In and out, in and out, in and out. Normal. For just this second, it was going to be all right.

Anne Marie looked down at her soup. She picked up her spoon. She put it down again. Split pea, heavy and thick.

"Bennis?" she said.

"I'm here, Anne Marie. I've always been here. I always will be here."

"Yes," Anne Marie said.

She felt very floaty, very floaty, adrift on an imaginary sea. It was all right. It really was. It was just Bennis here, after all. Nobody she had to be afraid of. Even though she was afraid.

From the moment she had known Daddy was dead, she had been afraid. And what she had been afraid of was here, now, in this room.

Anne Marie started to move. As she did, she turned away from the light. The hand was there, disembodied, a man's hand. It hovered in the darkness, something that could not be real. I'm losing my mind, she thought.

Then the hand came closer and touched her, circled her wrists, held them tight. It took a moment for her to realize what was happening, and then she screamed.

She screamed and screamed and screamed. And as she screamed, the hand on her wrist tightened and twisted. She felt her own hand turn and her fingers loosen. She watched her hand come open in the air.

What fell out of it was a tiny plastic bottle that had once held aspirin—and what fell out of that was powdered Demerol, spilling over the tablecloth like fine-grained snow on a pastel garden shelf.

SIX

1 When the lights came on, Gregor Demarkian got hold of Anne Marie Hannaford's other wrist. He blinked into the glare and told himself he was going to kill Bennis. He was going to kill her. He'd called her right after he'd called Evers and John Jackman. He'd explained the problem to her. He'd gotten her to call the gate and make sure they could get in without a call to the house. He'd involved her completely —but she was supposed to set things up for the police, and for him. She wasn't supposed to go out and do everything possible to get herself murdered.

Instead, he looked at her standing against the sideboard, watching him hold down Anne Marie, and said, "Where's Jackman? She's in shock now, but she's going to come out of it any minute. Then we're going to have a problem."

"No we're not," Bennis said. She was grinning.

"Miss Hannaford," Gregor said, "once, just once, in this year of our Lord, I would like you to do what you're supposed to do instead of what you want to do. I would like to be reasonably sure we're not all going to get killed here—"

"We're not all going to get killed here," Bennis said. "What do you take me for? She's not in shock, you fool. She's stoked to the gills on Demerol."

"What?" Gregor said.

"Well, she's already killed three people, hasn't she? She made herself a cup of tea about half an hour ago. She always fills it full of sugar. I put the Demerol in that. I mean, for God's sake,

Gregor. I'm not Nancy Drew. As soon as you told me what was going on, I wanted her out of commission."

Gregor looked down at Anne Marie. She had stopped screaming. She had stopped everything. She was the next best thing to catatonic.

He dropped her back into her chair. "You," he said to Bennis Hannaford, "are a very dangerous woman."

Bennis shrugged. "There's your Detective Jackman," she said. "He's out in the hall. Can't you hear him screaming at Teddy to get out of his way?"

Now that he was no longer desperately concentrated on keeping Anne Marie in check, Gregor could certainly hear Jackman screaming. Or shouting, at any rate. He could have heard him back in Philadelphia.

And just for the moment, he no longer cared.

Bennis Hannaford, Gregor thought. Bennis Hannaford is not only dangerous, she's crazy. She ought to be locked up for her own good.

EPILOGUE

FRIDAY, JANUARY 6

EPIPHANY

ONE

1 At six o'clock on the evening of January 6, the Feast of the Epiphany, Gregor Demarkian stood in the snow in the courtyard behind Holy Trinity Church and rang the bell to Tibor's apartment. He was feeling a little nervous. In the days since the Hannaford case had been brought to a close, he had been keeping out of sight. For one thing, he was tired. He had forgotten about murder cases. They took a lot of energy and they took a lot of emotion, and when they were over what you really wanted to do was sleep for a week. He hadn't been able to manage that. He'd spent so much time thinking about the Hannafords, and about Donna Moradanyan and her little "problem," he hadn't paid bills or done laundry in he didn't know how long. He had a lot of details to take care of, and he was too restless not to take care of them. That was the other thing. He was *very* restless. Now that he was no longer walking around in a fog, now that his life no longer felt like one long wound caused by the death of Elizabeth, he was in mortal danger of being terminally bored. What he was going to do about that, he didn't know. There would be more Donna Moradanyans and more little problems in his life if he wanted to let them in, but that kind of thing wouldn't really occupy his mind. And problems like the Hannaford case came up once or twice in a lifetime.

He pressed the bell again, readjusted the box of chocolates he was carrying under his arm, and waited. Because this was an Armenian neighborhood and Tibor was an Armenian priest, the Christmas decorations were still up. Tiny lights were strung through the one anemic tree that had grown up between the courtyard's tiles. Holly wreaths and plastic Santa Clauses were stuffed into all the observable windows. He could even hear faint strains of Steve Lawrence singing "The Little Drummer Boy"— Tibor must have bought one of those mail-order Christmas records. Here was the great thing about being Armenian. If for some reason you couldn't celebrate Christmas properly on December 25, all you had to do was wait for Epiphany and you got another shot at it.

In front of him, the doorknob rattled, the door frame shuddered, and finally the door came open. Tibor was standing just beyond it, a sprig of bright red plastic holly pinned to the shoulder of his "best" dayrobes.

"Gregor," he said, "Gregor, Gregor, come in. We have everyone here now."

"Everyone?" Gregor said.

"Yes, yes," Tibor said.

Tibor stepped back, and Gregor came in from the cold. He found himself in a small, cramped foyer that looked even smaller and more cramped because it was stuffed with books, piles and piles of books, pushed against the walls in unsteady stacks that looked ready to avalanche. He saw Paul Johnson's *History of Christianity* and Hardon's *Catholic Catechism* and three paperbacks by Mickey Spillane. The paperbacks had been read to shreds.

Tibor came up behind him and said, "Mr. Spillane, yes. Mr. Spillane has a very interesting mind, Gregor."

Gregor had read a book by Mickey Spillane once. It had been called *The Body Lovers,* and it had gone into sadomasochism in detail.

Tibor saw the look on his face and was hurt. "Gregor, Gregor. You must stop being so dependent on the obvious. Mr. Spillane has a very interesting moral sense. It is a form of barbarism, yes, but it is the right form of barbarism. It is a barbarism out of which civilization can grow."

"Right," Gregor said.

"Never mind," Tibor said. "Thank you for the chocolates. I will put them out in the living room. Do you want to go into the living room? Donna Moradanyan is there with her Peter."

"Ah," Gregor said.

Tibor nodded. "If she wants to marry him, we'll just have to put up with it. But I will tell you. I have thought once or twice about giving him knockout drops and putting him on a train."

"You've been reading too much Mickey Spillane."

"Gregor," Tibor said, "this Peter Desarian, he has a brain the size of a pea."

"But we *knew* that," Gregor pointed out. "If his brain had been any bigger, he wouldn't have gotten her pregnant in the first place, and if he had gotten her pregnant, he wouldn't have gone running home to his mother."

"I think it was a much better thing when parents arranged the marriage," Tibor said. "Donna's mother would have known better than to arrange *this* one."

Gregor wasn't sure about that—growing up among immigrants, he had witnessed a few arranged marriages in his life—but he let it go. The music had changed from "The Little Drummer Boy" to "Silver Bells," sung by a man whose voice had been trained out of all personality. He looked into the living room and saw Donna and her preppy Peter, George in the biggest armchair, Lida in red silk and diamond earrings. In the corner near the window was an overdecorated Christmas tree. As he watched, a very tiny child, a girl no more than two, walked up to it and took a candy cane.

"Who's the baby?" he asked Tibor.

"Baby?" Tibor brightened. "Ah, Gregor. I'm so used to them. I forgot. My houseguests."

"Houseguests?" Gregor said. And then he remembered. The day he had taken Tibor to lunch. The discussion about the "homeless problem." Oh, *God*.

Tibor was moving to the other side of the foyer, to the door that led to the kitchen. "Come on, come on," he was saying. "You will come in here, you will meet my houseguests, you will have a little talk with Bennis."

"Bennis?" Gregor said. "Bennis *Hannaford?*"

"Yes, yes," Tibor said. "George, he invites her here, she gets all dressed up and comes. She is a very nice woman, Gregor. I like her very much."

Mickey Spillane and Bennis Hannaford.

Well, Gregor thought, why not?

2

The smallest houseguest was still in the living room, of course, but the other three were with Bennis in the kitchen, a couple in their teens and yet another baby daughter. This baby daughter looked to be about three, and she could talk. A lot. She was sitting on the kitchen table, next to Bennis's piles of flour and eggs, singing "Jingle Bells" to herself in a high, clear, tuneless voice. Her father was sitting in a chair on the other side of the table, nearly hidden by yet more piles of books. Her mother was standing next to Bennis near the eggs. Gregor relaxed a little. When Tibor had first told him about taking in the homeless, Gregor had been half sure he'd gone off the deep end. A raving drunk who needed to be reformed. A crack addict who needed a personal relationship with Jesus Christ. Something. But this was all right. There were people like this all over Philadelphia, refugees from the hills of West Virginia and Kentucky, who had come north to look for work and not found it. Gregor came farther into the room and saw that at least one of the books on the table belonged to the male half of the couple. He was studying it.

Bennis, dressed in a beautiful red wool dress that was now covered with flour, was waving a rolling pin in the air. "It's a pain in the ass," she said, "but it saves a lot of money, and if you've got the time—"

"Oh, I've got the time," the mother said, making the word come out *tahme*. She looked seventeen, if that. "Around here, all I've got is time. I try cleaning up a little, but Father gets so *addled* if I move his books."

"Father *is* addled," Bennis said, "but nice." She put the rolling pin down and reached for a measuring cup. As she did, her head came up and she saw Gregor. "Oh," she said. "You. Father Tibor said you'd be here."

Gregor looked around for Father Tibor, but he was gone. "Do you mind?" he asked Bennis.

"Of course I don't mind." She pointed to the girl standing beside her. "This is Jenna Moore," she said. "And this is Donnie Moore, her husband. And *this*," she touched the three year old's hair, "is Suzanna."

"There's another one in the living room," Gregor said, "eating candy canes."

"That'll be Magdalena," Jenna said, and blushed. "I got that name out of the Bible. I thought it sounded—"

"Pretty," Bennis said.

Jenna nodded and turned away. Bennis put down the measuring cup. "So," she said. "It's good to see you. I've been thinking about you a lot, lately."

"Not bad thoughts, I hope," Gregor said.

"No."

"I think I'm going to go find Maggie," Jenna Moore said nervously, picking up her three year old. "Come on, Donnie. She's probably in there eating all the decorations off that nice tree."

The Moores disappeared through the door Gregor had come in by. Bennis and Gregor both watched them go.

"So," Bennis said again, when they were alone. "How have you been?"

"How have *you* been?"

Bennis shrugged. "Better. I've been to see her, you know. They don't seem to be inclined to let her out on bail."

"They wouldn't be."

"No, they wouldn't be. You know what I can't get over? She hates me. She really *hates* me. And hard as I try, Gregor, I just can't come up with a reason why."

"What does she say?"

"Not much, and nothing that makes sense." Bennis started cleaning up the table, brushing piles of flour into her hand. "I stood bail for Bobby. I did a little magic to make sure Teddy still had a job—"

"A little magic?"

"Don't ask," Bennis said. "You wouldn't believe what it costs to get somebody appointed to the faculty of a tenth-rate college.

Especially if that somebody is about to be drummed out of the profession by a seventh-rate college. Whatever. Gregor, I don't know what I'm doing wrong. Anne Marie hates me. Bobby and Teddy—it's like they wish I didn't exist."

"What about Chris?"

"Oh, Chris is all right," Bennis said. "He went to that place in New England. I guess he's going to be there about three months. He says when he's out he may come and live in Boston."

"I don't think you ought to worry about Anne Marie," Gregor said. "She's a very disturbed young woman. Not insane in the legal sense, you understand, but very disturbed. And as for Bobby and Teddy—"

"They're very disturbed, too?"

"They're jerks. And the world is full of jerks, Bennis. Racist jerks. Sexist jerks. Envious jerks. If you worry about the jerks, you'll never have any kind of life at all."

Bennis put the measuring cup and the rolling pin in Tibor's sink. "You never did tell me how you figured it out. When you called up that night, there wasn't time, and since then—"

"We've both been occupied."

"You could put it that way," Bennis said. "Mostly I've been depressed. But you know, if I'd had to pick someone, the last person it would have been was Anne Marie."

"That's because you were worried about your mother. Anne Marie said to me once that nobody wanted to keep your mother alive as much as she did, and that was true. Your mother was Anne Marie's life. Once your mother was dead, Anne Marie was going to have nothing. Not a home. Not an income. Not a profession. Nothing. She's over forty, Bennis. When your parents were both gone, what was she going to do? Learn to type?"

"I never thought about it."

"Anne Marie did." Gregor took the dish towel off the refrigerator door. Bennis had started washing up, unthinkingly and automatically. He thought he could at least dry. "It was your mother who told me, you know, although she didn't do it directly. She told me she knew *who* it was, but she couldn't give me the name. She's very attached to all of you, Bennis. I couldn't understand why she'd shield one of her children when that child was killing the others. And then it hit me. She owed your sister Anne Marie. She owed her *everything.*"

"And?"

"She gave me some things," Gregor went on. "One of those things was a folder with newspaper and magazine clippings in it, all pictures of her with her daughters. The other of those things was a file with notes your sister Emma had written to you, false starts on Engine House notepaper. Once I understood the file, I understood the debris."

"Debris? Oh, I see. You mean candlesticks and all that sort of thing."

"That's right. It was all meant to point to Hannaford Financial —and to the boys. Once turning Emma's death into a suicide didn't work, everything was pointed at the boys. The only possible explanation for that was that the real murderer had to be one of the girls. And then that 'first' note—"

"There wasn't one, was there?"

"No, there wasn't one. There was just the note from your purse. But then you recognized it—you were never meant to see it, but you did. But your mother was better, there was no hurry at the moment. She wanted a suicide. Then, with Emma blamed, she could pick off you and Myra later. As accidents. So she said she'd found a different note, and she got one of the ones from the file and put it in Bobby's wastebasket. With money from the briefcase she'd taken from your father's study the night of the murder."

"They still haven't found it you know," Bennis said. "I keep expecting it to turn up under one of the carpets or something."

"Maybe it will," Gregor said.

"But what about the brooch?" Bennis said. "Jackman said you'd found part of it right there in the study. I would have thought—"

"We'd see it immediately?"

"Well, those tin things are all over the house."

"Yes," Gregor said. "They are. But the decorations are the wrong size. They're too small. And I saw your sister Myra wearing one, and you wearing one—but not the right kind. You had a bell. Myra had a ball. Oh, there was one in Emma's room, too. After she died. It was a cupid."

"A cherub," Bennis corrected.

"A cherub. You know, that day I went to talk to your mother, the day she gave me the file, she was wearing a hair comb with all four of the figures on it. It was so painful for me, to be there with her the way she was after the way my wife had died, that I noticed the comb but I didn't process the information. My attention was—elsewhere, let's say. And then I got home, and Lida Arkmanian started talking about your mother and how she was dying, and then it hit me. Always, four different things, the bell, the ball, the cherub, *and the angel*. Your mother had all four on her comb. You and two of your sisters had one each made into a brooch. It stood to reason that Anne Marie must also have had a brooch, and the only thing it could have been was an angel. And an angel brooch of a size comparable to the bell or the ball I'd seen would have been the right size and shape for that piece of tin."

"She snooped, didn't she?" Bennis said. "That was how she knew about Bobby's financial problems."

"About the fact of them, yes," Gregor said. "And about the money in Bobby's safe, of course. I don't think she had any details."

Bennis laughed. "Bobby thinks she's a witch. He thinks I'm a witch, too. Oh, well. We always knew he wasn't too bright."

Gregor took a spoon out of her hands and started wiping it. "It wasn't until later that I understood about the folder. A mother and her daughters. A mother who loved her daughters, loved them extravagantly. Who protected them. And was married to a man who not only hated them, but had gone to equally extraordinary lengths to disinherit them. He couldn't have done that with a will, you know. The courts wouldn't have allowed it. So there it was, this woman with a tremendous sense of obligation, an old-fashioned woman with an old-fashioned sense of family."

"And no money," Bennis pointed out.

"That's true," Gregor said, "but she did have jewelry, and she had that insurance policy. You see, once you begin thinking of the implications of the fact that your mother is so ill—"

"Dying," Bennis said shortly.

"Dying, yes. Once you start from *that,* everything begins to make sense. Your mother has no money, but if your father dies before her she has the proceeds from an insurance policy. Those proceeds are doubled if your father is murdered, and if she cannot be proved to have committed that murder. So, your father *is* murdered, and in a way that makes it blatantly clear that the one person in the house who cannot be guilty is the beneficiary of his insurance policy. Now, you see, your mother has two million dollars. Tax free."

"Yes," Bennis said.

"Anne Marie's next problem," Gregor said, "was to get hold of that money intact. You see, she knew what was in your mother's will—"

"How?"

"She took it," Gregor said. "It was in a wall safe in a room off the main balcony. That's where Floyd Evers had seen her put it. Anne Marie took it, and read it, and found what you'd expect to find, if you thought seriously about your mother. Your mother had a need to compensate you—all of you daughters—for what your father had done to you. So she made a will leaving everything she had, unspecified as to particulars, to her girls."

"But that gave any of the four of us a motive," Bennis said.

"Oh, yes." Gregor put down the spoon and took the measuring cup. "But two of you were already dead, Bennis. And you didn't need money."

"No," Bennis said, "the one thing I don't need is money."

"There were other things, you know. Your mother didn't have the depth of obligation to you she had to Anne Marie. I don't think she would have felt such a duty to shield you. And there was the hundred thousand dollars."

"The hundred thousand dollars?"

Gregor nodded. "We tried and tried to think of what might be important enough for your father to spend that kind of money, just to have me come to the house for one night. We won't ever know for certain, of course, but my guess is that he already suspected Anne Marie of wanting to kill him, maybe even of having tried to kill him all those years ago."

"Did she?" Bennis said.

"Try all those years ago?" Gregor said. "I think so. If she's convicted, you can ask her. She'll probably tell you. But the point is, if something was going on that your father needed help with —and there must have been—then that something was going on when you were away from the house, living in Boston. It had to involve someone your father saw frequently, you see, because the offer came to Tibor before you came home for the holiday. And then Chris kept telling me how paranoid your father was, and how much worse he'd gotten lately. Finally, I asked him."

"What did he say?"

"He said the last time he'd talked to your father, your father had complained about someone coming in to his study and moving things, trying to make him think he was going senile."

"Oh, dear."

"Yes," Gregor said. "That was what was going on in Robert Hannaford's life when he showed up at Tibor's door with a suitcase full of money. And that made sense. Someone was thinking of killing him. He'd pay to get that to stop. But that had to be Anne Marie, Bennis. Nobody else went into that room except by invitation."

"And Anne Marie had to make sure the other three of us were dead before Mother died," Bennis said, "because if we weren't and we'd made wills, we'd inherit the money and it would pass to our heirs. And mother was worse that night. That's how you knew—"

"She was going to try then," Gregor said. "Yes. She had to.

But I'll repeat what I said to you at the time. I told you to set me up for her, to put yourself in a position where she would try to put Demerol in your coffee. I did *not* ask you to goad her beyond all endurance. She could have picked up one of those center-pieces and brained you with it."

"No she couldn't," Bennis grinned. "I *told* you about that."

"About giving her one little Demerol pill, yes," Gregor said. "It was intelligent as far as it went, Bennis, but that wasn't very far."

"It was far enough."

Gregor threw up his hands. "Remind me never to involve you in something like this again. You're much too much of a roman-tic."

"Right now, I'm much too much of a hungry person," Bennis said. "Do you think, if we went out there with all the other people, they'd let us eat?"

"They'd *force* us to eat," Gregor said.

"Let's go then."

She put the wet rolling pin in the dish rack, took the towel out of Gregor's hands, and wiped herself off. She was still covered with flour, but she looked lovely.

"Mother," she told him, "is in the hospital. Believe it or not, she's better."

"I do believe it."

"I don't think Mother kept Anne Marie home at all," she said. "I think it was Anne Marie who kept Mother. So that she could go on living in the house, and Daddy wouldn't be able to throw her out."

"Maybe," Gregor said.

"I don't have the guts to ask," Bennis said. "Not either one of them."

She walked by him, right out the kitchen door.

3

Gregor was still standing in the kitchen, thinking about Bennis, five minutes later, when Tibor came looking for him. He was drying the rolling pin, and had been, for what seemed like forever. Tibor frowned at the rolling pin and shook his head.

"I'm glad I have you here," he said, "by yourself. There was something I wanted to ask you."

"Ask." Gregor dropped the rolling pin back in the dish rack. He had no idea where it lived when it was "away."

"I have this friend," Tibor said, "another priest, but a Roman Catholic priest. Father John O'Bannion."

Gregor dropped the towel in surprise. "John *Cardinal* O'Bannion?"

"Yes, yes," Tibor said, nervous. "Now Gregor, I know you say you're retired, but John is a very nice man, an exceptionally holy man, and he has this problem—"

Gregor dropped into a chair to listen. John Cardinal O'Bannion had a problem, did he? Suddenly, he no longer felt terminally bored.

And Elizabeth would approve. He'd ask, when he got back to the apartment, but he knew what her answer would be.

She would definitely approve.